Praise for Marie LaT res

"Please never stop putting pen to paper. I love your books!"

"You've established yourself as a legitimate writer of historic fiction."

"Great read that kept the pages turning. Characters worth cheering for! Can't wait for the next book. And more adventures."

"I ended up staying up until 1 in the morning finishing your book!"

"Your writing is so clear and inviting!"

"I literally found myself awake all night last night reading the first book again. I simply love the way you have written all of the stories."

"Another awesome book. Great storyline and hard to put down!"

"A total surprise and loved the ending! Read it in a day!"

"I highly suggest it if you love history and a bit of romance!"

"Get in your comfy chair!"

"Another winner! Brings the past alive and includes some suspense, love, faith and hope…a talented storyteller!"

Other Books by Marie LaPres

The Turner Daughters Series

Though War Shall Rise Against Me: A Gettysburg Story

Be Strong and Steadfast: A Fredericksburg Story

Plans for A Future of Hope: A Vicksburg Story

Forward to What Lies Ahead: A Petersburg Story

Wherever You Go: A Turner Daughters Prequel Novella

Whom Should I Fear? Middle Grade Novels

Sammy's Struggle

The Key to Mackinac Young Adult Series

Beyond the Fort

Beyond the Island

Beyond the Mill (Coming Soon)

Beyond the Light (Coming Soon)

This book is dedicated to my sisters, Alecia and Tina. Like the Bennett sisters, we may argue or disagree, but we are always there for one another.

Thanks to cover models: Grace Strong and her horse Hondo.

Photo by: Susan Emelander

Wisdom and Humility

A Novel

Marie LaPres

Family Trees

The Bennetts

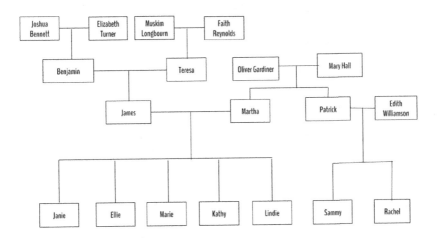

The Callahans

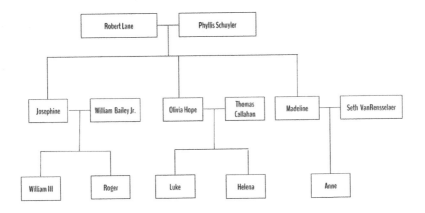

Part 1: Spring of 1928

Chapter One

Longbourn Ranch
South of Spearfish, South Dakota

"*James!*"

Eleanor Bennett jumped at her mother's shriek. She looked across the table at her grandfather, Benjamin Bennett. The two were playing a game of cribbage on the front porch of their modest, five-bedroom home.

"What is your mother yammering on about now?" He asked. Ellie's father, James, was Benjamin's son, and it was no secret that Grandpa Benjamin thought Martha Bennett ridiculous.

"I'll go see." Ellie, as Eleanor preferred to be called, put her cards into a pile and stood. She had wanted a nice, quiet evening after working on the family ranch, but apparently that wasn't to be. She crossed the porch, stepped inside and headed to her father's office, where she assumed her mother would be.

Ellie loved her family's home south of Spearfish, South Dakota. The town had been around since the Black Hills gold rush of 1876 and sat at the mouth of the beautiful Spearfish Canyon. Longbourn Ranch was her most favorite place on earth. His family owned 2,450 acres of land and had over 5,000 head of cattle. Spearfish Creek ran through the ranch, and since their land was surrounded by the canyon, the family had a majestic view of the mountains. Ellie had grown up working alongside her father and grandfather, learning everything there was to know about running a successful cattle business. At the age of 23, she still lived at home, unmarried, with her parents and four sisters.

"James! Have you heard the news?" Martha Bennett had made it to her husband's office, and Ellie's two youngest sisters, Kathy and Lindie, crowded around the doorway.

"What in the world is going on?" Ellie asked in a hushed voice. Lindie shrugged and giggled. Though she was the youngest of the Bennett sisters, she looked more mature than her 17 years. Tall, with sandy blonde hair and brown eyes, she was pretty, yet frivolous and silly. She spent most of her time worrying about boys and gossip, qualities that annoyed Ellie very much. She may look older, but she definitely didn't act older.

"Someone bought the Verbena Meadows Ranch." Kathy stated. Kathy was a year older than Lindie, but she was the follower of the two. She had similar features, but was plumper than the classically curvy Lindie. Kathy always had her nose in everyone else's business.

Ellie was intrigued at the information. "Did they now? That's interesting." Verbena Meadows Ranch had the largest, most elaborate house in Lawrence county, and also had more acres of land than any other ranch in the area. They boasted not just cattle, but the most beautiful herd of thoroughbred horses in all of South Dakota. The current owners, the Carlisles, had been very quiet and kept to themselves. None of the local citizens had ever been invited to see the inside of their sprawling ranch home. It had only been used as a summer getaway for the wealthy family and their elite guests. The new owner must be quite wealthy to have purchased the property. Ellie concentrated on her mother's words.

"The Carlisles have sold their house! Don't you care who bought it?" Martha was easily excited and quite dramatic, much like Lindie.

"You want to tell me more than I wish to know, but go ahead. Do tell." Mr. Bennett clenched a cigar between his teeth. Ellie smiled at her father's humor. He was always teasing his wife.

"It is a Mr. Brantley, from the big city. Chicago. He apparently comes from very old money, and he bought the ranch as a place to stay for the summers, just like the Carlisles used to do. I heard he may want to invest in the area as a tourist destination."

Ellie nodded to herself. That made sense. Many people were discussing ideas of how to bring people to the Black Hills for vacations ever since it had been designated a National Forest back in 1897.

"What is going on?" Janie, the oldest and most beautiful of the Bennett sisters had heard the commotion as well and joined the other girls outside the office. She had a desirable figure, luxurious blonde hair that always fell in perfect ringlets and bright sky blue eyes. But what made her most beautiful was her kind disposition; Janie was sweeter than anyone else Ellie knew.

"They're talking about a very wealthy man, a Mr. Brantley, who bought the Carlisle property," Ellie replied.

"My, he must be very rich indeed." Janie smiled. "If he's young and unmarried, I wonder how long it will take mother to get us an introduction." Ellie smiled and nodded in agreement. Janie, at 24, was also unmarried. She was most proficient in the kitchen, though her mother would have preferred that she never work.

"Yes, you know what Mama always says. Every single young man that has money must be looking for a wife." Too bad that in the Black Hills of South Dakota, single men with money to spare were few and far between, but that didn't stop Martha Bennett from looking everywhere to make a good match for her daughters.

"What's going on?" The middle Bennett sister, Marie, joined the group in the doorway. Marie was widely considered the plain sister, with drab brown hair and pale brown eyes. She was usually only concerned with reading and music, and she disliked most forms of socialization, yet Ellie had a soft spot for her. Marie was extremely conservative for her age of 20 and had few friends.

In the study, Mrs. Bennett continued prattling on about Mr. Brantley and his wealth. Ellie even thought she heard the name 'John Jacob Astor' in association with the new neighbor, so he was clearly well-connected. Ellie quickly informed Marie of what was happening.

"Oh, is that all?" Marie rolled her eyes and went back to her room.

Finally, Mrs. Bennett noticed her daughters at the door and put her hands on her hips.

"Listening in again?" she asked.

"You have to admit, Mama, you make it easy enough to hear." Janie smiled and the girls entered the room.

"Well then, I am sure you all realize how important the party at the Austen house will be." She focused on Janie and Ellie. The Austens were a neighboring family and good friends with the Bennetts. They were having a barbeque and bonfire next weekend in honor of their oldest daughter's engagement. "I heard the new neighbor will be there. First impressions are key and if any of you are to win over this Mr. Brantley, you will have to put your best foot forward." And with that, she flounced out of the room.

"Why is she always insisting that we find husbands?" Ellie groaned, pretending to bang her head against the doorframe.

"She is a mother! Besides, if this Mr. Brantley is half as nice as he is rich, I might already be in love with him!" Janie smiled, and the two laughed and went back to what they had been doing.

"You find out about the yapping?" Grandpa Benjamin asked when Ellie sat back down. She quickly filled him in. Benjamin rolled his eyes.

"That fool mother of yours needs to be careful. If she's not, she may push one of you girls into a bad marriage."

"I doubt that would happen." Ellie picked her cards back up. "You and father would be sure to stop us if we even thought of someone unworthy."

"We'd try, well enough." He sat back and examined Ellie. "I know you though, Ellie. You don't care about money or status in anyone, much less a prospective husband."

"That is true." Ellie nodded. "I'm waiting for a man who has goals, a decent job, a good work ethic and a love of God. I want a man who will want me for all of my good traits, as well as bad. You know I don't have many of the graces that most women have." She paused, then shook her head. "I'll probably end up an old maid. You know as well as anyone that I never receive much attention from any man beyond that of friendship."

"Because they're all fools." Grandpa Benjamin looked at the cribbage board, then the cards in his hand. "You'll find someone, Ellie, my dear. Though I don't know if any man can be completely worthy of you."

"Thank you for saying so, Grandpa." She smiled. What would she do without her family?

~~~~~

"*Such* a good sermon," Janie said the next day as they exited St. Joseph's church in Spearfish. "We seldom hear readings from the Book of Proverbs."

"You're right about that." Ellie agreed. "'When pride comes, then comes disgrace, but with humility comes wisdom.'" She looked across the churchyard and noticed her father talking with two unfamiliar young men, both good-looking. The shorter one, with dark hair and an impeccable navy suit, looked over and met her eyes. He was extremely handsome, but looked as though he was sucking on a lemon. "I wonder who Papa is speaking with."

The two unknown men tipped their fedoras and walked toward a sleek-looking blue and white Rolls Royce with the top rolled down.

"I wonder if one of them was this new Mr. Brantley," Janie replied. "They both fit the description of what we know about him. If that is the case, Mama will be ecstatic that Papa introduced himself to them."

"Well, I fear that the task of marrying well for her sake will fall to you," Ellie pointed out. "You're by far the best candidate. Marie is considered too plain, Kathy too much a follower. Lindie is far too immature, and I'm…"

"You're the least ladylike of us all." Lindie stood behind Ellie, hands on her hips, clearly upset about hearing what Ellie had to say about her. "You'll likely be single for the rest of your life. A spinster! I'll bet you've never even been kissed!" And with that, she flounced away.

6

"Don't listen to her, Ellie. You know it's not true." Janie tried to reassure her sister.

"Actually, what I was going to say isn't that far from what she said. I'm not much of a catch for any man and I'm well aware of it. My hair is the color of mud and far too unruly, I work quite physically on the ranch so I'm too muscular and I'm really not good at the social graces that the rest of you take to so easily." Janie took Ellie's arm and they walked toward their Ford Model T Truck.

"You're beautiful and you know it and any man would be lucky to earn your love. Even this Mr. Brantley."

"Doubtful, but if I did, I would then have to move east and I could never give up the ranch." Just the thought of living in a crowded city like Chicago made her shudder.

"For the right man, you would." Janie told her.

"Yes, but the right man would never ask me to," Ellie replied.

Chapter Two

The following Friday, Ellie and Janie were helping their friend Rosalie Austen with last-minute preparations for the party to be held at her family's ranch. It had been a busy week so Ellie was glad to help with minor chores and just relax. The event was to be a small affair, a barbeque dinner with a campfire and dancing later in the evening. It was a way for the ranchers and families in Spearfish to get together before the busy season of calving, followed by branding. Rosalie was quite excited that her family was hosting the gathering and had gone up to the front to help greet the guests.

"Today will probably be the day that we officially meet Mr. Brantley." Janie said as she placed a tablecloth onto a table with Ellie's help.

"Yes, and you'd better be prepared to have Mama pushing you quite forcefully in his direction." They looked over at their mother, who was supposed to be decorating, but was instead talking loudly to some of the other ranchers' wives. Her words carried over to her daughters.

"My Janie will shine tonight! I just know that Mr. Brantley will immediately notice her beauty." Mrs. Bennett gushed.

Ellie noticed Lindie and Kathy in the corner, tinkering with a phonograph. Dennis Warslow, the son of the local Spearfish grocer, was helping them. Lindie was being her normal, immature self, flirting unabashedly with the poor young man. A loud, screeching sound emitted from the phonograph, and then Vernon Dalhart's pleasant voice was heard. Lindie immediately grabbed Dennis's arm and they swung into a dance, leaving Kathy there, to look through the rest of the disks.

Ellie rolled her eyes. "Another community event where Lindie will make a fool of herself, and us." She brushed a hand down her loose blue dress. It was comfortable enough, with short sleeves and a skirt that fell below her knees. She was much more comfortable wearing a split skirt or Levi trousers, but she knew that she couldn't embarrass herself or her family for Janie's sake.

"Don't be so hard on her." Janie smiled. "You know that's just how she is."

"She is the silliest tease who ever made…" Ellie started to speak but her mother interrupted.

"Ellie! Janie! You must come at once!" Mrs. Bennett called from the back porch, waving her hand wildly.

"I would assume this means the new gentleman is here." Ellie said as she and Janie headed toward the back of the house.

Janie and Ellie's assumption about one of the new men from church being Mr. Brantley was correct. He was the tall one, with curly blonde hair, and a smile that could light up the horse stable. He was surrounded by guests, talking and laughing with them like they were all old friends. When Rosalie saw Janie and Ellie, she grabbed them and hastily pulled them through the crowd. Ellie couldn't help but notice her mother beaming from the porch.

"Mr. Brantley, these are the friends I was telling you about, the sisters. This is Ellie and Janie Bennett."

Charles Brantley turned to greet the two women, then caught Janie's eye and could not look away.

"I am very pleased to meet you ladies. How lucky for me that we have the whole spring and summer to get to know one another." He took Janie's hand and kissed it like a Victorian gentleman would. "A real pleasure."

"And this." Benjamin McFadden, Rosalie's fiance, pushed through the crowd, bringing another handsome young man to the small group. It was the other man from church who had locked eyes with Ellie. "This is Lucas Callahan. He is a good friend of Mr. Brantley's."

"I am very pleased to meet you, Mr. Callahan." Ellie smiled and held out her hand. Mr. Callahan took one sullen look at the hand, then briefly shook it. He smelled faintly of root beer.

"A pleasure." He stepped away, putting distance between himself and Ellie. As she had noticed at church, Mr. Callahan was extremely attractive, with dark hair and blue eyes that contrasted with his tanned complexion, strong features and a well-defined body. He wore brown pants and a dark blue button-up shirt, underneath a maroon vest and brown blazer. He was buttoned up so tightly that Ellie felt the urge to unbutton the blazer just to frazzle him. She shook her head. She usually didn't have thoughts of that nature about men. However, as attractive as Lucas Callahan was, he clearly wasn't as friendly as Mr. Brantley.

Ellie took another look at Charles. He was talking to Janie, a cup of lemonade in one hand, looking very much at home, even though both men were obviously big city-boys. Mr. Brantley was even dressed opposite Mr. Callahan. He wore Levi's and a Henley shirt that hugged his upper body perfectly and a brown Stetson covered his head. The outfit made him look like he had grown up next door. All the young ladies in the room wanted his attention, but true to her beauty, he was only focused on Janie. Ellie decided to leave the two alone and walked away, in search of other friends.

"Mr. Brantley is quite wealthy, a Chicago lawyer who is first in line to take over a firm from his uncle. He's here to relax after graduating, and is supposed to join the actual partnership this winter when another partner retires. A very good catch for any girl." Mrs. Ingraham, another friend of the family, spoke to Martha as Ellie walked past. Great. Even more reason for her mother to pressure Janie about the young man.

"Ellie!"

At the sound of her voice Ellie turned and smiled.

"Charlotte." Ellies's best friend Charlotte Ingraham approached. "I was just thinking about you. I saw your mother talking with mine and knew you wouldn't be too far away."

"Yes Ma'am, I am here, and I can't wait to eat some of that delicious food I smell!" Charlotte was a plain girl, with mousy brown hair, brown eyes and a nondescript face, but she made up for it in her personality, humor and a zestful love of life. Unfortunately, she also had a love of food, as did Ellie, but Ellie worked so hard on the ranch, she didn't easily gain weight. Charlotte, on the other hand, had a plumper figure. At 27, she had all but given up hope of finding a husband and was content to teach at the Spearfish school.

"I agree, let's go," Ellie said, "and we need to catch up. I know with your mother being the town gossip and your father the sheriff, you must know all about these new visitors from the East."

"Oh, I do indeed." Charlotte smiled.

The two found a place to sit and as they ate, Charlotte told Ellie all about Lucas Callahan and Charles Brantley.

"Mr. Brantley is a lawyer, but he really doesn't need to work because he's already rich. His father owns a prosperous lumber business in Chicago, and they are relatives of the Astors. He just bought the Verbena Meadows Ranch, which you probably already knew. He has two sisters, one married, one not, they both came with him, as well as his brother-in-law. They're all somewhere around here. As I said, Mr. Brantley has a law degree and his uncle will be giving him the law practice eventually." She looked around and spotted the other man, Mr. Callahan. The dark-haired grouch stood on his own, eying the guests with disdain clear on his face. Charlotte gestured at him and continued. "His friend there, Mr. Callahan, is quite well-to-do also. I think the family started with the railroad and steel business. His father was savvy and made some smart investments in the stock market and now they have more money than they know what to do with. Callahan also has an aunt, Mrs. Madeline VanRensselaer, who is close friends with the Vanderbilts, so both men have connections and money."

"And Mr. Callahan has a bad attitude." Ellie added.

"Yes, he does seem a bit pretentious."

"That is an understatement." Ellie looked at him again. He was still standing off to the side, not talking to anyone, watching as some of the boys started the bonfire and brought some chairs over. Three other guests that Ellie did not know had joined him, two women and a man. They were

12

probably members of Brantley's family. "Look at him, he's just standing there. I tried to be friendly earlier and he basically walked away from me. Incredibly rude. At least Mr. Brantley is having a good time."

"As are your sisters..." Charlotte nodded in the direction of Lindie and Kathy, who had obviously manipulated one of the boys to get them some home-distilled whiskey. Even though alcohol was prohibited by the 18th Amendment, folks in town were able to brew their own beer and distill their own whiskey and the local law didn't seem to pay much mind, unless the drinkers became disorderly. Lindie was giggling and hanging all over Dennis Warslow and Kathy was whispering and laughing with another boy who Ellie recognized, but didn't know by name. Marie was on the porch, curled in a chair, reading, occasionally giving disgruntled looks at those people who were being boisterous. Ellie and Charlotte moved to join Janie and Mr. Brantley.

"I really do enjoy this song." Charles Brantley was saying as he listened to the tune on the gramophone. "I love jazz. Do you enjoy this type of music, Miss Janie?"

"I do, though I'm afraid I don't recognize many of the songs."

Charles smiled. "I've had the pleasure of hearing a man named Louis Armstrong play in concert. Mark my words, he'll go down in history."

"So do you enjoy dancing also, Mr. Brantley?" Ellie asked.

"I do, very much," He replied. "I was glad to hear we would be able to do so once the band is ready."

"They likely won't compare to the big bands back east, but it will be quite enjoyable." Ellie smiled, then turned to Mr. Callahan, who had joined their group quite subtly. He was looking disapprovingly at Lindie, Kathy,

13

and some of the other younger girls who were acting quite immature. "Mr. Callahan, do you enjoy dancing?"

He met her eyes. "No. Not if I can help it." He then looked away.

Mr. Brantley continued his conversation with Janie. "I love music and dancing, but I'm afraid I am not much of a reader. I prefer being out of doors, which is why I love being here. So much open space, so much beauty. I cannot wait to see the buffalo that I hear still roam around the area."

"Ellie can drive you down to Custer State Park." Janie suggested. "I mean, I would love to go as well, but she is the outdoorsman-or should I say outdoorswoman-of the family. She is a wonderful guide."

"That would be very nice. I look forward to it." Charles smiled.

Finally, the band finished warming up and the dancing began. Charles's eyes lit up and he grabbed Janie's hand. "Come, will you dance with me?"

"Of course, Mr. Brantley." Janie laughed and allowed him to pull her to the dancing area.

Charlotte nudged Ellie with her hip and gestured to Mr. Callahan. Ellie turned toward the man. "Are you sure you're not up to a dance, Mr. Callahan?" She hoped she sounded enthusiastic about the invitation.

"No, thank you." He quickly tipped his hat and strode away, leaving Ellie and Charlotte behind.

"Do you see what I mean?" Ellie asked. "It's like he would rather be anyplace else but here."

"I think he's just shy," Charlotte stated. "I've seen similar behavior in a few of my students."

"He's shy, so he's rude to me?"

"Maybe he's attracted to you and doesn't know how to act around you."

Ellie looked at her friend in total disbelief. "Surely you're joking. That's much less likely than him just being shy."

"I'm not at all joking," Charlotte replied. "I've noticed him watching you quite a bit tonight. Perhaps you should give him a chance to get to know you."

Ellie sighed. "I'm trying. Did you not just hear me ask him to dance?"

"You did, you did. But you could have been more genuine about the invitation."

"But he…"

Charlotte held up a hand. "I'm just telling you what I notice. I think you need to give him a better chance."

Ellie shook her head. "I don't think he wants one. But I'll try."

~~~~~~~

Ellie amused herself by dancing with some of the local boys and elderly men. Her dance partners were either too young for her or unavailable, as usual, but it was a splendid time nonetheless. She continued to notice Lucas Callahan, and wondered if Charlotte was right about him being shy. He only danced once, with the red-haired woman who looked as though she belonged in an encyclopedia under the entry for "Flapper". Ellie discovered the woman was Isabella Brantley, Charles's younger sister. Mr. Callahan refused to talk with anyone else, from what Ellie could tell and spent the evening skulking around the yard. Mr. Brantley's other sister,

15

Mrs. Louisa Hurst, kept to herself, looking down her nose at everyone else while her husband apparently found the whiskey barrel much to his liking.

When the band took a break, Ellie walked toward Charlotte, passing her mother's group of friends.

"Mr. Callahan has the most deplorable character," Martha Bennett stated. Everyone in the group seemed to agree.

"I have never met anyone so moody and unfriendly." Another woman added.

Ellie frowned, feeling a little sorry for the man. Even if he were those things, these women shouldn't be openly discussing it at a party. Charlotte hadn't thought him horrible, and she was a fairly good judge of character. Ellie changed her destination and made her way across the yard to where she had last seen Mr. Callahan. She was determined to visit with him and give him another chance, and maybe ask him to dance again, but Charles Brantley beat her to him.

"Come on, Luke." Charles begged. "You know I hate to see you stand around all by yourself. Parties are so much better if you get out there and dance. Mingle!"

"I prefer not to, thank you." Mr. Callahan clasped his hands behind him. "You know full well I dislike dancing unless I know the person whom I am dancing with."

"Luke." Charles coaxed his friend. "I know this isn't the kind of company you're used to, but there are plenty of nice, pretty girls here."

"Charles, you are taking all the dances with the most beautiful woman at this party, truly the only one who would be worth my time." Lucas and Charles both looked over at Janie. Ellie was so happy to hear them speak highly of her sister that she ignored the fact that they had insulted her, along with every other girl at the party.

"She is, isn't she?" Charles' face lit up with a smile. "She is the most amazing girl I have ever met! She is sweet and kind and simply the best. Let's go find her sister, Ellie, she's quite pretty herself."

Lucas Callahan glanced over at Ellie, who immediately pretended to be checking on the supply of lemonade.

"She's all right, but not good enough to tempt me." He said coldly. "Besides, why would I dance with her when no other single man has? The only men paying attention to her are married, old enough to be her father or way too young for her."

Ellie's mood immediately changed. *How rude!* Her heart pounded with anger, and she had to admit, with hurt. Lindie said condescending things like that all the time, but Lucas Callahan didn't even know her. *Who does he think he is? The men I have danced with are quite kind. And why would he even care? Why did he even notice?* Granted, he was right that none of them could be considered suiters, but really. She shook her head. Mr. Callahan had just run out of chances to get into her good graces.

Chapter Three

A little later, Ellie and Janie sat on camp chairs in front of the fire, resting a bit. Janie always had the young, single men wanting to dance with her, yet tonight, Charles Brantley had been monopolizing most of her time.

"I cannot believe Charles Brantley left Janie to dance with Charlotte Ingraham, of all people," Martha Bennett said to Mrs. Austen as they walked behind them. Ellie sighed. Why couldn't her mother just talk about normal things instead of constantly gossiping?

Lucas Callahan sat on a chair a few feet away and kept looking over towards Ellie. She met his gaze and his eyes raised as someone came up behind Ellie and Janie and threw his arms around both their shoulders.

"Hello, ladies." Charles Brantley smiled, then came around and sat between Janie and Lucas Callahan.

"Did you enjoy dancing with Charlotte, Mr. Brantley?" Ellie asked.

"Oh, yes, she has such a great sense of humor, quite fun to talk with." Charles Brantley laughed.

"It is a pity she's so plain." Martha Bennett spoke from Mr. Callahan's other side.

"Mama, you shouldn't say things like that." Ellie spoke up. "Charlotte is one of the best friends I could ask for." The way her mother was acting, Ellie had no doubt she had found the whiskey.

"Oh, you are too kind to her, Ellie. Besides, it's Janie who is the real catch of the county." Martha walked around to put her hands on Janie's shoulder. "Why, not even two years ago, a young senator's aide passed through this way, you remember, to report on the National Forest, and he fell head over heels in love with her."

"He was actually a cad, among other things." Ellie muttered and tried not to shudder. "Mr. Clark Mercer." She hadn't cared for him at all, and was still unsure of why he made her feel so uneasy.

"He even wrote my Janie a song," Martha ignored Ellie. "It was simply lovely."

"And that ruined everything." Ellie tried desperately to ease the awkwardness her mother had created.

"I would think writing a song for your beloved would strengthen the relationship." Lucas Callahan spoke.

"If it were a true love, perhaps, but the song Mr. Mercer wrote was superficial and trite." Ellie stood, needing to get away from the man.

"So what would you suggest then, if a man wanted to show a woman how he felt?" Lucas Callahan asked.

She looked back and met his eyes. "He would dance with her." She couldn't help but grin. "Even if she was simply 'all right'." After throwing his words back at him, she walked away.

~~~~~~

Luke Callahan sighed and rubbed his temple as Ellie Bennett stormed off. He admired her pluck, and her chocolate brown eyes had caught his attention from the moment he first saw her. He never found it easy to talk with people he didn't know, but for some reason, he wanted to be able to converse with this cowgirl. It didn't make sense. He stared into the bonfire flames.

"Luke, here you are." Isabella Brantley snuck up to his side. He tried not to show his annoyance. Charles's sister had made it obvious that she would be open to a courtship, but she wasn't the one for him for a variety of reasons, including the fact that she was a flapper, an incorrigible flirt, overly critical, shallow and most of all, she had no faith in God. Luke would accept many flaws, but his future wife had to be a woman of faith. He had met Charles his first year at Harvard and Isabella a few months later during a visit to Boston and had soon found her to be nothing like her brother.

"I cannot believe Charles is actually considering buying more property out here," she said, then took a puff on her cigarette.

"And why not? I am." Though South Dakota was a little farther west than he ever thought he would want to live, he enjoyed riding and the outdoors and could see himself staying here for extended periods of time.

"You're considering it as a business opportunity. Charles wants a residence here." Isabelle scoffed. "I'm glad he brought you along. He trusts you, Luke. If you tell him not to keep that ranch, he won't."

Isabella was right. When he had first met Charles, he was a first year student, like Luke, but was far too trusting and naive. Luke quickly became the friend who guided Charles and always watched his back, and kept Charles from getting in over his head. That was the main reason Luke had come to South Dakota, but he also wanted to investigate the possibility of opening a resort in the Black Hills. In fact, he wanted nothing more than to leave the party and focus on his business, but he had promised Charles he would come to some social gatherings.

"Why would you care so much whether or not Charles keeps the ranch?" Luke glanced at Ellie, who was dancing with a tow-headed young man who couldn't be older than fifteen. "You'll never have to come out here again if you don't want to. In fact, I'm surprised you and the Hursts came out in the first place."

"Let's just say I want to make sure my brother doesn't do anything rash that he may regret." She didn't even try to hide the glare she gave Janie Bennett.

"You don't even know these people, Isabella. Perhaps you should get to know them first."

"As if! Janie Bennett seems sweet enough, but not even she could do justice as the wife of my brother. You can't possibly tell me that your Aunt Madeline and all of your friends and business associates from back home would approve of the future Mrs. Callahan hailing from Ranchtown, South Dakota."

Isabella was right, irritatingly so. His Aunt Madeline VanRensselaer would never accept a woman like Ellie Bennett, and in all probability, Ellie would be miserable trying to fit into his world. He shook his head. What was he thinking? He had just met her, and had not even had a successful conversation with her.

"You're right, of course, but I wouldn't worry about Charles. You know how easily he falls in and out of love." Luke couldn't help but think that maybe that wasn't true this time.

21

"He has such a tender heart." Isabella pursed her lips. "Which is why we need to keep an eye on him, just in case."

~~~~~~

*L*ater that night, Ellie tied off the braid in her hair and slipped under her covers. It had been a long, but enjoyable evening.

"What do you think of Charles?" Janie wanted her sister's opinion more than anyone else's. The two girls shared a room and often talked before falling asleep.

"I like him well enough, but the more important question is, what do you think of him?" Ellie asked even though she knew the answer.

"Charles Brantley is everything I would ever want in a man. He is kind, funny, sensitive, and he has impeccable manners…"

"Don't forget good-looking and conveniently rich." Ellie teased.

"You know I don't care about money," Janie replied.

"Maybe not you, but Mama is beside herself with happiness. A wealthy husband for her beautiful Janie."

"I couldn't believe that he asked me to dance so many times. I didn't expect that. It was such a compliment."

"Don't be ridiculous. I most certainly can believe it. But, as usual, that's the one big difference between you and me. You're so modest that you can't accept compliments, and yet I expect people to compliment you. Why wouldn't Mr. Brantley want to dance with you time after time? How could he not help but notice that you are ten times more beautiful than any other woman in this county." She leaned forward. "It was nice of him to ask me to dance and I really appreciated the fact that he asked Charlotte to dance. It was such a kind gesture, it made her feel so special. Men in this town rarely see what a wonderful person she truly is." She tapped her chin and pretended to think. "Mr. Brantley seems to be a fine man, and I do believe I approve of a relationship between the two of you. There have been several other men you've liked that were far worse."

Janie shuddered. "Yes, and I am glad you warned me against them. They weren't bad men, just not the ones for me."

"I'm not sure that's true, you so often like people, whether they deserve it or not. You rarely see a fault in anybody. Everyone is good in your eyes. Come to think of it, I don't recall ever hearing you speak negatively of anybody in your entire life."

"That's just not true!"

"Name me one negative trait that you have found about anyone."

Janie thought for a moment, and then said: "Mr. Callahan! I still can't believe what he said about you! Very rude."

Ellie frowned. "Lucas Callahan?" She paused, thinking about the night and the man. "I wonder if I would have liked him if he hadn't said that. Charlotte thinks he's just shy, but even if that were the case, he certainly didn't need to act the way he did, even though I know he didn't mean for me to hear." She shook her head. "But that's not the point. The point is that you are kind and beautiful and I think Mr. Brantley is the one you have been waiting for."

Janie smiled and stared up at the ceiling, hoping Ellie was right.

~~~~~~

Across the valley, Luke and Charles stood on the wraparound porch at the Verbena Meadows Ranch. The house was more like a mansion built of

23

logs and it overlooked the Black Hills National Forest. Duchess, Luke's black and white border collie and constant companion, laid at his feet.

"So, you had a good time tonight, Charles?" Luke asked.

"I did. I really did. You could have too." Charles chided his friend.

"No, I don't think so. I told you I wanted to focus on business dealings. I've been wanting to visit this area since my father spoke so highly of it before he died. I enjoy nature of course but I would rather be home in St. Louis." Luke loved St. Louis more than any other place he had been. He had an apartment in Chicago, but his house in St. Louis was where he called home. One of the reasons he had come to South Dakota was to make plans for an elaborate resort. Not only were the Black Hills beautiful, but the picturesque "badlands" were only 120 miles east of Spearfish. Some spectacular rock carving work was being done not that far away either. A man named Gutzon Borglum and 400 workers were sculpting US presidents into a mountain called Six Grandpas. When they were done, tourists would be coming from all around the world, and Luke knew that the potential of making money was immeasurable.

"I think I could live here." Charles stated. "Besides the view, I have never felt more comfortable and at ease than I do here. The people are so kind and courteous and of course, Janie Bennett is an angel."

Luke sighed. "Yes, but her mother is unbelievable. Coarse and unrefined and she also drank way too much tonight. Did you notice the younger sisters were drinking too? It's like prohibition was never passed."

"People are drinking in St. Louis and everywhere else in the United States, you know that, despite the 18th Amendment."

"Perhaps that is true, but your own sister agrees with me when it comes to these people." He thought back to Ellie. There was something

24

about her that made him more anxious than he had ever been. True, he never found it easy to talk to people he didn't know, but his anxiety was so much more prevalent around her.

"Louisa and Isabella told me they liked Janie." Charles defended her. "You can think what you want, Luke, but I don't care about Mrs. Bennett's actions. I intend to spend as much time with Janie as possible."

Luke groaned and his stomach felt queasy. That would likely mean he would be spending much more time with Ellie Bennett, as close as she seemed to be to her sister. He was definitely eager to see her again, yet at the same time, he didn't like that he felt this way.

Chapter Four

The next day, Ellie came in from the pasture, hot and sweaty and ready for a bath, but Charlotte had come over for a visit. The two of them and Janie sat on the porch, and the topic of conversation quickly turned to Lucas Callahan and his coldness.

"Isabella Brantley told me that he is quite loyal and usually only talks to his own friends," Janie stated. "She said that he is always kind and friendly to her."

"Well, that's all well and good, she can just have him," Ellie replied a little too flippantly. From what she had observed, the flapper wanted the gentleman.

Charlotte shook her head. "Maybe he has a reason to be prideful. He has family, fortune, and I would bet every single woman in Chicago and St. Louis is vying for his attention. He has everything going for him. Besides, I still think he's shy."

"That may all be true, but he doesn't have to be so arrogant!" Ellie was still hurt by the comment he had made about her. Perhaps she wouldn't be so affected by him if she had other men hanging on her every word, but that wasn't the case. Lindie could act that way, but not

Ellie. Seeing her friend was being stubborn, Charlotte changed the subject to Janie and Charles.

"You know, Janie, you really shouldn't hide your feelings." Charlotte warned her. "You need to make sure he knows you're interested. Don't play games like some other girls do, I don't think he's the kind of man to like that. Be sure to show your true feelings."

"I do let my feelings show. Just wait until tomorrow." Janie rebutted. "I have been invited by Isabella to visit the Verbena Meadows Ranch. So has Ellie, but she'll be coming later because she wants to complete her chores. I am so excited, finally, we will be able to see the inside of that vast home."

"I cannot wait to hear all about it," Charlotte said with a smile, "but heed my words!"

~~~~~~

"I think we should have a party here." Charles exclaimed. Luke looked up from the letter he was writing and frowned. He and Charles were in the huge front study. Luke sat at the large mahogany desk with a beautiful view of the rolling Black Hills and Charles lounged on a settee. Luke took his reading glasses off and gaped at his friend.

"Why? I cannot for the life of me understand why you want to socialize with these people so much. Besides, you'll be able to see them all at the church social this weekend."

"It would be fun to be the host. The social might not have any dancing and I would love to dance with the lovely ladies again, especially one in particular." Charles smiled as he pushed himself off the settee. "I'll go talk with Isabella to see what she thinks." He hopped up the stairs at the back of the room, his long legs taking them two at a time.

At this new thought, Luke stared, unblinking at the paper he had been writing on. The idea of a certain girl in his arms appeared in his mind and he was immediately distracted. As much as he hated to admit it, he couldn't stop thinking about Ellie Bennett and her most striking feature: those chocolate brown eyes. They were so full of expression that they nearly sparkled.

Luke groaned to himself when Isabella wandered into the room. She immediately noticed his stare. "I believe I can guess what you are thinking of, Luke." She teased, puffing on her long, thin cigarette. He hated the foul habit that so many had.

"I highly doubt that." Luke stuffed the letter he had been writing into an envelope. Why couldn't Isabella realize he had no desire to be with her?

"You are thinking of how bored you will be, spending so many evenings in the company of these country bumpkins this summer." She sauntered over to him and put her hand on his shoulder. "I must say, I am of the same opinion. Last night…well, let's just say that I have never been more annoyed."

"Well, you're wrong. I was thinking of something a little more…appealing." He stood and brushed her hand away. "I was thinking of how a woman's beautiful eyes can turn an average-looking woman into one who can bewitch a man if he's not careful."

Isabella pursed her lips in disappointment. "And whose eyes would those be?"

"Oh. Just…one of the local girls I saw at that gathering last night."

Isabella frowned. She should have known, but she also knew that Luke would never seriously consider a relationship with any of these uncivilized girls. She decided to push him even further.

"I am surprised at you, Luke. Who is this fine lady hidden among the country bumpkins? When will the date of your nuptials be?"

Luke laughed a short laugh. "I expected you would say something like that. A woman's imagination jumps right to marriage with very little encouragement."

"Well, I will wish you all the luck in the world." Isabella couldn't help but get one last dig in. "But I truly hope it isn't one of those Bennett girls."

Luke tried not to react to Isabella's words. No one could know that he had any interest in Ellie Bennett.

Isabella continued harping. "Good Heavens. You would have a most charming mother-in-law, and of course, she would probably move right into one of the guest cabins on your St. Louis property, or perhaps even the manor house itself. Wouldn't that be enjoyable?" And with that, Isabella strode out of the room.

Chapter Five

"Hya, Miss Ingraham!" A tow-headed boy ran by, then joined his friends who were playing baseball in the field behind the church. The whole town and many people from neighboring ranches had come out for the Black Hills State University's homecoming parade. Many churches had added events to expand the celebration into a day-long affair. Ellie had been looking forward to this 'Swarm Day' for quite some time.

"Do you ever regret not continuing your college education?" Charlotte asked. Ellie had gone to BHSU for one year, even played on the girls' basketball team, but she didn't return the following year because her family needed her help on the ranch after her father had fallen extremely ill. After a long, dry summer, the ranch was struggling financially, and paying tuition was an additional burden.

"There are times, yes," Ellie replied. "Do you ever regret not getting your teaching certificate through the college?"

"No, not really, I can still teach. Besides, I've learned more in the eight years I've been a teacher than I ever could have from sitting in a college classroom."

"Experience is the best education." Lucas Callahan and Charles Brantley had come up behind Ellie. Luke continued speaking, his breath again smelling faintly of root beer. "Still, there is no substitute for a formal education."

"I would expect you to say something like that." Ellie frowned. "Not all of us can afford to get degrees at…where? Harvard? Oxford? Yale?" *Where else would a man like Lucas Callahan go to college?*

He scowled at her. "I did get my degree from Harvard, yes, and I understand that not everyone is as fortunate as me in that respect. I'm simply saying that earning a degree is important, but you were right as well in regards to experience being valid."

"And it is something that all of us can afford." Ellie turned away from Luke and focused on Charles. "Are you enjoying our community celebration, Mr. Brantley?"

"I am indeed, Miss Eleanor. Good day, Miss Charlotte." He frowned as Luke stalked away. "I apologize for Luke, ladies. I'm not quite sure what's gotten into him. I will say he meant no disrespect to those with a limited education. His own father came from fairly humble beginnings and yet made quite a name for himself."

Ellie waved her hand. "It's no matter."

Charles nodded. "Have you seen Janie today? Well, of course, I'm sure you have, you came into town together I would assume, but have you seen her lately?"

"She's working for a bit at the church bake sale." Ellie told him.

"Splendid, thank you." He turned and made his way in that direction.

"Mr. Brantley is quite smitten with our Jane." Charlotte commented.

31

"Yes, I think he likes her very much." The two began walking toward the Ford garage, where they would be meeting the rest of the Ingraham and Bennett families for the parade. "I just don't understand why such a congenial and kind man like Charles Brantley is friends with a boor like Lucas Callahan."

"Mr. Brantley's sisters are interesting as well," Charlotte added. "My dad tried to be friendly and converse with them at the Austen bonfire but they were just downright rude to him."

"That doesn't surprise me. Did you notice that Mr. Hurst seems to drink way too much? I wonder if it's to get over the fact that he's married to Louisa."

"Now Ellie, you don't know that for sure, and even if it's true, it's certainly not for you to comment on." Charlotte admonished her.

"I know, I know, I'm sorry. The whole group just gets under my skin. Charles is the exception."

"Well, if all goes as we suspect, you will become family with Charles and that means Isabella and the Hurst family as well."

"I realize that," Ellie replied. "Perhaps my sharp tongue is why…" She shook her head. She couldn't let her lack of a husband bother her. After all, Janie and Charlotte were still unmarried and they had far better qualities in her opinion. God would show her His choice if that was in His plan for her.

"You just need to think before you speak." Charlotte replied.

"Thanks for reminding me," Ellie smiled. "And Janie did say that Isabella and Louisa were friendly to her, so that's good, at least." *Perhaps there is hope.*

That evening, St. Joseph's Church set up a dance area for anyone who wanted to continue socializing. The Bennetts, Ingraham's and the Brantley party were all in attendance. Charles continued to pay Janie very close attention, but Ellie was very concerned when she saw Lindie and Kathy running around with some unfamiliar young men. They had to be athletes from the college, wearing their dark green sweaters with a yellow 'H' sewn on front. Knowing Lindie, they played football, and they did not look like they had the best of characters. Ellie made her way over to her sisters, hoping to talk some sense into them. Lindie whispered into one of the young men's ears, and the two athletes walked away. Lindie turned and found Marie sitting off to the side.

"Marie! Quit being so boring."

Ellie's face scrunched in confusion. What was Lindie doing? Marie looked just as confused. She had just been sitting on a bench, quietly reading, and Lindie usually left her alone.

"Chase and Jason are going to find their friends and I promised to bring them some girls to dance with." She looked at Ellie. "You need to come too, Ellie. It's not like you can find a single man to dance with on your own."

Ellie blushed and groaned, especially because at that moment, Luke walked by them and didn't hide the fact that he was listening to everything they were saying. Why did he always seem to be around her at the most inopportune moments?

"What if I don't want to dance?" Marie asked. "You know I don't like to socialize in that manner."

"Come now, Marie, don't be a cancelled stamp. Even Ellie's going to dance with them."

"I never said that." Ellie protested. "And besides, Lindie, I'm not so sure you should be spending time with those men. They looked a bit...untrustworthy."

"Oh, Ellie, don't tell me you're going to be a bore as well. You'll never get a boyfriend, much less a husband if you don't take a chance."

"That might be partially true, but that doesn't mean you have to act immature and silly, much less settle for a disreputable young man." Perhaps it wasn't the best way to say it, but it was true.

A shadow crossed Lindie's face. "Well, fine then, don't blame me because the boys prefer to spend time with me over you!" She turned and stomped away, Kathy following like a little lost puppy. "Spinster!" Lindie yelled over her shoulder.

Ellie sighed and turned to Marie, who had gone right back to reading *Anna Karenina*. Marie was so engrossed in the huge novel; she didn't even realize when Ellie simply walked away. Part of her wanted to be in disbelief of Lindie's actions, but in reality, it didn't surprise her. She headed in the direction of Charles and Janie, who were on the far side of the churchyard, but before she could get there, the music started and Charles escorted Janie to the dancing area.

"Oh, my dear Eleanor, how are you?" She stopped and smiled at Mr. Ingraham, Charlotte's father, but she couldn't keep her cheerfulness when she saw who he was talking to. "You've met Mr. Lucas Callahan, correct?"

"Yes, yes I have." She nodded.

"Mr. Callahan, I must encourage you to ask Eleanor to the dance floor. She is quite the dancer."

"No, thank you, Mr. Ingraham, that's quite all right," Ellie blushed. The last thing she wanted was for Luke to ask her to dance just because he was pressured by the sheriff to do so.

"I was just telling Mr. Callahan how accomplished and multi-talented all of our Black Hills women are. Like you, for instance. Tough enough to bust a bronco, yet genteel enough to host an elegant dinner."

"I wouldn't say I'm accomplished…" Ellie insisted.

"And I know how much you love dancing, Miss Ellie, you can't deny that."

"That is true, I do, but…"

"That settles it, then." Mr. Ingraham beamed at the two. "Mr. Callahan…"

Ellie held up a hand. "I'm sure Mr. Callahan doesn't want to dance with me."

"And why not?" Mr. Ingraham asked, looking at Luke.

"Actually, Miss Eleanor, I would be honored if you'd be my dance partner," Luke said awkwardly.

"There, you see." Mr. Ingraham nudged Ellie toward Luke, who held a hand out to her.

"No, really. I'd prefer not to dance right now. If you'll excuse me." She then turned and walked away, pretending to have a specific destination in mind, when in reality, she just needed to get away from the odious, pompous man who was far too handsome for his own good.

~~~~~~

$\mathcal{L}$uke watched her stride away. Why did he feel the need to act so stiff and formal when she was around? He just wasn't savvy about conversing with people he didn't know well. Or was it more than that with her?

"I wouldn't worry about her, Mr. Callahan." Sheriff Ingraham slapped him on the back. "I've known Miss Ellie since she was a wee babe, and she's a busy one, always moving from one thing to another."

"I'm sure she has many friends and admirers." Luke replied.

"Friends, yes. She has been a dedicated friend to my daughter Charlotte since childhood, and as for admirers, I must say yes to that as well. There are many in town that respect her. She is a hard worker, and many were disappointed when she had to drop out of college to help her father run the ranch. She would have been quite the basketball star for our ladies' Yellow Jackets team."

"I hadn't realized any of that." Luke scanned the crowd and quickly found Ellie, laughing and talking with Charlotte, Janie and Charles. Why couldn't he say something to bring her joy like that? He thought of their earlier discussion. No wonder she had been so defensive of those who didn't have a college education: she had lost the chance to obtain one of her own. He admired the sacrifice she had shown her family.

"She is fiercely loyal and selfless." Sheriff Ingraham added as he spied his wife. "Excuse me, my boy, Mrs. Ingraham is summoning me for a dance."

Luke nodded, popped another root beer barrel in his mouth, then began to make his way towards Charles. He knew Miss Ellie wouldn't want to speak to him, but he didn't know anyone else well enough to simply walk up to them and start talking and he didn't want to be caught standing around all alone again. Charles had already scolded him about that. Oh, why couldn't he have been given the gifts of charm and mindless conversation?

"There you are, Luke." Isabella grabbed his arm and pulled him to her side. "I cannot believe this backwoods party. It's worse than the last one. No elegance, no eggs." Luke wanted to roll his eyes at her flapper word for people who lead an absurdly extravagant lifestyle. She continued. "I declare, I keep expecting a pig to dart through the streets and we'll all be expected to chase it down."

"That I would love to see." Luke answered dryly. "You in your flapper get-up."

She pursed her lips. "So Luke, where were you off to?"

"I was going to join Charles." He nodded in that direction.

"And the Bennett sisters, hmm?" Isabella chuckled. "I believe you're paying far too much attention to the younger of the two."

Luke tried not to show any emotion. Was Isabella fishing for information or had he given her hints of his interest in Ellie?

"I have noticed, Luke. Do you really think you should be looking at her that way? My goodness, can you imagine your Aunt Madeline receiving her in the parlor of her Charleston home?" She laughed. "I can see it now. Ellie Bennett, riding up on a horse in that split skirt she always wears with her braid and cowboy hat all askew, tracking mud and Lord only knows what else on her boots directly into your aunt's beautiful home."

Amazingly enough, Luke could picture it, and he had to admit to himself that he would most definitely enjoy seeing the scenario in real life. But of course Isabella was right. It would never work. Ellie would be miserable in his high-society life.

"I assure you, Isabella, I have no designs on Miss Eleanor Bennett. But it does appear as though your brother has them for Miss Janie."

"Yes, well, we'll just have to see about that." She frowned in the direction of Janie, Charles and Ellie.

Luke sighed. "Where are Louisa and Thomas?"

"Oh, Thomas had imbibed too much yet again, so Louisa took him back to Verbena Meadows. Luckily, the chauffeur wasn't off cavorting and had stayed where he belonged, with the car." The Hursts had brought their own car and chauffeur, saying that they didn't want to be at Charles's mercy.

"Thomas really should be careful with his drinking," Luke said.

"Yes, like your dear future mother-in-law." Isabella smirked.

Luke reddened. "I will not be marrying Ellie Bennett." He tried not to show his frustration with Isabella.

"I must say, that is good to hear." Isabella replied with a smug smile. She ran a hand down his arm and sauntered away. Luke sighed. When would he be able to go home?

Chapter Six

"*It* looks like it's going to rain, Janie." Ellie pulled her brown Stetson off and looked to the sky. "Are you sure you want to head over to Verbena Meadows?"

"Of course she does, she wants to leave right this instant." Martha Bennett insisted.

"I suppose I can drive you over in the truck and return later." Ellie replied.

"Absolutely not." Mrs. Bennett thrust her fists on her hips. "She'll go on horseback."

"Horseback?" Ellie looked at the sky again. "Mother, surely..."

"No, no, it is all for the best." Martha replied.

Ellie rolled her eyes "Oh, for Heaven's sake." She grumbled, then went back to work as Janie finished saddling her horse and rode off toward the Verbena Meadows Ranch.

~~~~~~

Luke stared at his friend, who was focused entirely on Janie Bennett. She was an extraordinary beauty and had quite a way about her, but Luke found he wasn't nearly as attracted to her as he was to Ellie. He would have danced with Ellie at the Homecoming social, but it appeared his shyness and awkwardness had gotten the best of him. It didn't help that his treatment of Ellie at the bonfire had given her a very poor first impression of him.

Janie had arrived just as a storm rolled in, and a part of Luke hoped the storm wouldn't keep Ellie away, yet he also thought it would probably be better if he kept his distance from her.

"I believe it's going to be quite the storm," Janie shrugged out of her rain jacket, then smiled at Charles.

"That's fine with me, I am sure we will find activities to keep us occupied." Charles replied. "You can stay for as long as you wish, and if you feel the absolute need to go home, I can drive you in my Phantom." Charles was very proud of his most recent purchase, a blue and white 1928 Rolls Royce Sports Phantom.

"Thank you so much for the kind offer," Janie smiled.

The trio took seats on the enclosed back porch that overlooked the forest and mountains. The view today was magnificent with the rolling thunder clouds contradicting the serene lands. The Black Hills really would be a perfect place to build a resort. The rain continued its gentle rhythm. Charles continued to lavish his attention onto Janie. Luke sat silently, looking across the pond, listening to Charles and Janie. Isabella and Louisa would not stop griping about their current situation and it annoyed Luke to no end. Thomas Hurst was in the billiard room, shooting pool on his own and drinking some local brew he had found. If Luke could stand the man, he would have joined him. Instead, he picked up some paperwork on the land he was considering to purchase and slid his reading glasses on. A bolt of lightning and a crash of thunder quickly turned the sky even darker, and rain began pouring down in earnest.

About two hours after Janie's arrival, a Ford Model T Truck drove up the road towards the house, and Duchess's head perked up.

"That's Ellie!" Janie exclaimed. Luke tried to seem unaffected with Ellis's arrival. Why on earth did she do that to him? He didn't even know her that well.

"I'll assist her into the house." Luke stood and went to greet Ellie at the front door, Duchess at his heels. He shrugged his jacket on and opened the door just as a very wet Ellie stomped up the steps and, not seeing Luke there, collided with him. He caught her by the waist and steadied her. She was a mess. Her brown hair fell in wet tangles framing her face, and mud covered her boots as well as the bottom of her split skirt. The dark blue shirt she was wearing clung to her body and she was breathing a little heavy. Luke thought she looked utterly breathtaking.

"Mr. Callahan! Hello." She said. "It's getting a bit messy out there."

"That is quite apparent." Isabella said sarcastically as she, Louisa, Charles and Janie came into the entryway. "Do you not have a rain jacket, Miss Ellie?"

"I was in such a hurry to get over here, I completely forgot, as silly as that sounds. I'm sorry to say that I don't believe Janie and I will be able to leave any time soon. I almost didn't make it here myself. The roads are becoming thick with mud and I would be willing to bet that there will be some washouts."

"What do you mean?" Isabella asked. "Are we stranded?"

Ellie laughed, her eyes bright. Luke tried to stop from staring at her, but was unsuccessful. "I'm saying that Janie and I are stuck here, at least

41

until the storm lets up and the roads can dry up a bit out there." She answered. "The creek's up over the bridge already and parts of the road are flooded too. I barely got through in the Ford. By now, it's impassable, even on horseback."

"That is more than all right." Charles said with a smile. "You are both welcome to stay here for as long as needed."

"You are so gracious, Mr. Brantley, thank you." Ellie smiled, then looked down as the black and white border collie nudged her hand.

"And who's this little beauty?" She smiled and knelt down to run her hand through her soft fur.

"This is my dog, Duchess." Luke replied.

"Luke and Duchess." Ellie chuckled. "Like Duke and Duchess." The collie licked her cheek and she laughed.

"Yes, well, she was already named when I got her." Luke shrugged.

Ellie stood. "Again, I am sorry for the intrusion. What were you all doing before I arrived?"

"We were just out on the back porch, talking," Janie replied, then rubbed her stomach.

"Well, now, won't this be just delightful." Isabella sighed, then huffed over towards where the magnificent stairs were. "I'm going to take a nap." Louisa followed.

"I must apologize," Charles said. "My sisters are not used to this country life. They're more city girls."

"Yes, I can tell." Ellie pulled off her muddied boots, then looked at Janie, who was quiet, even for Janie. "Janie, what's wrong?"

Oh, nothing." Janie said, but was getting paler as the moments passed. "Actually, I…" and with that, she raced to the washroom. Ellie was right behind her.

"Aww, Janie. Something you ate?" Ellie held Janie's hair and patted her back.

"Yes, most likely." Janie said, eyes watering.

"Let's get you to a more comfortable location. Come, we have many guest bedrooms." Charles stood in the doorway of the washroom and waved to one of the servants who led Janie and Ellie upstairs. As they walked, Ellie couldn't help but take in the beauty of the house. The rooms were each painted a different color, and accented with natural stone and beautiful wood that matched the exterior of the house. Electric light fixtures would light the hallway even in the black of night, and the room the servant led them to had windows that must have been five feet tall, giving a beautiful view of the forest in the distance.

"Well, thanks for leaving me to fend for myself with all of them." Ellie smiled at her sister after the servant had left them.

"You'll do fine. Isabella and Louisa have been relatively nice to me, and Mr. Hurst keeps to himself. You know how I feel about Charles. Just don't lose your temper with Mr. Callahan." Janie said weakly. There was a quiet knock on the door and Charles popped his head in.

"I must apologize for my condition, Mr. Brantley." Janie said quietly.

"No, Miss Janie, don't be. I only wish I could be of more help." Charles handed her a glass of water.

"Try to rest." Ellie said. "Holler if you need anything." She returned downstairs with Charles at her heels.

"Food problems?" Luke asked, concern in his voice.

"That's what I would suspect." Ellie looked around the great sitting room. "Goodness, your home is just beautiful." The floors were a high-polished wood that matched the rest of the house and had stunning imported rugs covering them. A leather couch, loveseat and armchair complimented the room they were in and the entire east wall consisted of a field stone fireplace with a hearth and built-in storage area for logs. The room was so massive, there were wood columns in the middle for stability.

Ellie was not one to just sit around, and so, while Luke and Charles found a deck of cards to play with, she wandered around the room, then sat and began reading the new Agatha Christie book she found on the bookshelf. *The Mystery of the Blue Train*. After about an hour, Isabella and Louisa returned from their naps and sat down. They immediately began complaining about the rain and anything else they could think of. Annoyed, Ellie excused herself to check on Janie. The moment she was out of earshot, Isabella's complaints turned to Ellie.

"That Ellie Bennett! Really! I don't know what anyone could possibly see in her. She is after all, just a rancher's daughter. I will never forget her appearance this afternoon. She looked literally barbaric."

"I thought she looked quite splendid," Charles said.

"Really?" Isabella said, disdain dripping from her words. "Charles, she drove out here all by herself with no escort and didn't even think to bring a rain jacket. She trekked mud and water all over the house. It's almost as if she is trying to prove something. Mustard Plaster."

Luke gritted his teeth. He wanted to defend Ellie, especially with Isabella using the current slang for someone who isn't wanted, and won't leave, but he held back. No one in the room could know that he wanted to champion her.

44

Isabella continued her rant against Ellie. "She's so annoying, far too independent, it's like she doesn't need anything else but her precious ranch and she wants everyone around her to know it." She turned to Luke with a smirk. "I would hope that her little adventure over here has affected any admiration you may have had for her. Those eyes you were talking about."

"Not really." Luke focused on his playing cards. "The eyes were actually brightened by the excitement, and she did remove her boots before entering, so really did no damage to the house."

Isabella sighed. "Well, at least Janie is a sweet girl, and I do hope she feels better. However, with that family of hers...please. I am afraid anyone who thinks of marrying her will be immediately turned off by that horrid mother."

"How...what...that doesn't make Janie one bit less wonderful." Charles stuttered.

"But it most definitely could lessen her chance at a good marriage," Luke said honestly. "Most men believe that old saying about women turning into their mothers..."

"Yes, well that is not always the case." Charles dearly loved his own mother, her kindness and generosity, but those traits had not been passed on to his sisters.

~~~~~~

Later that evening, as the storm continued, with Janie still feeling poorly, Ellie returned downstairs and picked up the Agatha Christie book she had found earlier and continued reading. Isabella, Luke, Charles and the Hursts sat at the sitting room table, playing cards again. Part of Ellie wanted to join, but she didn't want to intrude. Charles Brantley had been more than courteous, but the rest of the guests staying at the house had done nothing much to make her feel welcome.

Isabella looked at Ellie and spoke with derision in her voice. "I would gather that Miss Ellie over there dislikes playing cards. She must be one of the best readers and perhaps doesn't enjoy doing anything else."

"I don't know about that." Ellie laughed. "I am hardly the best reader in my family and I do in fact like doing many other things."

"I'm not much of a reader myself, but I own quite a few books." Charles said, then gestured to Ellie. "Come, Ellie, play cards with us."

"Thank you for the invitation." She stood and approached the table, heart pattering just a bit when she noticed that the only open seat was next to Luke. He didn't even meet her eyes as she sat down and Charles dealt her in.

"Luke, by the by, I've been meaning to ask, how is Helena?" Isabella inquired. "I admire her so much for all of her accomplishments, and now she has been accepted to the music conservatory. Miss Mary must be one of the finest music teachers for hire."

Luke simply nodded.

"I find it amazing how in this day and age, young women can still be so accomplished," Charles added. "So many can cook and sew and knit, raise a family and still look beautiful. Some even work outside of the home now." He smiled at Ellie. "They can even manage a ranch."

She smiled back in thanks to his complement.

"I don't agree with you." Luke stated. "I'm not sure that I know even half a dozen women who I would consider perfectly ideal. Accomplished, if you will."

46

"I suppose your ideal woman must be proficient at a good many things." Ellie tried to restrain from smacking the cards on the table and focused her attention on Luke. Bad idea. Why did he have to be so handsome? This evening, he was wearing khaki pants and a blue wool sweater that made his eyes as blue as the sky.

"I remember Luke's list for the ideal woman." Isabella interjected, then ticked the points off on her fingers. "She has to be smart, speak a few languages, be athletic, graceful, witty, confident..."

"Isabella..." Luke said, a bit irritated.

"And in addition to all this, she must have something more, a kind of elegance in her posture, and the tone of her voice must be sweet, yet steady. And of course, she must want to constantly improve her mind by reading. Don't deny it Luke, darling, I remember you saying this. Then, to top it all off, she must be a Christian, a woman of strong faith, something about charm being deceptive, and beauty fleeting."

Proverbs 31. Ellie put her cards down and leaned forward towards the table. "No one can be all of that. I am very surprised to hear that you even know six of these ideal women." She rested her elbows on the table as she looked at Luke's blue eyes. "I find it hard to believe that you know any."

"Are you so negative about women that you doubt one could have all these traits?" Luke raised his brow.

"I've never met a woman like this. If I did, I would be quite intimidated."

Luke studied Ellie as she looked back at her hand of cards. He hadn't expected that answer from her. She wasn't just light and teasing in her words, she was also quite thoughtful, but what he really noticed and liked was the fact that she wasn't afraid to stand up to him like so many others

47

were. Ellie had wit and intelligence; two things he wouldn't have expected from a girl who lived quietly, and simply, and happily on a ranch in the middle of nowhere. He caught her eye and gave her a quick smile.

"Maybe I have been too selective and unrealistic in my ideas." Luke admitted.

Isabella looked at him, as if upset about something he said, then slammed her cards down. "I'm going up to my room."

Ellie sighed. "I should check on Janie and then turn in for the night myself. Thank you for your hospitality, Mr. Brantley." And with that, she went upstairs.

Chapter Seven

The rainstorm continued throughout the night, but lessened in its intensity. The next morning, Janie's queasiness had turned to a minor cough, and she remained in bed. Ellie started to wonder if she had caught a cold, or perhaps was just overly fatigued. Ellie tried to keep herself occupied by reading, playing cards and keeping Janie company, but her mind was filled with all of the things that needed to be done back on the ranch. She disliked being away from home.

"I believe we will be here for a while." She told Luke and Charles as they entered the dining room. Charles still looked slightly sleepy, Luke, on the other hand, was as alert as ever, his shirt buttoned all the way and his dress slacks appeared to be freshly pressed. Isabella then sauntered in, dressed to the hilt as if she were ready for a big city flapper party.

"Good morning, all." She said with forced happiness.

"You seem to be in a better mood this morning, Isabella." Charles said as a servant set a cup of coffee in front of him. He nodded his thanks. Ellie appreciated the fact that he was kind to the hired help. Another point in his favor.

"Well, I have decided to just make the best of the situation." Isabella sat close to Luke and gave him a sly smile. Ellie rolled her eyes and continued to eat her breakfast.

The rain, now just a misty sprinkle, continued throughout the morning. Isabella flirted with Luke shamelessly, and he continually tried to put her off. Why couldn't she understand that he had no romantic interest in her? After lunch, Luke was able to procure some paper to write letters and take care of other business. Even though the storm had somewhat lessened, whenever Ellie went to check outside, she would come back to report that the road still looked impassable.

Isabella glanced at Luke as he wrote.

"You write uncommonly fast, Luke. I don't know that I have ever noticed," she stated.

"I've never thought that about myself." Luke's eyes never left the paper he was writing on. Was she seriously commenting on his writing pace?

"So much business you must have to take care of, especially with your plans to expand into new territory. I will not lie, I'd find that work annoying and boring." Isabella didn't seem to realize Luke was trying to brush her off yet again.

"Lucky for all involved then, that they are my responsibilities instead of yours," Luke commented, adjusting his reading glasses. "Right now, I am just writing a letter to Helena."

Ellie sat on the settee, again reading, and looked up at the mention of a girl in Luke's life. It was the same name they had brought up last night.

"Tell her that I can't wait to see her again." Isabella said. "I do so adore your sister."

Luke tried not to sigh. "I told her that the other day when I wrote to her, as you asked then."

Isabella would not stop talking to him. "You should tell her that I am delighted to know that she is now composing her own music, and also that I loved the sketches she sent you."

"Well," Luke folded the letter and put it into an envelope. "You must allow me to sing your praises of her when I write her next time. I don't have time to do so right now, or better yet, you can write her yourself."

"You truly do write so differently than my brother." Isabella droned on. Luke glanced up and met Ellie's eyes, just as she grinned to herself and looked back down at her book when she saw the exasperation in his face. "His writing is simply awful, with terrible penmanship and misspelled words."

"I can't help it, Isabella." Charles paged through the most recent copy of *The American* magazine. With how quickly he turned the pages, Ellie wasn't sure if he was actually reading the articles about economics and politics, which the publication was known for, or just bored. "I'm usually in a hurry."

Isabella turned to Ellie. "My dear Miss Bennett, would you like to stroll around the room with me? I have heard that it is quite refreshing to move about after sitting so long in one position."

Luke looked at the women out of the corner of his eyes. Ellie raised her eyebrows in slight confusion as if she wasn't sure why Isabella was suddenly being friendly towards her, but she was getting stiff, and physical movement would help, even though it seemed silly to just walk around the room.

"Would you care to join us, Luke?" Isabella asked.

"Well," Luke sat back, pulled his glasses off and looked directly at the two women. "I feel as though my joining you would ruin your motives."

"Di mi, whatever do you mean?" Isabella asked in a flirting tone, looking over her shoulder at him. If Ellie wasn't mistaken, 'di mi' was flapper-speak for 'my goodness'. Why couldn't Isabella just use regular English? Ellie decided she needed to speak.

"I think he is going to mock us," Ellie suggested. "We can disappoint him by not asking about his meaning." She continued to follow Isabella's lead. For once, she would try to tolerate the other woman. The walking did feel good, even if a little silly.

"I insist you tell us, Luke."

"Well, you either chose this method of stretching and passing time because you are telling secrets to one another, or it is because you know that your…figures…look very nice as you're walking around." Luke's hands started to sweat as he watched Ellie. She wore the split skirt and blue shirt that she had arrived in. Isabella had offered some of her clothes, but Ellie had declined. "If the former…" He continued, "I would be in your way. If the latter, I can… uh…admire you much better from here." He gave them what he hoped was an infectious smile, but he had always failed miserably at flirting.

"Shocking!" Isabella exclaimed. "How shall we respond?"

"We could always laugh at him." Ellie said, a smile on her face. She quickly noticed Luke's look of alarm.

"Oh, I think not." Isabella chuckled. "Luke hates to be laughed at."

"Ahh, that's too bad." Ellie smiled at Luke. "I truly love to laugh."

"I admit I have my faults." Luke set his right ankle over his left knee, trying to appear relaxed. "I have been told that I can be quite resentful. I find it difficult to forgive people who have hurt those I love. Once someone loses my trust..." Luke looked out the window into the rain. "It's gone forever."

"Well," Ellie walked back to where her book was. "I suppose I can't tease you for that." She then sat down and opened the book to continue her reading, yet she couldn't help but steal glances at the handsome, yet vexing man.

~~~~~~

𝒮ate that afternoon, Ellie quietly shut Janie's door. Her sister was feeling better, and even said she might try to bathe and join everyone for dinner later. Despite this, there was not much change in the weather, which meant that they would be staying at Verbena Meadows for a couple more days at least.

Ellie quietly made her way downstairs. She knew she should spend time with everyone else in the sitting room, but she had no desire to deal with Isabella Brantley and her not-so-subtle attempts for Luke's attention. She thought he would have welcomed the flapper's gushing, but he only seemed annoyed by it.

As she passed the billiard room, she heard the smack of clay pool balls crashing into one another and Charles laughing. Curious, she peered in the room to find Luke and Charles, a pool cue in each of their hands. Duchess poked her head up from the ground and looked at Ellie.

"Miss Ellie!" Charles smiled. "Come right in."

"I'm not sure I should intrude in this masculine domain." She stepped into the room anyways, eyes on Luke. Would he encourage her to leave?

"Nonsense." Luke answered. Ellie continued through the door and looked around the room. It was painted a light brown, with dark stained trim and taxidermied animal heads were displayed on the walls. There was another large field stone fireplace where several antique rifles hung above the mantle. Flames gently crackled in the firebox, giving the room a warm and comfortable atmosphere in spite of the cold drizzle outside. A solid-looking mahogany table was situated near one of the walls that had a large picture window with a view looking out across the mountains. Masculine chairs sat in each corner and the magnificent billiard table dominated the center of the room.

Luke bent over the table and took aim with his cue stick, then pulled it back and thrust it forward. The cue ball knocked two striped balls into the corner pockets.

"Nice shot." Ellie leaned back against the door frame, unsure if she felt comfortable enough to sit in one of the leather chairs.

"Thank you." He nodded and adjusted his maroon and black striped tie. The two men continued their play until Luke expertly knocked the eight ball into the side pocket he had called.

"One of these days, Callahan, I'll find a way to beat you." Charles playfully tossed his cue stick onto the table.

"Perhaps." Luke gave his friend a half-grin. Had Ellie ever seen his full smile? She felt for sure she would remember as it would likely enhance his handsome features. He turned his sky blue eyes to her.

"Would you like to learn how to play?" He asked Ellie. She chuckled to herself. When would men stop underestimating her?

"I was able to learn quite a bit from just watching the two of you play." She was telling the truth. She had learned that Charles was a good sport and that Luke had focus and a competitive streak. Well, so did Ellie. She moved to pick up the cue that Charles had discarded and Luke moved to each pocket to retrieve the balls and re-rack them.

"Let me show you how to hold the stick." Luke moved to stand behind Ellie and she got a whiff of sandalwood and root beer. His arms came around her and he positioned her hands on the cue stick, then he demonstrated how to lean over and move the stick. Her heartbeat accelerated and she felt his muscles tighten, as if uncomfortable, then took a step back. Just to be contrary, Ellie slipped her hand to an incorrect position.

"Like this?" She tried not to chuckle.

"No." His hand covered hers and adjusted it. "Like this, here."

Charles sat back in one of the chairs and smiled.

"Oh. Thank you," Ellie replied. He backed away, then gestured for her to break. While she wanted to draw out the charade she was playing for just a bit longer, she decided it would unnerve him more if she played for real. She drew back the pool cue, took aim, and broke the rack in a way that would make Grandfather Benjamin proud. Two solid-colored balls fell into the pockets. Ellie stood, unable to hide her smile.

"So does that mean I get to go again?" She asked innocently. Charles laughed and Luke looked surprised. Ellie walked around the table to line up her next shot. Three shots later, she finally missed and lost her turn.

"So I'm guessing you're not just benefitting from beginner's luck." Luke commented dryly.

"No, not at all." Ellie smiled. "My Grandpa Benjamin started me playing the day I could see over the pool table." She leaned against the table, hoping to distract him. "Not only that, I've also had a lot of practice. Remember, winters here can be very cold and long. One thing my father indulged in was a nice pool table. Not as grand as this one, though. It is beautiful."

"So why didn't you just say that you knew how to play?" Luke knocked the '11' ball into the corner pocket, then moved to take his next shot.

"You didn't ask. You only assumed I needed to be taught." She shrugged and he missed the pocket he was aiming for as the cue ball slowly rolled to a side pocket and fell in. Luke groaned as Ellie pulled it out and placed it back on the table. "Men often underestimate women and what we can do." She knocked the '2' ball in, then moved to line up the '4' ball.

"I'll be sure to never do that again." Luke sighed as she hit the purple ball into a corner pocket.

"That is a wise decision. Corner pocket." She gestured, then struck the cue ball a final time and it clanked into the '8' ball, which then rolled into the pocket she had indicated. "I believe that means I win, right?" Ellie smirked.

"You know it does." Luke placed his cue stick on the proper rack.

"Sorry, I couldn't resist teasing you just a bit more."

"I think you need to give me lessons." Charles spoke up. "I don't think I've ever seen Luke lose at pool and I've seen him play hundreds of times."

"So you're telling me that I am the first person who finally bested Mr. Lucas Callahan." She put her own cue stick away.

"I've lost before, believe me." Luke protested, then was interrupted by a knock at the door. An older woman, the housekeeper if Ellie remembered correctly, stepped in.

"Mr. Brantley, dinner is ready."

"Thank you, Mrs. Eastman," Charles said, then offered Ellie his arm to escort her. "Shall we, Miss Bennett?"

"Yes, Mr. Brantley, we shall," she replied, and they walked towards the dining room.

Chapter Eight

The next day, Luke peeked into the back sitting room and, seeing it empty, slipped in, Duchess padding in behind him. The rain was still lightly falling and Isabella was becoming even more moody. He needed some time away from her and the Hursts, just a moment to himself. Solitude was difficult to come by in the house at present, yet he didn't really want to stay in his bedroom. Even time away from the maddeningly distracting Ellie Bennett would be welcome. He wished he could ride through the countryside, but the weather prevented that. He was feeling pent-up. At least the rain added a relaxing, calming melody.

Luke settled into a comfortable chair, slipped on his glasses and opened the book he had brought down. Duchess lay at his feet.

As he read, his mind settled and he began to doze off. In his dream, he and Ellie raced on horses, she was beating him by just a head, hair flying from underneath her hat.

"Ellie…" He muttered, coming slowly awake.

"Hello, Mr. Callahan."

He jerked all the way awake and saw the focus of his dream softly close the door leading into the room. Duchess immediately went to greet her and Ellie knelt down to pet the border collie.

"I'm sorry to disturb you, but I had to..." She stood and looked around as if trying to figure out how to word what she was trying to say.

"Just get away?" He pulled his reading glasses off and finished the statement for her.

"Yes." She smiled, her warm brown eyes finding his. "I didn't know you were in here. Am I intruding?"

"No, not at all. How is your sister faring?" Jane had come to dinner last night, but missed breakfast this morning."

"She's doing better, obviously, as she was at dinner yesterday. Perhaps tomorrow, if the weather lets up, we can head home." She looked unhappy at the idea.

"Well, I hope you're not too disappointed about that." He placed his book on the side table next to his chair as she sat across from him on the settee, her own book in hand. Duchess followed her and sat at her feet. *Traitor.* Luke thought.

"No, you all have been terribly kind to allow us to stay here, it's just that there is so much I can be doing back home. I'm just not used to being so idle." She reached down to pet Duchess, who rose up on his hind legs and placed his front legs on her lap.

"Duchess, down." Luke said firmly. Most women he knew would be upset with a good-sized dog in their surroundings.

"It's quite alright, Mr. Callahan. She's just curious." She dropped a kiss on the furry black head.

He nodded, then referenced her earlier comment. "Believe it or not, I feel the same about not being used to sitting around idle."

"I'm sorry if I disturbed you. I can find somewhere else to read."

"You're no bother, Miss Bennett."

"Thank you." She smiled, continuing to scratch Duchess's head. "And please, call me Ellie."

"Of course, and you should call me Luke." His heat warmed just a bit.

"All right." She patted her lap, and Duchess jumped up onto the settee and laid down with her head in Ellie's lap. "I'll let you get back to your reading."

He nodded, put his glasses back on and picked up the book he had brought down. The two each read their own novels quietly, though Luke was constantly aware of Ellie, noticing little things, like the way she absentmindedly stroked Duchess, and occasionally bit her lip, perhaps when her mystery novel got intense. He wanted to give her his full attention, but couldn't let her know that. He wasn't sure how long they sat there when she spoke up.

"You must be a serious reader if you're taking on Dostoevsky."

He met her eyes. He really hadn't been able to focus on the Russian literature since she had walked into the room.

Ellie continued when he didn't answer. "I've tried reading *Crime and Punishment*, but it's quite complex."

"Yes, it is. I try to read many different subjects." He hoped his answer didn't sound too lame.

"Broadening your mind is always a good thing," She replied. "It must help you in your business."

"Yes, I suppose it does." He answered, and was about to ask what her favorite genre was when Isabella burst into the room. "Oh, here you are, Ellie." She hesitated when she saw Luke as well, then focused back on Ellie. "Janie is awake and asking for you."

"Thank you, Isabella. I'll see you later, Luke." Ellie stood, gently nudging Duchess from her lap, and hurried out of the room. Isabella turned to Luke with a perfectly manicured eyebrow raised.

"Consorting with the cowgirl. Won't her mother be so delighted to hear about that?"

"We both just wanted to read in peace, Isabella." Luke stood and patted his thigh. Duchess immediately came to his side.

"You'd better hope that's all it was." She replied, then flounced out.

~~~~~

The rain had finally ceased a few hours ago, and Janie was feeling much better, but continued to be tired. Ellie was sitting in Jane's room, reading, when she looked out the window to see one of the hands from Longbourn Ranch drive up in a farm wagon with her mother and other sisters in the back. "Oh, no, what are they doing here?"

Ellie hurried downstairs to intercept her family, but didn't make it in time. Her mother was already blathering on and on to Luke, Charles, Louisa and Isabella as they sat in the formal sitting room. She had no idea where Mr. Hurst was. Probably sleeping off his latest overindulgence of Coffin Varnish.

"I do not wish to take Janie home until she is absolutely well enough to travel," Martha said as Ellie sat down on a couch in the great room.

"She's fine." Ellie spoke up, but her mother ignored her.

"And Ellie must stay with her. Propriety, you know."

61

"I wouldn't dream of sending her home before she is ready to travel," Charles replied. "She and Miss Ellie are more than welcome to stay for as long as they need."

Ellie tried not to let her frustration show. Why did she have to be the chaperone? Then again, looking around at the other options, she had to agree that she was the most logical choice. Perhaps Grandpa Benjamin would be willing...

Martha continued. "I do believe if it were not for such good friends, my dear Janie would be on her deathbed. Goodness, she does have the sweetest disposition. I always tell my other girls that they are nothing compared to her."

Ellie blushed and glanced around at the others. She caught Luke's eyes and he was studying her once again. Isabella, as usual, had a look of disgust on her face and Louisa appeared unable to hide her amusement.

Martha continued. "Mr. Brantley, your home is simply magnificent, you should host a barbeque and dance here at Verbena Meadows. The Carlisles never had anyone over. Such a waste."

"That is true, Mr. Brantley," Lindie said with a toss of her head. "They were practically hermits."

"Oh, please have a dance, Mr. Brantley," Kathy squealed.

Charles smiled. "Once Janie is well enough to attend, I will make sure we have a shindig. I was thinking of having one anyway. It is a wonderful way to get to know the community."

"I don't agree that a dance is the best way to get to know one's neighbors." Marie spoke up. "Conversation would be the more fitting way to do so."

"But not nearly as fun." Lindie scoffed. "Oh, Marie, you're such a bore."

"Lindie, please, that comment was truly unnecessary," Ellie pleaded with her sister. Why did their mother never scold Lindie?

The rest of the afternoon passed by awkwardly, and Ellie heaved a sigh of relief when her family departed. She really wished she could return home with them, but Janie needed her and she wasn't about to let any other family members stay to care for her.

~~~~~~

Later that evening, it started to sprinkle once again, and somehow, Ellie and Luke found themselves alone in the sitting room for the second time.

"Please tell me, Ellie," Luke asked, "do you believe Charles should hire a jazz band or should he have a local group play for his dance?"

Ellie raised her eyes from the book. She had felt him watching her, but couldn't imagine why. She was by no means the type of woman he would be interested in.

"I believe you want me to say a local band. That way you could criticize my taste in music." She watched his reaction, but he remained stoic. "However, Mr. Callahan...Luke, I have figured you out. I would actually enjoy either. I may not be a...posh flapper, but I do enjoy jazz as well as a variety of other music types. I would, however, have to point out that it is unlikely Mr. Brantley will be able to find a jazz band out here in the Black Hills. You'll probably have to add that to your list of reasons why South Dakota is not good enough for you."

"Why are you so convinced that I dislike everything about your community?" he replied. "Ellie..."

"Oh, Luke, here you are." Isabella entered the room looking gorgeous in a fashionable, flowing beaded crimson dress, immediately trying to get Luke's attention. He was polite to Isabella, and to Mr. and Mrs. Hurst when they entered the room as well, but Ellie couldn't help but notice that he continually looked over to her. And she had no idea why.

~~~~~~

The next day, Janie was well on her way to recovery. Ellie began to pack the few items they had assembled so they could leave for home. When the preparations were complete, Ellie helped the still weak Jane descend the stairs to the grand entryway.

"Thank you so much for your hospitality." Janie smiled at Charles.

"I found our time delightful." Charles said. "I'm sorry your stay can't be longer, and I am sorely distraught that we couldn't spend more of it together."

"Yes." Isabella said, a strong hint of sarcasm in her voice. "We most definitely need to visit more often."

Ellie turned to Charles. "I'll come by on Friday and we can go to Custer like we talked about."

"I look forward to it." Charles escorted Janie to the Rolls Royce. Since Janie wasn't up to full strength, it had been decided that Charles would drive Janie back to Longbourn in his automobile while Ellie would ride Janie's horse, Princess, home. Luke would follow behind in the Bennett's truck and drive Charles back to Verbena Meadows. Why none of her siblings had thought to ride Princess home the other day was beyond Ellie, but she loved riding, so she had no problem with the arrangement. Just as she was about to mount Princess, she felt strong hands encircle her waist to help lift her up. Her heart pounded as she turned to see Luke step back.

"Thank you, Mr. Callahan."

"Remember, it's Luke." He nodded and walked stiffly back to the truck. Ellie shook her head and pressed her heels into Princess's flanks, so ready to be home.

Chapter Nine

The following Friday, Ellie and Janie pulled up to Verbena Meadows in the family truck to pick up Charles, Luke and anyone else who wanted to go on an excursion to Custer State Park. The trip had been discussed while Janie had been sick, and though Ellie wanted to get some work done at the ranch, she loved going down to the park. Charles had wanted to take his car, but Luke had been the voice of reason, pointing out that they would be driving through the National Forest and his car could get damaged. Charles had relented; obviously he listened well to what Luke had to say.

"Miss Ellie, hello! Miss Janie, you look absolutely lovely. So much better...uhh...healthier than the last time I saw you." Charles bounded down the steps of the grand wraparound porch to the truck. Janie and Ellie got out of the truck to greet him. Luke joined the group at a more sedate pace, and he balked and reddened at the sight of Ellie 's outfit.

"Ellie, I...I suppose I should have expected you would be one to wear trousers..."

"I find them to be most sensible, with the work I do around the ranch." She glanced down at her Levi's and red button-up shirt, then shrugged. She didn't need his approval for what she wore.

"Did Isabella not want to join us?" Janie asked. She had worn a button up shirt with a split skirt, a combination of practicality and gentility.

"She decided to stay here with Louisa." Charles replied. "It didn't surprise me in the least. Neither are very interested in nature."

Luke doesn't appear to be either. Ellie kept that thought to herself, though he looked the part today. He wore his Stetson with a button up green and white flannel shirt, Levi's jeans and a sensible pair of leather boots that looked like they were specifically made for hiking.

"All right then, let's be on our way." Ellie settled her own hat on her head. Charles pulled Janie into the bed of the truck to sit next to him, which left Luke to sit in the cab with Ellie. She tried not to groan as she slipped behind the wheel and started the truck.

The hour-long drive was quite awkward for Ellie. Charles and Janie were entertaining each other in the back, and both attempted to talk to Luke and Ellie through the window, yet they were obviously preoccupied with each other. It didn't help that Luke said not a single word to her. She really didn't understand this man. They had several nice conversations while she was at Verbena Meadows, but today, the only thing he did was suck on his infernal root beer barrels.

"Ellie, what animals might we see?" Charles asked, leaning through the back window.

"We could see pronghorn, whitetail, or mule deer. If we're lucky, we might see some elk and bison. Eagles and hawks are always flying overhead, with a variety of other birds. My personal favorite, though, are the prairie dogs, despite them being a nuisance with all of their tunnels." She couldn't help but smile at Charles's enthusiasm. "We'll drive the loop here, but if you see anything and want to stop and observe in more detail, just holler."

"Perfect. I have my Brownie." Charles held up the Kodak box camera he had brought.

"I'm excited to see the pictures you take with that," Janie said.

"Lord, what a beautiful sight." Luke finally spoke. Ellie had driven around a bend and just below them, on a gradually sloping hill, was a herd of bison. These majestic animals always tugged at Ellie's heart.

"Holy smokes, will you look at that! There are so many." Charles tapped on Ellie's shoulder through the window. "Could we stop here?"

"Of course." She pulled to the side of the gravel road and they all piled out of the truck. Charles readied his camera and snapped some pictures. He had Ellie and Janie pose for one, then had Luke take one of him and Janie. Ellie wasn't sure, but she thought Luke may have taken one of her, looking off in the distance. She wondered what he was thinking. One minute, he seemed to strongly dislike her, but other times, it was as if he was constantly watching her. This man confused her so much.

~~~~~~

Luke couldn't keep his eyes off Ellie. If he thought her captivating at a bonfire or a church picnic or at Verbena Meadows, she was stunning when she was in her element, hiking through nature. If he did build a resort here, he would have an excuse to come back and visit her and...wait. He shook his head in frustration. Why was he entertaining these thoughts? It would never work between the two of them. He had to get Ellie out of his mind.

68

"I thought I heard most of these animals were killed decades ago." Luke asked. He should know as much as possible about the land.

"That is true." Ellie nodded. "They were almost extinct. From 1872 until 1874, five-thousand bison were killed each day."

"Why were they being slaughtered like that?" Charles asked.

"Mostly because buffalo skinners wanted their hides and tongue, but some hunters came out just to be able to brag that they could kill a bison." Ellie's tone darkened. "Such a senseless waste."

"I agree." Luke couldn't understand why anyone would want to destroy the stunning creatures.

Ellie continued. "By 1884, only 325 remained in the American West. People started realizing that and trying to figure out ways to bring them back."

"I know Teddy Roosevelt helped with that." Luke stated.

"He did," Ellie replied. "Roosevelt and other supporters formed the American Bison Society in 1905 to help the bison survive. We also had the Bronx Zoo in New York and Yellowstone National Park over in Wyoming establish bison preserves. About twenty years ago, the federal government created the National Bison Range in Montana."

"And to think if that hadn't happened, we wouldn't be able to see them today." Charles shook his head.

"Indeed." Ellie adjusted her Stetson. "We are very lucky for the individuals and organizations that were able to bring them back."

They continued watching the bison and Charles shot some more photographs.

"Shall we move on?" Charles asked after a time, and they climbed back into the truck and continued on their way. Luke envied his friend. How did Charles always manage to adapt to his surroundings so well? It had long bothered Luke, but this trip in particular and getting to know the Bennett family made it much more obvious that he couldn't easily make conversation with people he just met, unless it had to do with business. He needed to remedy this somehow.

Throughout the drive, every time Charles saw something interesting, they stopped and took more pictures. Luke knew they would stop for anything he wanted to look at as well, but the most interesting subject in the whole state was sitting next to him in the Model T.

"Luke, you will have no problem bringing in tourists if you decide to build that resort," Charles said after taking another beautiful shot of a stand of Ponderosa pines in a stunning rock formation.

"As long as you don't ruin any of the landscape, you could really do some good for the community," Ellie added. "Spearfish would be ideal for a Black Hills resort. It's only an 80-mile drive here to Custer, and the badlands are not that much farther.

"Badlands?" Charles asked.

"They are magnificent buttes that have eroded over time and their color...well, it's hard to describe, but it's almost as though God painted horizontal lines across them. Purple and yellow, tan and gray, red, orange and white. They are simply magnificent, more picturesque than you can even imagine. As I said, I can't describe them, you just have to see them for yourself. There is also Devil's Tower, that's only 60 miles away to the west in Wyoming. It's a huge butte, close to 1000 feet tall. It's made of igneous rock. And now they have started carving the sculpture over at Six Grandfathers. Rushmore, they're calling it. We drove quite close to it on our way down here."

"So you would approve of a resort being built," Luke had assumed Ellie would balk at any change. Her attitude encouraged him. "I had expected you to be against any kind of development."

"I can see the benefits of tourism, though I also realize there are drawbacks. As long as you respect nature and keep the development simple, a resort would be quite beneficial for Spearfish." She smiled.

They pulled off to the side for another spectacular view of the rock formations and prairie vegetation. A small furry critter poked his head out of a hole in the ground. It scurried up into the grass and stood up on its hind legs, looking around curiously.

"I say, what is that little brown animal there?" Charles had noticed the 4-inch-long mammal as well. A couple more joined him on the mound.

"Those are prairie dogs." Ellie answered. "I mentioned earlier how they are one of my favorite animals, but most ranchers around here don't like them at all. I understand their reasons why, as the critters dig holes and tunnels and live in colonies. It can be dangerous for a horse or a human to step into one of the holes and twist their limbs."

"They are rather amusing." Luke continued to watch as they darted around, went in and out of the holes, and barked at each other. Ellie smiled at him and wandered away as Charles took some more photographs. After he had gotten some good shots, he handed the Brownie to Luke again and then took Janie's hand and pulled her across the meadow. Luke slowly made his way to Ellie, who was sitting on a small grassy hill, leaning back on her hands and staring off into the distance. Some of her hair had escaped her braid, and Luke longed to reach out and tuck it behind her ear. He restrained himself and continued their earlier conversation.

71

"So you don't think I would face opposition from locals?" Luke wanted to sit next to her, but didn't know if it would be considered too forward of him.

She met his eyes. "Of course you will. Any change will meet with some resistance. But if your plan is in good taste and you present your proposal in the right way, you'll get your approval."

"Luke, take a picture of that buffalo over there!" Charles pointed to a buffalo who was near a small pile of rocks.

Luke shook his head. "There's too much grass in the way."

Ellie chuckled at his excuse. The grass there was rather tall, but it seemed as though he was getting irritated by being designated the photographer. Luke was finally holding a conversation with the lovely Ellie Bennett and not tripping over his words and he didn't want to be interrupted.

Charles and Janie returned to where Luke and Ellie were.

"We just decided that here would be a good place to have our lunch." Charles stated. He gripped Janie's hand tightly. Luke pursed his lips. How attached was Charles already? He had fallen for girls before, but he seemed to be very serious about Janie. However, the question Luke had was in regards to Janie. Did she care for Charles in the same way, or was she simply hoping to snag a wealthy husband? Luke would have to watch them carefully, especially Janie. He couldn't let Charles be taken advantage of. It had happened before.

"This is a perfect place for lunch," Ellie agreed.

"I'll grab the basket." Charles offered. "Come, Miss Janie, I may need help with some of the supplies." He almost skipped off, pulling Janie behind him.

Ellie began picking at the long grass next to her. "Are you hungry as well, Luke?"

"I am. Being out here in the wide open spaces is very invigorating." He looked off towards the majestic rock spires rising from the ground, surrounded by tall evergreen trees. The rocks almost looked like fingers reaching up to Heaven. Luke took the time to take in the beauty of the day, a blue sky with fluffy white clouds, cumulus, if he remembered the term correctly, bright yellow sunshine and a gentle breeze.

"It is. Though I am sure it's nothing compared to the skyscrapers of Chicago and New York City." He couldn't tell if she was being sincere or sarcastic.

"They are impressive, it's true. New York City is in the middle of a construction boom right now. Builders just finished a magnificent tower on Madison Avenue, and another one is being planned for East 40th street. And in Chicago there was a building boom after the Great Fire of 1871, and it's never slowed down." He hoped he wasn't boring her with his words. Should he offer to host her if she ever wanted to visit? He tried to imagine her in East Coast society and his thoughts flashed to the conversation he had with Isabella. Then he wondered, if he did ask her, would it sound too forward? Would she believe he was interested in hosting her, as a beau hosting his love interest? Again, he just wasn't sure how to act around Ellie Bennett, and what were his true feelings for her? "It's all very impressive." He finished his statement a bit lamely. "You really should visit someday."

"Well, I'll probably never make it as far east as New York, but maybe Chicago someday. I'm not much of a city girl."

"I have noticed that." Luke replied. Ellie raised her eyebrows and he wondered if she had taken his words the wrong way. He hadn't meant any offense. "I understand how you feel. Chicago and even St. Louis, where I spend most of my time, has the hustle and bustle with beautiful architecture, but I must admit, I prefer the creation that God has given us, like these majestic mountains and valleys."

Ellie gave him another puzzled look, as if she had never expected him to admit something like that. Luke nodded at Charles and Janie, who had returned, set out the picnic blanket, and were unpacking the roast beef sandwiches and fruit.

"Charles can take as many pictures as he'd like and they'll turn out well enough and provide a nice memory of the day, but they will never quite do this beautiful scenery the justice it deserves." Luke added.

Ellie stood and brushed her hands on her jeans. "Now there, you are correct." She walked over to Janie and Charles. Luke followed her, hoping he had finally made a good impression on Ellie.

~~~~~

Ellie was having a difficult time figuring Luke Callahan out. Since her stay at Verbena Meadows, he appeared to be trying a bit harder to be friendly, but he still came off as being pretentious.

After lunch, they continued driving and stopping along the trails. Ellie took them to many of the park's highlights, including her favorite granite rock pinnacle that looked like the eye of a needle.

"It just towers above us!" Charles exclaimed in absolute awe.

"If I remember my geology correctly, a formation like this is formed by centuries of rain, ice and wind." Luke commented.

"I have heard that as well." Janie nodded. Since lunch, she had become a bit more reserved, and Ellie wasn't sure why, but she was likely just tired. She was still recovering from her sickness, after all.

"I hate to be the bearer of bad news, but we should probably start heading home," Ellie stated. The sun was starting its descent and she wanted to be out of the mountains before dark.

"It has been such a pleasant day." Charles smiled. "We will have to make plans for another road trip. As you said, we can visit this Devil's Tower, the Badlands, and I'd love to see the progress Borglum is making on Mount Rushmore."

"God really has created some beautiful landscapes around here." Luke commented yet again, as if he just couldn't contain his wonderment.

Ellie looked at the man. She recalled that 'a Christian, a woman of strong faith' was on Luke's list of an ideal woman, so he had to be a man of God himself, but she hadn't expected him to make such a comment. Maybe there was more to him than she had expected.

~~~~~~

"We really must go on another excursion with the lovely ladies of the Longbourn Ranch!" Charles gushed. "I am so anxious to develop these photos."

"Good luck finding a photo developer around here." Isabella scoffed.

"There might be one in Spearfish." Charles insisted. "I must say, Isabella, I don't understand why you're so snippy lately. If you don't like it here, why did you come in the first place? I'm glad to spend time with you, don't get me wrong, but I don't want you to be unhappy either."

"Mother insisted that I come to look out for you. Lord knows you need guidance." She patted her curled bob haircut and lit a cigarette.

That explains a lot. Luke thought. He had wondered why Charles's sisters had accompanied him, and when Isabella smiled and winked at him, he realized she had her own ulterior motives.

"I saw Miss Ellie Bennett from the window when she arrived to drive you." Louisa chortled, then lit her own cigarette. "Was she really wearing trousers? What a reuben."

"She was indeed." Luke hoped he didn't blush at the memory.

"I thought she looked delightful in them." Charles defended Ellie's attire, always the gentleman. "And you really have no reason to call her a country hick."

Isabella wasn't even trying to hide her disdain. "Yes, I'm sure you thought her delightful. What did you think of her pants, my dear Luke? Will you make sure Helena has a few pair of her own?"

Luke took a deep breath.

"Isabella, really." Charles sighed. "I wish you would at least try to enjoy yourself without being negative towards others."

"What I wouldn't give for a speakeasy in this town." Isabella muttered, ignoring Charles. "Now that would allow me to enjoy myself."

"I can take care of myself, you know." Charles was actually getting annoyed with his sisters. That didn't happen often. "Please feel free to leave at any time."

"Of course you can." Isabella laughed and rolled her eyes. Luke shook his head. There were many reasons he didn't care for Isabella, and her poor treatment of Charles was a big one. Charles loved deeply and fiercely and would do anything for his friends and family, yet she continually berated him. Luke felt lucky that his own sister was more like a friend to him, though they were almost ten years apart in age. Charles deserved better treatment.

"Don't mind her, Charles," Luke said. "We all know you can take care of yourself just fine."

"Of course. Thank you, Luke." Charles smiled. "I should at least start planning my party. I want it to be quite the sockdollager."

"I am most certain that will not happen here." Isabella blew out a puff of smoke, then rose and left the room.

"It will take a strong man to put a manacle on Isabella." Charles shook his head. "I love her, but it's true."

"As long as she realizes it's not ever going to be me." Luke added. "All right then, what can I do to help with this party?" If Charles was going to go through with the event, the least Luke could do was make sure it was the best party the town had ever had.

Part 2: Summer of 1928

Chapter Ten

"I hope, my dear, that you are able to set an extra plate for dinner, because we will have a guest." James Bennett folded the telegram he had been reading. A week or so had passed since Ellie and Janie had gone to Custer State Park and Lindie and their mother were still barraging Janie with questions about the outing. It was just after lunch and Ellie was taking a short break from work to play a quick game of cribbage with Grandpa Benjamin.

Martha looked up, shock on her face. "Who? And why are you telling me only now?"

"I received the message yesterday and only read it this morning." James shrugged. "It is my cousin, Mr. Richard Sutton."

Grandpa Benjamin couldn't hide his laugh. "Odious man." He said, only loud enough for Ellie to hear.

"The man who will supposedly inherit Longbourn Ranch when you die, Papa?" Ellie couldn't keep the bitterness out of her voice. "I still cannot believe that Great-Grandpa Longbourn…"

"Do not speak that horrible man's name in this house." Martha cried, interrupting Ellie. "It is the cruelest thing in the world to know that the ranch my husband has slaved over and his daughters have worked so hard on, will be given to some unknown Easterner." She glared at Grandpa Benjamin as if it were all his fault. Ellie knew it wasn't. Benjamin Bennett had done all he could to fight the will of his father-in-law, which stated that the ranch should be passed down to males only. Unfortunately, since Grandpa Benjamin had married into the Longbourne family, he had no legal claim to change anything, and neither could James. It was iron-clad.

James ignored his wife. "Mr. Sutton is a well-respected solicitor for the George Vanderbilt family and a few other wealthy individuals. He is living on the Biltmore Estate near Asheville, in the mountains of North Carolina. He feels badly about the inheritance, so he says."

"Clearly not enough to sign over his interest in the ranch." Ellie muttered.

"He could do that." Grandpa Benjamin nodded. "Unfortunately, I believe it is too profitable a ranch for him to consider."

James looked at his father, then continued speaking. "Sutton somehow wants to promote peace between us. He will be here sometime between 2 and 4:00." Mr. Bennett went back into his office.

"As much as I hate the fact that Richard Sutton will have control over my ranch, I must admit I am curious to meet the man." Ellie said to her grandfather.

"I have." Grandpa Benjamin played a card and won the game. "I thought him quite awkward, a strange mix of humbleness and self-importance. It will be interesting to see him out here, not in his element."

Ellie nodded, moved a peg in the cribbage board, then stood. "I hate to leave you, Grandpa, but I have more chores." She leaned down and kissed his weathered cheek. "I'll see you at dinner and later we can start another game."

Benjamin looked at her with pure affection, and nodded. "Until then, my dear."

~~~~~~

Ellie shoved her hat on her head as she stepped outside, then found the ranch foreman, Matthew Shaw. Matthew was one of the best men Ellie knew and was like an uncle to her. Half-Negro, half-Lakota Indian, he had been working the ranch since both he and James had been teenagers. He knew the land well, and had infinite amounts of wisdom. His wife, Hattie, cooked for the ranch hands and helped Martha up at the main house.

"What is left to do for today, Matthew?" Ellie asked.

"I could use your help checking on some sick cows." He answered. Ellie pulled on her riding gloves, then followed Matthew to the barn to saddle their horses. As they worked, Ellie couldn't help but vent, and Matthew, as always, listened patiently.

"I just can't believe my great-grandpa Longbourn had such an archaic view of things. You know that he specifically wrote in his will that the ranch was only to be passed to males?" She rambled.

Matthew nodded. "I know it and agree that it was a bad idea, but when he wrote his will, things were different in these parts. I don't think he

81

realized any of the women in your family would be as tough and smart and capable as you."

Ellie looked around her horse at the kindly man and smiled at the complement. "Thank you for saying so." They mounted their horses and began to ride. As they rode, Ellie shared with Matthew about her time at Verbena Meadows and the trip to Custer.

"Charles seems very enamored with Janie. I hope it will become something more serious. He is a fine man and they would complement each other."

"Miss Janie needs a thoughtful, kind man like that. I've heard good things about both he and his friend." Matthew replied.

"Luke Callahan?" Ellie asked. She still wasn't quite sure what to think of him. At first, he had been snobbish and rude, but he was a bit friendlier when Janie was sick. Then at the state park, he had been a mix of awkwardness and decent conversation.

"Yeah, heard real good things 'bout both of them."

"I'm still trying to figure Luke out." She admitted. "Perhaps I was too quick to judge him."

"That can happen, Miss Ellie. That can surely happen."

They finished checking the cows and headed back to the main barn. Ellie hadn't been rubbing down Naomi for five minutes when a very giggly Lindie ran into the barn

"Di mi, Ellie! Mr. Sutton is here and, oh my goodness, I have never seen a sillier man."

"He's here already?" Ellie pulled her hat off and wiped her forehead with a handkerchief.

"Yes, and he wants to meet you. He wants to meet all of us. He's talking like he wants to marry one of us. You may have a chance for a husband after all."

"And of course, Mama will throw me at him." Ellie leaned into Naomi, hoping for some comfort. The horse nudged her playfully.

"Well, how else will you find a man willing to marry you?" Lindie teased then ran off back toward the house. Ellie finished taking care of Naomi, then dragged her feet to the house herself.

"Ellie, Ellie, good here you are!" Martha pulled Ellie over to the man who had to be Richard Sutton. "I do wish you had taken a moment to freshen up."

"Lindie made it sound as though I must be here as soon as possible," Ellie replied, though she likely wouldn't have freshened up to meet the man before her no matter the circumstances. He was slightly overweight, a bit shorter than Ellie, and he appeared to be in his mid-thirties. He wore cowboy boots, Levi jeans, a brightly-colored button-up shirt and a pure white Stetson. The getup made him look quite ridiculous. For once, Lindie hadn't been exaggerating.

"It matters not to me, Mrs. Bennett, I can appreciate the fact that your second daughter was out working the land. She is surely a most beneficial person to have around." He smiled at her, though Ellie couldn't get over his puffed-up chest and stiff manners. "Miss Eleanor here is a beautiful young woman, as are all of your daughters." He took Ellie's hand and bowed over it, as if trying to be a debonair gentleman.

Ellie stepped back. "Well, I really should clean up and then help Janie and Hattie finish dinner preparations. It's almost that time." She nodded politely to Mr. Sutton. "I will see you later, sir."

Lindie followed Ellie to the kitchen and continued to pester her. "You'd best be careful, Ellie. Just being polite to that man might encourage him to think you're fond of him and he's already anxious to propose marriage."

"I'm well aware of that, Lindie." Ellie tried to hide her annoyance. "Did you come down here to help or gossip?"

Lindie gave a 'humph' of indignation, then flounced off. Ellie sighed and washed her hands, then soaked her handkerchief in the cool water to wipe her face. The stuffy Mr. Sutton, her overbearing mother, and her annoying younger sister, all together at dinner? She would have to muster all her patience to survive this fiasco. "Just remember, Ellie." She spoke to herself. "Hot tempers cause arguments, but patience brings peace."

"What was that child?" Hattie asked.

"Oh, just praying for dinner to go well, Miss Hattie."

Janie smiled. "Everything will be perfectly fine. No need to worry, Ellie."

"I hope you're right, Janie. I really hope you're right."

~~~~~~~

Mr. Sutton dominated the conversation in his irritating, abrasive voice. Back east, he worked as a solicitor for some very wealthy people, including George Washington Vanderbilt's widow, Edith and daughter, Cornelia, as well as a Charleston socialite, Mrs. Madeline VanRensselaer. Mr. Sutton talked excessively about these women, and especially the latter, as well as many of the elite in the East.

"Mrs. VanRensselaer is all one could wish for in a person of importance. She comes from very old money and had the wherewithal to

84

marry a prestigious steel baron from Pittsburgh, and her nephew, Mr. Lucas Callahan, is very successful."

Ellie's wandering mind halted when she heard Luke's name. She should have known that he would have a pretentious aunt like Mr. Sutton was describing. The man continued rambling.

"Mrs. VanRensselaer has the utmost manners, grace and style. She advises me to marry as soon as possible."

Ellie caught Janie's eye and shook her head. Lindie and Kathy giggled. Marie, strangely enough, seemed enraptured with Mr. Sutton, and Martha hung on his every word. Grandpa Benjamin and James looked like they wanted to oust him from the table and then out of the house.

"Mrs. VanRensselaer is so gracious whenever complimented. In fact, I often practice, for Miss VanRensselaer and others, to plant little compliments whenever I can." Mr. Sutton took a bite of beef stew, continuing his blathering.

"You practice compliments?" Ellie raised her eyebrows. Could this man be any more nonsensical?

"Well, many of them come to me in the moment, I always try to be as complimentary as possible, but there are times when I purposely plant compliments, with as much subtlety as possible, of course."

"Oh, believe me, no one would accuse you of being insincere," Ellie replied as sincerely as possible. Lindie laughed so hard, she choked. Janie patted her on the back. Grandpa Benjamin tried to hide his laugh behind a cough.

"I felt tonight, we could discuss the farmer's almanac. I have been reading and studying these fascinating papers since I was a boy and learned that I would be inheriting this ranch. I also brought with me a book about

85

Butch Cassidy and the Sundance Kid. I could read it to you. I know we're not that far from the town of Sundance."

"No, we're not," Martha stated. "Ellie could take some time out of her busy schedule to drive you out there. I am sure she would be most delighted to do so."

No, I would not be delighted at all. Ellie wanted to protest, but knew it would do no good.

"Splendid. Perhaps a visit to the town would be in order." He turned to Janie. "Would you care to accompany me on a drive to Sundance, Miss Bennett?"

Janie looked panicked for a second, but Martha spoke up quickly.

"Mr. Sutton, it would probably be good for you to know that my Janie is courting a wealthy young lawyer who is staying at a nearby ranch."

Janie's eyes widened even more. "Mama…"

Martha continued. "They will likely be engaged before long."

"Engaged." Mr. Sutton looked crushed.

"Mama…" Ellie spoke up.

"But Ellie here is the next oldest, and she has by far the most practical experience in running this ranch. She would be the perfect choice for you to marry."

"Mama!" Both Janie and Ellie exclaimed, and Ellie actually pushed to her feet. Mr. Sutton focused his buggy eyes on her.

"I have complimented you on your beauty as well, Miss Ellie."

"Mr. Sutton, I…" Ellie started to speak at the same time as her mother.

"Ellie, dear, you should…

86

"Let us table this discussion until later." It wasn't often that James Bennett spoke sternly, but when he did, the family listened.

Ellie was distracted through the rest of dinner, then claimed a headache after helping clean up and went right to her room. An hour or so later, Janie joined her.

"Such a nauseating little man!" Ellie exclaimed. "I just couldn't be in the same room with him anymore. How long will he be staying?"

"I don't know, exactly. A month, at least."

Ellie thumped back on her pillows. "It will be the longest month of my life." She shook her head. "Perhaps I can find an excuse to ride the trail for a few days. There has to be work in the far pastures."

"I had a chance to speak with Grandpa Benjamin about Mr. Sutton." Janie sat at her vanity and began taking pins out of her hair. "Mr. Sutton is 'as absurd as he remembers', Grandpa's words, not mine, and he does not appear to be a sensible man at all. Apparently as a boy, he was taught that flattery was the answer to everything, especially ignorance and fear, and that is why he speaks the way he does."

"Well, that's just not true." Ellie folded her arms over her chest. "I'm sure he's full of both ignorance and fear."

"You're probably right." Janie began brushing her hair.

"I imagine he spent most of the time after dinner singing the praises of this Mrs. VanRensselaer."

"He did," Janie replied. "He seems to almost worship her."

"Unbelievable." Ellie muttered. "I can't believe Mama thinks I would ever consider marrying a man like him. You know I prefer someone more independent and honest. Empty compliments are just that. Empty."

"You would be miserable with Mr. Sutton." Janie finished her evening toilet and slipped into bed. "But you must admit, he has a fine house and a good income, and he will inherit this ranch, so he could be considered quite a catch."

"So he has said repeatedly." Ellie stared at the ceiling.

"He does seem legitimately sorry about inheriting the ranch and he is trying to be friends with us."

Ellie sat up. "Yes, and his solution is to marry one of us. Me in particular." She flounced back down. "He thinks that will make up for everything. He doesn't realize just how ridiculous and archaic he sounds. I wish Grandpa Benjamin would have complete say in what happens to the ranch."

"But that's not the way it is. I wouldn't worry over much, Ellie. Mama might pressure you, but Father would never force you to marry someone you didn't want."

"That is a true statement, thank the Lord." Ellie pulled her covers tightly around her and prayed to God that Janie was right.

Chapter Eleven

The next day, Ellie and Charlotte rode their horses back from the east pasture of the Longbourn Ranch. Ellie had wanted to count head and Charlotte had been anxious to go riding for weeks.

"Do you mind if we stop at the bunkhouse? We have a few new hands I'd like to meet." Ellie asked as they headed to the stables. Charlotte shook her head.

"I can't believe you haven't said much about this Richard Sutton," Charlotte commented. "Why is your mother so insistent that you or one of your sisters marry him?"

"I'm trying to forget him, and am surprised you don't remember the story." Ellie took a breath and began the tale. "My great-grandpa, Muskim Longbourn moved out here before the War Between the States, leaving one brother, Victor, behind in South Carolina. Muskim established our ranch and married great-grandmother Sophia. They had one child, a daughter, my grandma Teresa. My grandpa Benjamin grew up in Virginia and moved out here in...1879, I believe. He fell in love with Teresa and they were married. Now, Muskim approved of Teresa and Benjamin taking over the ranch, but he still put in his will that the ranch should thereafter be passed down through a male line whenever possible."

"Ahh, yes. Like a British title or some such thing."

"Exactly. Grandpa Benjamin didn't even know about the will stipulations until Muskim died, so there was no way to talk him out of it." Ellie sighed. "Since my father has no sons, upon his death, the ranch will pass to Richard Sutton, who is the oldest grandson of Victor. Richard, the silly easterner, who is playing dress-up and has no idea what to do on a ranch. He'll likely be killed his first day in charge." She groaned as they neared the bunkhouse and saw the very man they were talking about. Mr. Sutton was once again dressed as he was yesterday. He was talking with some of the ranch hands. He gestured towards Spotted Demon, one of the meaner bulls at Longbourn Ranch. One of the hands shook his head.

"And there's nothing anyone can do?" Charlotte asked. "No loopholes?"

"Mr. Sutton can sell his stake in the ranch, but after listening to him yesterday, there is very little chance of that. Grandpa Benjamin tried everything he could, and even contacted some distant cousins of his who are lawyers to try and find some way out of it. They couldn't. It is ironclad." Ellie often wanted to cry with the injustice of it all. She had been raised on this ranch, loved it, and couldn't imagine living anywhere else. To have the city-born-and-bred Richard Sutton take it over just because he was a man? It seemed grossly unfair.

"And what is he doing now?" Ellie squinted as they rode closer to the pen next to the bunkhouse. Mr. Sutton was climbing the fence.

"Is he doing what I think he's doing? Good gravy, he's going to get himself killed!" Ellie nudged her horse, Naomi, to a run, hoping she could get to the man in time. Just as Mr. Sutton moved to jump into the pen with Spotted Demon, a man that Ellie didn't recognize grabbed the back of Mr. Sutton's shirt and hauled him away. Sutton fell into the dirt just as Ellie and Charlotte rode up. Mr. Sutton scrambled to his feet and stood as tall as he could, though he was still a head shorter than the cowboy who had thrown him to the dirt.

"I say, man! What did you do that for?" Mr. Sutton demanded. "I'll have your job for this blatant display of disrespect."

Ellie dismounted and strode over to the two. Matthew Shaw approached from the other side of the barn.

"Mr. Sutton, what on earth were you trying to do?" She stood next to the man who had tried to save Mr. Sutton and couldn't help but notice how handsome he was. Dark blonde hair that curled around his ears, green eyes, and a few days' worth of scruff on his face. She smiled and nodded at him in thanks. He tipped his hat.

Mr. Sutton sputtered. "I was going to ride the bull. Since I am going to one day run this ranch, I must have some practical experience."

The handsome man, who Ellie hoped was one of the newly hired hands, tried to hide his laugh behind his fist.

"You cannot just jump on a bull, Mr. Sutton, and I can guarantee that particular bull would have killed you." She gestured to the handsome man. "He has undoubtedly saved your life."

"Davis Martin." The handsome man tipped his Stetson. "Newly hired as a ranch hand."

"I would have been just fine." Mr. Sutton insisted, picking his own hat off the ground. "Rest assured, I will be discussing this with cousin James." He then stormed away.

91

Ellie turned to Mr. Martin, who was now laughing unabashedly. "Please tell me that shrimp was mistaken. He can't possibly think he will one day take over this ranch. The boys 'round here say one of Old Man Bennett's daughters will take over. Word is she's what keeps this ranch going right now anyways."

Ellie pushed a strand of hair behind her ear. "I wish that were true, Mr. Martin, but that man, Mr. Sutton is indeed a relative." She pulled the leather glove off her right hand and held it out for him to shake. "I'm Miss Eleanor Bennett. One of Old Man Bennett's daughters."

Mr. Martin smiled brightly. He shook her hand firmly. "Most pleased to meet you, Ma'am. You're much prettier than I would have expected."

Ellie hoped he didn't notice the slight blush she could feel at his words. It wasn't every day a handsome man told her she was pretty. "Well, thank you, Mr. Martin." Her heart fluttered just a bit at the contact of his hand with hers. "I was aware we'd taken on some new hands. I'm glad to know at least one is as capable as you are."

"I'll do whatever is necessary to help." He began to walk beside Ellie as she headed back to the barn, leading her horse with its reins. Charlotte dismounted and came to walk with them and Ellie made the introductions. Martin was just the type of interesting man Ellie enjoyed being around. Friendly, pleasant, witty...the exact opposite of a certain gentleman with sky-blue eyes that she couldn't stop thinking about. Perhaps Mr. Martin would be the perfect diversion.

When the trio reached the barn, Charlotte remounted her horse and said her goodbyes. Mr. Martin followed Ellie into the barn and they put up the horses. Mr. Martin relegated her with tales of his past, and she quickly surmised that he moved around a lot. He was a good conversationalist, and though they hadn't talked long, it seemed as though they had known each other for years. When the horses had been cared for, Mr. Martin offered to walk her up to the house and Ellie readily agreed. Just as they reached the front porch, Lindie and Kathy scurried down the steps, giggling hysterically. Ellie hoped Davis Martin wasn't put off by their silliness.

"Oh, Mr. Martin, there you are!" Lindie grabbed onto his arm flirtatiously, and Ellie wondered if they had been waiting on the porch for him to come by. "Whatever did you do to annoy Richard Sutton so? I must learn your secrets."

"I did nothing but save the half-wit's life." Martin swept his hat off his head gallantly. "He thought he could simply jump on that bull and ride him like Bill Pickett."

"Who's Bill Pickett?" Kathy asked.

"A Negro cowpoke from down Texas way. One of the best cowboys I've ever ridden with. He now travels around to fairs and other exhibitions all over the west. His signature move is coming to be known as bulldogging."

"And what's that, Mr. Martin?" Lindie asked. Did she really just bat her eyes at Martin?

"He jumps from his horse's back onto a steer's back and throws him to the ground by grabbing and twisting his horns. Very dangerous, but impressive, it takes a lot of practice to accomplish such a feat."

"Well, gracious me, he may be good, but I'm sure you're a far better cowboy than him." Kathy gushed.

"I don't know about that," Mr. Martin replied. Ellie was impressed by his modesty. "Pickett will likely go down in history. I'm just a lowly ranch hand. Though I hope one day to own a spread of my own."

"Well, who knows, Mr. Martin. Anything is possible." Ellie smiled.

Chapter Twelve

"Grandfather, how could you do such a thing?" Ellie looked at Benjamin in shock.

"I didn't even consider that you would be so opposed to it," he retorted. "You brought him over to Custer and you didn't come to any harm."

"No, but that was with Janie and Charles as well." Ellie shook her head. Apparently, Luke Callahan had been talking to Grandpa Benjamin about scouting for some land to buy for his resort and the old codger had volunteered Ellie to escort him and show him some good possible locations.

"Do you feel you need a chaperone, my dear? I didn't think you had any romantic feelings towards him, so I didn't feel it would be a problem."

"I don't...it's not..." She sighed. "I just have a lot of work to do here and I already missed a day when I took him to Custer in addition to all those days I spent at Verbena Meadows with Jane."

"Your skills are invaluable, of course, but we can handle things for a few hours." Grandpa winked at her. "Besides, now we have the new hires here to help." He paused. "On second thought, perhaps you should stay. I can have that Mr. Sutton shadow you and learn the ropes."

Ellie glared at her grandpa. He knew he had her. "Fine, I'll escort Callahan, but please don't corner me like this again." She kissed him on the cheek as she passed by him and headed out to meet Luke. The businessman had arrived unbeknownst to her, and so certain she would be his guide. Ellie was sure he now thought her to be an imbecile for not knowing about the excursion. He looked up at her and adjusted his Stetson nervously as she exited the house. Like the excursion to Custer, he had dressed appropriately, Levi's jeans and a green and white plaid button-up shirt over a green cotton Henley shirt. A cowhide jacket completed the outfit.

"Miss Ellie, if this is an inconvenient time…" He actually sounded nervous.

"No, not at all." She waved her hand. "My grandfather simply forgot to tell me that he spoke to you. I can escort you, it is no problem." She was about to go to the truck, but decided that taking the horses would actually be quicker based on where her grandfather had suggested she take him.

"I hope you ride, Mr. Callahan." She looked towards the stables, not caring if it would be uncomfortable for him.

"I actually enjoy riding very much." His answer surprised her. "You may have more hills than I am used to, but I enjoy a challenge."

"Perfect. You can head to the stables, Matthew should be in there and can help you find a suitable mount. I'm going back inside to get us some vittles for the trail." She spun around and went back inside. What was it about this man that constantly threw her off guard?

Hattie had already prepared a lunch for Ellie and Luke.

"Mr. Benjamin, he sprung this on you quick-like, didn't he?" The plump, motherly woman commented.

"He did, and I suppose I'm the best Bennett daughter for the job, but I still wonder why he offered to help in the first place."

"He's just trying to be neighborly, you know. Helpin' a man like Mr. Callahan now may pay off in the future. His fancy hotel will need plenty of beef."

"That's true, though I hope we never become completely dependent on that kind of man." Ellie picked up a fresh green bean and popped it into her mouth.

"You speakin' like he's a monster, Ellie. From what I've heard and seen, he's a fine, upstanding young gent. She placed a fist on her ample hip and looked at Ellie as if she were her own daughter. "You treat him right, Ellie, unless he gets fresh, of course, then you give him a solid kick to the you-know-what."

Ellie smiled. Hattie and Matthew should have raised a slew of children, but only one had lived to adulthood, and he was now a preacher in Bozeman, Montana. Ellie missed David, who had been a good friend growing up. To make up for her lack of biological children, Hattie was a mother figure to all at the Longbourn Ranch, including the Bennett girls and often even Martha, though they were about the same age,

"I will, Hattie. Thank you." Ellie laughed and grabbed the packages of food, glad that Hattie had wrapped them to fit in her saddlebags, then left to begin her duty.

~~~~~~

97

The weather couldn't have been more perfect. The summer morning was cool, and Luke didn't even need the lightweight leather jacket he was wearing. And thinking of clothing, he couldn't help but notice that once again, Ellie was wearing trousers. He didn't know if he would ever get used to that.

"Are we still on your land?" Luke asked.

"Yes, we will be for a while. It might seem faster to go by vehicle, but there are many shortcuts, mostly paths that the truck wouldn't be able to get through. It would take much longer to go around the hills."

"I trust you," he replied, "and I must thank you, yet again, for showing me the area. I appreciate your expertise and the fact that you took time out of your day to help me."

"It will be nice to get away for a spell." She led him between two buttes. He marveled at the rock walls on either side of him. The pass was very narrow and Luke had to follow behind Ellie in order to get through. When they emerged at the other end, he nudged his borrowed horse to ride beside her.

"Do you ever have trouble with cattle wandering through here and getting lost?" He asked.

"Occasionally, yes, but we ride the paths often and you'll see some barbed wire at the edge of our property, which helps keep them contained. We also have the canyon and buttes to create natural barriers."

"Ahh, yes. I gather barbed wire is one of the rancher's favorite inventions." He knew from his research that barbed wire had been patented in 1874 by a man named Joseph Glidden.

"Indeed," she replied. "It has made keeping the cattle contained much easier."

"Do you have problems with rustlers?" He asked, wanting to learn everything he could about the land.

"I think ranchers will always have problems with rustlers." She commented. "The barbed wire certainly helps, but all it takes are some good wire cutters and there goes the fence."

"I suppose that's true." Luke flicked the reins.

"Barbed wire also creates some problems for the wildlife." Ellie added. "Cattle and bison, all animals really, can get ensnared and trapped, especially when their thirsty and looking for water. It's also hard to see sometimes and can hurt the horses."

"I hadn't considered that." Luke nodded. "But it seems as though the good outweighs the bad."

"It does," Ellie replied.

They rode in silence for a while. Luke couldn't get over the beauty around him. Rolling hills covered with grass and wildflowers were beginning to pop up everywhere. He could possibly use a botany expert to lead tours at his resort. "The wildflowers are beautiful around here. Do you know the names of all of them?"

"I know a lot of the more prevalent ones. That's sagebrush..." She gestured to a green bush close to the ground. "However, if you want to know about all the plants and gardening here, you would do best to talk to my sister, Marie. She's the horticulturist of the family."

"I'll have to keep that in mind." Luke replied. They continued riding for a while, then came to a barbed wire fence. Ellie dismounted and opened the gate. She led her horse through, and Luke followed, then she closed the gate and swung back up onto her horse.

"Another mile or so is the first place Grandfather thought you might be interested in."

"That's quite close to your ranch." He pointed out.

"Yes, but there is a beautiful spot another hour or so away from here that I believe would be the perfect location for your resort. It has a wonderful view of the mountains."

"I can't wait to see it." He trusted Ellie so much, he believed this spot would be a perfect place without even seeing it.

"I must say, you're quite adept at living out here," he commented.

She looked at him as if surprised that he would make such a comment. "I dare say there is much I still need to learn, but with time comes experience. I just try to do what God has planned for me."

"I agree with that philosophy wholeheartedly."

She looked as though she wanted to add something, then closed her mouth.

They rode on for a bit, then she finally spoke up. "Tell me, what ideas do you have for this resort? Why did you even choose South Dakota as a possible site?"

Luke smiled and began telling her all his plans, of how his father had visited the Black Hills decades ago and had always talked about its beauty, making Luke want to visit. "And now with Borglum creating his sculptures, even more people will want to come out here. I can offer day trips, hikes, and even overnight trips where guests can sleep under the stars like they're on a cattle drive. I was also playing around with the idea of eventually running my own cattle and even some buffalo. I'd like to try and make it as self-sufficient as possible."

"That's a good idea for you," she replied, then nodded to a ridge about half a mile away. "If I were you and I bought this land, I would construct my main complex there. Once you're up on that ridge, you'll see why."

They spurred their horses on and quickly made it to the destination. Luke drew in a breath. The mountains rose in the distance with many buttes in between. The land appeared to roll as a breeze whipped through the meadow grasses and the effect made it look almost like water cascading over the land.

"In case you got turned around, you're facing west, so when the sun sets, it's simply spectacular, like God has painted a masterpiece just for you." She smiled and he almost fell off his horse it was so breathtaking. "It's one of my most favorite places in the area to visit. The current owners are kind enough to let me come here whenever I have extra time, however, there is a place on our property that I love even more."

"You don't ever want to live anywhere else but your ranch, do you?" Not that he was seriously thinking of a relationship with her, but if he did…

"I don't want to, no, but it's not my choice." She stiffened, her whole demeanor changing.

"My apologies. I just assumed your father and grandfather know how well you manage the ranch and would hand it off to you."

"They would without a doubt. Unfortunately, my great-grandfather had other ideas." She proceeded to tell him the basics about the will of Muskum Longbourn.

"That is quite unjust," he replied. "I believe I know this Mr. Sutton. A little, squirrelly kind of man."

"Yes," Ellie smiled at his description, "he quite idolizes your Aunt Madeline VanRensselaer."

"Ahh, that's right. Her solicitor." He couldn't imagine the man who resembled a pompous weasel would be capable of running a ranch.

"Yes. I suppose I could entice him into marrying me, it wouldn't take much. However, I can't even begin to imagine a life with him." She shuddered. "I'd rather be an old maid living in New York City than be forever tied to that man."

"I don't blame you one bit." Luke's stomach churned at the thought of her marriage to another man, especially Sutton. He also didn't like the idea of a complete stranger taking over a family business just because the person who should inherit happened to be a woman. Ellie knew more about running a ranch than Richard Sutton could learn in a dozen lifetimes.

They rode down the ridge, then around another butte that linked up to another path.

"I know a nice place where we can stop for lunch, then we can head over to the other property," she said. He nodded and followed her.

~~~~~~~

Ellie found it a lot easier to be with Luke than she had anticipated. He was different out here away from wandering eyes, not as uptight. He wasn't as pretentious as she initially thought either. Perhaps Charlotte was right and he was just shy. Then again, she had to remember the fact that he had said she was just 'good enough'. That still stung.

After eating the delicious lunch Hattie had made, Ellie showed Luke a few more sights and before she knew it, it was time to head back to the ranch. Just as they neared the Longbourn property line, she frowned to see the glint of flames and smoke about a mile away.

"Is that a fire?" Luke asked as Ellie drove her heels into Naomi's flanks and rode quickly toward it. She heard Luke right behind her. As they drew closer, she saw that it was indeed a fire. She couldn't quite tell what was burning, but they appeared to be brown lumps.

"What on earth?" Beside her, Luke coughed, no doubt from the stench and smoke. She dismounted quickly and unhooked Naomi's saddle to access the blanket underneath. A shadowy figure on a horse caught her eye from a hill about half-mile away, riding toward Longbourn, and she waved, praying they were going to get help.

Luke stripped Samson's saddle off and they both rushed to the flames, beating at them with the blankets. Sweat poured from everywhere on Ellie's body. Her hat had fallen off and her hair began to unravel. The smoke was unbearable, and she felt as though her throat was closing up. Her eyes watered and her vision blurred. The flames had been fairly well-contained around the brown lumps and they managed to extinguish them. If only they had water or at least wet blankets, but she knew the nearest watering hole was too far away to do any good. After walking the fire's perimeter, which felt like hours, Luke stomped the last of the burning embers out. Ellie wanted to cry in relief. The muscles in her arms burned and each limb felt like they weighed more than a bale of hay. She collapsed to her knees, tears slipping down her face. Luke stumbled towards her, exhausted as well.

"Are you all right?" His chest heaved from breathing so hard, and his face and hair were covered in soot and sweat. He knelt down and reached out as if to touch her face, then dropped his hand and placed it on her back.

Ellie nodded, trying to still catch her breath. "Are you?" She finally panted. He took a deep breath and nodded, then pushed to his feet.

"Why does the fire actually smell appetizing?" He walked over to one of the piles that was still smoldering and bent down. Ellie stood and joined him, then scanned the burned area. The sight she saw made her quickly turn and retch. Cattle, just as she had suspected at first. From what she could tell, three cows and two calves had been slaughtered, then burned.

"Why?" She gasped out. Luke patted her back comfortingly.

"Do you think rustlers or squatters took them to eat and then burned the evidence?" He asked, his brow furrowed.

"I don't think so, no. They wouldn't have killed the calves and it doesn't look like any meat was taken, not much at least." She stared at the smoldering carcasses. "Lord, I thank You for keeping this fire contained, but why?"

"And there's no chance it could have been an accident?" Luke asked.

"Nothing is impossible, but I can't see how this wasn't deliberate." She took another deep breath and stepped away. Goodness, she must look atrocious. "I think it's safe enough to head home. We'll probably meet some of the hands on the way back. They can continue to monitor the site to be sure the fire doesn't spark back up again. I need to get you home."

"Are you sure you're ready to ride?" He asked. "I saw the man ride away as well, hopefully to get help. Although in reality, he could be the one responsible for this."

"I suppose that's true." She smoothed her hair back from her face, grabbed her dusty hat from the ground and put it back on. "He was too far away to recognize. I couldn't even identify the horse."

"I didn't either."

She strode over to her earlier discarded saddle blanket and shook it out. Luke did the same. She then went over to re-saddle Naomi as Luke saddled Samson. Luckily, the horses hadn't been spooked by the flames. They both finished their tasks, mounted up and rode close to the pile of cattle carcasses to look one final time. Ellie sighed heavily and they rode off in silence.

Chapter Thirteen

"So there is absolutely no trace as to who set the fire?" Ellie asked the next day. Davis Martin had found her at the stables after she had checked the fences of the north pasture riding Naomi. Davis had been one of the hired hand who had ridden out to monitor the scorched area, and apparently, he had gone out again this morning to see if there were any clues to what might have happened.

"Nope, not a trace." Davis shook his head. "They were slaughtered before they were burned though, but I don't know..."

His statement trailed off as a blue and white Rolls Royce came up the drive, Charles Brantley behind the wheel and Luke sitting next to him. Ellie glanced at Davis, who clenched his jaw at the sight of the car. What was his change of demeanor all about?

"Mr. Brantley!" Lindie dashed out the front door, danced over to the car and smiled at Charles. "I am so glad you have come for a visit. Janie will be ever so sad she missed you."

"She's not here?" Charles swept off his spotless black Stetson and frowned.

"She went into town to run some errands." Ellie explained. "You are more than welcome to come in for some refreshments. She shouldn't be more than an hour or so."

"We can't stay long," Charles said. "I have come to invite your family personally to a barbeque at Verbena Meadows Ranch." He handed Lindie an envelope and looked up towards the porch, clearly searching for Janie.

"Oh, Mr. Brantley, you must include all of our ranch hands in this invitation." Lindie looked back at Davis and winked. "Men like Mr. Martin here will surely add much enjoyment to the festivities."

Ellie glanced at Luke and was shocked to see him glaring at Davis. If a simple look could kill a man, Davis Martin would be stone dead. Davis didn't look any happier to see Luke.

"Of course, Mr. Martin, you and the other men must come." Charles turned to Luke. "Didn't you need to speak with Miss Ellie?" Luke shook his head, which surprised Ellie. He didn't even want to inquire about any information regarding the fire yesterday? Charles waved to the group, then put the car back in gear. "We must be off, I can't wait to see you all again on Saturday."

Lindie backed away from the car as Charles and Luke drove off, a cloud of dust following. "Come, Kathy, we must plan our outfits for the party." The girl gave one more flirtatious smile to Davis, then flounced away, Kathy right behind her, as always. Ellie knew she had an endless list of chores to complete, but her curiosity over the exchange between Luke and Davis won out.

"How long have those two been in South Dakota?" Davis asked before Ellie could bring the subject up. They began walking back toward the barn.

"Not long, a month or so maybe." Ellie stopped and looked at Davis as it dawned on her that he must know the two men from a previous encounter. "I didn't realize you knew them,"

"The blonde, Brantley, I've never officially met him. Lucas Callahan, on the other hand, I know very well. Probably was hard to tell, seeing as how happy we were to see each other, but we actually grew up together."

"Golly." Ellie surely hadn't expected that bit of information. "Sounds like a very interesting story there."

"You could say that." Davis stepped up to the fence, bent down, picked a long weed and stuck it in his mouth. He rested his arms on the fence and looked across the valley. "I can never quite get over the beauty of this land." He remarked, then turned and smiled. "Beauty all around me."

Ellie was a bit disappointed that he wanted to flirt instead of telling her about Luke. She didn't really have time for that, though compliments didn't happen often and she should relish it. She turned toward the barn, but Davis reached out and grabbed her arm. Her sleeve pulled up a bit and he ran his thumb over the front of her wrist. As he moved to pull her close, she gently stepped away. He let go of her arm, smiled and leaned casually against the fence.

"As I was saying, Luke and I grew up together in St. Louis. My father was the family chauffeur. We used to scamper around together all the time, pretending to be pirates on the Mississippi River, fishing and playing baseball. We were the best of friends. Luke's father, Thomas, was a great man, very supportive of me. He knew I wanted to study law, so after my parents died, he paid for me to attend college. I was doing well, was on the baseball team, made good friends and contacts that would help me get a job when I graduated. I was a year away from obtaining my degree when Thomas Callahan died. Heart issues. Luke immediately stopped paying for my classes. I had no other source of income, so I had to drop out of school and quit the baseball team. I tried to find a job, unfortunately, no one would hire me, not even as a legal assistant. I couldn't even get a job as a chauffeur, which I had been trained to do by my own father."

"Why would no one hire you?" She asked.

"Luke's influence, of course, and that of his more powerful aunt." Davis threw up a hand in frustration. "So I had very few options left. I had as much experience with horses as I did anything else and had always wanted to see more of the country, so I headed west." He slid his hand down to hers and squeezed. She looked over his shoulder towards where the Rolls Royce had driven away.

"It does surprise me. I know Luke can be proud, arrogant and perhaps even a bit prejudiced, but I wouldn't think he could be so heartless."

Davis nodded in affirmation. "Trust me, he can be."

"Why did he treat you with such disrespect?" There had to be a reasonable explanation. Even Luke Callahan couldn't be that petty. She may have thought that when she initially met him, but her more recent encounters with him gave her pause.

"He was jealous, plain and simple. Thomas Callahan always treated me like a second son. I even believe he liked me better than Luke, and the young Mr. Callahan couldn't stand that, so he did whatever he could to make my life miserable." Then, Davis smiled. "But he has failed. It will take more than the mighty and powerful Luke Callahan to keep my spirits down." His hand moved from her wrist to her waist and he pulled her closer, then reached up with his other hand and touched her cheek. Ellie's

109

heart pounded. "Miss Bennett, I really want to kiss you right now." He leaned down. Ellie gently pushed him away and shook her head. He was exceedingly handsome and someone she could be attracted to, but…

"Mr. Martin, your attention flatters me, really it does, but we've only known each other for a few days. There may be girls around who would allow such…liberties…after so short a time, but I'm not one of them."

Davis nodded and stepped back. "You're right, of course, how forward of me. I usually don't make advances so quickly myself. There's just something about you that I cannot resist, Miss Ellie."

"Well, you'll have to, until we get to know each other better."

"Yes, of course, my apologies." He took her hand and placed a kiss on the back of it. "I'll be sure to dance with you this weekend at this barbeque of Brantley's, if that's okay with you."

"I look forward to it." Ellie smiled.

~~~~~~

"What is he doing here? And with her?" Luke couldn't control his anger. What were the odds, with all the ranches in the west, that the betraying lout Davis Martin would be working at Longbourn? And why was he following Ellie around like a cougar stalking its prey?

"I can't honestly tell you, Luke." Charles answered. "A crazy coincidence for sure."

"Or the devil working to torment me." Luke wanted to slam his fist on the dashboard. He had wanted to talk with Ellie, to see if she had learned anything new about the fire they had put out the day before. He wanted to make sure she was all right after the terrifying incident, but he had lost his chance.

Charles nervously tapped his fingers on the steering wheel and glanced at his friend. "You know, you never told me exactly what happened between you and Davis. I mean, I know he used all his money indiscriminately at school and that made you mad. It would me too, I suppose, but I don't understand the complete disdain you have for the man that used to be your best friend."

Luke thought back. He could have excused Davis's lack of motivation, self-centered behavior and sense of entitlement. He could have forgiven Davis for misusing the inheritance Luke's own father had given him, and even dropping out of college. Luke could have gotten over the feelings of betrayal when he realized that Davis only believed Luke was good for doling out money and bailing him out when he was in trouble. But what Davis Martin did to Luke's sister, Helena...Luke could still see the tears cascading down her face and hear her sobs...Luke knew he needed to forgive Davis, and someday he would, but he would never, ever forget what he had put Helena through.

Charles interrupted his thoughts. "I mean, you don't have to tell me, I know you like your privacy, and I respect that, but if you're really worried about him being here, perhaps you should tell Ellie. I know you have an interest in her..."

"I don't," Luke said a bit quickly. "Not really,"

Charles shook his head. "At any rate, the Bennetts are a delightful family, well most of them, that is, and if he's going to cause trouble for them, it would be wrong not to say something." The car pulled up to Verbena Meadows and Charles turned to Luke. "Personally, I think we should say something about Davis."

Luke wanted to, but didn't know if it would do any good. It looked as though Ellie had made up her mind about both him and Davis, and if what he had just witnessed was any indication, she preferred Davis. The last thing he wanted was to say something and have her think him petty, or get mad that he wasn't allowing her to form her own opinion. She was independent and would want to make her own decisions. He felt she already had a pretty poor opinion of him.

"No, not just yet, I'll watch him closely at your gathering. See if I can determine what he actually thinks he can get from the family. I wonder if he realizes they won't inherit the ranch and don't have the kind of long-term income like those he usually chases." It would certainly fit with Davis's previous actions if he were trying to get into Ellie's good graces because he thought she would inherit a large sum of money or property. He had chased after socialites before.

Charles frowned. "If that's what you think is best." Luke could tell he wasn't happy about the decision, but he would respect it.

"For now, I do." Luke opened his car door and stepped out of the Phantom, then changed the subject as they walked up to the sprawling ranch house. "I have been meaning to ask you. What is your impression of Janie? You're spending a lot of your time with her."

"Luke, I must admit, I think she might be my future bride. I could spend the rest of my life with her."

"Already? Come now, Charles, you've fallen before…"

"That may be true," Charles interrupted, "but I realize now I was never really in love before. My feelings for Janie are so different than any other relationship I've had."

"And you're not at all concerned about the differences in your social standings?" They both sat down on the wicker chairs situated on the front porch. Luke was a little shocked when he realized that he could be content looking at this view for the rest of his life. If only he didn't have so many responsibilities, so many expectations to live up to, so many people whose livelihood depended on him.

"No, I'm not, not at all," Charles replied. "I think Janie could charm Queen Mary of England if ever given the chance. I truly love her, Luke."

"But does she feel the same for you?" Luke couldn't help but ask the question that had been plaguing him since he first saw the two together. Janie Bennett was indeed sweet and kind, but from what he'd observed, she acted that way with everyone. Was she simply leading Charles on, hoping to snag herself a kind, handsome, and especially wealthy husband? Luke just couldn't tell for sure, but he definitely couldn't let Charles enter into a bad marriage.

"I'm sure she does." Charles answered, but Luke could sense the doubt in his friend's voice. "And I have to say, Luke, I simply cannot wait to see her again at our soiree."

Luke could wait for the day of Charles's party, especially now that he knew Davis Martin would likely be there. But at least he would be able to observe him and perhaps discern his end plan. He could also watch Janie Bennett to see how she responded to Charles. Did she really have feelings for his best friend or was she a gold digger like so many others? He would have to discern that. If he was lucky, maybe he would even be able to persuade Ellie to dance with him.

Chapter Fourteen

The week dragged on, but finally the day of the Verbena Meadows barbeque was upon them. As Ellie brushed her hair, she couldn't help but wish she had the natural ringlets that Janie had. But to no avail, her hair was neither straight nor curly. It was simply wavy, or depending on the day and if it was humid enough, embarrassingly frizzy. Hopefully, Janie would be able to work her magic and design an elegant hairstyle for her today. Ellie looked back at her bed where she had laid out her best dress for the occasion. She sighed. Her wardrobe consisted mostly of practical clothing, not much in the way of elegance.

"Here you are, Ellie." Janie entered their bedroom. "Marie said you needed my help."

"Yes, thank you so much. I was hoping you would style my hair; you have such a talent for it."

"I most certainly can. Why today, though? You usually don't get all gussied up for a barbeque. You're not looking to impress someone in particular, are you?" Janie smiled slyly and nudged her. Ellie had told Janie all about Davis, including his history with Luke and the way Ellie's heart had fluttered when he had almost kissed her. Ellie hadn't been able to see him since the day he told her about Luke, as they had both been very busy.

"You know I am." Ellie blushed. She couldn't hide anything from Janie. "I've been looking forward to this all week."

"We all have." Janie smiled, clearly thinking of dancing with Charles again. "I'll have to ask Charles about Davis Martin and Luke Callahan. I find it hard to believe that he would be friends with Luke, if what Mr. Martin says is true about Luke's character."

"You don't need to do that. Luke should defend himself against these stories." Ellie ran a hand through her plain brown hair. "I was beginning to think he may be a decent man despite his pompous attitude, but now after hearing what he did to Davis, I know better. Davis is twice the man Luke will ever be."

"Then let's hope Mr. Martin is more willing to dance with you." Janie laughed as she put the last pin in Ellie's hair and moved to tend to her own wardrobe. "Perhaps we can find an even nicer dress for you in here."

~~~~~~

"I'm so excited. This party will be so much fun!" Kathy squealed as they walked up the few steps to Charles's home for the evening affair. Verbena Meadows hadn't been built for functionality and was a bit too ostentatious for Ellie 's liking, but she had to admit, it was still magnificent.

"I do hope Dennis is here." Kathy looked around for the young man from town who always had a good time with Kathy and Lindie. "He promised to dance with me."

"He promised me as well." Lindie smirked. "I just can't wait." The front door opened and a well-dressed butler escorted the family to the back of the house where the party was taking place. It appeared that Charles had spared no expense for the event. Lanterns hung everywhere, though Ellie

115

knew the house was equipped with electric lights. Several tables covered with silk maroon tablecloths lined the back porch, already piled high with food. There was a pit for the campfire, likely to be lit when it became a little darker, and Charles had even had a wooden dance floor constructed outside with lanterns encircling it. Almost every family from the surrounding community and their ranch hands appeared to have come out for the gathering, as well as many townsfolk from Spearfish.

"Miss Bennett!"

Everyone in the family turned to see Charles striding towards them, away from Luke and Isabella. Ellie met Luke's eyes briefly, but she quickly looked away. She didn't need to be vexed so early in the evening, and that would happen if she dwelled on that man. Ellie was at the party to have an enjoyable time.

"I am so glad you were all able to join us." Charles addressed the whole family, but his eyes were transfixed on Janie.

"Thank you so much for having us." Martha Bennett took both of Charles's hands in hers and kissed him on the cheek.

He chuckled nervously, then told the family where they could get plates for their food. As he led the family to the location, Janie's arm tucked in his, Ellie broke away from the group and began looking for Davis. She was searching so intently that she didn't even notice that Luke had approached her.

"Are you looking for someone or something in particular, Miss Ellie?" He asked. She tried not to look too intently at him. He had embraced the attire of a rancher again tonight. Levi's, a forest green button-up shirt, tan vest and tan Stetson. It was a good look on him, but she couldn't dwell on that.

"No one in particular, no, I'm just...taking everything in. I can never get enough of the view of those hills. Aren't they magnificent"

"They are quite splendid. I've never seen their equal."

"Is that a fact?" Ellie looked at him, doubt in her eyes. "I'd be willing to bet you've traveled all over our country and probably even much of Europe."

"That is true, and the Swiss Alps are quite a sight to behold, but I still believe…"

Ellie saw Charlotte over Luke's shoulder. She waved her friend over. "Charlotte!" Feeling slightly rude for interrupting Luke, she gave him an apologetic smile. "Will you please excuse me?"

Charlotte met her and gave her a quick hug. "I've been trying to find you. I saw Lindie and Kathy running around with Angelina, looking for all the eligible cowboys." Angelina was Charlotte's younger sister.

"I wish they weren't such a bad influence on her." Ellie shook her head. "Your sister is so sweet. Don't get me wrong, I love my own sisters, but…" She looked over to see Marie, standing awkwardly near the doorway of the house, likely hoping to find an excuse to go inside and find a piano to play. "they just always seem to make such fools of themselves." At that moment, her mother walked by, talking loudly with some of the local women.

"Mr. Brantley dotes on my dear Janie ever so much, even more so than Clark Mercer did, he even allowed her to stay…"

Ellie sighed again. Sometimes her family could be a bit tedious, even for her.

"Everyone knows your family means no harm," Charlotte replied, trying to be kind, then smiled and waved at a young towhead that Ellie

117

presumed was one of her students. "Now, why were you talking with Mr. Callahan?"

"He ambushed me." Ellie rolled her eyes. "I was so intent on finding Davis Martin when suddenly, Luke was standing there talking to me. On that matter, have you seen Mr. Martin?"

"I have not." Charlotte looked around. "Perhaps he's by the corral. Many of the ranch hands are going to try and ride one of the Verbena Meadows bulls."

"A Verbena Meadows Rodeo. I can see Davis participating in that." Ellie tucked a fallen tendril of hair back into her chignon.

"Davis, is it now?" Charlotte smiled. They began to walk in the direction of the barn when Janie approached them.

"Ellie, I have news for you." She looked slightly concerned. "Mr. Martin isn't here. He's not coming."

"What?" Ellie's shoulders drooped and her chest tightened. "He has to be here. Father gave all the hands the evening off so they could come."

Janie shrugged. "He apparently had some business to attend to in Spearfish, though Dennis Warslow mentioned that he could have put it aside for later, but he hinted that he didn't want to take a chance of running into someone that he'd rather not see." With the knowledge that Davis wasn't at the corral, the trio began walking back to the food table as the band began to warm up for the dancing.

"Callahan." Frustration coursed through Ellie. Something else that pretentious man had ruined by his arrogance. "I will have you know..."

"Miss Ellie." The three stopped short when Richard Sutton stepped into their path. She couldn't help but notice, once again, that he was half a head shorter than she was, and again looked ridiculous in his attire, almost like a child dressing up as a cowboy. "Miss Ellie, may I have the honor of the first dance tonight?"

"I...well...that is..." Ellie wanted to say no with everything in her, but couldn't. "I suppose."

"Splendid." Richard took her arm and all but dragged her to the dance floor. She stumbled behind him, shocked at how strong he actually was. She looked behind her to see an amused look on Charlotte's face. As Richard pulled her into his arms for the dance, Ellie saw Lindie and Kathy openly laughing at her predicament. The music started, and Richard began to awkwardly move his feet to the steps of the dance.

"Mr. Sutton, I am surprised you know this dance."

"I know a great many things about life out here," he replied pompously.

"I thought this was your first visit to our state." She tried not to wince when he missed a step and stomped on her foot.

"It is, but I have been doing much reading about the area in order to prepare for when I take over Longbourn." He rambled on as Ellie clenched her teeth to keep from speaking out against him. Nothing angered her more than being reminded that the ranch she had poured her own sweat and tears into was going to be stolen out from under her and given to an easterner who only knew about ranching and the area from reading books. It was infuriating. He stepped on her foot again.

"Have you ever thought of selling your stake in the ranch?" Ellie asked when she could finally get a word in.

"Oh, no, not at all," Richard replied, and her heart sank once again. She had no means to buy him out and really didn't know of anyone else who could either, at least no one that she would want to own her home.

119

"It would take quite a bit for someone to entice me away from the ranch." Richard continued. "It is very agreeable out here. Though I must say, where I live back in North Carolina in the Blue Ridge Mountains, now those are a sight to behold. I am very honored to be the solicitor of the Vanderbilts and I live in a lovely cottage in the village, near the Biltmore Estate. A home that rivals any grand manor in Europe. I do hope you can see it some time."

"It sounds lovely." *When will this dance end?* Richard continued blathering on about Biltmore, the Vanderbilts, Madeline VanRensselaer, who he explained was another of his primary clients and who seemed to be as perfect as Mother Mary. He stepped on her foot yet again. She tuned him out until he brought up a familiar name.

"Is that Mr. Lucas Callahan? Here?" Nervous excitement laced Richard's voice. "Here at this party? I must make myself known to him. He is a dear friend of Cornelia Vanderbilt Cecil, friends since they were children, and of course, he is the nephew of the esteemed Mrs. VanRensselaer."

"Yes, you already told me that, Mr. Sutton." She followed his gaze and spotted Luke almost immediately, standing stately and aloof on the porch. He locked eyes with her. Had he been watching her dance? He didn't even like dancing, not if he could help it. Isn't that what he had said?

She looked at Richard, who had once again brought his focus to her. "Now, Miss Elizabeth, I must let you know that it is my intention to stay close to you all evening…"

Well, that will be annoying. Ellie thought about the many ways she could avoid the man as the music came to an end.

"May I have the next dance, Miss Ellie?" A voice from behind her asked. She was saved! Hallelujah!

"Yes!" She spun around, not caring who was asking; she just wanted to get away from Richard. Her heart sped up just a bit when she saw who it was.

"Luke. Yes, of course."

"Ahh, Mr. Callahan." Richard, quite rudely pushed in front of Ellie. "I must make your acquaintance…"

Ellie stepped away, knowing that Luke would find her when he was ready to dance. She had to get away from Richard Sutton and in her haste to get away, she almost ran into Charlotte.

"So, I see you just agreed to dance with Mr. Callahan." Charlotte grinned. "Be careful, you might actually enjoy it."

"No, he's just the lesser of two annoyances at this point. It was either him or Mr. Sutton, and in reality, I prefer neither." Charlotte shook her head, and Ellie changed the subject.

"Have you noticed how much time Charles has been spending with Janie? I think he likes her very much."

"But does she like him?" Charlotte asked

"You know Janie, she's always been shy and modest." Ellie shrugged.

"Well, she must be careful in regards to her actions. If she doesn't prove to Mr. Brantley that she likes him, he may move on. She needs to snatch him up now while she has his interest."

"He must have at least an inkling of how she feels." Ellie replied, and almost ran into Luke, this time as they came around a corner. He steadied her with his hands.

"I came to find you…are you ready for that dance…with me?"

121

~~~~~~~

 Ellie nodded, and Luke cradled her forearm in his as he politely led her to the dance floor. He was still shocked that she had even agreed to dance with him. Luke pulled her close and locked eyes with Ellie as the band began playing Aura Lee and all the couples started two-stepping to the Civil War-era song.

"This song may be old, but it is quite a favorite around Spearfish," Ellie started the conversation, then waited for him to reply. He took in a breath and stared over her shoulder.

"It's your turn to say something, Mr. Callahan." Ellie reminded him. His mind blanked and Luke couldn't think of anything to say. All topics flew from his thoughts, except for wondering why Ellie was back to calling him 'Mr. Callahan'.

"Do you always talk while dancing?" He finally asked.

"It would feel quite awkward to be entirely silent."

"Well, then, I have been meaning to ask: have you learned anything about how that fire started?"

"Unfortunately, no. Not a trace of the person or persons who killed the cattle or set the fire. It's as if a ghost were the culprit."

Luke nodded. He didn't want to bring up the scumbag who was Davis Martin, but he really had to learn why he was at Longbourn Ranch. With her. "Does your father often hire new ranch hands?" He met her eyes for a second.

"Only when we are in need of them, the majority of our crew is temporary help. They come and go. The rest are very loyal to our family. The ones we just took on may become permanent if they work

122

hard." Ellie spoke in such a way that Luke knew she was really speaking about Davis. He felt his face redden and he paused before finally answering, searching for the right words.

"Davis Martin makes friends quite easily and he can secure a job almost anywhere, that's true. The real question is, however, does he have any qualities that allow him to keep or maintain the position?"

"Well, he apparently lost your friendship." Luke could see the anger boiling in Ellie. "And because of that, his dreams have been shattered!"

Luke clenched his jaw and didn't reply, too afraid of what he would say if he lost his temper. Davis Martin had clearly already gotten inside her head and spun some fine tales about him. All lies, if he knew Davis. Why couldn't Ellie see that? Finally, he shook his head. "I noticed you had started reading the new Agatha Christie book when you stayed here a few weeks ago. I'm sure Charles would allow you to borrow the book if you wanted to finish it." *I can't believe I just changed the subject to books.*

Ellie looked at him with a raised eyebrow and ignored the question. "I remember you once told me that you hardly ever forgive anyone. If that is a true statement, you'd better be careful about making snap judgements about people."

"I am careful." He searched Ellie's eyes. How could he tell her the real story when Davis had likely already poisoned her against him? Not to mention the fact that Luke found it difficult to speak coherently around Ellie and she already had formed negative, preconceived notions about him.

Her eyes narrowed. "And are you never blinded by prejudice? Never wrong?"

"I know I am far from perfect, but I do consider myself to be a good judge of character." He focused on her so intently that she could not look

123

away. For just a moment, it seemed as if they were the only two people in South Dakota. How he wished it were so. "Why are you asking me all of these questions anyway?"

"I'm just trying to figure you out, Mr. Callahan." The music ended and Ellie moved to leave the dance floor, but he gently grasped her wrist.

His heart pounded. "And what exactly do you see?"

Ellie shook her head. "I haven't quite decided yet." She then turned and left him standing alone on the dance floor. He watched her as she made her way to the refreshment table. Why was his heart set on this girl? He had been ready to share with her a little of his and Davis's backgrounds, but if she didn't want his advice, she could just learn about the lout the hard way. She clearly had no affection for him and a relationship would never work between them anyway.

Chapter Fifteen

Ellie had to get away from the pompous, arrogant man. Not only did he make her blood boil, but dancing in his arms had made her heart pound. What was wrong with her?

"Ellie Bennett?" The refined voice of Isabella Brantley spoke. Ellie steeled herself for more insults and turned. Isabella did not look happy at all. "I must say, Ellie, you have some of the most truly...interesting relatives." She nodded at Mr. Sutton, who was talking earnestly to some ranchers, most likely about Biltmore or the Vanderbilts or VanRensselaer or himself.

"You have no idea." Ellie muttered.

Isabelle continued. "I just heard the most distressing news about how you are spending time with Davis Martin. Please tell me the rumor is not true."

"And what if it is true, how does it affect you? Why would you care?" Ellie's defenses rose. She had been spending extra time with Davis this past week, but it wasn't any of Isabella Brantley's business. And who had she even gotten this information from?

"Has Mr. Martin shared with you anything about his past? Specifically, in regards to Luke. Did he tell you he grew up with Luke? That his father was employed as a chauffeur by the Callahan family? I'm sure you know that Davis will tell anyone who will listen that Luke left him penniless, and unable to find a job, but that isn't quite the truth, I can promise you that. I don't know all of the details, I'll admit, but I do know that Luke is not to blame, and I have it on very good authority that Davis Martin is nothing but a Forty-niner."

Ellie bristled. She didn't know many flapper terms, but she knew Isabella was calling Davis a gold-digger. She shook her head. It almost sounded as if the woman was trying to warn Ellie, but that didn't seem right. Isabella didn't even like her. She was likely protecting Luke's reputation because she wanted to marry him. "According to you, then, the only thing Davis has done wrong was to be born the son of a chauffeur and that he wants to better himself. You make it sound like it's a crime to want more out of life." She threw up her hand, frustrated with all these pretentious easterners. "For your information, Davis did tell me he was the son of a servant, and that at one time, he and Luke were best friends, so if you're trying to make me dislike Davis because of that, it won't work. You are completely misguided if you believe Davis is less of a man because of his history. And you shouldn't blindly believe the ramblings of Luke Callahan either." She spun and stomped away, back towards the corral. She was intercepted this time by Janie, who immediately noticed Ellie 's anger.

"Ellie, I spoke with Charles about Luke and Davis Martin." Janie spoke softly. "Charles wouldn't give me all of the details, but he said he would bet his entire fortune that Luke wasn't at fault. He doesn't believe Davis Martin to be very trustworthy."

126

"Does Charles even know Davis?" Ellie asked. Charles sounded quite biased, just like his sister.

"Well, not really, they've met a few times, and…" Janie admitted.

"Well, it stands to reason, then," Ellie interrupted, "all of what he knows is from Luke's perspective. I can appreciate Charles defending his friend, it does show his immense loyalty, but I just don't believe the information. Like you said, Charles barely knows Davis, so how can he form an accurate opinion of him?"

"Yes, but…"

"Enough, Jane." Ellie interrupted again, this time with a smile, not wanting to talk about Luke any more. "Let's talk about you and Charles…I see he's hardly left your side this evening."

"Well, I suppose that's a fact." Janie blushed, clearly smitten, perhaps even falling in love. "I'm embarrassed to admit though, Mother can speak of nothing else. I overheard her telling Mrs. Ingraham that an engagement is all but guaranteed."

"Personally, I don't think Mother's wrong this time." Ellie smiled. "But on the other hand, she shouldn't be saying such things, it makes for gossip. I truly love Mother, but she can be so dramatic and even embarrassing, much like Kathy and Lindie."

"I suppose she's just excited about the prospect of my being married." Janie blushed again.

"Now that is an accurate statement." Ellie looked off into the fading sunlight. The colors against the Black Hills were breathtaking. It was as though every shade of red, yellow and blue were used in one of God's paintings. It had a most calming effect on her.

~~~~~

"Mr. Callahan, how are you this fine evening?"

Luke turned to see Benjamin Bennett, Ellie's grandfather.

"Very fine, Mr. Bennet, and yourself?" Luke shook the offered hand.

"Quite well, thank you. I trust you were able to see most of the available land before your day with Ellie came to a complicated end."

"Yes, she was very knowledgeable and helpful." Luke cleared his throat. "It has been a pleasure getting to know all of your granddaughters."

"Ellie in particular, I would wager."

Was Luke that transparent? First Isabella guessed and now this old man? Though Benjamin Bennett appeared to be a very sharp observer.

"I don't know what you mean, sir," Luke replied. Benjamin chuckled.

"Come now, Mr. Callahan. You haven't danced with nary a one of our local gals at any of our shindigs, and then all of a sudden, you're asking my Ellie to dance. Not to mention you've spent time with her when she was at Verbena Meadows as well as on your trip to Custer. It was also at your suggestion, rather your hinting, that she escort you on your quest to see the land in the first place, and I see the way you look at her."

"With the exception of the scouting, she and I were simply chaperoning Janie and Charles. He's the one you should be conversing with if you're talking with men who wish to court your granddaughters."

"Oh, young man, I plan to, believe me." Benjamin nodded. "I just found you alone first."

"I don't have designs on Ellie, sir. She's a lovely, fascinating young woman, but a relationship with her would never work. Even if I was interested in her in that way." He quickly added.

128

"What do you mean by that?"

"Well, sir, first and foremost, she doesn't like me much. If you've been watching, which apparently you have been, you'd notice that. And besides…" Luke stopped, not wanting to voice any more thoughts, especially ones that would insult this old cowboy.

"Besides what? The fact that you're from two different social groups?"

Luke didn't nod, but he feared his lack of denial was telling.

"Callahan, I know my granddaughter. She has a special place in my heart that's for certain, and let me tell you, I honestly believe she likes you more than she may let on, but she can be terribly stubborn. Gets that from my side of the family, I'm afraid. My Aunt Belle, she was especially stubborn. Oh, the stories I heard about her, especially during the War Between the States."

"I don't recall South Dakota being affected by that war." Luke commented.

"I'm sure it was in some ways, but I didn't grow up here. I was born and raised in Fredericksburg, Virginia."

"I had no idea, sir." Luke understood well that the town played a significant role during the war, and that several major battles occurred in and around the town.

"I still have many vivid memories, though I was only a young lad of four when it started."

"I imagine that experience must have severely altered your life." Luke had always been fascinated by the War Between the States.

"It did indeed. My father, Joshua, was a blacksmith and lost an arm during the siege of Petersburg. He was a special man: kind, patient and devout. I couldn't have asked for a better Pa." Benjamin had a far-off look in his eyes. "We lost my Uncle James at the Battle of Glendale. That's who I named my son after."

"I'm sorry to hear of your loss, sir."

Benjamin nodded. "I know you feel there could be potential problems because of the differences in your family backgrounds, and I can appreciate that you recognize that. But if you feel that these differences are a deterrent to having a friendship with Ellie, don't. My brothers and sisters and I are proof that any relationship, no matter what the origins, can work."

"Sir?" Luke was confused.

"My mother, Elizabeth married a man that many considered to be beneath her." Benjamin explained. "She was a true Southern lady, the daughter of one of the wealthiest planters in Spotsylvania County. Mama fell in love with a simple blacksmith. Several of her friends refused to associate with her because of it and even her sister, Belle, who she considered to be her best friend, snubbed her nose at Mama for years. As I said, my Aunt Belle was very prideful and stubborn. However," the old man gave Luke a very meaningful look, "though my parents struggled through some hard times, they were the happiest couple that I ever knew, and I have tried to model all aspects of my life after theirs. Trust me, my boy, societal differences can be overcome by any couple as long as love and God are a constant in their lives."

Luke was taken aback by the story and the man's advice. He could almost believe it was what his own father would say under these same circumstances. However, knowing Benjamin was right and having the courage to follow through were two different things. There was also the nagging feeling that Luke wasn't even sure if Ellie liked him. Benjamin saying that she did was not proof of her feelings.

"Thank you, sir, for this talk. I will certainly keep all you've said in mind and take it to heart."

Benjamin tipped his cowboy hat and walked away. Luke hoped the old gentleman was right, that maybe Ellie did hold some affection for him, but there were still many other obstacles to overcome. He had to be sure of his own feelings before taking a chance.

"Di mi, I thought that old codger would never leave you alone." Isabella latched onto Luke's arm.

Luke tried not to sound exasperated. "What can I do for you, Isabella?"

"I actually need you to come with me. I'd prefer Charles, but he's currently playing the host. Come." She all but dragged him around the side of the house. "I'm afraid I saw Janie go off with one of the cowboys. He had his arm around her."

"What?" Luke was taken aback. Janie Bennett wouldn't do that, would she?

"I didn't believe it myself, but I saw it with my own eyes." The two walked around a corner and Luke stopped dead in his tracks. The light was fading, but there was no mistaking what he saw. Janie Bennett in the arms of another man, hugging him tightly. He moved to confront her, but Isabella pulled him back out of sight. Luke looked at Isabella, confused.

"I'll go find out what's going on. There must be an explanation."

"Of course there is, she's been toying with Charles's affections all this time just to make a good match. She wants to get out of this wretched

131

town. I don't blame her for that, but not at the expense of my brother." Isabella argued.

Luke feared she was right, and he dreaded telling Charles. But he would have to. Charles needed to know.

"Surely I can go and ask her…"

"Oh, and be forced to engage in fisticuffs with a cowboy who has likely been in more brawls than you can count."

Luke knew he could hold his own, but the last thing he wanted was to cause a ruckus and spoil the party for Charles. His friend would be crushed soon enough. He nodded.

"And you'll tell Charles what you saw here tonight?" Isabella asked. "He'll listen to you, Luke."

"Of course I will." Luke suspected that once his illusion of perfect Janie was shattered, Charles would want to leave posthaste. He hated conflict of any kind, but perhaps it would be best for him. He looked over at Ellie, who was laughing with Charlotte Ingraham and some young ranch hands. She must have felt his gaze because she turned to look at him. The moment she locked eyes with him, she frowned. Perhaps leaving would be the best for Luke as well.

Chapter Sixteen

The next day, Ellie came in from morning chores, a bit breathless and dusty. She went to the sideboard and piled her breakfast plate with scrambled eggs, sausage, and potatoes, thanked Hattie for the wonderful food, and sat with her family to eat.

"Where's Father?" She asked Janie as their mother droned on and on about how perfect Mr. Brantley was and how much she would miss Janie when she moved to Chicago.

"He's in his study." Janie answered. No one noticed Richard Sutton entering the dining room until he loudly cleared his throat. Then, everyone looked up.

"Ladies, I hate to intrude, but may I have a moment alone with Miss Bennett? Miss Eleanor Bennett, that is."

Ellie almost choked on her coffee. Slowly, her mother and all her sisters stood and made their way out of the dining room. Kathy and Lindie couldn't help but giggle and Janie grimaced as she stared at Ellie and had to be pulled away by their mother. Grandfather Benjamin gave Richard a stern look, then patted Ellie on the shoulder as he reluctantly walked past her. The moment the door closed, Mr. Sutton set his hat on the side buffet table and clasped his hands in front of him. His awkwardness was as thick as molasses.

"I am sure you already realize this, Miss Eleanor, but I must confess that from the moment I arrived at Longbourn, I knew you would be the one. My future wife."

"Oh, no, please." Ellie's face heated in embarrassment and anxiety.

"First, let me explain to you why I feel the need to marry. I believe I should set a good example for the people of Biltmore Village and Asheville, as I am a leader in that community. So many of them look to me to set the standards of a good and moral life. I also believe that marriage will add greatly to my happiness. Lastly, it has been the wish of Mrs. Madeline VanRensselaer that I marry and she commented on my bachelor status when I last saw her at Biltmore. I do believe she is right as she is about most everything, if not all things."

"Mr. Sutton." Ellie tried to interrupt him, but he held up a hand and continued speaking.

"Of course I could have found a woman more than willing to become my wife back home in North Carolina, but I feel I owe it to your family. As you know, I will inherit this ranch, so it is only fitting that I marry one of my charming cousins, to keep this ranch in your family. I find that you, Miss Ellie, will be a charming companion and the most helpful when I do inherit." He slid down on one knee and took her hand in his already sweaty one.

"I am terribly flattered, Mr. Sutton, truly I am, but I really must decline." Her stomach ached, hating the feel of his hand on hers. Why on earth had he decided on her? He would be much better suited to anyone else. Marie, for example.

134

"It is highly unusual for a young lady to reject a man she secretly admires. Come now. I know you want to accept." Mr. Sutton said smugly.

"Excuse me, Mr. Sutton, but no! I don't want to accept!" Ellie stood and pulled her hand from his. "I'm very sorry, but I know for a fact that you couldn't possibly make me happy and quite honestly, I'm probably the last woman in the world who could make you happy. Believe me when I say that being married to you... it just wouldn't work. I could never live back east and I am far from being the charming and elegant woman you're looking to marry. Perhaps..."

"You are most charming." He stood, reached out and snagged her hand again. "And I'm sure you will eventually accept my proposal. Why wouldn't you? You'll never receive a better offer."

Ellie's temper flared. Why would he not listen to her? He was such a pompous and arrogant man. She pulled her hand away. "Mr. Sutton, you're quite wrong. Why won't you take me seriously? I can't marry you. Ask someone else!" She stormed out of the room and grabbed her hat from the entryway.

What on earth would possess Richard Sutton to propose to her? They had absolutely nothing in common and there were certainly no sparks between them. Luke Callahan had a much better chance of getting her to accept a marriage proposal than that self-obsessed weasel. She slammed the front door behind her as she stomped down the steps, jammed her hat on her head, then tromped to the barn.

"How could he ever think I would marry him? Just like that?" She said to herself, then stopped and surveyed the pastures, hoping to find Davis. She wanted to talk to him about last night, but didn't know where Matthew had sent him for the day. Unable to locate Matthew or Davis, she

135

went into the work shed, grabbed a hammer and nails, and headed back to the house. She needed to get her aggressions out, and there were some loose boards on the porch.

"Eleanor Marie Bennett!" Her mother's screech echoed in the morning air as she stormed out of the house to the front porch. By that time, Ellie was on her hands and knees, pounding nails into a porch floor board. Her father followed at a more sedate pace. Ellie stood and pulled her hat off and thumped it against her thigh as she braced herself for the argument that was sure to happen. Grandfather Benjamin stepped into the open doorway, arms crossed. His presence gave Ellie courage. "You get back in this house and tell Mr. Sutton you've changed your mind."

"Mother..." She tried to interrupt.

"You're always saying that you want to own and run this ranch, that you never want to move away. Now is your chance."

"I'm sorry, Mama, but I can't do it." Just the thought of marrying that simpering cousin made Ellie sick to her stomach.

"You do realize this isn't just about you, young lady. This union would benefit our entire family." Martha turned to her husband. "Tell her, James. Tell her now! If she doesn't marry Mr. Sutton, I'll never speak to her again. Do you hear me? Tell her!"

Ellie's stomach ached, but she couldn't give in. Martha continued her tirade.

"Tell her I will refuse to even see her again unless she goes back in there right this instant and accepts Mr. Sutton's proposal before he decides to ask someone else. I know she will regret turning him down. For goodness sake, Ellie, no other man will ever want you, and you will become nothing but a pathetic spinster!"

136

"Please, Father…" Ellie could feel tears forming in her eyes. She knew deep down she would comply if her father insisted. The silence between them seemed to last forever as both women and Grandfather Benjamin looked at James. Finally, her father spoke.

"My dear Ellie, your mother wishes you to marry Mr. Sutton."

"Yes, or I will never speak with you again." Martha repeated.

"So I hate to tell you this, Ellie, but you have a difficult choice to make."

Ellie's heart leapt just a bit. Her mother looked incredulous, but continued to listen.

"Your mother will disown you if you do not marry Richard Sutton, but I will disown you if you do."

Ellie smiled and tears of relief formed in her eyes as his words sunk in. He would support her decision. "Thank you, Father!" She kissed him on the cheek, smiled at Grandfather Benjamin and made her way back to the barn to put the tools away, leaving her father to deal with her disgruntled mother. When she came back out, Charlotte was dismounting her horse and Kathy and Lindie were chatting with her from the porch.

"Oh, Charlotte, you must hear the news." Lindie called out. "Mr. Sutton has proposed to Ellie but she has turned him down! He's in the house causing an awful ruckus now."

Charlotte looked at Ellie and raised her eyes in question. "I'll tell you the entire story later." Ellie promised her. "What brings you out here today?"

"I just wanted to visit. When I was riding past Verbena Meadows, I saw Annie Elliot, who is helping out as a maid there. She asked me to bring this letter to Janie."

Annie Elliot was a young woman Marie's age who lived in town and helped her family earn money however she could. She was engaged to a Naval sailor, Captain Frederic Wentworth, who was on the high seas at present.

"Janie and Marie are washing the dishes." Lindie informed Ellie. "They saved the rest of your breakfast, in case you're still hungry."

"That confrontation made me lose my appetite." Ellie said, but proceeded to the kitchen. She sincerely hoped that Mr. Sutton had gone to his room, as she didn't want to see him now, so soon after turning down his proposal. Charlotte gave Janie the letter, who went out back to read it privately. Ellie and Charlotte went into the sitting room where they could visit.

"Oh, I can't deal with him right now." Ellie grumbled.

"I assume you mean Mr. Sutton. Honestly, Ellie, do you even want to try and understand him?" Charlotte asked. "He really can't be all that bad."

"Other than being a pompous, arrogant know-it-all?" She proceeded to tell her friend about the dreadful proposal.

Charlotte thought for a moment. "What if I were to invite him for dinner with my family? You know my father will talk with anyone and it might give the two of you some distance."

"You would do that for me?" Ellie asked, grateful for Charlotte's insight into the situation.

"Of course I would. When we're done chatting, you can go back to your work, and I'll handle Mr. Sutton."

~~~~~~

When Charlotte and Ellie had finished visiting, Charlotte quickly found Mr. Sutton to invite him for dinner, then returned home, which Ellie found strange. Would Charlotte really ask Mr. Sutton to dinner simply to be a good friend, or did she have some other reason? What could it possibly be? She headed out to the barn to saddle Naomi when a voice sounded behind her.

"Ellie, how are you this fine morning?"

Ellie threw her saddle on Naomi and turned to see Davis in the entryway of the barn, framed by the sunlight behind him.

"Davis! How nice to see you." She turned toward him, a smile on her face.

"I heard you had some excitement this morning." He smiled back. "All the hands are talking about it." He chuckled. "Don't know why Sutton ever thought you would say yes. You're way too much of a woman for him to handle."

"I missed you yesterday, at the barbeque." Ellie changed the subject, not used to such praise from a handsome man. "I heard you had errands to run in town."

"I did." Davis pulled his hat off. "But the real reason I decided not to go was because I didn't want to cause any problems for Luke Callahan." The two walked outside. Ellie was touched at the courtesy Davis showed the businessman.

"He doesn't deserve your kindness." Ellie told him. He spun to face her and stepped closer.

"I suppose that's just the kind of man I am. Forgiveness is the way of a Christian." He spoke softly, his eyes falling on hers. He slid a hand around her waist and leaned forward.

"Ellie, come quick!" Lindie's voice called from the other side of the barn. Martin stepped away as she rounded the corner. "Oh, there you are. Come, Janie needs you."

"Do you know why?" Ellie's heart was still racing from Davis's nearness as she was sure he was going to kiss her if Lindie hadn't interrupted.

"She's terribly upset. She went straight to her room after reading the letter from Verbena Meadows and she won't come out."

"Oh, dear." Ellie went back to Naomi's stall and removed her saddle, threw it back on the paddock post, settled her hat back on her head and hurried to the house and up into their room. She found Janie on her bed, face down, crying. Kathy was trying her best to offer comfort.

"Janie, what in the world happened?" Ellie sat on Janie's other side. Janie handed Ellie the letter.

"It's from Isabella Brantley." Janie wiped a tear from her cheek. "They've all left Verbena Meadows. They're on their way back east already." *Sniff.* "It doesn't sound as though they will be coming back any time soon, if at all." She took a breath.

"What?" Ellie was stunned. Charles hadn't even had the decency to say goodbye? She would expect that from Isabella, and probably Luke, but not Charles. Janie choked back a sob.

"I don't understand why, Ellie. I wonder..." Janie hiccupped. "Isabella does go out of her way to say that Helena Callahan is

140

a most accomplished young lady. She even wrote that she hopes to one day be able to call Helena her sister."

"It's more likely that she wants to marry Luke, but perhaps she wants Charles to marry Helena. Or she could be saying spiteful things just to hurt you."

"I find it hard to believe that she would do such a thing." Janie shrugged, looking miserable, yet her trust in the goodness of mankind evident.

"Well, I believe Isabella knows that her brother is in love with you, but she wants things her way. She probably wants Charles back in Chicago so he will forget all about you. Luke is probably on her side in that respect. Of course, we're not rich enough or dignified enough for their hoity-toity society." She shook her head. "But you shouldn't worry, Janie. Charles loves you, I know he does. No one, not Isabella, not Luke, or even this sister, what's her name? Helen? Not even she can change that fact."

Janie nodded, and Ellie's heart ached at the pain her sister was going through.

"Miss Ellie! We need your help out in the west pasture." Matthew yelled up into the open window. "You and the Ford." Ellie got up and waved in acknowledgement, then turned back to Janie. "Will you be alright if I leave?"

"Yes, of course. I have my own chores to take care of." Janie stood and tried to make herself look presentable. Ellie rubbed her temple, walked back to Janie, gave her a hug, then left to drive the truck out to the west pasture.

Part 3: Fall 1928

Chapter Seventeen

St. Louis, Missouri

It was obvious that Charles was unhappy. The group had stopped at the Callahan's home in St. Louis for an extended stay. The Brantleys didn't have any pressing matters in Chicago for a few months, as they were still supposed to be in the Black Hills. Luke looked up from a business proposition he was considering to see Isabella talking on his Ameche telephone, no doubt making plans to go to a speakeasy. His suspicions were confirmed when she said Blind Pig, caught Luke looking at her, and winked as if they shared a secret.

Luke shook his head and went back to his work, but it was difficult for him to stay focused. He didn't want to admit it, but he missed South Dakota. Even St. Louis seemed too busy; he shuddered to think of how he would feel when he was stuck in Chicago or New York. He wasn't quite sure why he longed for the peacefulness of Spearfish. He often visited the Pisgah National Forest in North Carolina and enjoyed it, but had never before felt the sense of yearning to go back to a place the way he did now. He dreaded the reason and feared it had everything to do with a cowgirl who had chocolate-colored eyes and had stolen a piece of his heart.

"Charles is back!" A blonde-haired, blue-eyed sprite skipped into the room.

"I didn't know you were home, my dear Helena." Isabella had hung up the Ameche and sat on the sofa. Luke groaned when she pulled out a cigarette. Now the whole first floor would smell of rancid smoke.

"Where was Charles? I didn't even realize he was gone." Luke asked, not caring that he interrupted Isabella. A part of him regretted agreeing with her so quickly when they witnessed Janie's supposed offense. He wished he had asked Janie about the circumstances instead of jumping to conclusions. When they had told Charles, he was appropriately crushed, yet acted as if he almost expected something to ruin his happiness.

"He went to pick up the pictures from his Brownie, they were being developed. He said he would show me all of them and it would be almost like I took the trip with you."

Luke raised his eyebrows, surprised that Charles wanted memories of the past few months. He had been putting on a happy face, but Luke knew he was still upset.

"I don't know why anyone would want to go there in the first place, much less revisit that place." Isabella shuddered.

"Then I suppose you don't have to stay here, if you really don't want to." Helena looked earnest, but Luke knew she wouldn't care one way or the other if Isabella was around. She had told Luke several times that she didn't care much for the woman. He agreed with his sister.

"You're so sweet." Isabella stood. "I do have some friends to meet up with. I'll be back for dinner."

144

"She'll be going to get a jorum of skee," Helena said as soon as Isabella was out of earshot.

Luke looked at her, surprised that she knew the jargon for drinking alcohol.

"What?" Helena smiled innocently, as if she didn't know what he was shocked about. Luke just shook his head in amusement. He loved his sister dearly.

"How are you both doing this fine day?" Charles entered the room, a package in his hand.

"I am ready to see your pictures." Helena looked at Luke. "Can I come with you the next time you go to South Dakota? You still want to build your resort, right?"

"I do. You can come as long as you don't have school." Luke promised. Charles sat on the sofa next to Helena and Luke stood and went behind them to look at the images. He had been looking forward to seeing them as well, in spite of himself.

Charles thumbed through the black and white pictures, telling Helena about the mountains and wildlife. Luke tried to see if the pictures of Janie affected Charles, but his friend remained calm and unaffected, on the outside, at least.

"Who is that?" Helena asked, pointing to a picture.

"That is Miss Ellie Bennett." Charles looked back at Luke, questioning in his blue eyes. "Though I don't recall her posing for any solitary photographs."

"I was just playing around with the camera." Luke's heart skipped a beat when he looked at the image. Even a black and white photograph of Ellie affected him unlike any other and brought him back to the Black

145

Hills. The picture had turned out well; she had just turned around, was looking at the hills and had a slight smile on her face. The spires of Custer park framed her and the sunlight lit her just right, making her almost glow.

"You took that?" Helena smiled up at Luke, as if she suspected his feelings for Ellie. An infatuation, that's all it must be.

"I did." He nodded and leaned over to take it out of Charles's hand.

"Are you going to send it to her?" Helena asked.

Luke looked at his sister. "Yes, of course. I'll make sure she receives it." He would hold onto it, hopefully he could give it to her in person. He went back to his desk and placed the photograph on it, then walked back over to Helena and Charles.

"South Dakota is so beautiful, Luke. I won't take no for an answer. You must bring me with you next time."

"Such demands for a girl who is not yet 18." He reached out and tugged a strand of her hair.

"I know you'll bring me. You always give me whatever I really want. You find it impossible to say no." Many people might call Helena's words spoiled or haughty, but Luke knew it was more a confidence in him that he would always see to her wants and needs, if it was reasonable and in his power.

"As I said before, you can come as long as you won't miss any school."

"Thank you, Luke." She stood, kissed him on the cheek and skipped out of the room.

"She has you tied right around her little finger." Charles tucked the rest of the pictures into the envelope.

"Yes, well, she deserves it after all she's been through," Luke answered. Charles agreed, even though he didn't know the details of the worst that she had experienced.

"So you really think you'll be going back to South Dakota?" Charles asked casually.

"Yes, eventually. I'm very serious about building a resort near Spearfish and I have agents looking into purchasing some land. It should be a profitable investment."

"And the Bennetts? Would you see them?"

Luke looked at Charles, who was staring down at the packet of pictures.

"I...I really hadn't considered that," he lied. He wanted to see Ellie again, very much, but wasn't sure if she ever wanted to see him again.

"You know, I wouldn't begrudge you pursuing a courtship with Ellie. I sensed something there and I would hate for you to miss out on a good relationship because Janie wasn't who I thought she was."

"But if she deceived you..."

"No, Luke, I'm not sure she ever did." Charles admitted. "I was the one pressuring her to spend all of her time with me. She was simply being polite, as she is with everyone. Perhaps her mother pushed her to do so. I feel it is just who she is. I don't know. I hold no ill will toward her."

Luke nodded. Charles's current musings matched what he had observed in South Dakota as well. "Be that as it may, as far as the Bennetts are concerned, I don't believe Ellie will ever care for me in that way."

"If she's smart, she would." Charles smiled sadly.

"And if it's God's will that you end up with Janie, that will happen as well."

147

Chapter Eighteen

Longbourn Ranch

The days passed, and one evening, after dinner, Ellie rode out to her favorite spot on the ranch, needing some quiet time to think and pray. There were so many things on her mind: Mr. Sutton, the ranch, Janie and Charles, Luke and Davis. Her mother still wasn't speaking directly to her, but didn't hesitate to make her miserable by making rude, hurtful comments whenever Ellie was in earshot. Thank goodness Charlotte had been bringing Mr. Sutton into town. In fact, he had dined there two to three times a week since she had rejected him. It was a nice reprieve not to listen to his monotone ramblings, much less have to face the accusatory looks he threw her way when he did see her.

Ellie sat and braced her back against a boulder. Naomi was tethered nearby and would occasionally nudge her shoulder sensing Ellie needed some comfort. She looked out across the terrain. It was views like this when Ellie wished she were a more accomplished painter. The sun had just started its descent over the green hills, creating a beautiful blend of oranges, reds and purples. Tall grass rustled around her. She knew that before long, the sky would burst with orange and yellow and pink. It seemed as though

God was painting His masterpiece to be seen for just those few minutes, and Ellie wanted to capture the vivid colors in her mind. She knew that even a gifted painter like Marie would never be able to do the scene justice.

A horse approached behind her and she turned around.

"Charlotte!" She smiled at her friend and stood to greet her.

"I knew you would be out here." Charlotte dismounted.

"What in the world are you doing here so late in the day? You're usually planning your weekly lessons. Did Mr. Sutton need you to guide him back to the ranch?"

"Partly, yes, but I wanted to talk to you." Charlotte didn't meet Ellie's eyes.

"Thank you for distracting that man these past few weeks. I know it couldn't have been pleasant."

Charlotte blushed just a bit. "It hasn't been...that unpleasant."

Ellie leaned against a taller rock and crossed her arms over her flannel shirt. "What have the two of you been talking about anyways?"

"Many things." Charlotte took a deep breath. "Ellie, he has proposed to me and I have accepted. We are engaged."

"What?" Ellie's jaw dropped. "It's been barely a month! You seriously mean...you're going to marry him?"

"Yes, I am. That's what it means when two people are engaged."

"But...what about your job? Your family? You can't just move across the entire country. Besides, you can't marry him, he's ridiculous!"

"Ellie, please." Charlotte's eyes shimmered with tears. "Not everyone can turn down perfectly good marriage proposals. We can't all afford to be romantic and just wait around for the perfect match. Mr. Sutton is a good man."

"But, Charlotte…"

"I am 27 years old, Ellie, and I will soon be without a job. I will not become a burden to my parents."

"What do you mean you'll soon be without a job? You're a wonderful teacher, all of your students love you."

Charlotte crossed her arms. "Yes, well, the mayor has a niece that needs a teaching job and she actually has a college degree with a teaching certificate, so she will be taking over next term."

"What? Mayor Gilmore cannot do that!" Ellie protested.

"Apparently he can, and the school board agrees. His niece has more education, more training and they feel she will be a better fit for the students. What am I supposed to say?"

"I would argue for my position, for what I love to do. You're too good a teacher for them to just let you go. I will argue for you. When did you find out about this? Why am I now just hearing about it?"

Charlotte shook her head. "I wanted to tell you weeks ago, it's why I came out, but then I heard about Mr. Sutton's proposal, I figured I would try and help my own situation as well as yours. I appreciate the fact that you would argue with the school board, really, I do. But I have accepted the loss of my job and Mr. Sutton's proposal, and I…" She shrugged. "This is what I have chosen. So please don't judge me."

Ellie shook her head, still in disbelief. "Charlotte, I'm not…" She wasn't quite sure what to say.

"I want to do this, Ellie. I promise." Charlotte took Ellie 's hands in hers.

"I suppose I can accept that, I just..." She looked up at the sky, praying for wisdom in her words, then looked back at her friend. "I'm going to miss you so much."

Charlotte pulled her into a hug. "We can write and still visit. The train makes travel so much easier now. This won't be goodbye forever."

"I know, but still." Ellie pulled away and wiped at her cheeks. "I really do wish you all the happiness in the world, Charlotte. You deserve it."

~~~~~~

The next few days dragged on. Martha still wouldn't speak to Ellie at all, and made her feel her anger in other ways, complaining to anyone who would listen, especially if Ellie was in hearing distance. According to her mother, Ellie was a selfish, ungrateful child who would never get another proposal in her life, and now Charlotte was counting down the days until Mr. Bennett died so that she could come back to South Dakota as owner of Longbourn. Whenever she went off on one of her tangents, Ellie simply left the room.

Ellie continued to be concerned about Janie, as she was more forlorn than Ellie had ever seen her. It was obviously because of her feelings for Charles and his sudden departure. Isabella had sent another letter, from Chicago this time, telling Janie that they were settled in the 'Windy City' for the coming winter. To Janie, that meant all hope was gone. Ellie had wanted to ball up the letter and toss it into the fire when she read it. Isabella actually had the impertinence to brag about Charles's new affections for Helena Callahan.

Ellie knew it wasn't possible, as he had mentioned he considered the girl a sister. It had been obvious Charles had strong feelings for Janie and

Ellie thought them a perfect match, but she was so miffed with the man. Why would he lead Janie to believe that he cared for her? He had showered her with attention, and everyone who had seen them together had thought them to be a perfect couple. Why would he break her heart? Why would Charles throw away his relationship with Janie? Janie would never blame Charles, but Ellie certainly could. She liked him well enough, but was beginning to think of Charles as weak and unable to think for himself much, less fight for his own beliefs.

"How can everyone be so insensible?" Ellie asked Janie, trying to make sense of everything one evening while sitting in front of the fire. "Charles's leaving! Charlotte getting married! I still don't understand either of these decisions, though I try and try. That Mr. Sutton is a conceited, narrow-minded fool. No self-respecting woman would ever marry a man like that, yet Charlotte has chosen to. I know she believes there is no other alternative. Oh, if only Mayor Gilmore hadn't used his powers to get his niece to take Charlotte's position, she would not have felt the need to leave. She was forced into making a decision she would never have made otherwise.

"I don't know what to say about Charlotte, except that she chose her own course. I know you blame Charles for leaving, but really, you mustn't. I don't. Young men don't always act responsibly. It was my own fault, my own ego getting the best of me. I must have misread his intentions the whole time."

"He led you on!" Ellie exclaimed.

"Do you think it possible that Charles's sisters influenced him?" Janie ignored Ellie's statement. "If they did, I'm sure it was because they only want him to be happy."

"I think they want more than that." Ellie turned to stare into the flames. "All the east coast families like theirs just want more money and prestige. His friends and family only want him to marry a wealthy girl with powerful connections."

"But if they thought he loved me, why would they discourage him from courting me?"

"Because they're the selfish ones."

Janie picked at her blouse "Besides, if Charles truly loved me, they wouldn't have been able to lead him away." She sighed. "He must not have loved me as I thought he did, Ellie. Mama won't leave the subject alone, so please, when she's not around, can we please not talk about Charles? It's really still upsetting to me."

"Of course, Janie. I am so sorry to have brought it up." Ellie decided she could at least do that for her sister.

~~~~~~

Before Ellie knew it, Charlotte's wedding day had arrived. Though she didn't understand the reasons why, Charlotte was excited, and had asked Ellie to be her maid of honor, while Angelina, Charlotte's sister, and Janie would also stand up with the bride. The groomsmen would be two of Charlotte's male cousins and James Bennett.

"Oh, Ellie, this will be so nice for you." Lindie flounced into the room where Janie was doing Ellie's hair.

"What do you mean, Lindie?" Ellie had tried to hide the exasperation in her voice.

"This will be the closest you'll ever get to the altar."

"Lindie, be kind." Janie always tried to be the peacemaker.

"In case you forgot, Mr. Sutton proposed to me first." Ellie countered. Not that the fact was anything to brag about.

"Only because he'd need your help on the ranch. Besides that, he really wanted to marry Janie first, we all know that. And who can blame him? What man would have you as their first choice for a wife?" She cackled and darted out of the room.

"That's not true, Ellie, really." Janie pinned a curl up. "And don't think I haven't noticed that Mr. Martin is still paying close attention to you."

"I'm not convinced he likes me. I think he may just want the ranch."

"Aren't we a pair." Janie nodded her head. "I love Charlotte dearly, but who would have thought she'd be the first married of the three of us."

"Which leads me to believe that I will end up being the spinster of our little group." Ellie grumbled.

"Don't let Lindie get to you. Personally, I think she's jealous."

"Of who? Me?" Ellie didn't believe that for a moment. "What does she have to be jealous of?"

"You're smart, driven, would have a college degree by now if Papa hadn't gotten sick, and every man, woman and child in town and on the ranches in the area likes and respects you. Besides," she smiled, "we all know you're Papa's favorite, as well as Grandpa Benjamin's."

"I don't think that's true." Ellie hesitated. She could understand how her sisters might believe that, though. "And even if it were true, I'm certainly not Mama's favorite. Lindie is. Or maybe you." She shrugged. "I'm definitely at the bottom of that list."

"I also feel that Lindie is jealous of your relationship with the ranch hands, specifically one Davis Martin. I think she actually likes him." Janie continued.

"Oh Heavens no, that can't possibly be true. She wouldn't lower her standards for one of the ranch hands. She wants one of the students from the college."

"Well, all that aside, we're very lucky that we have two parents who love us and sisters who are as close as friends."

"That is true." Ellie gave a smile in the mirror. "And a sister who can actually make my hair look beautiful, as you have done again. Thank you so much."

"Any time. And you never know, the man of your dreams could make an appearance at any time, when you least expect it."

"The same goes for you." Ellie was so thankful God gave her this sister.

Part 4: Winter 1928-1929

Chapter Nineteen

St. Louis

"Merry Christmas, Luke!" Helena bounded into the library where the balsam fir had been set up and decorated for the holiday. She was such an effervescent young girl. Luke looked up from the Dickens novel he was reading, and smiled at his sister. Duchess lifted her head to greet Helena as well.

"Merry Christmas," he pulled his reading glasses off. "And how are you this fine morning?"

"I am quite well." She sat next to him and scratched Duchess's head. "Shall we open our presents from each other before everyone else comes down?" Aunt Madeline, Cousin Anne and Cousin Roger had arrived three days ago to celebrate the holidays, but they were all late sleepers. This gave Luke and Helena time in the morning to spend alone together, and today they would be able to exchange gifts, just the two of them.

"I believe that is a great idea!" He set *A Christmas Carol* aside and sat forward as Helena retrieved two presents and proudly handed him a neatly-wrapped package about the size of his hand. He tore off the brown paper and smiled again to see a W.H. Morley multi-tool pocket knife.

"I figured it would be good for you to have since you spend so much time riding and hiking. Do you like it, Luke?"

"This is a very thoughtful gift, Helena." She knew him so well. "I love it. Thank you." The girl glowed with pride.

"Can I open mine now?" She asked excitedly.

"Of course."

Helena shook the box, frowned in confusion, then tore off the wrapping and pulled a folded piece of paper from the box. "What is this?"

"Read it." Luke stood, knowing they would be leaving the room soon. Helena unfolded the note and then jumped to her feet after reading the message. "What's in the parlor?"

"Let's go see." She hadn't taken long to decipher the riddle he had spent an hour composing. He followed her out of the library and into the parlor, normally a room decorated for the lady of the house, but Helena refused to claim it as hers, citing it had been their mother's, then insisting that she shouldn't use it, as the room would become Mrs. Callahan's once Luke found his future wife.

"Luke! Lucas Callahan, you didn't!" She squealed and dashed to the black Steinway Model D grand piano and touched the ivory keys.

"Of course I did." He stepped over to her. "You deserve the very best, Helena. Miss Mary said it is the finest piano to be had in the country."

"This model is too expensive, Luke, I don't need…"

"Hush. I insist."

"Oh, I shouldn't accept…" She sat down and began playing. *Abdelazer* by Henry Purcell, if Luke wasn't mistaken.

158

"But you will anyways." He chuckled. He enjoyed watching and listening to his sister play. She was truly talented, and was even starting to compose her own music. Helena smiled and continued playing. When she finished the complicated piece, she stood and threw her arms around her brother.

"Thank you, Luke. My old piano was quite sufficient, but this one sounds magnificent."

"You're welcome. I'm thinking of getting you a new violin for your birthday."

She shook her head. "My old one is just fine, really."

"Very well, then." Luke smiled, glad to see that she enjoyed the gift he had given her and appreciated it, yet didn't expect expensive gestures like so many other young women of her station.

Helena returned to the piano. "I must practice some carols for later on today." She immediately began playing one of her favorites: "Silent Night". He could tell it was an easy piece for her, and that thought was confirmed when she proceeded to have a conversation with him at the same time that she was playing. "Did you send a gift to your friend, Ellie?"

His heart sped up at the mention of the girl he couldn't get out of his head. "No, why would I do that?"

Helena looked at him as though he was daft. "Because you love her, that's why." She continued playing.

"What makes you say that?"

"You keep that picture of her in your study and she is the only girl you have ever spoken of to me."

"You asked who she was when you saw Charles's pictures." Luke pointed out.

159

"But the way you speak of her, Luke. I can tell she means the world to you. And she would be smart to reciprocate these feelings."

"If you say so, but I don't believe she held me in very high esteem when we parted. I'm afraid I made a poor first impression."

"You usually do." Helena replied with a roll of her eyes. Luke sat down to listen to Helena play.

"You know me too well." He set one ankle on top of his opposite knee.

"Better than anyone else." She transitioned to "Carol of the Bells", a little more challenging piece that was only about a decade old.

The door to the parlor opened and the formidable Madeline VanRensselaer entered.

"Good morning, Lucas, Mosby told me you were in here, and of course, I could hear the music."

"My butler's name is Mason, Aunt Madeline." Luke reminded her.

"Of course." She waved her hand. "I take it you have had your time just the two of you to exchange gifts."

"Yes, Aunt Madeline and look what Luke has given to me!" She ran her hand across the grand piano's lid.

"It is very beautiful, indeed. Your brother is quite generous."

"He is, and any woman would be lucky to marry him."

"I have long believed that." Aunt Madeline sat down, avoiding Duchess. The dog looked up and thumped her tail. "And he will do well to remember what is expected of his future bride."

Luke sighed. Aunt Madeline was constantly reminding him of her expectations in the woman he should marry, and they were quite different than his.

Even Helena knew. "Yes, she must be graceful, genteel, well-connected, traditional, and certainly not a flapper." She repeated the list as if she'd heard it thousands of times.

"Gracious, no!" Aunt Madeline would have clutched her pearls if she had been wearing them. "Those women bucking all convention and flaunting against tradition just to be contrary." She shook her head. "I cannot imagine how Cynthia Brantley can cope with it, what with her daughter Isabella falling in with that crowd." She looked directly at Helena. "You'd better not get any ideas, young lady. Your mother and father would both turn over in their graves."

"Of course, Aunt Madeline."

"Now, continue playing, if you please. I enjoy your music. I trust you know 'O' Holy Night'." Aunt Madeline leaned her head back and laid her hands on her stomach.

Helena began playing as Luke's cousin and loyal friend entered the room.

"Mason told me you'd be in here, though I should have known by the sounds of this Heavenly music." Roger Bailey was the same age as Luke, born just a month later. Roger's mother Josephine, Luke's mother, Olivia and Aunt Madeline were all sisters, Madeline being the bossy oldest sister. Roger was considered plain-looking, he was tall and thin with dreary brown hair, and dull brown eyes. He currently worked for Luke in New York City, managing many of his investments and helping him plan other ventures.

"I take it you appreciate Luke's gift to you, Helena." Roger nodded.

Helena smiled at her cousin. "Most definitely."

"Have you seen Anne yet this morning, Aunt Madeline?" Luke asked.

161

"Yes, she'll be down directly, I'm sure," Madeline replied.

Mason entered the parlor. "Brunch is ready."

"Thank you, Mason." Luke nodded. They all went into the dining room where the cook had set out a beautiful display of foods on the sideboard.

"I thought you were giving the servants the day off." Roger remarked.

"I gave them the option, but Mason wanted to be here, and as always, Mrs. Dennison looked apoplectic at the thought of someone else feeding us."

"She doesn't like the idea of anyone else in her kitchen," Helena added.

"That's true as well." Luke smiled.

"I must say, Lucas, I am very glad you've continued the Christmas traditions of your mother and father." Aunt Madeline smiled after they had all been seated and prayed. Luke wanted to send someone up to inquire after cousin Anne, as she was usually tired and sickly. At least, that's what they were always told by Aunt Madeline. Helena had different ideas and thought Anne was just spoiled and lazy.

"Thank you for saying so, Aunt Madeline. I can't see myself ever forgetting the traditions." These traditions included reading the Nativity story on Christmas Eve to anyone who wished to join, from the lady of the house to the stable boy and his family, attending Midnight Mass, on Christmas Day, giving the servants the day off, exchanging gifts with family, and eating a delicious Christmas brunch. After brunch, the extended family would gather together for games and music and then they would have a splendid dinner. Luke's father had worked hard to accumulate the wealth he had, and had taught Luke and Helena to care for those who had less. Thomas Callahan's favorite scripture verse had been from Zechariah: *Do not despise these humble beginnings, for the Lord rejoices to see the work begin.* In fact, his mother had cross stitched the verse on a sampler, framed it and hung it on the wall of his study. Luke never intended to take it down.

"I'd bet Ellie Bennett would appreciate the traditions as well." Helena grinned at Luke.

"Who is Ellie Bennett?" Aunt Madeline's head flew up. Luke sighed.

"She's just a friend I met in South Dakota when I was there with Charles this past summer." He stated, not wanting to explain his relationship to anyone before he could determine exactly what his feelings were.

"And why, pray tell, are you commenting on her, Helena?" Madeline glowered at the girl.

"She's just...from what Luke told me about her, I think she would like a good many things about our home here in St. Louis."

"I see. Lucas, why are you telling your sister about some cowgirl from the backwoods of South Dakota?"

"Charles Brantley was showing Helena some photographs of our trip and Miss Ellie was in some of them. That's all." He gave his sister a brief look and slightly shook his head. Helena grinned just a bit guiltily then focused on her food. Luke smiled back, hopefully letting her know that there were no hard feelings.

"That better be all there is to this story, Lucas," Aunt Madeline concluded. "You know the kind of woman you must marry, and no one from South Dakota would fill those requirements." She looked at Roger. "Same goes for you, young man. You will one day be taking over several aspects of the family businesses, so you also must take care in the choice of woman you marry. As for you, Helena…"

Luke interrupted. "Helena is far too young to be worrying about that, Aunt Madeline, and Roger and I hear your words."

"Indeed, now, how about we end this discussion for today," Roger replied, good-natured as always. "We should be celebrating the birth of our Lord."

"Here, here." Helena spoke up, a grin on her face. Luke smiled, took another sip of coffee and thanked God for his blessings.

Chapter Twenty

Longbourn Ranch

Ellie leaned back in her chair and gazed into the crackling fire. It had been a good start to the Christmas celebration. Her mother's brother, Patrick, his wife, Edith, and their two children, Sammy and Rachel, had all come for the holiday. Since Sammy was eleven and Rachel nine, it was good to have younger children around, making the season more enjoyable. The family had gone to church that morning, exchanged gifts, then had the traditional Christmas luncheon with all of the ranch hands. It was now time to relax until dinner was served.

"Cousin Marie, will you play us some songs on the piano?" Rachel asked. "It would be ever so much fun to sing some carols."

"Yes, Marie, do play, but make sure they're fun songs." Lindie added.

"All right. What would you request?" Marie moved to the upright piano in the corner.

"Start with 'Joy to the World!'" Kathy suggested.

Marie nodded and began playing. The whole family began singing, with the exception of Mr. Bennett. Matthew and Hattie had also joined them for the day, though Hattie spent much of her time preparing the prime rib dinner.

After 'Joy to the World', Marie played 'Up On the Housetop', then after a few more songs, Marie took a rest, Hattie went to check on dinner, and Ellie and Janie left the sitting room to set the table.

"You're quieter than usual, Janie. What's wrong?" Ellie asked.

"Oh, nothing. I'm just being sentimental." Janie folded a napkin and placed it on the table.

"Come now, you know you can talk about anything with me."

"I just...I had it in my heart earlier this year that this Christmas, I would be able to spend it with Charles. Perhaps even as his..." She shook her head and wiped at an eye. "It's silly, I know, but I really thought he was going to propose to me. I really thought we were headed in that direction. I thought..." She drew in a breath. "I feel so stupid, Ellie. I truly believed he loved me." She sank into a chair.

"I thought that as well, Janie." Ellie moved to give Janie a comforting hug. "I believe anyone who saw the two of you together thought the same thing." Frustration bubbled up in her. "I tell you, it wasn't Charles who made the decision to leave. It was probably his insufferable sisters and that...smarmy Luke Callahan."

"No. I'm not so sure about that. You've said that before and I have considered it as well, but Charles is a man that makes his own decisions." She took a breath, then stood and continued setting the table. "Sometimes I wonder if I missed my chance for love and marriage when I broke it off with Clark Mercer."

Ellie shook her head. "Absolutely not." She thought back to the smooth man who had swept into their town several years ago. He was

166

handsome and had a good job with the federal government. He had charmed their mother, Lindie and Kathy, and had almost swept Janie off her feet, but something never felt right. Ellie had supported Janie in that sentiment. She didn't trust him, and she had let Janie know about it. "Like we agreed at the time, he just wasn't right for you. When he looked at you, Janie, it wasn't with love, it was more like he just wanted to...possess you." At least Charles looked at her with interest and adoration and what Ellie believed to be love. "You will find the right man, Janie. I just know it. It still may be Charles Brantley even though he doesn't deserve you after leaving like he did. Don't worry, it will all work out."

Janie shook her head. "You, at least have had a formal proposal, and I see Davis Martin as a possible suitor for you also."

"Oh, for Heaven's sake, Sutton would have proposed to you first and you know it. Mama told him you were all but engaged elsewhere." She shuddered. "We both dodged a bullet there." She let the matter about Davis drop. She still wasn't sure about him.

"Yet Charlotte ended up married to Mr. Sutton, and thanks to great-grandpa Muskim, he'll be in our lives forever."

"I don't like thinking about that fact." Ellie took a breath and stepped back to study the table. It looked good, if she did say so herself. "And I still can't believe Charlotte married the nincompoop. Even if she thought she'd never have another offer."

"We all make different decisions for certain reasons," Janie responded, then looked at the door as Hattie came through, platter of prime rib in hand.

"Ohhh, Hattie, the ham this afternoon was delicious, but this smells simply divine." Ellie's mouth watered.

167

"Appreciate ya sayin' so, Miss Ellie. I thank ya both for your help as well."

"We are all happy to pitch in." Janie smiled, brightening her mood. "It is, after all, to celebrate this wonderful holiday with our loved ones."

Ellie put an arm around her sister. "That is certainly true."

~~~~~~

After the new year started, Ellie began seriously looking at Davis Martin and how he acted around her. She enjoyed his company for sure, and he seemed to reciprocate. She knew he was attracted to her, as he also constantly found excuses to be with her and even tried making passes at her a few more times, but Ellie avoided that. It never felt quite right, and she wasn't sure why. He was handsome, attentive, and funny, but he seemed to...there was just something she couldn't quite place. It annoyed her that she was unable to understand what it was.

The Ingraham family held their traditional Epiphany party twelve days after Christmas, and the entire Bennett family, along with the ranch hands, were invited. Ellie desperately missed Charlotte's company, but she had received a letter from her friend saying that all was well and she was settled in North Carolina.

"My dear Ellie." Aunt Edith Gardiner sat next to Ellie. "I have been meaning to talk privately with you. Could we speak for a moment?"

"Of course, Aunt Edith." Ellie smiled at her kind aunt. She was only in her late thirties, and was oftentimes the voice of reason for her nieces, much more so than their own mother. "What's on your mind?"

168

"I'd like to know more about this Mr. Charles Brantley that your mother has been telling me about, but only from your perspective, not hers."

Ellie shook her head and explained her understanding of the story. "I would swear that I have never in my life seen a man so in love, Aunt Edith." Ellie replied. "The whole fiasco has been so frustrating. It still is."

"Do you suppose we could persuade Janie to come back with us to Kansas City? A change of scenery may do her good. I doubt she'll run into this Mr. Brantley there, it's far enough away from Chicago. What do you think?"

"I think that is a splendid idea." Ellie nodded. "I'm sure I'll be able to talk her into going."

"Marvelous. Now, the next person I wanted to speak to you about is that handsome cowboy you've been spending time with. He appears quite attentive to you. Is there anything special there?"

Ellie blushed. She was unsure of her exact feelings for Davis. She liked him well enough, but Ellie was becoming more and more aware of the fact that his conversations were mostly about their mutual dislike for Luke Callahan. Was that really a good basis for a relationship, if that's where they were even headed?

"I know you're much too sensible to fall in love with a lout, but I feel uneasy about the gentleman. I'll just warn you to be on your guard," Aunt Edith continued.

Ellie opened her mouth to interject, but her aunt held up a hand.

"I have nothing to say against him and he appears to be an interesting young man. I am sure that if he had stable employment or was more committed to settling down, I daresay he could be very good for you, but

169

as I said, there is something not right about him. You have a good head on your shoulders, be sure you use it."

"Aunt Edith, please." Ellie spoke up. "I'm not in love with Mr. Martin, if that's what you're thinking. I like talking with him, he's paid me more attention than any other eligible man ever has and that makes me feel special, but I can promise you that I will not rush into anything. I, like you, have some misgivings about him."

"Very good." Aunt Edith hugged Ellie. "Now, let's discuss how we can talk your sister into traveling to Kansas City with us."

~~~~~~

_It_ hadn't taken much convincing for Janie to agree to go to Kansas City, and Ellie fell into a routine of doing the winter chores on the ranch and living without her two best friends around. As winter warmed slightly, Ellie came to the conclusion that Davis Martin was avoiding her. At least that's what it seemed like. It shouldn't surprise her that he had lost interest over the winter, but it still stung.

One afternoon, Ellie was looking for Davis, as Matthew had requested some help with checking on some cattle in one of the pastures. Something else she had learned was that Davis seemed to disappear when there was real work to be done, which was often.

Ellie entered the storage barn and almost jumped at what she saw. Lindie was leaning against a post and Davis was standing close with an arm braced above her head. Shock and indignation coursed through Ellie. No wonder he had stopped talking with her. Lindie was much more adept at flirting and far more feminine. What man would ever choose

Ellie? She stepped closer and cleared her throat loudly. Martin saw her and straightened.

"Ellie!" He waved as if nothing were wrong.

"Matthew needs you at the southeast pasture, Davis." She tried not to let her discomfort show. He nodded, tipped his hat to Lindie, moved to saddle his horse and headed off. Ellie turned to her sister. She had no idea what to say to Davis, but she definitely had to say something to her baby sister. Lindie spoke first.

"Oh, Ellie, isn't he just delectable?"

Ellie didn't like Lindie's lovesick expression. "He's far too handsome for his own good, Lindie. You should probably keep your distance from him."

Lindie stood tall and gave Ellie a spiteful look. "You didn't have that opinion when he was sparking you."

"He was never...I never...we didn't..."

"Well, that's probably why he moved on, then. It's 1929, for heaven's sake, Ellie, you don't have to be engaged or married to let a man kiss you. No wonder you can never keep anyone interested."

Ellie reddened. "Well, you shouldn't be kissing just anyone who strikes your fancy, Lindie. They'll think you want more. Besides, Davis is almost ten years older than you."

"That doesn't matter, Papa is much older than Mama. You're just jealous that Davis is seeking me out now, instead of you. You were fine with him when he was paying attention to you, but now he knows you aren't worth the effort. What do you find so wrong with him anyway?"

"I can't put my finger on it, but..." Ellie couldn't explain it to herself, much less Lindie.

171

"Because there's nothing," Lindie continued. "You are simply jealous that he likes me now and you'll be a spinster for the rest of your life." With that, a now angry Lindie stormed out of the barn.

Ellie shook her head, a painful tightening in her throat. "You will not cry. Not over Davis Martin. Not over Lindie's comments." She had worth, no matter what Lindie said. She just had to remember that.

Part 5: Spring 1929

Chapter Twenty-One

Ellie straightened the hat on her head and made her way out to the barn. Standing right in front of the stable were her grandpa and Matthew, both with concerned looks on their faces. When they saw her approach, Matthew frowned and Grandpa Benjamin walked slowly towards her. Ellie felt a sinking in her stomach.

"Grandpa, what's wrong?" She really didn't want to know the answer.

"We're not sure how or why it happened, but Naomi…"

Panic coursed through Ellie and she pushed past her grandpa and into the stable. Naomi lay on her side, nickering softly, her breaths quick and shallow. Matthew moved to kneel next to the sick animal, patting her swollen belly.

"What's wrong with her?" Ellie went to the back of the stall, sat down and pulled Naomi's head into her lap. "Oh, girl, what happened?"

"We're not sure how, Ellie, but somehow green potatoes got into her food." Matthew replied.

"That can be deadly to horses-all animals! How could this have happened?" A tear slipped down her cheek.

173

"There's no telling how it got mixed in with her food. From what we can surmise, it was only her trough. None of the other animals have been affected." Grandpa walked through the barn. "I have an idea; I'll be right back."

"We figured out the problem pretty quick, Miss Ellie." Matthew rubbed the horse's stomach. Ellie rubbed her head, tears still falling. She'd raised Naomi from a foal. What would she do if she didn't get better?

"Roll her up a little and see if we can get her to her feet at least." Grandpa Benjamin returned with what looked like crushed coal in his hands. Though she was confused, Ellie helped Matthew get Naomi into a standing position. Benjamin carefully opened the horse's mouth, then forced the coal powder inside. "Hold her mouth closed; we've got to try and make her swallow it."

"What is it?" Ellie was sure her face was blotchy with tears, but she didn't care.

"Activated charcoal." He replied, steadying himself against the stall wall as Matthew and Ellie worked together to calm Naomi and get her to swallow the charcoal. "I saw my Uncle Aaron use it back home when one of the horses got into the trash pit and ate what he shouldn't have. Aaron was a man of science, a doctor during the War Between the States and then afterwards. Said the charcoal will absorb the poison." Benjamin ran a hand through his white hair. "It worked back then, I pray it will work now."

"How long until we know?" Ellie asked, stroking Naomi's muzzle as the horse nickered and lay back down.

"About an hour or so," he replied. Matthew helped Benjamin straighten up.

174

"You stay with her, Miss Ellie," Matthew said. "We'll make due with chores until we see how she's progressing."

"Thank you," Ellie said quietly.

"I'll check on you in half an hour or so." Benjamin added. Ellie nodded and hugged Naomi's head as the two men walked out of the stables.

~~~~~~

" *Ellie*."

Ellie jerked. She had been laying down, her head on Naomi's neck, curled up in a wool blanket, praying that her beloved horse would survive. Marie stood at the stall, a look of concern on her face. "How is she doing?"

"How long have I been out here?" Ellie murmured.

"An hour or so," Marie replied. Ellie rolled to her knees and looked at Naomi. Her breathing was steady and her heart rate seemed normal.

"She seems a little better." Ellie breathed a sigh of relief. Naomi whinnied, then pushed herself to stand as Ellie backed out of the way. Standing shakily, Naomi nudged Ellie with her head. Ellie hugged her horse's neck. "Oh, girl, I'm so glad you're feeling better."

Marie smiled. "We should find Matthew and Grandpa, they've been worried, in fact, everybody has."

Ellie's relief quickly turned to anger as she stormed out of the barn with Marie. "Yes, we can assure everyone she's okay, and then find out who put that poison in her food. Someone tried to kill my horse and I'll be..."

"Ellie, we'll all do our best to find the culprit and what exactly happened," Maria said, "but it's going to be a difficult task. Remember, Matthew generally feeds the horses himself."

"Yes, he always does, and unfortunately, everyone in the county has access to her trough. Anyone could have put those potatoes in there." She saw Matthew about 100 yards away in the pasture. "You can go tell everyone in the house, I'll go tell Matthew."

Marie nodded and they parted. Ellie quickly made her way to Matthew.

"Naomi up and better, Miss Ellie?" He asked, wiping his handkerchief over his face.

"She is," Ellie smiled. "Thank you so much for all your help." Matthew nodded and Ellie continued. "Now we just have to figure out who could do such a thing."

"I can tell you, I didn't see anyone around the stables that shouldn'a been." He shook his head. "Miss Ellie, I wonder…" He paused, then rubbed his head. "We still haven't figured out who killed the cattle and set them on fire those months ago and I chalked it up to an isolated happening, but this…I wonder if there's some connection."

"That crossed my mind as well." She admitted, crossing her arms over her chest. "Perhaps I shouldn't go to North Carolina." Ellie had received a letter from Charlotte a few days ago, inviting her to come for a visit in the summer. She was excited at the prospect of traveling and seeing her friend, but didn't want to just leave the ranch work behind.

"No, Miss Ellie, I don't think that's necessary. You haven't had any time away from work since you were in college, and even then you still lived and worked here. You need to go visit Miss Charlotte."

"I was really looking forward to traveling, but if there's going to be danger here, perhaps I should…"

"If the same person did do both deeds, he waited months to strike the second time. You'll only be gone a month or so. We'll be just fine."

Ellie nodded, though she was still unsure if it was the best idea.

~~~~~

Marie entered the barn a few days later where Ellie while repairing some harnesses. "A letter for you. It's from Janie."

"Thank you, Marie." Ellie took the letter, sat on a wooden chest of tools and opened it. She hadn't been reading long before her temper erupted.

"Arrogant, conceded family. They don't deserve her."

"I imagine you're talking about the Callahans?" Ellie looked up to see Davis step into the barn, a brown cowhide jacket over his usual attire. Marie looked from Davis to Ellie, then slipped back outside.

"No, but just as bad." She held up the letter. "I received a letter from Janie." She shook her head. "She says here that Isabella Brantley wrote to her in Kansas City and told her that Charles has no intention of ever returning to South Dakota. None of them do, except perhaps Luke for business. She just wanted Janie to know so that there wouldn't be any misunderstandings about Charles's future plans. Can you believe that? The audacity of that woman is beyond my belief. She had no reason to write to Janie except to drive the knife in deeper."

"That doesn't surprise me at all." Davis leaned on a post directly across from Ellie, then crossed his arms over his chest. "They're all selfish and pretentious, and that includes Luke's sister. Little Helena used to be

177

so cute and pleasant. She followed me around everywhere. Unfortunately, the last time I saw her, she acted just like everyone else and wanted nothing to do with me. They're all the same."

"I thought you told me that you didn't know Mr. Brantley well." Ellie pointed out.

"No, I don't, but if he's friends with Luke, I know all I need to know."

It struck Ellie once again that most of what she and Davis discussed in their conversations were Luke and his family's flaws. "What brings you in here today, Davis?" She wanted to talk with him about his actions toward Lindie, but didn't want to sound like the jilted lover or the overbearing older sister.

"I actually came to say goodbye." He twisted his hat in his hands.

"Where are you going?" Ellie was a bit surprised that his leaving made her feel relieved instead of sorrow. She didn't like the feelings that consumed her when she talked with Davis and if he left, Lindie wouldn't be able to get too attached. As bad as it sounded, she was actually glad he was leaving.

"I have an opportunity for a foreman's job on a ranch down in Texas. A good friend wrote to me about it. I told Shaw and he said I could leave whenever I needed to, so I'll be heading out in the morning. But I couldn't leave without saying goodbye to you." He straightened and moved to stand in front of her and drew her up next to him. The harness Ellie was holding fell to the ground and he wrapped his arms around her waist. Knowing what he was likely going to try again, Ellie tried to outsmart him by pulling him into a hug.

"I wish you all the luck in the world, Mr. Martin. I'm glad I was able to make your acquaintance." She pulled back and patted his arm. "Feel free to write and tell us how you're doing." She turned and picked up the harness again. Davis settled his hat on his head and walked out the barn door. Once he was gone, Ellie let out a breath and leaned back against a post, rubbing her temples. All this drama over the past few months was giving her a headache.

Chapter Twenty-Two

The calving and branding season flew by, and before Ellie knew, it was May and time for her to travel to North Carolina. She was a bit annoyed that Charlotte's father and younger sister, Angelina were also traveling to Asheville to visit Charlotte. Ellie would now have to share her time with Charlotte, but at least she would have some traveling companions. Though she didn't want to see Mr. Sutton, Ellie desperately wanted to see Charlotte and the change in scenery wouldn't hurt either. She hoped this new adventure would help her to relax and forget her pent up anger in regards to the Callahans, and Brantleys.

Ellie had never traveled east of the Mississippi River, so much of the trip was new and interesting. The Blue Ridge Mountains were beautiful, but in her opinion, they couldn't compare to the view of her Black Hills. They disembarked the train at the Biltmore Depot, and Charlotte and Mr. Sutton were waiting for them with their automobile.

"Papa!" Charlotte hugged her father warmly, then turned and did the same to Angelina and Ellie.

"It is so good to see you." Ellie said. Charlotte did look well, happier than she had in years. Mr. Sutton's demeanor, on the other hand, had not changed as a result of his marriage, still annoying and overbearing.

"I have missed you so much!" Charlotte replied.

"You too! Oh, we have so much to catch up on that can not be told well in any letter."

Biltmore Village was quaint, and Mr. Sutton immediately showed Ellie and the Ingrahams all about the town and told of its history. George Vanderbilt had created the village as a "company town" for his estate workers. It had been planned and designed to reflect the qualities of an English country village, with its own church, a small hospital, multiple shops, a school, and even the railroad depot.

"I am so glad you are visiting and able to see our splendid home and mountains." Mr. Sutton continued to gush and speak over Charlotte. "And you have come at the best time possible. Mrs. Madeline VanRensselaer is visiting the Vanderbilts and we have had the very fine privilege of dining with them twice a week. The magnanimous Mrs. VanRensselaer never allows us to drive ourselves. She always has her chauffer pick us up and bring us back to our humble abode." He adjusted his jacket primly, then stood tall. "I am pleased to say that we have already been invited to dine there again tomorrow." He was beside himself with joy. Charlotte blushed at his eagerness, but was able to ignore his annoying ways.

"I am most excited for you to see the grandeur of Biltmore. The Vanderbilts, and Mrs. VanRensselaer of course, are the best employees one could ask for." Mr. Sutton added.

The Sutton home was small, but comfortable. Angelina and Ellie would be sharing one of the guest bedrooms and Mr. Ingraham would be in the other. After dinner, Mr. Sutton took Angelina and Mr. Ingraham on a walk about the village, and Charlotte and Ellie were able to sit on the back porch and talk. Ellie told Charlotte all about Lindie and Davis, Davis's departure, Janie's trip, and how she still thought Isabella Brantley and Luke Callahan were responsible for breaking Janie and Charles up.

"We may never know what really happened," Charlotte pointed out, "but if they were meant to be together, God will find a way."

"I suppose you're right." Ellie chuckled. "You see why I need you in my life? You put everything into perspective for me." Not wanting to pry too much, Ellie looked at her hands. "How is married life?"

"Richard isn't really a bad sort, not at all," Charlotte said. "In fact, many of the quirks that annoyed you about him, I actually find endearing. His parents didn't give him any help when he was growing up regarding social graces. I feel I have made progress in teaching him in some aspects, and will continue to do so. He treats me better than I ever expected, and is often quite sweet."

"It's good to hear you say that." Ellie nodded. "You do look so happy, Charlotte, and I am so glad for you."

~~~~~~~

The next evening, the group drove to the Biltmore house through the forest with its various hardwood trees, and rolling hills. The mountains with their infamous smoke hiding the top peaks filled the backdrop. As they rode, Mr. Sutton rambled on about the house, estate and family. He was like a walking encyclopedia.

"Elegance and grandeur abound at Biltmore. The manor was built in the French Renaissance style, and has over 250 rooms, including 35 bedrooms, 43 bathrooms and 65 fireplaces. In addition to the house, the 8,000-acre estate is home to forested trails and beautiful gardens designed by the extraordinary landscape architect, Frederick Law Olmsted. The azaleas here are superior to those anywhere else." They came around a bend and the house loomed in the distance. It was the largest building Ellie had ever seen. It could have been mistaken for a limestone castle, with its entrance tower and steep roof and over a dozen chimneys. What really took Ellie's breath away was the view of the mountains behind it.

"It's magnificent." Ellie murmured. For once, Mr. Sutton had not been over exaggerating.

"My goodness!" Angelina gasped as they pulled up in front of the house. A footman greeted the group at the front door and escorted them into the vestibule where they were greeted by a liveried butler. The man led them into the entrance hall and Ellie couldn't believe all the splendor. The hall had high limestone arches and a smooth marble floor. In the middle of the hall was a huge oak table with bronze statues displayed. They passed through one of the arches to enter another impressive room. It was clearly a garden room, with it's glass roof and exotic plants in pots everywhere. The room was furnished with pieces that looked like they came from the French countryside, and in the middle of the room was a marble fountain with a bronze sculpture of a little boy and goose.

"This is the winter garden." Mr. Sutton announced. "The rattan and bamboo furniture was purchased by Mr. Vanderbilt from France; indoor gardens like this one were considered quite stylish in the Victorian era."

The party passed through another couple of doorways and entered an area that appeared to be a sitting room for the women of the house, with floral covered furniture, including a settee and loveseat with ornately carved tables that accented the fireplace. Floral wallpaper covered the walls and there were large windows with a view of the majestic mountains.

Ellie immediately noticed a woman who must be Cornelia Vanderbilt-Cecil. She looked to be in her late 20's, appeared elegant and refined, with dark hair and eyes, yet she had a genteel manner about her. She greeted the visitors and Ellie was immediately put at ease. Cornelia turned to make introductions. Her mother, Edith, was welcoming and gracious. George Washington Vanderbilt, Edith's first husband, had passed away in 1914, and she had remarried a US Senator from Rhode Island, Mr. Peter Gerry. He was currently in Washington DC, but Cornelia's husband, John Francis Cecil was in attendance. The British aristocrat was very friendly, quite handsome and debonair.

The final member in attendance was Mrs. Madeline VanRensselaer. She was a tall, larger-built woman with strong features and dark hair streaked with gray. She had a commanding tone and was a bit intimidating, not welcoming at all. Ellie realized right away that Davis had described her perfectly during one of their conversations about the family. Her daughter, Anne was also at Biltmore, but had stayed in her room as she wasn't feeling well. Davis also commented that Anne had been pale and sickly her whole life.

They moved to the dining hall and that space was just as splendid as the other parts of the house. Ellie could easily imagine this room in any medieval castle. The wooden vaulted ceiling had to be over 60 feet tall. There were two built-in throne chairs against one of the walls, and a huge dining table in the center of the room. Tapestries lined the walls, and the front of the room boasted a fireplace with three fireboxes and a beautiful carving of men on the mantle. There were also pennants hanging

184

in the room, and Ellie immediately noticed the state flags of Virginia, Maryland, and the other 13 original colonies, with a few more that she didn't recognize.

"This room is where the Vanderbilts dine, whether it is just the family or a large party. There are 67 chairs here in total. The tapestries are from Paris and were woven in the 1500's, and the carving on the mantle is called *The Return from the Hunt* which illustrates a scene from Wagner's epic *Tannhäuser* opera." Mr. Sutton could easily be a tour guide for the Biltmore Estate.

"So beautiful." Ellie nodded.

The group took their seats and servants dressed in fine livery began serving them the first course of what would be a delicious meal. Throughout the entire dinner, Mr. Sutton used every opportunity to praise the Vanderbilt family and Mrs. VanRensselaer.

"Mr. Cecil, you esteem us with this most beautiful dinner. Each delicacy is a treat for us."

Ellie tried not to roll her eyes or sigh in despair. What a brown-noser. In spite of Charlotte's happiness, Ellie still didn't believe that Richard Sutton deserved a woman as wonderful as her friend.

"Miss Bennett, I understand you are acquainted with my nephew, Mr. Lucas Callahan, are you not?" Mrs. VanRensselaer asked coolly.

"Yes, ma'am, I met him while he was visiting my home state of South Dakota last year."

"Hmm." She pursed her lips. "Your relationship was mere business, I assume."

"I would hardly call it a relationship, ma'am...I was able to escort him to view some land that he might purchase for the resort he's planning." The real question for Ellie was how she would react the next time she saw Luke, suspecting that he had a role in Charles's leaving, in turn breaking Janie's heart.

"Ahh, yes. His father enjoyed that part of the country as well. I could never understand why." Mrs. VanRensselaer added haughtily.

"I hear it is quite beautiful," Edith Gerry smiled graciously. Ellie smiled back and took a bite of her boiled potatoes.

"Mr. Callahan was a very pleasant guest in our town." Mr. Ingraham spoke up. "The entire party was, and many locals appreciate the fact that Mr. Callahan wants to bring tourism to our area."

"Lucas is an excellent businessman." Mrs. VanRensselaer smiled smugly. "Willing to do what it takes to be successful, but never ruthless in his ways."

"I can imagine," Ellie focused on not rolling her eyes, especially since the woman's statement was so contradictory.

"He is quite handsome as well," Angelina chimed in. Ellie couldn't argue with that statement. She took a sip of her wine, then glanced at Mr. Sutton, who was also tasting his wine.

"Such a delight to have wine with dinner, Mrs. Cecil." Sutton then turned to Ellie. "Miss Bennet, you are aware that private ownership and consumption of wine is not prohibited by our federal law."

"Yes, I am aware of that," she replied. It was not illegal to drink alcohol under the 18th Amendment, but local and state laws were often stricter. If she remembered correctly, North Carolina had actually been one of the first states to prohibit the sale of alcohol.

"We were able to purchase a large quantity before the ban," Mrs. Cecil stated. "And we only serve it when we have guests."

Ellie nodded. Everyone knew it wasn't that difficult to obtain alcohol if you were discrete and had connections. She did find it interesting that Mr. Sutton all of the sudden approved of alcohol. She recalled him making it perfectly clear that he disapproved of spirits when they were back in South Dakota.

When the meal was finished, the ladies went back to the salon while the men convened in the smoking room. Ellie couldn't help but feel for Mr. Ingraham and Mr. Cecil for having to put up with Mr. Sutton for an extended period of time. On the other hand, Ellie and the women had to deal with Madeline VanRensselaer, who dominated the conversation and was clearly not used to having anyone question her.

"You have four sisters, Miss Bennett, is that correct?" Cornelia asked as if she were truly interested.

"I do, we are all quite close," Ellie replied. "I'm the second oldest."

"Are any of your sisters out in society?" Mrs. VanRensselaer demanded to know.

"Well, we don't really have 'society', as you call it, in South Dakota, but if we did, I suppose I would have to say yes, we all are."

"All five out at once? And none of you married?"

"No, ma'am." *No thanks to your pretentious nephew.*

"All of you searching for a husband at the same time? How young is the youngest?"

"Seventeen, but I see no reason why we shouldn't all be able to...court. It would hardly be fair for the younger ones not to enjoy the men just because the older ones haven't married yet."

"My goodness, you give your opinion quite...vehemently for such a young woman. How old are you?"

187

"With three adult sisters younger than me...well, I prefer not to answer that." Ellie tried to keep her voice light.

Cornelia chuckled, but Mrs. VanRensselaer was taken aback. It was obvious she wasn't challenged like this often.

The evening continued with small talk and Ellie was reminded of just how little she enjoyed trying to force conversation. Mrs. VanRensselaer continually asked questions that Ellie was certain were meant to demean her: Does she know how to swim? Helena Callahan is a wonderful swimmer. Does Ellie actually ride the bulls? How unladylike. Did you really drop out of college? How unfortunate.

Cornelia and Edith continually tried redirecting the conversation to a friendlier thread, but Ellie still didn't feel welcome by Mrs. VanRensselaer. She didn't understand at all why the Vanderbilts were friends with the woman. Overall, Ellie enjoyed herself, though she would much rather have been out hiking in the National Forest that surrounded the estate. Perhaps she would be able to spend time doing just that tomorrow.

Chapter Twenty-Three

The next few days passed quickly. Ellie was able to do a good amount of hiking and visiting with Charlotte. Another dinner engagement at Biltmore approached for the Sutton's and their visitors, and Ellie once again put on the best outfit she had brought, which was truly put to shame by the elegant apparel of the Vanderbilts. Even Charlotte had a more appropriate dress to wear.

The group was once again escorted to the sitting room to wait for dinner to be announced. Just as they were about to go through to the dining room, the door opened and two more gentlemen entered, one wearing a sharp, but worn brown suit and tie and the other...

"Luke!" Ellie's stomach fluttered just a bit. He was dressed in a finely tailored suit; like the first time she had seen him.

"Luke Callahan!" Cornelia greeted her childhood friend warmly. Ellie wondered, not for the first time, how people who seemed as nice as the Vanderbilts, were friends with Luke and his family.

"It has been too long, Cornelia." Luke smiled at the hostess, and then turned to Ellie.

"Miss Bennett, it is so good to see you again."

"It is good to see you as well." Ellie nodded. He looked aristocratic in the grand manor, wearing black pants, a white undershirt, and a black vest with white stripes. "How are Charles and the Brantley women?"

"All were well the last time I saw them." Luke nodded. He seemed a bit uneasy at seeing her again. She waited for him to talk and when he didn't immediately say anything more, she asked another question.

"I had no idea you would be here. When did you arrive?"

"My cousin, Roger and I came in this afternoon."

Ellie moved her attention from Luke to his companion, who heard his name and approached Ellie and Luke.

"Ellie, this is my cousin, Roger Bailey. Roger, this is Miss Bennett."

"Miss Ellie Bennett." Roger smiled. "A pleasure to finally meet you. Luke has told me so much about you."

"Is that a fact?" Ellie looked at Luke, then back at Roger. "And, pray tell, what has he said?"

"Oh." Roger glanced at Luke. "Just…how helpful you were when he was in South Dakota." He ran a hand through his shaggy brown hair. Roger appeared to be about the same age as Luke but not nearly as handsome, with dull hair and brown eyes and a crooked nose. She could immediately tell that he was a polite, friendly gentleman, more like Charles than Luke.

"Ellie, I…" Luke started to speak, but then dinner was announced and the party all moved into the dining room. Ellie couldn't help but shake her head at the general splendor of the hall. It was as impressive the second time as it was the first.

"My dear Roger, what have you been doing of late?" Mr. Cecil asked once they had been seated.

"I have been helping Luke with his resort in upstate New York, but it's running quite smoothly now, so we're just making plans for our next venture. It's been my pleasure to be able to relax and read and simply enjoy the company of dear friends for a change."

"You enjoy reading, Mr. Bailey? Who is your favorite author, may I ask?" Ellie asked.

"I enjoy the works of many authors, but I just finished a novel by the fascinating F. Scott Fitzgerald," he replied amiably. *"The Great Gatsby.* Have you read it?"

"I haven't been able to yet," Ellie replied. "Though I dearly love to read, I don't often have the time."

"Ellie practically runs her family ranch back home." Angelina piped up.

"Impressive." Roger smiled. "Impressive indeed." Ellie smiled back, then caught Luke watching her. Why was she always so aware of him?

During dinner, Ellie couldn't help but notice that Luke acted bored, or perhaps distracted. A part of her couldn't blame him, as he was attempting to listen politely as Mr. Sutton blathered on and on about nothing interesting. It wasn't long before Madeline VanRensselaer took over the conversation and focused solely on her nephews, especially Luke, who was clearly the favorite. When dinner was over, the entire party went into the tapestry gallery, which was instantly one of Ellie 's favorite places in the mansion. It was another sitting area in the colossal house, right off the Entrance Hall. The room displayed three huge tapestries and three Persian rugs. Three portraits hung on the far wall, George Vanderbilt, his mother, Maria Louisa, and Edith. On the opposite wall was another painting of Edith. The best part of the room, from Ellie's standpoint, was

191

that it had a completely picturesque view of the mountains. It also had a Steinway concert piano.

"Miss Bennett, I have heard that, in spite of your country upbringing, you and your sisters were all given lessons on the piano." Mrs. VanRensselaer spoke up, a challenge obvious in her voice.

"Yes, ma'am, that is true." Where had the woman heard this tidbit of information? Ellie's mother thought it would bring some culture into her daughters' lives that may one day assist them in snagging a husband, but Marie was the only one who was truly proficient in the art.

"Then you should play for us." Mrs. VanRensselaer stated.

"I don't really play that well, and I haven't practiced in years."

"Well, I happen to enjoy music and I would like to hear you play." Mrs. VanRensselaer insisted.

"My dear Madeline, if Miss Bennett is uncomfortable, she doesn't need to entertain us." Edith Vanderbilt-Gerry smiled gently at her guest. "We can certainly bring the phonograph in if you would like to listen to music."

Ellie stood. "Thank you, Mrs. Gerry, but if Mrs. VanRensselaer wants me to play, I suppose I should at least try." She made her way to the beautiful piano and sat. Luckily, Ellie remembered enough to play some music that was simple enough, but sounded good.

Roger sat as close to the piano as he could while she played, and it wasn't long before Luke himself came and stood nearby. Still playing, Ellie turned towards Luke.

"Are you trying to intimidate me, Mr. Callahan?" She asked with a smile. "If you are, it won't work. You have never frightened me."

"I don't try to intimidate you," he replied. "And besides, I know you well enough that you don't frighten easily. I have noticed that at times, you

192

enjoy giving your opinions simply to challenge others." He paused. "And remember, you agreed to call me Luke."

"I suppose I did agree to that." Ellie grinned. "I think you try to antagonize me on purpose, though I'm not sure why. What would happen right now if I were forced to say something that would shock your family or embarrass you."

"I don't try to antagonize you, Ellie." He smiled, showing a dimple in his right cheek. How had she not noticed that before? Was this really the first time she had seen him smile so genuinely?

"I would be interested to hear how he behaved among strangers in South Dakota." Roger grinned. "If you don't mind telling me."

"Oh, I would love to," Ellie promised, "but you should prepare yourself for something fairly dreadful." She continued plinking at the keys. "The first time I saw Luke was at a barbeque for some friends of ours. He only danced twice, though at that particular party, there were many more women than men present. Some women were actually forced to sit dances out because they had no partner. And there stood Lucas Callahan, who I happen to know can dance, standing on the sideline like a statue in the Louvre." She looked up at Luke again. "You have to admit I'm right."

"I didn't know any of the ladies, other than the ones in my group." He tried to make excuses.

"Of course, and no one ever meets someone new at a party." She responded.

"You're right, of course," Luke admitted. "I could have managed the situation better. I'm just not comfortable talking with strangers."

193

"Because he usually just doesn't want to be bothered to do so," Roger replied with a grin.

"Some people find it easy to make small talk," Luke said. "I'm not one of them."

"I can certainly understand that." Ellie nodded. "I can't play the piano nearly as well as others, my sister Marie, for example, is a very talented pianist. However, the fact that I am lacking in this endeavor is entirely my fault. I simply don't practice enough."

"No, you're too busy roping and riding." Luke smiled again. "But I get the point you're trying to make. You're right. I should practice my social skills."

"Roger, Lucas, whatever are you talking about?" Mrs. VanRensselaer interrupted from across the room. Ellie smiled to herself and continued playing the piano. She wished their conversation could have continued, but Mrs. VanRensselaer seemed determined to dominate the evening.

~~~~~~

The next day, Ellie sat on the Sutton's front porch in Biltmore Village, which had a wonderful view of Mt. Pisgah. She was writing a letter to Janie, who had recently arrived back home in Spearfish. Charlotte had taken her father and sister to Asheville to go shopping, and Mr. Sutton was at the Biltmore Village train station. His cousin Edward from his mother's side of the family was arriving to take a new position as minister of the church. Ellie wasn't sure if she would be able to tolerate another Sutton in the same vicinity. Hearing a car approach, Ellie looked up to see a green Strutz Bearcat coming up the drive. Luke stepped out, wearing perfectly pressed casual tan trousers, a blue button up shirt and a tan derby hat.

194

"Ellie." He took off his hat and looked around as if he expected to see someone else.

"Luke." She gestured to the chair next to her. "Please, have a seat."

He nodded and tossed his hat on the seat of the car, then moved to sit stiffly with perfect posture in the chair next to Ellie. He didn't speak.

"What brings you here today, Luke?"

"I was just driving by," he replied, then fell silent.

"How is everyone up at Biltmore House today?" She asked.

"Quite well." He nervously met her eyes, then looked away, not offering anything more to the conversation. The awkward silence stretched while Ellie tried to think of something to say.

"If you don't mind my asking, I have been curious as to why you all left Spearfish so quickly. The Brantleys were all well, I hope. No emergencies?"

"No, nothing like that," he replied. "Everyone is fine."

"I heard Mr. Brantley has no plans of returning to Verbena Meadows." Ellie glanced at him out of the corner of her eye. He had been watching her as well, but looked away when their eyes met.

"He hasn't really mentioned anything definite to me." Luke replied. "But I don't believe he will. He saw the sights of the area that he wanted to see, and he has a lot of work to keep himself busy, as well as many friends in Chicago. His friends and family life are important to him. I'm sure you also noticed that he loves socializing and meeting new people."

Ellie paused. That sounded just the opposite of Luke. She didn't want to discuss Charles Brantley overly much, but she did want to bring up Mr. Brantley's treatment of Janie. Unfortunately, she felt she might get too emotional and she definitely didn't want to cry in front of this man, so she waited for him to continue the awkward conversation. He had been the one to drive down here after all.

"This is a quaint house," he finally said. "It has a beautiful view. I know Cornelia and her family take pride in just about everything around here, even the homes of their employees." He paused again and Ellie was unsure of what to say. The awkward silence stretched. Luke finally spoke again. "Mr. Sutton made a good choice when marrying Miss Charlotte."

"Yes, indeed. He is very lucky. Charlotte is extremely kind, intelligent, and has the biggest of hearts. I still don't know why she accepted his proposal. Marrying Mr. Sutton definitely came as a surprise to me, but she does seem rather happy, or at least very content. And there is the fact that one day they will inherit our ranch, unless he sells his stake in it, which is highly unlikely." She looked around. "I just wish Charlotte wasn't so far from home now; I do miss her dearly."

"But as you say, she will return to Spearfish eventually."

"Not for many years, I hope." Ellie replied, then clarified. "They won't move back until my father dies and Sutton takes over. Not only that, despite having a comfortable income, she can't just travel across the country on a whim like you can, just for a visit."

"Have you ever thought of leaving Spearfish?" He leaned forward and rested his elbows on his knees.

Ellie was surprised at the question, but before she could answer, Charlotte, Angelina and their father returned. Luke scrambled to his feet.

"I just wanted to stop by for a short visit." He stammered to them. "I didn't realize Ellie would be alone." He backed up as if embarrassed to be found talking to her, then quickly walked to his car and drove away.

Charlotte gave Ellie a curious look. "What on earth did you say to Mr. Callahan to make him run off like that?"

Ellie shook her head and watched the Bearcat kick up dust as it headed down the road toward the mansion. "I have absolutely no idea."

"Maybe he's in love with you, Ellie." Angelina's eyes lit up. "Why else would he have visited?"

"I don't think so, Angelina," Ellie smiled at the girl's innocence. "His actions in the past have shown that he has nothing but scorn for me and my family."

"Well then, why did he come?" Charlotte demanded, seeming to agree with her sister.

"I really have no clue. It's definitely not for my company. He barely said anything, and what he did say was fairly unimportant. It actually was a very awkward visit. No, he's not in love with me, he doesn't even like me, at least I don't think he does."

"Personally, I believe Mr. Bailey would make a good match for you," Charlotte stated. "He may not be as handsome as Mr. Callahan, but he is kind and hardworking. He would definitely be able to care for you. I hear he is quite well off and he runs many of Luke's businesses, as well as his own. Perhaps he would purchase a ranch and allow you to run it someday. He does seem to be very attentive to you."

"Perhaps." Ellie smiled. She liked Roger, but couldn't see him as anything other than a friend. "I'll just have to keep trusting that God will nudge me in the right direction."

Chapter Twenty-Four

Ellie continued to spend most of her free time exploring the paths around Biltmore. Many women preferred to walk through city parks or gardens, but Ellie liked more of a challenge. She also thought that walking the trails would help her avoid a certain businessman, but she soon learned that wouldn't be the case. Luke crossed her path almost every day and he always seemed just as surprised to see her. The third time they intersected each other's paths, Ellie had to make a comment.

"I never imagined you to be a hiker, Mr. Callahan."

"I've always enjoyed being outside. I actually met Teddy Roosevelt as a child and I believe he helped inspire me in that respect. After my business meetings, I find a brisk walk in the great outdoors very invigorating."

"I agree, I can't imagine being pent up inside all day," Ellie said as they walked up a narrow trail. It was only wide enough for one at this point, so Luke followed behind her. "I need the fresh air and open spaces to feel alive."

"Indeed. I can tell you are at your best out here."

The trail widened and he stepped next to her.

"I suppose I am." She agreed. He could be so pleasant; it was times like this that Ellie found it hard to remember why she didn't like him.

"You made a comment the other day about Mr. Sutton having a stake in Longbourn and I recalled you saying something similar when I was in South Dakota. I don't understand the reason your father would trust Sutton with the future of your ranch, especially since you seem so competent. Makes no sense."

Ellie told him in more detail about Great-Grandpa Longbourn's will. Luke nodded.

"That is a very unfortunate situation," he replied, "but perhaps God has something bigger and better in mind for you."

She smiled. "I would have never guessed you to be the kind of man to say something like that."

"My faith has gotten me through much pain in my life," he admitted. "My parents both died young, and I was barely an adult when I found myself the guardian of my younger sister and the Chief Executive Officer of our family business. I never would have gotten through those early years if not for my belief in God, and I'm not ashamed to admit it."

She nodded. "I feel the same way, and I am terribly sorry to hear about your parents."

"It hasn't been easy, but I have learned a lot about myself, and what is truly important. I couldn't have done it without my faith."

They walked in comfortable silence, just enjoying the peaceful surroundings. Ellie couldn't help but wonder why he acted so snobbish if he had such a deep faith.

"So tell me, what do you think of Edward Stewart?" Luke asked, referring to Richard's newly-arrived cousin.

"Much more likable than Mr. Sutton himself." Ellie replied. Edward was a bit dull, but he could at least hold a conversation without coming across as annoying and pretentious. He was a minister and had just taken an assignment in Biltmore Village. Ellie hadn't determined if she would enjoy a sermon of his or not. His voice was monotonous and she didn't feel he would relate to the average parishioner, but he was quite intelligent.

"I suppose you'll be returning to Spearfish soon?" Luke asked.

"Yes, in about a week," Ellie replied. "I am anxious to get back, there is much to do, and yet, I will miss being here." *Including taking these walks with you, strangely enough.* She was shocked at how true that thought was.

"You can always come back for another visit. There are many rooms available at Biltmore if you wish to stay there. Cornelia would love to have you."

"Goodness, I wouldn't want to be any imposition." She glanced at him, curiosity in her eyes. Did he want her to return as his guest? Or perhaps Mr. Bailey's? And for that matter, if she did return to the area, why did he not think she would stay with Charlotte?

"You could never be an imposition, Ellie." His reply was so earnest, so heartfelt that Ellie took her focus off the path she was walking on. She tripped on a large root that was growing in the path; her arms flailed as she caught her balance, and she almost smacked Luke in the face. He grabbed her arm and steadied her, then wrapped his other arm around her waist, pulling her so close she could smell root beer on his breath.

"Ellie..." He whispered her name. He bent down and her heart pounded.

"Ellie, where are you?" Angelina's voice pierced through the woods. Luke quickly stepped away.

"I'm right over here, Angelina." Her voice cracked a bit. What on earth was Luke doing to her state of mind?

200

"Oh, good. I'm glad to have finally found you. You've been out here so long, it's almost time for dinner." Angelina came around the bend and saw that Luke was with her. "Oh, hello, Mr. Callahan."

"Miss Angelina." He nodded, not able to meet Ellie 's eyes. Had he really been about to kiss her?

"Come now, Ellie, Mr. Sutton is hungry and that means he's getting grumpy," Angelina said.

"He doesn't need an excuse to be grumpy." Ellie muttered. She turned back to Luke. "Would you like to join us for dinner, Mr. Callahan? It won't be as grand as what the Vanderbilts are having, but…"

"That's quite all right." Luke quickly checked his Rolex wrist watch. "I'm expected back at the estate but thank you for the invitation, and the company." He smiled, then strode away in the direction of Biltmore.

Angelina giggled. "He is so in love with you, Ellie. I would stake my life on it."

Ellie tried to refrain from rolling her eyes. "I still don't believe that, though he isn't nearly as insufferable as I initially thought, yet I don't believe his feelings are anything more than a friendly acquaintance."

"Whatever you saaaay." Angelina said in a singsong voice, as the two made their way back to the Sutton home.

~~~~~~

"This is just plumb crazy, Charlotte! I should never have let you talk me into this." The next day, Ellie gripped Charlotte's arm as they made their way down the steps to the basement of the grand manor, Angelina right behind them. "It's hard to imagine that this house is so ostentatious that it even has an indoor pool."

Cornelia had invited Charlotte, Ellie and Angelina to go swimming, as it was supposed to rain all day.

"I agree with you to a point, but I have seen the pool area before and it is really quite nice. The water is even heated."

"But why would they have a pool? It's not like that many people even know how to swim." Ellie continued.

"More and more are learning, and many resorts are starting to build pools. Besides, we've been swimming in the pond and river back home for years, so this will be fun. It's an opportunity that you'll never get again."

"That is true." The maid showed them to the dressing rooms, and Ellie stepped inside one and changed into a one-piece bathing costume that Cornelia had let her borrow. It was a modest navy blue and white striped suit. The trouser went almost to her knee, and a thigh length skirt helped cover her bottom half. The top was tighter than she was comfortable with, and barely covered her shoulders.

"Oh gracious, why can't we just swim in our clothes like we do at home?" Ellie stepped out of the changing room, a towel wrapped around her.

"When we were children, we swam in our underclothes." Charlotte reminded her. "This is considered much more appropriate."

"I still don't like it." They followed the maid through a corridor, then entered the pool room.

"Holy smokes, it is impressive." Ellie gushed. Charlotte had been right. The pool was enormous; Mr. Sutton had informed her earlier that it held 70,000 gallons of water. It was surrounded by a railing, and had

202

underwater electric lighting, safety ropes and a diving platform. The ceiling above was arched with white terra cotta tile and electric chandeliers illuminated the entire room.

The Vanderbilts and some of their guests were already in the pool. Luke swam from side to side with powerful strokes, Roger Bailey and John Cecil were hanging onto the safety ropes talking, and Cornelia sat on the far side of the pool in the shallows, playing with her four-year-old son who was usually with a nanny. Little George Cecil had a look of absolute glee on his face as he splashed around. The guests and hosts all wore swim costumes similar to hers, only the men's shorts had no skirts, and also...good heavens...no sleeves to fully cover their shoulders. Ellie tried not to stare at Luke's physique. For a businessman, he had muscles that could compare to any cowboy.

"Charlotte, Angelina, Ellie, welcome!" Cornelia waved. "Come, join us, please."

Charlotte and Angelina moved to enter the pool demurely and ladylike, but Ellie longed to show off some skills. She moved to the platform at the deeper end of the pool. Luke touched the far side of the pool and shook his head, spraying water everywhere. He met her eyes and she couldn't help but see a silent challenge in his gaze. Did he think she wouldn't get in the pool?

"Miss Ellie, is everything all right?" Roger asked.

"She's a little shy about her bathing costume." Angelina's reply echoed off the walls. Ellie blushed just a bit, but let her towel drop to the ground and stepped up on the platform. She glanced over at Luke, who looked away, then she took a breath and dove into the water. When she surfaced, she swam expertly over to Roger and John Cecil, who were clapping, along with Cornelia, Angelina, Charlotte, and little George. Luke clenched his jaw in frustration and glared at her, causing Ellie to recall, then dismiss Angelina's claim that he was in love with her. Clearly, he only felt distaste.

"I would give that dive a 9.4." Roger smiled.

"I can't say that it was of Olympic quality, but not bad for a farm girl." Luke said dourly approaching the trio. His demeanor reminded her of the time they were back at the Austen's barbeque when they first met.

"And what would you know of Olympic-caliber dives, Mr. Callahan?" Ellie asked.

"Didn't you know that Luke is quite the athlete, Miss Bennett?" Roger explained. "He lettered at Harvard."

"In what?" *Probably in rowing or fencing or some elitist sport.*

"Roger, is this really necessary?" Luke asked. Roger ignored him.

"Both baseball and rugby, actually." Roger almost sounded like he was defending Luke for some reason. "In fact, he could have been on the Olympic rugby team in '24 if…"

"Roger, thank you for your high praise, but it's not really necessary." Luke's eyes flickered to hers, then lowered, then quickly went back to his cousin. Ellie softened her expression.

"That is quite impressive, Mr. Callahan. I had no idea you were such an accomplished athlete."

He met her eyes again. "I daresay there is much you don't know about me, and there is likely much more for me to learn about you."

The look he gave her made her heart skip a beat. "That's likely very true." She couldn't help but tease him just a bit. "Even if you consider me to be just 'good enough'?"

He clenched his jaw and looked at the ceiling, knowing exactly when he had said those unflattering words. "I didn't mean to speak in that context when we talked back then." He moved towards the shallows where he could stand.

"Well, that's exactly what you said. How else was I supposed to interpret it?" Unconsciously, she moved toward him until she could touch the brick tiles on the bottom of the pool. As always, he smelled faintly of root beer barrels.

"You weren't supposed to hear it at all!" He retorted.

"Oh, so that makes it okay for you to say?"

He glanced around at the others in the pool, none of whom were hiding the fact that they were watching the sparring.

"If you were so intently listening to my conversations with Charles when you were a guest at Verbena Meadows, you would have also heard me compliment your eyes."

She took a slow step back. "What do you mean? Are you referring to when I was tending to Janie when she was sick? You think I was snooping around and listening in on your conversations? As if I needed to know what you think of me. Your opinion has always been quite clear."

"You have no idea how I feel about you." And with that, he sloshed out of the pool, wrapped himself in a towel and stalked off towards the doors that led to the gymnasium.

Roger made his way to the ladder, John Cecil right behind him. "We'll make sure he cools down," Roger said. "We wanted to get some time in with the Indian clubs anyways and perhaps some fencing is in order."

"I knew he fenced. How could he not?" She muttered, though she had to admit, the baseball and rugby information had been a pleasant

205

surprise. His reaction to her was baffling, however. They had been getting on so well on their hikes and now, suddenly he changed again.

"You certainly know how to rile Luke up." Cornelia smiled. Ellie swam over to the others. "Like lightning striking dynamite."

"It was like that when they first met as well." Charlotte remarked.

"I don't try to annoy him," Ellie admitted, "It just happens. He's so insufferable."

"That's because he's in love with you." Angelina stated once again. "He was probably skittish after seeing you in your bathing costume."

"I told you, Angelina, he's not in love with me." Ellie insisted.

"It seems to me that Miss Ingraham may be correct." Cornelia held George by the waist as he practiced paddling with his arms and legs. "I've known Luke for as long as anyone, and I have never seen him act the way he does when he's around you. He's really not as bad as you seem to think Ellie, he has his faults of course, but we all do. I'd be lying if I didn't admit to having a bit of an infatuation with him myself once upon a time."

"He'll end up married to someone posh and elegant, like Isabella Brantley." Ellie huffed.

"You don't mean Charles Brantley's sister, do you? I'm acquainted with her through Luke. She is attracted to him like a moth is to a lantern, but Luke has never indicated that he reciprocates those feelings. Quite the contrary, he would never consider Isabella for a wife. He's polite to her, of course, but he's polite to everyone."

Ellie scoffed. "Not in South Dakota, he wasn't! He was downright rude and prideful. He could stand to find some humility."

"I will admit, he's shy," Cornelia admitted, "and it takes a while for him to warm up to people, but he is a true and loyal friend." Cornelia

206

brushed some of George's wet hair from his forehead and gave him a kiss. "You should give him the chance to show you his true personality."

"I told you he was shy." Charlotte nudged Ellie with her shoulder.

Ellie nodded, deep in thought. Perhaps she should do as Cornelia suggested. And maybe then she could ask him some long-wondered about questions. Like why he and Charles Brantley had left South Dakota in such a rush, and why he disliked Davis Martin so much.

Chapter Twenty-Five

"Well, fancy seeing you here." Ellie shook her head and smiled. Once again, Luke had intercepted her on her daily hike. He just couldn't seem to stay away from her.

"I hope you're not overly distressed about seeing me again," he replied. "I'd actually like to...umm...apologize about how I reacted at the pool yesterday."

Her face softened. "I suppose I did provoke you just a bit. I seem to do that quite often."

"Well, I seem to let you." He wondered again if he should actually tell her how he felt about her. Perhaps it was time, though he was still not sure how to broach the subject. He had come to the realization that he cared for Ellie more than he cared to admit. "Do you mind if I take you to a special place on the estate?"

"Not at all, lead the way." She walked beside him. "Did you feel better after fencing with Roger?"

"I did, actually. Nothing like physical activity to keep your mind focused."

"I agree with that. It's one of the benefits of working on the ranch that I find so fulfilling."

He could just imagine a red-faced Ellie pounding a nail to fix a fence when her anger got the best of her.

"I think yesterday might have been the first time I actually saw you lose your temper though." She continued. "You're usually just aloof."

"I can assure you, that is not always the case." Should he tell her of his past? He had to take a chance. "In fact, as a young man, I had a fairly bad temper that began after my mother died. I was so angry at her for leaving me and angry at God for taking her away. My father taught me quite diligently to control my temper through activities like fencing, rugby and football. He would constantly steer me in the right direction, even when I was cruel to him." He paused. "He just kept loving me and helping me and teaching me. He was a good father."

"It sounds like it," Ellie replied. They continued to walk.

"After he died, I was afraid I would fall back to my old ways, but by then, I had my sister Helena to worry about and Roger was always there to remind me of my father's lessons. He remembers the times when I was at my worst."

She nodded. "I'm sorry for all your losses, Luke."

He gave her a half-smile. "Thank you for saying so."

"May I ask where you are taking me?"

"My mother's favorite place on the estate, the Lagoon. Have you been there yet?"

"I have not, but Charlotte told me about it and said I had to see it before I leave."

"Splendid! I'm glad to show it to you then." They continued walking, and he told her a few stories about spending time at Biltmore as a child and she responded with tales of growing up on the ranch.

"You know, I'm surprised you haven't embraced the flappers' lifestyle more, what with your avoidance of traditional female roles." Luke stated.

"I may not be the ideal, traditional woman, but I'm not about to be rebellious just for the sake of rebellion. I'm just trying to discern God's plan for me so I can follow it."

Luke's heart warmed at her words. Could she be any more perfect for him? They came around a bend and the lagoon could be seen in full view.

"Goodness, Luke, it's beautiful." Ellie's face all but glowed. "If only we had Charles's Brownie." She paused. "Though I don't think a photograph would do the view any justice."

"That is true." He would remember this view with Ellie's smile for a very long time. The man-made lagoon boasted a mirror image of the western part of the mansion. Maple, sweet gum, and river birch trees were also reflected in the waters. "Frederick Law Olmstead himself designed the plans for this lagoon, as well as Bass Pond. Are they not beautiful water features for the estate?" He impulsively took her hand and brought her to the tree line where he knew Cornelia kept a rowboat. "The view is even better from the middle of the lagoon. Would you care for a boat ride?"

"That would be…"

POP! CRACK! A tree splintered beside him and shards of bark hit his face.

"Get down!" In a move practiced many times from his rugby days, he tackled Ellie to the ground and covered her body with his, but not before another shot rang out. He rolled and pulled them both behind a fallen tree.

"What on earth?" Ellie asked, breathing heavily. Luke's own heart pounded. Who was shooting? And were they trying to hit him or Ellie?

They waited in silence as Luke thought of what to do. Ellie was likely doing the same. He heard rustling; it sounded like whoever was there was moving away from them. The shots would undoubtedly bring some of the estate's workers, gardeners and the like. He peeked his head over the fallen tree and didn't see anyone. He cautiously stood.

"Are you crazy, Luke? What if he's not gone?" She grabbed at him to try and pull him back down. Just then, footsteps came from behind them.

"Mr. Callahan!" One of the gardeners ran up to the duo. "I heard gunshots! Are you all right?"

"Yes." He turned to Ellie and wiped at a scratch on her cheek. "Are you okay?"

"I'm fine, just scraped it a bit when you dragged me down." She brushed her walking skirt off. "That was quite an impressive tackle, I must say."

"Thank you." He turned to the gardener. "I don't imagine you saw anyone?"

"No, just heard the shots." The young man looked around. "It could have been a careless hunter. They traipse through here looking for game even though they're not supposed to, but usually not this close to the main house."

"I hope that's all it was," Ellie whispered.

"I'm sure that's it." Luke had to think positive in this. He was a powerful businessman and had made some enemies because of it. He tried to be as Christian as possible in his dealings, yet some people didn't like that about him. Could someone dislike him so much that they would follow him here to kill him? He couldn't imagine that. The only other alternative was that someone was shooting at Ellie, which was a less likely scenario.

"Let's get you both back to the house." The gardener said. "We'll contact the sheriff, I'm sure he'll have some questions."

"Yes, of course." Ellie whispered, as they all walked up the path to the house.

~~~~~~

Ellie hoped her trembling wasn't obvious. She was a rancher and didn't consider herself a weakling, but the shooting had shaken her a bit. Someone had just tried to kill her or Luke. It could have been accidental, but that didn't seem likely. Luke had offered his arm to her and she was thankful for it. His thoughts were also consumed with what had just happened. Who had tried to kill them? Which one of them, if either, were they actually after? They entered the manor through a side door and Luke brought her to the library where he helped her sit down. Ellie's thoughts raced as she tried to think of who might want her dead. The more she thought about the shooting incident, she didn't believe it was a hunter who mistook them for prey. The gun sounded more like a handgun than a rifle or shotgun.

"You're quiet, Ellie. Are you sure you're alright?"

"Yes." She looked at him and reached up to touch his bloody sleeve. "But you're not. You're bleeding. Why didn't you say anything?" She was irritated with herself for being so distracted that she had just now noticed that Luke had been injured.

Luke looked down. His shirt was torn and blood seeped from it. Ellie pulled the hole in the shirt open wider to look and saw a deep, smooth gash

212

on his upper arm. She pulled the ruined sleeve off and wrapped it around Luke's arm, hoping the makeshift bandage would work until someone could properly tend it.

"I honestly didn't realize I'd been hit." Luke said. "I felt something, I just thought it was bark from the tree that hit me. The bullet must have grazed me first."

"It appears so." Ellie finished tying off the bandage. "I hope this wasn't your favorite shirt. We're going to have to get the wound cleaned out well so it doesn't get infected, but it doesn't look too bad."

"I didn't know you were so good at doctoring people up." He commented.

"We get a lot of scrapes and bruises back home. You can't be skittish living on a ranch. Even Lindie knows how to patch up the most basic injuries." She couldn't help but roll her eyes. "And she never loses an opportunity to show off those skills to any attractive cowboy she can get her hands on."

"She is quite the flirt, isn't she?" He winced slightly as she tightened the makeshift bandage.

"Yes, unfortunately." She didn't want to get into a discussion on Lindie's supposed attributes. "We really should have a doctor look at this, to be sure it's okay."

Luke reached up and touched her cheek and Ellie looked into his deep blue eyes. Her heart pounded.

"Thank you, Ellie." He spoke quietly.

"Merciful heavens, Luke, what has happened to you?" Madeline burst into the library, Cornelia, Roger and Edith behind her.

213

"I'm fine, Aunt Madeline." Luke leaned back and Ellie steadied her breath. "Ellie has taken good care of me."

"Remember, Luke, you still need to cleanse the wound thoroughly," Ellie stated. Luke nodded.

"What on earth happened?" Cornelia asked. Luke explained what had happened at the lagoon.

"You were definitely right to send for the sheriff." Edith stated.

"Whoever would want to shoot you, Luke?" Madeline asked. "It's unconscionable."

"I really have no idea," Luke replied, then glanced at Ellie, a question in his eyes.

"I can't think of anyone either." Her mind brought her back to the fire on the ranch and Naomi's food being poisoned. Could the shooting be connected? Had trouble followed her to North Carolina?

"Don't pretend you haven't wanted to shoot me a time or two." He joked, echoing her earlier thought.

"I'll admit I have had that desire on occasion, but I was standing right next to you."

"Well, I suppose that gives you an alibi, at least."

"I am a pretty fair shot, though not an expert. I'd find a cleverer, less dramatic way to do you in." She tried to lighten the mood with humor.

Luke smiled at her. "I'm surprised a ranching expert like yourself isn't a sharpshooter."

"Well, I can't be perfect at everything." She teased back.

"Mrs. Cecil, Mrs. Vanderbilt, Mr. Callahan, the sheriff is here." A butler announced. Ellie took a deep breath, ready to give her story yet again. Hopefully, the sheriff would have an idea or two on how they could go about finding the culprit in this incident.

~~~~~~~

The next day, Ellie sat near the Bass Pond, reading a letter from Janie. Apparently, a rumor in Spearfish was that Mr. Davis Martin was engaged to a young woman from Texas. Good riddance.

"Miss Bennett!"

Ellie looked up from the letter and shaded her eyes with her hand. Roger Bailey smiled and strode up to her.

"I'm glad to see you have recovered from your unfortunate scare yesterday." He came to stand before her.

"Yes, it was quite an eventful day, but my Grandpa Benjamin has always told us to 'be not afraid'. It's one of his favorite Bible quotes."

"It is a good one." Roger nodded.

"I didn't realize you enjoyed straying this far from the house, Mr. Bailey." She teased. "So far away from your aunt. She won't like that."

"Ohh." He pressed a hand to his heart. "I feel as though you just fired verbal insults at me from a rifle." He nodded at the grass next to her. "May I?"

"Of course." She smiled. "Though I must tell you that I was planning on heading back in a few minutes."

Roger offered his hand, then helped her up. "Then instead, I shall accompany you back to the Sutton's house, if that's all right?"

She nodded and took his offered arm, glad to know there were men that still practiced chivalry. "I heard you might be leaving on Saturday. Is this true?"

215

"Yes, unless Luke decides to delay again. I am completely at his mercy regarding this trip. He often times arranges my travel plans around important meetings for the business."

"Heaven help us. Luke always does what he prefers and expects others to just fall in line after him, doesn't he?"

"He does like to have his own way, I suppose." Roger admitted. "But I think if we were honest with ourselves, we all want that. He's just more likely to get it. He's wealthy, others are not."

Ellie rolled her eyes. "Please. We're living in a new century; this is not the 1800's. Any man can do just as he wants if he works hard for it and if he doesn't, well then, it's just an excuse. I very much doubt you've ever gone without."

"That is true. I haven't ever experienced any hardships, but I've never felt as though I had much of a choice in my careers. It was either helping my older brother, Samuel, at our Boston shipping company or working with Luke, which was a much better fit. He has allowed me a lot of opportunity to grow and has supported me in many things. He and I think alike and he treats me like a partner, more often than not. Like Luke, though, I fear that I'll not have much of a choice in whom I marry. My family has certain expectations and I will have to stay within those guidelines."

"Well now, that would be much of your own doing, blindly obeying your family, and for what? Money? Prestige? This is America, for goodness sake." Ellie shook her head. All of these medieval traditions were driving her batty.

"Steady on! I suppose you are right about that, but I have grown to like the life of leisure I can live if I follow my parents' dictates. Besides, there are several pleasant young ladies my family would no doubt approve of and would make me happy."

Ellie shook her head slightly. "When you do marry, what are your plans? Will you continue working for Luke?"

"Yes," he replied, "I would eventually like to manage his Black Hills resort. He's offered me the opportunity. I'm not sure I will enjoy a small town over New York or Chicago, but I would give it a try."

"I imagine you accompany him on many of his travels so he can have someone he can dictate to. You know, I'm actually surprised he's not married yet, that way he'd always have a wife to boss around too. But perhaps his sister fills that role for now. He is her guardian after all."

"That's not Luke's way at all," Roger replied, a little perplexed. Ellie was slightly confused at her own line of questioning. She was actually starting to like Luke, yet her line of questioning didn't reflect that. Why did she even care so much about him and his relationships? Even with that thought in her head, she asked more questions.

"Well, pray tell, what kind of guardian is he? Does his sister give him troubles? She must be difficult to manage if she's anything like her brother."

Roger gave Ellie a questioning look. "Why would you think she'd give him any trouble? She's the sweetest girl I have ever met."

Ellie shrugged. "No particular reason. I've just heard conflicting reports about her, although Louisa Hurst and Isabella Brantley can't stop singing her praises. You are familiar with those ladies, if I am not mistaken?"

"Of course. I know Charles well, he's a good fellow, and Luke's good friend, of course."

"Oh, yes." Ellie said, sarcasm dripping from her voice. "Luke and Charles! They are such wonderful friends." She still wasn't sure why she was getting so irritated about Luke when she had just had some very good conversations with him over the past few days. Not to mention the fact that he probably saved her life yesterday. There was just something about him that got under her skin.

"Luke is a great friend to many, and from what I understand, Charles is indebted to him," Roger stated.

"How so?" Ellie asked.

"Luke recently saved him from a bad marriage. You know Charles, so you're well aware that he would be the type of fellow to blindly follow his heart instead of making a well thought-out decision. Luke had to step in."

"Did Luke say why he thought it necessary to interfere? Why was this girl such a bad match?" Ellie tried to stay calm as she realized that she may actually get some answers to questions that had been plaguing her for months.

"There were strong objections to her." Roger hesitated, then looked at Ellie. "Why are you so curious about this?"

Ellie clenched her jaw. Did Roger really not make the connection between her sister and Charles?

"Who does Luke think he is? Why should he judge the situation? What right does he have to decide what and who will make Charles Brantley happy?"

Roger held up his hands. "I don't know, Miss Ellie. I don't know anything more about the situation, but I can tell you that Luke will do whatever he needs to help and support his friends." The two came to a fork in the path where they would go in their separate directions and stopped to finish their conversation. "You should come by after dinner tonight. We're going to test our skills at bowling." A two-lane bowling alley was another part of the Biltmore mansion.

"That actually sounds quite fun. I have never tried that sport." Ellie bit her lip and tried not to show how upset she was. "I will check with the rest of my party." She had no intention of going. Seeing Luke...she wasn't sure she could control her anger. Luke was the one who had talked Charles into leaving Janie. She had believed it was his family, but to learn it was all Luke? How could he do such a thing to her beloved sister and then talk with her as though he had done nothing wrong? He had ruined Janie's chance for happiness and acted as though it didn't matter. He had to know how upset Ellie would be or he would have said something to her. She felt betrayed, and just when she was beginning to like him.

"Very well." Roger tipped his hat. "Even if they don't want to come, you still should, it will be fun. I hope to see you later."

"Yes, of course." Ellie nodded as she turned and walked back to the Sutton's, consumed with her thoughts.

"Ellie, good Heavens, you look as mad as a thundercloud, is there something wrong?" Charlotte asked when she arrived. It didn't take long for Ellie to tell her about the conversation with Roger.

"He said there were strong objections to the lady." Ellie ranted. "No one in their right mind could have objections with Janie. She's sweet, kind, thoughtful and practically perfect. It has to be her lack of money and social connections. Those families are obsessed with status! It can't be anything else." She paced as she talked to Charlotte, who listened intently. "And it's not like we are destitute; we are financially well off right now."

"Maybe it was your family." Charlotte suggested.

219

"I suppose that could be true." Ellie plopped down into a chair. "My mother is always embarrassing herself, and Lindie and Kathy as you are well aware are simply annoying. Poor Marie just wants to live in her music and books and Papa is so wrapped up with running the ranch that he just doesn't care to deal with any of them." She thought for a moment, then shook her head. "Oh, I don't know anymore. I really can't see Janie's family ties carrying so much weight with Luke. His opinion would only be affected by Janie's lack of social connections." She shook her head. "That and the fact that he still wants his sister to marry Charles one day, which is why he must have convinced Charles to leave Janie without any notice." Frustration boiled within her again. *How could he be so heartless?* "I am so disappointed about this, Charlotte. Furthermore, I don't believe I can go with you to Biltmore any more. Make my excuses, tell them I'm sick, tell them I'm packing, tell them the truth, I don't care. But I cannot be in the same room with Luke Callahan."

Chapter Twenty-Six

Ellie's only comfort came from the knowledge that she would soon be home on her ranch where she would never have to see Luke again. She would miss her free time and the ability to explore so often, but mostly she would miss Charlotte. The day before she was to leave and three days after learning of Luke's role in Charles's departure from South Dakota, Ellie decided to take one more hike along her favorite path. When she was still quite far away from the Sutton home, it started sprinkling. She dashed into the Bass Pond boathouse so she could escape getting wet and leaned against a post, a bit breathless.

"Ellie…"

She was so caught up in her thoughts that she jumped at the voice. The one person in all of North Carolina that she didn't want to see entered the boathouse. Luke. His hair was damp, his button-up shirt was untucked, with the top button undone and she could see a Henley undershirt beneath. The rain began to fall harder outside. Drops of water pitter-pattered against the leaves on the ground around the boathouse and the wooden roof.

"What are you doing here?" She moved back against the latticed corner wall of the building and tried to control her temper.

"I was out for a walk. I was hoping to see you. I know you leave tomorrow." He paced a bit in front of her. "How have you been?"

"Ready to go home," she replied coolly. He turned away and was quiet for a few moments, then returned to stand in front of her.

"I can't keep my thoughts to myself anymore." He ran a hand through his hair, rumpling it. His words were fast and frenzied. "I find I must tell you how I feel."

He hesitated for a few seconds, then continued to babble. "I care for you, Ellie, and I have from the moment we met. As I said, I have kept my feelings to myself and although I have tried to deny them, I find I can't anymore. These feelings I have for you are absurd, and these last few months have tormented me. I must admit, I came to Biltmore because I heard you would be here and I had to see you again. You must understand that I'm expected to marry well, to a woman in my own social circle and you are certainly not that woman. And your family can be a bit…well, a bit much. But frankly, I don't care!"

Ellie stared at him, mouth agape, speechless. A blush crept up her cheeks. She didn't know what to say, how to react. He was trying to tell her that he cared for her, which touched a place in her heart, but at the same time, he was ridiculing her and his comments about her family just plain humiliated her.

"Just what exactly are you saying?" She finally asked.

"I am in love with you, Ellie, and I can't deny it any longer. I…I would like to marry you."

Ellie shook her head in disbelief, her chest tingling. She didn't have the same feelings for him…or did she? Perhaps she realized that he was not exactly the cold, callous man she had first met months ago, but she certainly

222

didn't love him. She couldn't lie to him and say she did, but she didn't want to hurt his feelings. He continued his ramblings.

"In spite of all the obstacles between us, you have stolen my heart. I would like to ask you...I must ask you, Ellie...will you marry me?" He reached out to take her hand, and she immediately pulled it away.

"I'm sorry you've had to endure so much...torment because of your feelings for me. I certainly didn't mean to cause you pain. I truly do appreciate your sentiments, but I don't feel the same way."

"So you...you're rejecting me?" He was crestfallen.

"Yes, yes I am. I surely never expected for you to fall in love with me, and I apologize if something I said or did led you to believe otherwise." She brushed back a strand of wet hair from her cheek. Had she done something? She had begun to think of him as a friend, up until her last conversation with Roger.

"So you'll go back and tell Mrs. Sutton of my proposal and you'll both have a good laugh at the pathetic Mr. Callahan." He spun away baffled, almost incredulous that she would turn him down. Ellie could tell that he was struggling with his composure and was forcing himself to stay calm.

"No, not at all, I would never do such a thing." Ellie insisted. "But I'm sure what you said about this being a difficult decision for you will help you to overcome my answer."

"Can I at least ask why you're turning me down?" He twisted his hands together and stepped closer.

"Besides the fact that I don't know my feelings for you in return? Please explain to me how you have the audacity to insult my family and myself in your proposal. You say you love me, yet your better judgement made you question your own feelings? How is that supposed to endear me to you?"

"No, I didn't mean it that way..." He tried to answer, but she interrupted him.

"Honestly, I might have considered you a suiter at one point, but there are other reasons I can't marry you and you know full well what these reasons are."

"I have no idea. What exactly are you in reference to?" He raised his voice louder than he meant to.

"Do you honestly believe I could ever be friends with, much less marry someone who ruined the happiness of my sister? You caused Janie's heartbreak, you can't deny it."

His face paled as he looked at her. She continued.

"You just took it upon yourself to separate Janie and Charles, despite the fact that they obviously loved one another. You completely destroyed Janie's hopes and dreams of a future with Charles."

"I'll admit I'm the one that told Charles to cut ties with your sister and I'm glad I did."

"Why?" She looked at him, horrified. "How could you do such a thing?"

"Janie doesn't love Charles. She was completely uninterested."

"Uninterested?"

"I watched them carefully when they were together and it was quite obvious to me that Charles liked Janie much more than she liked him."

"Oh, for Heaven's sake, you can't tell that from just watching them, besides, Janie is very shy, especially when it comes to romance!" Ellie exclaimed and threw up her hand.

"I disagree with you! Charles was quite easily persuaded that she didn't really care for him."

"Of course he was! Because you told him so!"

"I discouraged him for his own good, he's my best friend!"

"Janie rarely tells me what she's thinking and feeling, and she's not only my best friend, she's my sister. Even I have a difficult time trying to read her like a book, so tell me how can you know her thoughts just by observing?"

Luke looked at her without a response. Ellie glanced down, took a breath and voiced what had been on her mind of late. "I suspect her lack of money and social standings had more to do with…"

"No, I would never say that, though it was quite obvious…" He turned around.

"What was obvious?" She grabbed his arm and turned him back towards her.

"It was obvious that your mother wanted the marriage because of Charles's money."

"Did Janie ever give you that impression…"

"No, not her, just your mother, and of course there is the matter of the rest of your family…"

"Because we're ranchers from South Dakota and not snobbish Chicago socialites? Charles didn't seem to care about that."

"No, it's not that."

"What then? Explain it to me, please." Frustration mounted.

Luke looked away as if collecting his thoughts, then turned right back to Ellie. "It was the lack of manners. Your mother, your three younger sisters and even your father at times are seriously lacking in any social decorum and their manners can be quite atrocious."

Ellie looked at him, shocked that he would say such a thing.

"I must admit, I like your Grandfather and father and you and Janie have always acted completely appropriately. Well, usually."

"Usually?"

He looked away, as if he didn't want to elaborate on what he just said.

"What do you mean 'usually?'" She insisted.

"The night of Charles's party, Isabella and I caught Janie in a... peccadillo."

"A what?"

"A... compromising situation. An indiscretion with a man who was not Charles Brantley."

"What are you talking about?" Ellie almost shook with indignation. "Janie would never do such a thing."

"I wouldn't have believed it myself, but I saw her in the arms of another man, embracing him, in public, quite inappropriately."

Ellie's thought back to that night. Who would Janie have been hugging? The answer slowly dawned on her. "Did he have straight blonde hair and a missing front tooth?" She asked.

"The hair sounds right, but I didn't ask him to smile."

Ellie threw up her hands. "That was probably Jackson Roberts! They've been friends since childhood. They've never been romantically involved, and besides that, he's happily married, with two children and another on the way!"

"Then why were they embracing for so long?"

226

"I would suppose it's because Jackson's father had just died and she was comforting him. They were extremely close and Jackson loved him dearly."

Luke looked shocked, then a little remorseful. Ellie took a deep breath and shook her head. Perhaps he could have misread the signs and made a poor judgement, maybe he had seen things the wrong way and was just trying to do the right thing, but there was one other action he hadn't explained.

"And what about Davis Martin?"

He gave her a stormy look and stepped close to her, close enough that she could see a green speck in his blue eyes. "Davis Martin?" He almost growled.

"How can you explain the way you treated him?"

"Really? How I treated him? And why would you even be so concerned about that? I thought he left you..."

"He told me all about what you did to him."

"What I did to him?" Luke's voice was deep and low, but controlled. She briefly thought back to his story about his temper. Would he take it out on her? She didn't care.

"You all but ruined his future by making him drop out of college and quit the baseball team. You treat him as though he is not deserving of any respect, and you practically stole his money."

"Ahh, I understand now. This is what you think of me." He shook his head. "Well, thank you for explaining things. Perhaps you might have been able to forgive me and my shortcomings if it hadn't been for all the wisdom and pride you possess."

"My pride!" She clenched her hands into fists. He continued talking over her.

"...being hurt by my honesty. I felt it was the right thing to do, admitting that a relationship between us would have been complicated. Did you expect me to be happy that I had fallen in love with a girl that would never meet my family's expectations?"

"Well, aren't you the gentleman." She stepped so close that there was almost no room between them. "From the first moment I saw you, I disliked you. You are arrogant, conceited, and insensitive, Luke Callahan. You are the last man on this earth that I would ever consider marrying." He leaned toward Ellie. Her heart pounded. He was about to kiss her; she just knew it. He looked at her with pain in his eyes that made her almost want to pull him into her arms.

"Well then, there's nothing more to discuss." He backed away, eyes still locked on hers, then turned and quickly walked into the rain and down the path toward Biltmore. She leaned back against the wall. What had just happened? Luke just proposed to her? Angelina had been right. The wealthy entrepreneur businessman was in love with her, so much so that he had been willing to cross societal lines to marry her.

She shook her head. She had to remember what he had done to Janie and Charles and Davis. He hadn't denied any of the accusations and sounded like he would do the same things again if given the choice. Any feelings she felt for him were gone. There was a break in the rain, and Ellie needed to get back to Charlotte's home so she could finish packing. She had to get away from this place. She had to get away from Luke Callahan. She pushed away from the wall, ran out the door, and hurried as quickly as she could to the Sutton's.

228

$\mathcal{L}$uke trudged to Biltmore, a combination of frustration and heartache coursing through him. How could he have let this happen? He had been so sure she would accept his proposal. It never occurred to him that she would reject him. No woman he had ever met before would have considered saying no. He was always so concerned that people didn't just like him for his wealth, well, he had finally found someone who didn't. Ironically, it was just the opposite, she seemed to dislike him because of it. He snuck into the house, not wanting to see anyone. He knew he wouldn't be good company at the moment.

"Luke, what on earth happened to you?" Roger came around the corner just as Luke had started up the elegant staircase to his suite in the bachelors' wing.

"I just got caught in the rain while hiking." And encountering the biggest disappointment I have ever faced.

"I know you better than anyone, Luke. Something has you riled up. Go on up and get dried off and change your clothes, then meet me on the back porch." Roger spoke in an uncharacteristically forceful tone. Luke sighed. His cousin was one of the men he trusted most in the world. Perhaps Roger had some thoughts on what he should do next. Was there a way he could somehow get back into Ellie's good graces?

"All right, I will join you shortly."

As he dried off, Luke went back and forth between being distraught and being frustrated. He realized that he may have been proposing a little sooner than he had anticipated and it may have come as a shock to Ellie. Thinking back, he had tried to hide his feelings for so long that she

229

likely had very little warning that he wanted a serious courtship. It had surprised him, so he supposed he couldn't blame her for not knowing him well enough to accept. At least he knew she wasn't after his money. He just hadn't expected such a harsh reaction when she spoke to him, he had never seen her so upset. How was he to know that Janie was shy, and that the cowboy was a good friend? He also knew he needed to defend himself in regards to Davis, and warn her about the man's true character. He had to respond to her accusations, but how? She'd never want to speak to him again.

Luke joined Roger on the back porch, which overlooked the lush green rolling hills in the foreground and hardwood and evergreen trees of the Pisgah National Forest behind them. The Blue Ridge Mountains loomed in the distance, not unlike the Black Hills he so enjoyed. With Ellie. Why, oh why did everything remind him of his time spent with her? It was still raining, just sprinkling really, but the limestone roof over the porch kept them dry.

"So, did you see Miss Ellie Bennett while hiking?" Roger asked, though his tone and relaxed posture suggested he already knew the answer.

"I did." Luke nodded.

"You finally tell her the depths of your feelings for her?"

Luke looked over, a little surprised. "Who said I had any feelings for her?"

"Your face says it every time you look at her or when someone mentions her name and especially when you talk about her." Roger smiled. "I must say, I'm surprised she's the one you chose, but pleasantly. She's perfect for you, in my opinion. She's not afraid to stand up to you and she can make you laugh, which on both counts is difficult for any man to do, much less a pretty woman."

"And here I thought you might find her attractive and want to court her yourself." How could any man not? Ellie did seem to get along well with Roger.

"Perhaps I would have, but I could tell from the first time I saw you together that you both shared something special." Roger shrugged. "So, did you? Tell her, that is?"

Luke sighed and explained to his cousin what had transpired. Roger shook his head over and over as he listened and then interrupted before Luke could get to the part about Charles, Janie and Davis.

"Seriously, Luke, it's no wonder she refused! I don't blame her at all, and neither should you. Even a man with very limited experience in the field of romance can tell that you don't insult a woman or her family while you're proposing."

"I didn't think I was insulting her. I just wanted to explain to her that I know we have our differences, but that they don't matter to me. That's all." Luke shook his head. "Perhaps I should have worded it differently."

"There's no perhaps about it." Roger rolled his eyes.

"I'm thinking now that none of this probably matters. She really despises me. You may have realized that the young woman I warned Charles Brantley about was Ellie's sister and..."

Roger interrupted. "No, no, actually I didn't. Well, blast, it certainly explains a lot of things. I apologize, Luke, but I may have said some things to her regarding Charles that validated what she already suspected."

Luke sighed. "It's no fault of yours, I would have told her eventually. Besides, she was already poisoned against me by Davis Martin."

231

"Davis Martin? That miscreant? I didn't know she was acquainted with him."

Luke told Roger about seeing Davis in South Dakota, as well as his suspicions that Davis had followed him out there to try and cause trouble.

"I don't know about that." Roger stroked his mustache, the same style made popular by Douglas Fairbanks in the Zorro film. "It's a coincidence, to be sure, but he can't reasonably believe you'd give him any help after what he did to Helena."

Luke nodded, then remained quiet for a moment. "Should I have told Ellie about that?" He finally asked. "I just don't want to spread our family secrets far and wide, though I know Ellie would use discretion. I do trust her." He sighed. "It's hopeless. I've lost her, probably forever, though I'm not sure I ever really had her. I just don't want her thinking badly of me. I would at least like to be on friendly terms with her if we ever meet again."

"So go talk to her."

"I doubt she'll want to see me, besides, I'll muck up my words again."

"Then write her a letter. You usually have a way with the written word. I can help make sure she receives it."

"That might work." Luke leaned forward, elbows on his knees and rubbed his face. "I'll wait until later, however. Let my emotions settle down."

"That is the smartest thing I've heard you say all day." Roger smiled.

Luke smiled back. "Thank you for your advice, Roger. I don't know what I would do without you."

"No problem, cousin." Roger nodded.

Chapter Twenty-Seven

*E*llie, Angelina and Mr. Ingraham were loading their luggage into the Sutton automobile when Angelina pulled at Ellie's arm. "Look who's here." She whispered. Ellie turned and saw Luke pull up in his Bearcat. She hadn't told anyone what had happened at the boathouse the day before. She wasn't sure if she would ever tell anyone.

"Is there something I can help you with, Mr. Callahan?" She stood her ground as he stepped closer to her. He spoke softly.

"I believe you said all that you felt was needed yesterday, but will you at least give me a chance to explain myself and please read this?" He handed her a letter. She took it from him and nodded, trying not to let the brush of his fingers affect her pulse. He turned and strode back to his car and drove away. Ellie shrugged at Charlotte's questioning look, then hugged her friend and said her final good-byes. The Ford pulled away from a visit she would never forget.

Ellie could barely contain her curiosity about the contents of the letter. She didn't want Angelina or Mr. Ingraham to see how anxious she was to read it, so she waited until they had pulled out of the Biltmore Village train station before she carefully tore it open.

My dear Ellie,

There are two things you have accused me of. First, ending the relationship between Charles and your sister. Second, the part I played in Davis Martin leaving college. I'm sorry if anything I share with you upsets you, but I want you to know the truth. My actions were only done for what I believed to be good reasons.

First, about Janie. Charles liked your sister from the moment he met her, but he had fallen for another girl in a similar manner before and it did not end well. I watched them both closely and Janie was cheerful and friendly, but didn't seem especially interested in Charles, which convinced me that, although she is a wonderful girl, Charles cared for her far more than she did him. I thought she was friendly to other men at the parties we attended and felt she was indifferent to Charles, but upon further reflection, I find that she was probably being her kind, gentle self. I truly believed that Charles's feelings were unreturned. You told me otherwise, so I must take your words as truth. I can certainly understand why you may resent me for my actions regarding their relationship. I believed from Janie's behavior that she didn't care for my friend as he did for her. I didn't want Charles to be stuck in a loveless marriage, as he deserves the best. And there was the situation that I misinterpreted with her embracing the cowboy. I should have asked more questions.

I must admit that the inappropriate actions of your mother and sisters were concerning to me as well. However, even your family's behavior wouldn't have prevented a relationship if Charles hadn't been so easily convinced that Janie didn't care for him. At the time, Charles truly believed that she did, so I will take responsibility for planting seeds of doubt in his mind. I don't blame myself for that, as I thought I was doing the right thing. Please believe me when I say that I never wanted to hurt Janie, I only wanted to protect Charles.

Now, as for Davis Martin. I can only tell you about his connection to my family. Davis's father was an extremely respectable man and a hard worker. He was not just an employee, but a good friend to my father. Davis is actually my father's godson and we were very close growing up. Unfortunately, Steven Martin died eight years ago, from a cancer of the lungs. It was at that time that I decided to stop smoking, as I thought maybe this had contributed to his disease though Davis continued to do so. I admit, my habit of sucking on root beer barrels comes from when I was trying to quit. But I digress.

My father paid for Davis to attend good preparatory schools and after Steven died, he continued to support him in college, but Davis had no intention of focusing on his education. As you know, my father died five years ago. He had informed me long ago that he wanted me to continue to support Davis and help him get started in whatever business he wanted. Davis was also a beneficiary in my father's will and was left a tidy sum of money.

Davis often wrote to me saying that he needed more money for school and I always sent it to him, despite knowing that he already had a large monthly income. Keep in mind, I was still attending college and trying to run a business. I had quit playing baseball and rugby to focus on my family and business. By this time, I knew Davis wasn't as trustworthy as my father believed him to be, and I told him that he should have more than enough money to finish his degree, but he continued to request more and more.

I soon found out that he lied about his college attendance, including the fact that he made the baseball team. Instead, he was spending all of his time drinking and gambling away the money that I had sent him. I heard nothing from him for the next year. Finally, he wrote to me when he heard I was opening a resort in the Catskill Mountains of New York. He told me he had graduated, which was a lie, but could not find any employment. He thought he would do well as a resort manager with his talents of conversation. He quickly reminded me that my father had requested I help him to get started in whatever business venture he desired.

I offered him an entry-level position, thinking he could work and prove he was worthy to be a manager, but he declined. No one could blame me for refusing him such an important position right away, with no degree and a background of irresponsibility. He was angry and knew just what would hurt me the most. I beg you and trust you to keep secret what I tell you next.

Last summer, Davis sought out my sister, who was only sixteen at the time. She was staying at a boarding school, and unbeknownst to me, he began courting her. She quickly fell in love with him (you know how charming he can be) and he persuaded her to elope with him. My sister and I are very close, and I luckily happened to visit with her the day before they were to run off. I could tell she was excited and holding back a secret and was finally able to get her to tell me her reason. I immediately confronted Davis and told him I would cut Helena off from any allowance and all income she was to receive when she came of age if they married. When he heard this, he left without even saying goodbye to Helena. She was devastated. I suspect he wanted not only her money, but to exact his revenge on me, to make me pay for everything he believed I had done to him.

I hope you have read all the way to the end of this letter, and I pray you can understand my position, and forgive me for any mistakes you feel I have made. If you need to verify any of this information, you can write to Roger. He knows of my father's will and is one of the few people who know what Davis did to our dear Helena.

I do still love you, Eleanor Bennett. I believe I always will. I don't know exactly when it happened, but it did, and I feel as though I am a better man because of it. I regret hurting you and mucking up my proposal. You are one of the finest women I have ever met. I hope you realize and always remember how special you are. Never let anyone else tell you differently.

I pray you have a safe trip back. South Dakota and your Black Hills are truly one of the most beautiful places I have ever been. I plan on returning for business and hope that if we see each other again, we can be on friendly terms.

Yours affectionately,

Lucas Callahan

~~~~~

*E*llie spent the entire train ride home pondering and re-reading Luke's letter. She still thought his excuse about Janie and Charles was a bit weak. How could he honestly believe she was indifferent to Charles Brantley? Anyone who saw them together could tell they adored one another. Ellie thought Luke's interference was all about his pride, his sense of dignity and his ideas about Janie marrying outside her station. But on further reflection, Luke couldn't take issue with an ordinary woman marrying a wealthy man, as he had just proposed to her.

The information about Davis Martin was another story. Much of Luke's version made sense, and it certainly explained some misgivings she had concerning Davis. *One of those men is lying,* she thought to herself as she watched the great plains roll by, *and deep down, I know it's Davis.* There had always been something about the cowboy that she didn't trust. Not for the first time, she wondered if he paid attention to her to get the ranch, then after he learned she would not inherit anything, he didn't find her worthwhile anymore. She continued to think about the letter after she finally arrived home, when she was working, and always before falling asleep.

"Luke must be the one telling the truth." She spoke to her horse, Naomi, while sitting and watching a herd of buffalo pass by. The herd

237

reminded her of Luke when he first saw the majestic buffalo at Custer State Park, the awe and wonder on his usual calm and poised face. It had been the first time he had shown any true emotion in front of her.

"I always figured him as a man to be trusted."

Ellie turned around and smiled at the ranch foreman, Matthew Shaw as he came up beside her.

"Though I am unsure of why you continue to dwell on him. He hasn't been here in months. Have you learned something new?"

"Oh, have I." Ellie told Matthew all about what had happened in North Carolina, including the details of the letter. "So now you know what I know," Ellie said. "I should have realized how strange it was that Davis told me so much of his past when essentially I was a total stranger. And I should have known that he apparently worked on other ranches in the area before coming here, but I had never heard of him before. They must have been all lies. Did you know any of his background?"

"Nope. Took a chance on him like your Grandpa Benjamin took a chance on me all those years ago."

Ellie nodded. "I keep trying to think of even one instance where Davis Martin showed true integrity or goodness that might make me think better of him, but I just can't. I try to think back in my memory about every conversation I ever had with him. He claims he had no fear of Luke, yet he avoided that barbeque."

"True. Shore puts things in a different light, don't it?" Matthew replied.

"Davis clearly left here because he realized none of the Bennett daughters would inherit the ranch, so he had no reason to trick us into marrying him." Thank goodness Ellie had put off his advances.

238

"I did hear tell of him being practically engaged to the daughter of a wealthy rancher down Oklahoma way."

"I heard she was from Texas." Ellie sighed, feeling about as low as she could. Used and discarded. "I have no doubt now that Luke was telling the truth on that score."

"I done my own observing and I find that Mr. Luke is far more trustworthy than Davis Martin will ever be." Matthew always read people so well, she should have confided in him long ago. Feelings of embarrassment washed over her. Luke may have been arrogant, but she had been prejudiced and quick to judge.

"I'm afraid to admit that I fell for Davis's lies initially because I was so excited about all the attention he gave me. He is devastatingly handsome and so few men have really paid much attention to me beyond my ranching ability."

"Well, you grew up with most of the young men around here and it would be hard to find one who doesn't care that ya can outride and out-ranch them. Can't imagine what they would think of ya if ya could outshoot them too. But someday ya'll find the right man. Maybe it is Mr. Luke, maybe someone else. Only God knows."

"I've made so many terrible mistakes, Matthew." She felt tears threaten. "I've been so blind, acted so foolish. I always thought I was so smart, perhaps not book smart, but I thought I had the wisdom to make the best decisions. Instead, I find that I need more humility in my life."

"Now, now, Miss Ellie, what's this all about? Don't fret none. You's a strong and loyal young woman. Unfortunately, that can sometimes blind us to reality. We all have stubborn moments in our lives. I sure had mine when I was courting my Hattie. A miracle that woman ever agreed to marry

239

me." He smiled as if caught up in a memory. "If something is meant to be, it will be. Ya just gotta put yo work in. If ya see Mr. Callahan again, ya talk to him."

Ellie continued thinking out loud. "Was Luke right about Janie and Charles? Obviously, he misunderstood the relationship between Janie and Jackson, but could he have been right about the other situations?"

"Don't know about that. Aside from being the sweetest gal I ever met, it's not always easy to tell what Miss Janie's feeling." Matthew replied.

"Charlotte warned me about that, now that I think about it. She told both of us, me and Janie that Janie should allow Charles, of all people, to know and see her true feelings."

"I gotta agree with that, Miss Ellie. Woulda been a good idea for Janie to be more open, it's just not her way."

"And Luke can't be blamed for judging us based on Mama, Lindie and Kathy's ridiculous behavior, and Marie who doesn't always act appropriately in certain social situations."

"Ya know that be the truth, but again, ya cain't change who a person is meant to be."

Ellie wiped at a tear that had fallen to her cheek. "Yes, I've been such a numbskull. I can see now that Luke did have reasons to sway Charles's feelings." It was tough to admit, but true. Luke wasn't the hateful vindictive man she had made him out to be, he was simply a man trying to be a good friend.

"And to make matters worse, Matthew, I was so terribly deceived by Davis." She felt dejected.

"Wouldn't worry 'bout that much more, Miss Ellie. Davis will get what's comin' ta him someday. Seems he fooled lotsa people. What's important is that ya know who he is now an' he wasn't able to do any lastin' damage. Ya know better now."

"Thank you so much, Matthew." She turned and embraced the man who was like an uncle to her. "Have I told you lately that I'm so glad you're in my life." The grizzled old man simply smiled and hugged her back.

Even though Matthew's words made her feel slightly better, she was still unsettled. Would she ever see Luke again? And could she find the words to apologize for misjudging him if she did?

Chapter Twenty-Eight

Lindie skipped up the porch steps the next afternoon, a letter in her hand. It was nice to have the entire family back home at the ranch together. Lindie, however, continued to be just as immature as ever, and Ellie had to focus on not getting too upset about it.

"Such interesting news, Ellie." She thrust the letter at Ellie, and continued to explain what the message said.

"Davis will not be marrying any old rancher's daughter after all. It turns out that Miss Mary King traveled all the way to New Orleans to see her uncle and promptly fell in love with a Louisiana steamboat company owner. Davis is safe and still available."

"More like that young lady is safe from him." Ellie whispered to herself. Her sisters continued to talk endlessly of the two new ranch hands the family had recently hired. Janie smiled and pulled Ellie away.

"You've been so pensive since you've been back," Janie said. "Won't you tell me what happened in North Carolina?"

Ellie sighed. She could at least tell Janie about part of Luke's letter, and about the proposal. The family would find out about Luke's presence in North Carolina eventually, as Angelina or Mr. Ingraham were bound to mention it.

"I know you will keep this in your utmost confidence and won't tell anyone else about this, but I actually saw Luke Callahan while visiting Charlotte."

"Oh, good Heavens, I hope he didn't spoil your vacation," Janie's eyes widened. Ellie proceeded to tell her an abridged version of the story.

"I still can't believe he proposed. I had no idea he felt that deeply for me."

"I think there were signs of it." Janie countered. "And from what you said, the two of you had some very good conversations on your hikes."

"That is true."

"But what I don't understand is why wouldn't you at least consider it? Perhaps not then and there, but tell him that you would think about it, or allow him to court you."

"I..." Ellie almost told her about Luke's role in Charles's leaving, but just couldn't bring herself to do so. "I just got so upset about him proposing after insulting me and our family, so I overreacted. I'll admit I did it badly. I wish I could take it back, respond to him differently, but I just get so frustrated with him sometimes."

"Those strong feelings may be love. Are you attracted to him, Ellie?"

"Yes." She could admit that at least. "I have been from the start. Perhaps that's what upset me so much." She readjusted her hat. "I thought I was so clever, disliking him as I did, not falling for his charm, which I must confess, he showed me eventually. He can be so cocky and arrogant and I must admit that it was fun verbally sparring with him." She shook her head. "As Grandpa Benjamin would say, dislike sometimes sharpens one's wit." Ellie felt like she was rambling, but Janie was understanding it all.

"How did he react to the refusal?" Janie asked.

"He seemed surprised, as if he couldn't believe a woman would reject his proposal," Ellie replied. "I am sorry that I hurt his feelings, though. I could have been kinder." She paused, then asked, "You don't think I was foolish for outright refusing him, do you? I still don't know him as well as I should, in order to consider marriage, but perhaps once I did, I might...I think I could...fall in love with him."

"I wouldn't say you're foolish, no. As you said, you don't know each other well enough, yet. I think you could have suggested that you court first. Get to know each other better. Truth be told, I believe the two of you would make a good couple. There are definitely sparks between the two of you, and he seems to respect you as a woman rancher, which is not common for a man."

Ellie looked at her sister in shock. "You can really see me married to him?"

"I can. I thought he might have a little interest in you last year, and I didn't think you minded him as much as you pretended."

Ellie thought back, especially to their time together in North Carolina before she learned of his involvement with Janie and Charles's relationship.

"It doesn't matter anymore one way or the other. I told him no, and I doubt he'll ever make an offer to me again."

"All I can say is, if it's meant to be, God will find a way to put the two of you together again. Luke did say he'll be back in South Dakota for business, right?"

"Yes, he did." Ellie realized that a part of her wanted him to show up again.

"You could always write to him."

244

"I suppose." Ellie wasn't so sure. How would she even start a letter to a man who admitted she stole his heart? Ellie wasn't certain that she loved Luke, but she now realized that she could, very easily, if they were able to have a second chance.

Ellie looked at Lindie and Kathy across the yard. "There is one more thing I didn't tell you," she said, then proceeded to tell Janie about what Lucas had written regarding Davis Martin. "What do you think? Should I tell the others about Davis's true character?"

Janie thought for a moment. "I don't feel we need to expose Davis at this time. After all, he's gone far away, and I doubt he'll be back around these parts again. Is that what your thinking?"

"Yes, that we should probably keep it to ourselves," Ellie replied. "Luke asked me to keep it private, and you're right, Davis won't be coming around anymore."

"Then we are in agreement." Janie looked in the direction of Verbena Meadows. "Did Luke say anything else?"

"No, not really." Ellie couldn't bring herself to tell Janie about the rest of the letter, how Charles had loved her. She wasn't quite sure why. Perhaps deep down, she wanted to hide Luke's role in it to protect him. If Charles was so easily persuaded against Janie and wouldn't fight for her, perhaps he didn't deserve Janie. Perhaps Janie and Charles would get back together only to have Charles shatter Janie's heart again. Whatever her reasoning was, Ellie could not bring herself to tell Janie.

~~~~~~~

The days continued to pass by while Ellie worked hard, Luke never far from her thoughts. There were especially times when her mother, Lindie

245

and Kathy were constantly complaining of all the tedious work they had to do and Ellie could almost hear Luke objecting to them. They became increasingly annoying and she could almost forgive Luke for interfering with Charles's life. Why would anyone willingly choose to attach themselves to this family?

"Father." Ellie entered her father's office on the particular day after she caught Lindie kissing one of the ranch hands in the barn. She didn't know what to do about the situation. "I am very concerned about Lindie and her actions. Are you aware of how her antics are making her look? She's going to get tangled into a situation that she won't be able to flirt her way out of. I'm worried about her."

"Why are you so concerned? Has she frightened away some suiter of yours?" He asked, clenching his cigar in his teeth.

"No, I'm first and foremost worried about her and her personal reputation, though it's true that our respectability in town and the whole county, for that matter is at stake. If you don't somehow restrain Lindie, she's going to find herself in trouble. She is the most outrageous flirt I've ever known and it's only going to get worse. She makes herself and all of us look ridiculous. I'm truly concerned for her, Father, and you should be too."

"Don't worry yourself, my dear Ellie. I have a plan for your wayward sister. I received a letter from the Foresters, over at Brighton Ranch."

Ellie ignored the fact that her father had changed the subject so quickly. "Your friends near Cheyenne?" She clarified.

"Yes." Her father nodded. "They have a daughter Lindie's age and they have invited her to come for a visit."

"And you're going to let her go?" Ellie was aghast.

246

"She will be just fine. She already knows about the invitation, so she'll complain until the day she dies if I do not allow her to go. The Foresters are good people; they won't let her get into any trouble. Perhaps this visit to Cheyenne will teach her that she's not the center of the world."

"But, Papa…"

He held up a hand. "I have made my decision, Ellie." He pulled out a ledger and opened it. Ellie sighed and stood, then walked out of the office. There was no reasoning with her father sometimes. She grabbed her hat and made her way toward the barn, but was stopped on the porch by Janie.

"You look like you're hot under the collar. What's wrong?"

"Lindie is what's wrong. She's an incorrigible flirt and one of these days, she's going to go too far or compromise herself and get…well, get into trouble with a boy that will have dire consequences that could permanently alter her life." She put her hands on her hips. "And when I try to tell Papa how much the situation concerns me; he tells me not to worry about it. Not only that, he's sending her to Brighton Ranch near Cheyenne, to stay with the Foresters."

"I think Lindie will enjoy that. It will be nice for her to get away from the family, and be close to a new town full of fresh faces."

"Really, Janie? Yes, fresh faces and new men to act foolish with. You do realize that Cheyenne is right next to Fort Russell, so she'll have cowboys and soldiers to flirt with. It's as if Papa's rewarding her for behaving poorly."

"He just doesn't know what to do with her any more." Janie defended their father.

247

"And he's too annoyed by her. He all but admitted it to me, though I certainly don't blame him." Ellie replied.

"Is that really what you think of me?" Angry footsteps hit the wraparound porch as Lindie came around the corner of the house. "That I am annoying and no one in this family wants me around?"

"Lindie, that's not…" Ellie tried to explain.

"Not what? Not true? I doubt I misheard you. You and Papa both want me out of your lives."

"Lindie, nobody…" Janie tried to keep the peace, but Ellie interrupted.

"Will you please stop being so dramatic?" Ellie stared at Lindie. "I'm worried about you and your behavior. I tried talking to you about it this spring, but you wouldn't listen. I was trying to get Papa to…"

"Oh, just stop it, Ellie. You're just jealous of the fact that I'm friendly and outgoing and pretty and that everyone wants to be around me more than you and you can't stand it."

"That is not true!" Ellie protested.

"You keep thinking that! Now, I must be off. I need to pack so I can leave and stop annoying you and Papa." And with that, she turned and stomped into the house.

Ellie squashed the urge to slam her hat against the porch post. "Why does she have to be so melodramatic? I'm more worried about her now than I was five minutes ago."

"I'm sure she'll be just fine." Janie tried to assure her. "The Foresters will keep an eye on her. Perhaps when she's able to get away, she'll mature."

"So you think I'm worrying too much?"

Janie shrugged. "I think that you have always felt as though you are responsible for all of your sisters. You're very protective, even of me and I'm older."

"I just...I don't really intend to. I just..." She didn't want to say that she sometimes felt she had to, as Janie was so meek and the rest of them needed so much guidance.

"It comes naturally to you, I understand." Janie smiled. "However, you shouldn't worry about Lindie. As I said, the Foresters will keep an eye on her, and I think she'll be better out from under all of our shadows."

That made sense. "I can only hope and pray you're right." Ellie nodded.

Chapter Twenty-Nine

Luke darted across the busy Chicago street, avoiding cars and carriages alike. The more he reflected on his life, the more he realized he didn't want to spend his days in the big city. He would continue to visit Chicago and occasionally New York, of course, to conduct his business, but he longed to be able to spend the majority of his time at his childhood home in St. Louis, or maybe further west. He could trust Roger to run the businesses based in Chicago. As plans moved forward with his Black Hills resort, he wondered whether or not he should reside out there permanently, but he was unsure if it would be uncomfortable with Ellie there. A month had passed since he had written her the letter, and he had hoped to hear from her, though he hadn't really expected it.

Luke quickly made his way to his business office.

"Good, you're here." Roger dumped a packet of papers on Luke's desk. "These need your perusal and signature if you want to move forward with the resort in South Dakota."

"Did everything go smoothly with the land acquisitions?" Luke sat, slid his reading glasses on, and flipped through the pages. He had decided to purchase one of the tracts of land Ellie had shown him, the one with the view she loved.

"Yes, it did, and the architects competing for the building contract will have their proposals ready in two weeks."

"Perfect." Luke paused as a name on a document caught his eye. He looked up at Roger, who smiled as if holding back a secret. "Meetings in St. Louis to contract beef for the resort?"

"I thought you might notice that." Roger nodded. "And a few of those Spearfish-area ranches look for investors as well. I've asked around and they're fairly safe investments. It's a good way to not only embed yourself further in the Black Hills, but also potentially profit from a ranch investment. With your newfound familiarity with ranches, I was thinking you should be the one to go to the meetings with the representatives."

Luke shook his head and ran a finger over the name on the list. *Ranch: Longbourn Ranch; Representatives: Patrick Gardiner and James Bennett.* "Ellie won't be there."

"Probably not, but if I'm not mistaken, James is her father. It wouldn't hurt for you to be reacquainted with him. See how she's doing, perhaps lay some new groundwork with him."

"If Ellie had read the letter and changed her opinion of me, she would have written back."

"I'm not so sure." Roger sat in the chair across from Luke's desk, leaned back and comfortably rested his feet up on the desk. "The way I see it, you have an opportunity here. Let's assume she read the letter, and I believe she did, as she would be too curious to resist, she has a lot of new information to process and may believe you're through with her. You're bound to see her again, what with the new resort, so perhaps the two of you can start anew and this time, show her the real you. It sounds to me that you acted like the pompous Lucas Callahan we both know you can be

251

at times, when you were in her hometown. Lay down your pride and let her breach those walls you build, like you started to in North Carolina. Your close friends and family know this side of you, let her know it too."

Luke thought for a moment. "What if she still doesn't accept me?"

"She isn't accepting of you now." Roger stood. "What do you have to lose?"

Luke nodded, still uncertain, but Roger was right. If he wanted Ellie in his life, and he still did, he would have to take another chance, which wasn't easy for him to do. The last time he put his heart out there for the cowgirl, she had crushed it.

"Well, then, I suppose I should be on my way to St. Louis." Luke smiled.

~~~~~~

The day before Lindie was to leave to visit the Foresters, Martha held a barbeque to send her off. Though it was smaller than most of the local festivities, Ellie couldn't help but remember Luke. Dancing with him, teasing him, watching the awe on his face when he looked at the majestic Black Hills. She stared into the fire now, so caught up in her memories that she didn't even see Davis Martin sit next to her until he spoke her name.

"Davis, what are you doing here? I thought you were in Oklahoma."

"Actually, I never got farther than Sundance. Found a good job there so I stayed. Just coming back to visit some friends."

"That's nice of you." She wasn't about to ask him about Miss Mary King. Anything out of his mouth was probably a lie anyways. The job in Sundance wouldn't last long either, she'd wager.

"I hear you went down to Asheville. Did you enjoy your time there?" He asked.

"I did. In fact, Luke Callahan and his cousin, Roger Bailey were visiting Biltmore with their aunt and cousin Anne. Have you met Mr. Bailey?"

Davis's initial reaction was shock, then displeasure, then alarm, all quickly covered by his affable nature. "Of course I have."

"He's different from Luke, very pleasant and friendly. I was able to speak with both men at length. Funny thing is, I found that Luke was much friendlier and more talkative as I got to know him better. He's not nearly the arrogant man I once thought him to be." It was true, though she had to admit that she wasn't able to know him as well as she was making it sound. She really just wanted to see how Davis would react.

"Really?" He raised his brow, surprised.

"I mean, the more I got to know him, the more I understood why he acts the way he does."

Davis looked off in the distance, nervousness on his face. "He probably just looks like he's doing what is right, you know, for appearances sake. That's different from actually doing the right thing." He turned back to face her and gave her his most charming smile. "I just hope that in the future, he won't harm others the way he hurt me."

Ellie shook her head and looked into the crackling flames. Davis stood and said his goodbyes, though Ellie got the impression he never wanted to see her again. That was fine with her, as she felt the same way.

253

"*Matthew*, you've known my parents since before they were married, correct?" Ellie asked as they rode along the fence line, making sure there were no vulnerable places where cattle could wander away.

"Ya know I've been on this ranch longer than they've been married, so yes, I have. Why do ya ask?"

"I've just been thinking about my family quite a bit lately and I've been wondering why my parents even got married. Papa gets so annoyed with Mama and she is just...well, she doesn't fit the mold of a rancher's wife at all."

"Yer pa was taken with yer ma in her youth right from the start. Many young men in the county were, but he won her over. Unfortunately, he figured out she had a weak mind and selfish heart too late in the game, no real offense meant to her. She wasn't always the way she is now and she does have good qualities. Yer pa, though, he turned to his books and running this ranch when yer ma started acting like a shrew. I can't really speak for yer ma, but I do believe yer pa does love her, it's just that her foolish ideas don't interest him. He still wants what's best for her and he always wants her to be happy."

"That explains some things, thank you. I've just been very reflective lately."

"That's not a bad thing, Miss Ellie. Not at all." He reached down and took a drink from his canteen. "I hear tell your father's sending you to St. Louis with your uncle."

Ellie immediately brightened. Every summer, her father and Uncle Patrick Gardiner went to St. Louis. Uncle Patrick, being a lawyer, went to meet with business associates and buyers to plan for the next year. This year, because it was their fifteenth wedding anniversary, Aunt Edith, who was originally from St. Louis, would be traveling with them, leaving cousins James and Rachel in the capable hands of the Bennett women.

"Yes, Grandpa Benjamin suggested it. I'm very excited." Though it stung that she would never inherit Longbourn Ranch, Ellie enjoyed doing everything and anything to learn more about the day to day business of running a ranch. She hoped that when the time came, Mr. Sutton would allow her to run the ranch. Perhaps by then, Charlotte would have turned him into a more tolerable man.

"Ya'all be a fine representative for us." Matthew nodded.

"Thank you." Ellie nodded, then noticed a large tree branch that had fallen on the barbed wire fence, pulling the wire from the post. "Well, let's get at it." She dismounted, and it was back to work.

~~~~~

"Luke Callahan." Charles Brantley walked into the parlor of his Chicago townhouse, a smile on his face.

Luke stood. "Sorry to drop in unannounced. I hope you're doing well." Charles looked happy, but Luke could tell he wasn't quite himself.

"As well as can be expected," Charles replied. "What brings you here, my friend?"

"I'm heading home to St. Louis and wanted to see you before I left."

"I'm glad you stopped." Charles sat back and placed an ankle over his knee comfortably.

"I would be lying if I didn't tell you I had some business to discuss with you."

255

"Of course." Charles laughed. "You're usually thinking business. It's likely why people think you unapproachable."

"What makes you say that?" Luke asked, though he had been wondering how he appeared to others.

"Just a comment. My apologies. I meant no harm."

"You never do, Charles. I know that." Luke paused. "In fact, I have been doing some...well...self-evaluation. I have wealth, good friends, a caring family, though I often wonder about my Aunt Madeline." He shook his head. "I enjoy working with my business and I believe I have the respect of many..."

"And you've met many important people, like President Theodore Roosevelt." Charles interrupted.

"Yes, indeed." He smiled at the memory of meeting the man when Luke was a boy.

"So you have the ideal life. I know that, and it's not like you to boast about it. What are you getting at, Luke?"

"Yes, I have all this and yet I'm not content. Not really. God has blessed me with so much and I thank him for it every night. I just feel my life is missing something."

"You were stiff and unfriendly in the Black Hills at first, but later, you seemed to have a...sort of serenity there. Not sure why, but your attitude then took on an immediate change and we left abruptly. Maybe you need another change of scenery."

"That's why I plan on spending most of my time in St. Louis from now on. It's not as wide open as South Dakota, but it's definitely better than New York or Chicago. I'll probably be selling my Chicago home. Though I've also been toying with having Roger completely take over everything here, so perhaps I could sell it or rent it to him."

"Sounds like a good idea." Charles nodded.

"Why don't you come and stay with me the next few weeks." Luke suggested. "I'll have some business to attend to, but Helena would be there to entertain you, and you have other friends and acquaintances in the city to visit."

"I'd enjoy that, Luke, but I promised Isabella and Louisa I would spend time with them this month. They just returned from New York." Charles didn't look excited at the prospect.

Luke wanted to help his friend, but didn't want to spend any extra amount of time with Isabella Brantley. "You're family, Charles, and that means your sisters are always welcome as well." He finally said.

"You're a good friend, Luke." Charles smiled. "I remember when we first met at boarding school. I know it takes a while for you to warm up to people and you still act aloof when you're nervous, but by golly, you've become a true friend. To be honest, I'd really enjoy a trip to St. Louis. I'll talk with Isabella and Louisa and see if they want to spend some time at Hope Gardens. I'm sure they won't be opposed."

"All right, then. I'll make sure rooms are ready for the three of you, unless I hear otherwise." He knew Isabella wouldn't miss an opportunity to spend time with him. "My train leaves this evening. You can all follow when you're ready. Telephone Hope Gardens and tell us what you decide." Luke stood.

"Sounds like a plan." Charles stood as well. "I take it you can't stay for dinner, then."

"Unfortunately, no," Luke replied, "but I look forward to sharing many meals with you at Hope Gardens."

"As do I." Charles smiled.

Part 6: Summer of 1929

Chapter Thirty

St. Louis in late June was splendid, and Ellie felt so lucky that she was able to enjoy two excursions out of South Dakota in less than a year. On her hikes in North Carolina, Luke had told Ellie that St. Louis was in the midst of making many civic improvements, including building many parks and playgrounds. They now had baseball fields and tennis courts in many of the parks as well as two professional baseball teams, the Browns and the Cardinals. The city even had a zoo located in Forest Park, which was the largest park. Ellie wanted to hike through all 1,000-plus acres and learn more of its history, but she also knew she was in the city for business, not pleasure. Luckily, her aunt assured her that there would be some time for leisure while they were there.

As Ellie, her aunt and uncle rode from the train station to the hotel, Aunt Edith talked about some of the activities she wanted to do during their stay in St. Louis.

"My dear, I know you'd like to see Forest Park, but there is a lovely privately-owned conservatory that is open to the public. I've wanted to see it for years." Aunt Edith had grown up in St. Louis, she had been fortunate enough to experience the Exposition and Summer Olympics, both held in 1904. She now wanted to experience some of the newer attractions.

"Of course, that would be lovely." Ellie looked down at the list of meetings she was to attend. Her stomach fluttered at one of the names: Lucas Callahan. She took a steadying breath. Luke was a businessman who had many different holdings, and he had spent time on a ranch, so it made sense that he would at least look into investing in one. She thought about what she would say to Luke if they happened to meet up. He most likely wouldn't be the one attending the meetings. Men like him sent representatives to take care of most of their business. Perhaps it would be Roger Bailey. She wouldn't mind seeing him again.

"My dear, what is wrong?" Aunt Edith had noticed Ellie's reaction to the list.

"Nothing," Ellie shook her head. "I just recognized a name, that's all."

"I see," Aunt Edith gave her a sly look. "A single gentleman, perhaps?"

"Yes, as a matter of fact, Lucas Callahan, I know you've heard of him."

"Of course I have. In fact, the conservatory I'd like to visit, Hope Gardens, is one of his properties. He has a beautiful home on the grounds."

Ellie's heart fluttered. "You didn't mention that."

"I forgot you had even met the man, to be honest."

Not just met. I could be engaged to him, I could have a home in Chicago, practically have a home in Asheville, a home in St. Louis and countless other possible homes across the United States, maybe even the world. I could have a husband who seems to be much more than what I thought.

"I wouldn't worry about seeing him, my dear, if that's the case." Aunt Edith continued. "He's likely not even going to be there. He has employees that maintain Hope Gardens and many assistants to meet with business associates. Men with such fine upbringings seldom do their business without assistants."

"I'm not worried. I realized the same thing," Ellie replied. "Let's go see these magnificent gardens tomorrow after we've settled in." Uncle Patrick had thought it wise to leave a day open in case their travel was delayed, so they had the first day free to themselves.

The next day, Ellie and her aunt and uncle rose early and made sure everything was in order for the rented room they would be using for meetings over the next few days, then they headed out to Hope Conservatory. The drive to Luke's estate was beautiful. The majestic Mississippi River flowed alongside the road and beautiful trees lined the other side. A sense of longing filled Ellie as they approached. If she hadn't trusted the wrong people, like Davis Martin, even for a little while, and if she had allowed herself to get past her own assumptions, could she now be living in this city? In this house?

"Aren't the grounds just delightful?" Aunt Edith commented, and Ellie had to agree. The closer they got to Luke's home, the more nervous she became, and by the time they reached the conservatory building, all she could do was laugh nervously at the splendor of the entire property. Cottages lined the ridge that led down to the river, likely for visiting guests. A very large, brick manor that looked like it belonged in England stood a little bit further up the ridge.

Ellie and her aunt and uncle paid the modest admission to enter the conservatory, and Ellie was immediately swept away. Where it could have

261

been ostentatious, she found its simple elegance to be perfect. Most of the decor was stone with wood accents, and the flowers and other plants were displayed dramatically.

The trio continued to walk through the many rooms and Ellie was more and more impressed. Were all of Luke's properties this tasteful?

They entered a side room where a picture gallery was located. There were some beautiful landscape paintings, as well as some family portraits hanging. Ellie recognized one of the subjects right away and her heart leapt at his image.

"These are portraits of the Callahan family, the owners of the property." A tour guide spoke up.

"Are they good employers?" Uncle Patrick asked.

"Oh, yes, wonderful people. They are most generous, so much so, that all of this can be enjoyed at such a nominal fee. Any visitor can view the surrounding grounds at no cost. Back up the hill a ways, there is even a garden modeled after those in Japan. The family employs many people in St. Louis through their multiple businesses."

"Are the family members here often?" Aunt Edith asked.

"They visit when they can, in fact, I believe Miss Helena is coming to stay for a few weeks and should arrive here soon."

"Does Mr. Callahan make it down here often? From Chicago, that is?" Uncle Patrick remarked.

"Yes, sir, he considers this to be his main home. There have been comments that if he were to marry, he would stay here more often, but I highly doubt he will ever meet a woman good enough to truly deserve him." The man was clearly proud of his employer. "I am simply a tour guide who answers questions and helps visitors, yet he knows me and makes it a point to ask after me and my family whenever he is around. I have never heard him say a cross word to anyone, and everyone I work with agrees. He is most dedicated." The man continued. "There are so many young men nowadays who act wild and think of no one but themselves, but our Mr. Callahan is not like that at all. I have heard some say he is egotistical, but I don't believe it to be so. The only reason someone might say that would be because he has so many responsibilities to concern himself with, he just doesn't have time to flit around."

"Such a fine account of Mr. Callahan." Aunt Edith whispered. "Not quite in line with how Mr. Martin described him."

"Perhaps Mr. Martin was lying to us." She longed to tell her aunt the whole story, but it was not the time nor the place. The guide's words, however, touched a place in Ellie's heart. Luke appeared to treat his employees well, and she already had learned that he was loyal to his friends. It was hard to deny that she really did like him. If she hadn't been so angry with him when he proposed, things could have been so different. She had regretted her sharp words the moment he walked away from her that rainy day at Biltmore.

"He is a handsome man, that is quite evident in these portraits." Aunt Edith stated.

"And more handsome in real life." Ellie said to herself. He looked a bit stuffy in the painting. She was more of the opinion that he looked much better in Levis and a button-up shirt while riding a horse.

After exploring all the rooms indoors, they went outside to walk the grounds. Ellie eventually wandered off on her own to look at the banks of the Mighty Mississippi River. When she turned to rejoin her aunt and uncle, she noticed a green Bearcat parked near the main house. Luke was

263

here? The car hadn't been there when they arrived. She took a few steps back to get a better look and bumped into a solid body. She spun around and looked into the blue eyes of...

"Luke!" Her heart pounded. He looked well, very relaxed and smelled faintly of his root beer barrels.

"Ellie!" He smiled nervously. "I didn't realize you were going to be in St. Louis."

"My aunt, she wanted to see the conservatory and grounds. My apologies, we were told you would not be at home." She tried hard not to stammer and hoped he didn't notice her blush. She glanced down and smiled to see Duchess wagging her tail. She reached down and rubbed her head as Luke continued talking.

"Yes, that is often the case, but this is my childhood home, and I find myself staying here more often of late. I am actually in St. Louis to meet with several representatives from different ranches. I am quite interested in investing and perhaps making some deals with a few of the ranchers for the resort I am building."

"Yes, I saw your name on a list, but I assumed you would send a representative. My father thought it best to send me to meet with the investors this year."

"He's smart to do so, though it does surprise me."

"Grandpa Benjamin suggested it and I believe my father realized it was a wise decision."

"I always felt your grandfather to be a keen man. I like him." Luke smiled nervously. Ellie smiled back. She hadn't realized that he had actually held conversations with Grandpa Benjamin. Luke continued speaking. "How has your trip been so far?"

"We haven't met with anyone yet, we only arrived yesterday, but I have enjoyed being in St. Louis so far. I...I hadn't realized you stayed here so often. I assumed you spent most of your time in Chicago." She stammered. Her heart pounded and her mind forgot everything she had told herself she would say to him if she ever saw him again.

"Actually, the city life..." Luke was interrupted by a smartly dressed young man running up to him from the direction of the house.

"Yes, Zachary, what is it?" Luke asked.

"I'm sorry to interrupt, sir, but we need your assistance in the main house."

"I'll be right there," he replied, then turned to Ellie. "I must take care of this, but perhaps I will see you again while you're here. I'd like to meet your aunt and uncle."

"Yes, of course," Ellie replied.

He leaned in as if to hug her, then hesitated. Instead, he tipped his tan derby hat and sauntered back up the hill, Duchess at his heels. Ellie watched his retreating back, wishing he would have embraced her.

"Ellie, there you are!" Aunt Edith approached and Ellie had to pull her eyes away from Luke. "And who was that fine figure of a man?"

"That would be Luke Callahan," Ellie replied. "He had to attend to some business, but he said that he would like to meet you both before we leave St. Louis."

"I would really enjoy that, so long as it doesn't distress you." Aunt Edith smiled.

"Of course not," Ellie replied. The fact that he had even spoken to her was a miracle, and to be as kind as he had been was more than she could have asked for. They'd had many genuine conversations while in North

Carolina, but she never expected such a sincere greeting based on her reaction to his proposal. If only she could tell what he was thinking, did he still care for her? The more she learned about Luke, the more she regretted how she had treated him in the past.

The Gardiners continued walking and Ellie followed behind. They explored the grounds at a slow, meandering pace, and it wasn't long before Luke and Duchess found them again.

"Ellie, I apologize for having to run off earlier." He reached for her hands, then pulled back, just like he had with the hug earlier. Was he trying to be proper or did he just not want to touch her?

"I understand, Luke, don't worry yourself." Ellie turned and made introductions.

"Mr. Callahan, your conservatory and grounds are simply lovely," Aunt Edith stated.

"Thank you, but I cannot take any of the credit for them. My head groundskeeper and gardeners keep everything in tip-top shape." He smiled. "I am delighted to meet you, both."

Ellie was glad as well, especially since Luke could see that not all of her family was annoying and inappropriate. It made her smile to know that he seemed truly pleased to meet members of her extended family. The conversation between the two men quickly turned to fishing.

"Please, Mr. Gardiner, feel free to come and fish on my property while you're here. There are several access points to the river, but I also have a nice pond on the property that is fully stocked with bluegill, channel catfish, largemouth bass and fathead minnows. I have all the necessary equipment you might need."

"That would be very enjoyable." Uncle Patrick smiled. "Thank you so much for the offer."

"There is also a beautiful Japanese Garden on the grounds, though it is a bit of a walk. Most people rent horses from our stable to get there. They can also pay one of my stable boys to bring them over in a carriage if they don't want to ride. You really should see it." Luke's eyes were drawn to Ellie in a way that made her believe that the offer was clearly for her, as if he wanted her to see it.

Aunt Edith grabbed her husband's arm for support, and Ellie wondered if she was getting tired. They began walking toward the Gardiner's rented roadster. Luke casually walked beside Ellie.

"How is everyone at the ranch?" Luke asked.

"Quite well." She glanced at him and bit her lip nervously. "A few ranch hands left, as they always do. One in particular I think you would be glad to know of." She looked at her aunt and uncle, who were far enough away that she could be discrete. "Thank you for your warning about Davis. I'm glad he's out of our lives. I was wrong about him. I was wrong about a lot."

"So you read my letter?" He asked with a tentative smile.

"I did." She sighed. "Thank you for explaining everything. Many men wouldn't have done so. They wouldn't have taken the time."

"I know I may come across as stuffy sometimes, but I am trying to be better in that regard."

She smiled. "How is everyone in your family?"

"Actually, my sister, Helena will be arriving here tomorrow. She has wanted to make your acquaintance for quite some time." His hand incidentally brushed hers, which sent a pleasant chill up her spine. He drew

267

in a sharp breath, then continued, his hands clasped behind his back. "May I introduce you to her before you leave St. Louis?"

"Of course. I would love to meet her." Ellie smiled.

"I must also tell you that Charles Brantley and his sisters will be arriving with her. I do hope that will be alright."

"It will be nice to see them all again," she said honestly, then felt a pang of disappointment when they reached the Gardener's tan roadster. Her time with Luke was almost over.

"Are you sure you all wouldn't like to stop in for refreshments?" Luke asked as if he were unwilling to part with them. "My cook makes the best strawberry lemonade."

"I wish we could, but Ellie and I have meetings to prepare for," Uncle Patrick replied.

"Then I will be in contact with you later regarding your meeting Helena," He smiled at Ellie, "and I look forward to seeing you again."

"I look forward to it as well." She smiled back and moved to get into the car, but Luke gently grabbed her wrist and lifted her hand to his lips, then kissed her hand as if she were an elegant lady. Ellie tried to slow her breathing, but his nearness made her heart flutter. He smiled and tipped his hat, then headed back to the house.

"What a perfectly delightful gentleman." Uncle Patrick said as he started the roadster.

"There is something quite noble about him." Aunt Edith agreed. "I have heard some people refer to him as pretentious and prideful. I didn't see that at all."

"Why did you lead us to believe he was unpleasant, Ellie?" Uncle Patrick asked.

"I'll be quite honest; I have never seen him so content as I have today." She wanted to tell them more, especially about Davis, but didn't want to betray Luke's trust.

"I was under the impression that Mr. Callahan treated your Mr. Martin poorly." Aunt Edith stated.

"Let me clarify that for you, Aunt Edith! He was never my Mr. Martin." Ellie said a bit too sharply. "And yes, I did say that about Luke, but I know now that I was wrong. A reliable source recently told me that Davis is the one who betrayed Luke."

"My goodness. I must admit that I had a bad feeling about Mr. Martin. He just didn't strike me as a good sort." Uncle Patrick shook his head.

"And I should have listened to my own instincts." Ellie said to herself. She wanted to beg Luke's forgiveness for misjudging him, but she had no idea exactly what to say. She wondered why Luke was so excited to have her meet Helena? He was a very purposeful man, there had to be a specific reason and it certainly piqued her interest.

Chapter Thirty-One

The next day was filled with meetings, and as Ellie and Patrick were leaving the office building that afternoon, she saw Luke outside, leaning casually against his Bearcat. He wore a crisp dark gray suit with a dark green undershirt and the same brown Homburg he had on yesterday. He straightened and smiled when he saw her.

"I think that man is in love with you, Ellie." Uncle Patrick whispered to her.

"What makes you say that?" Ellie asked quickly.

"He is clearly smitten with you. You may take issue with him for whatever reason, but I believe him to be a good man. I've been subtly asking about him around town and he has many dedicated clients and employees, not nary a one spoke poorly of him. In fact, I learned that the infamous Davis Martin left many unpaid debts both here and in Chicago when he left to go west. It was Luke Callahan who made sure they were all taken care of."

"That doesn't surprise me." Ellie murmured as Luke swept the Homburg off his head. She preferred him in a Stetson.

"Ellie! I was hoping you were finished for the day. Can I interest you in a ride to Hope Gardens? My sister has arrived and is beyond excited to meet you. You could stay for dinner." He looked over at Patrick. "Of course you and your wife are invited as well."

"That would be very nice." Ellie tried not to sound too anxious. She immediately turned to her uncle. "As long as you didn't have plans for us, Uncle Patrick."

"Of course not, my dear. You go and have some fun. Fortunately, your aunt and I wanted an excuse to go see some old friends anyways, so we won't be able to join you." He patted her gently on the back and winked. She blushed and turned back to Luke. "So you two go and have a fun time."

"Thank you for the invitation, Luke." He assisted her into the Bearcat before getting in himself, then drove in the direction of Hope Gardens. She felt extremely conscious of the fact that she was riding alone with a man. It wasn't often done, at least socially, and Ellie could no longer deny that she had feelings for Luke.

"I really like your automobile," Ellie said, trying to make small talk. She wasn't an expert, but the car seemed older than what she would expect Luke to be driving.

"Thank you. It's a 1914 Strutz Bearcat."

"I would think you would have a newer model of a car, like Charles."

"I suppose, but this car has sentimental value, and I can't see myself ever getting rid of it. It belonged to my father."

"I see. Sentimentality is not a bad thing." She looked over at him. "May I ask how your parents died?"

He nodded. "My mother died of the Spanish flu towards the end of the epidemic. It was a horrible time for all of us. Helena was only six years old. My father, he died from heart issues. I blame it on the fact that he was

271

always smoking and the doctors do think it was a contributing factor, just like Steven Martin's lung problem. It's another reason I stopped smoking myself."

"You mentioned that in your letter." Ellie commented. "I had noticed you didn't smoke, when most other men do."

"Davis got me addicted when we were in our teenage years. We thought it would make us look older, more sophisticated." He shook his head. "I have to admit, it wasn't easy to quit, even knowing the habit contributed to both my father and Davis's father's deaths. It was Charles who suggested I suck on root beer barrels to help my cravings. Such a good friend." He laughed. "Strange as it sounds, it worked, though now I'm hooked on the root beer."

"I must say, I am glad you stopped smoking. I've always found it a distasteful habit."

"You wouldn't be a good flapper with that attitude." He teased.

She joked back. "Well, now, isn't that just a pity. And here I was trying so hard to be one." She looked around. "There are so many beautiful sights to view."

"That is true. Although, I have been to many cities across the nation and there are many scenic areas but I'd say your Black Hills are incomparable."

She smiled at him. "Do you really believe that?"

"Yes, I do." He smiled back at her. "The company was most pleasant as well."

Ellie knew he was in reference to her, but she couldn't forget his opinions of the rest of the Black Hills community. "Now, I know for a fact

272

you don't really feel that way. You made your impressions about the people in Spearfish quite clear."

He took a deep breath, glanced at her hesitantly, then spoke. "The next time I'm in South Dakota, I would like to see the area they call the Badlands. I was able to drive over to Devil's Tower and it was magnificent, but I really would like to see the Badlands."

"Oh, yes, you really should," Ellie said enthusiastically. "I would enjoy being your tour guide again, when you return to South Dakota. I don't believe you've seen any of our magnificent waterfalls yet either."

"I was hoping you would offer to escort me." Luke's hands seemed to relax on the wheel as he changed the topic. "Have you been able to stroll through Forest Park yet? I believe you would enjoy it very much."

"Not yet, but it is one of the places on my list that I'd like to visit before I leave."

"How would you like to have a picnic there tomorrow?" He asked as they headed closer to Hope Gardens. "You, me, Helena, Charles. Of course, we would have to invite Isabella and Louisa as well, but maybe we'll get lucky and they won't come."

"Yes, that sounds wonderful," Ellie replied, "even if they do decide to come."

"And if you're still here through Sunday, I'd be honored to escort you to church."

"That would be very kind of you. I might take you up on that invitation as well."

They reached the main house and as soon as Luke opened the door for Ellie, a blonde whirlwind darted out and threw herself into his arms.

"Luke!" She hugged him tightly, then turned toward Ellie and shyly tucked a blonde ringlet behind her ear.

"My dear sister, this is Miss Eleanor Bennett. Miss Ellie, I am pleased to introduce you to my sister, Helena Callahan."

"It is so good to finally meet you!" Ellie smiled at the girl. Though she was barely seventeen, she was just as tall as Ellie, and appeared to be graceful and well-mannered.

"Ellie!" Charles walked outside and gave Ellie a quick, friendly hug. "It is so nice to see you! How are you and your family?"

Ellie gave him a brief update regarding her family, which wasn't much, and he told her of his family. He informed her that Isabella and Louisa would be arriving tomorrow.

Luke gave her a complete tour of what he called his 'cottage', which was much larger than her ranch house. The home looked like it belonged in the English countryside, constructed of brown and tan stone. It had a large main entryway, a rounded turret directly to the left, and two wings, one on each side.

When Ellie had entered the home, she immediately felt comfortable. The interior was warmly decorated and elegant, with beautiful wood floors, colorful rugs, and electric lights that looked like lanterns.

One thing was quickly made clear: Helena Callahan and Charles Brantley were not romantically interested in each other at all. He teased her endlessly like an older brother would and she gave it right back to him like a good pesky little sister. Clearly, Isabella Brantley was wrong if she thought her brother wanted to marry Helena.

The four of them sat on the front veranda as they waited for dinner to be served. The house had a beautiful view of the Mississippi River. They spoke on many topics, from the history of St. Louis to Helena's dislike of many of the debutantes at her Chicago boarding school. She was a funny, animated young lady. After a time, Luke excused himself to see to dinner, and Helena left to visit the restroom, leaving just Charles and Ellie. Charles leaned over and rested his elbows on his knees, then clasped his hands together, a forlorn look on his face.

"I…how is Janie, Ellie?"

"As well as can be expected." Ellie wasn't quite sure how to answer. "She recently stayed with my aunt and uncle, the same aunt and uncle I am with right now, and has returned and settled back into her routine."

"I must confess; I miss her terribly. So much so, I cannot go a single moment without thinking of her. I miss her smile, her sweet disposition, her kindness. I miss everything about her. Does she…does she ever mention me?"

"I know she misses you as well." Ellie felt comfortable at least saying that. "She was very…surprised and even hurt when you left. Not that you left, necessarily, but the fact that you left so abruptly. She felt the two of you had become friends, and she thought you would have at least said goodbye." She thought of telling Charles that she knew of Luke's persuasion, but also felt as though that might be disloyal to Luke. The businessman would have to admit it to the lawyer on his own.

"I should have seen her one last time. I just…I heard some things and needed to leave very quickly." He sat back and puffed out a breath. "I suppose I was just too…upset to say goodbye to her. I never meant to hurt her."

But you did. Ellie couldn't say the words aloud. "I believe she still would welcome you back in her life. Perhaps you should write to her. Tell her you miss her and that you would like to renew your acquaintance."

"Perhaps I will." Charles looked up as Luke walked back onto the veranda.

"Luke! I was just telling Ellie how much I miss her family, especially Janie."

Luke glanced at Ellie, as if he was curious about what she had accused him of. She bit her lip and looked away. Charles continued.

"She suggested I write to Janie."

"That…" Luke looked conflicted. Would he admit his mistake now? "That might be a good idea."

The rest of the evening passed pleasantly, and the dinner of roast beef and potatoes was delicious. They returned back to the veranda and chatted about inconsequential subjects. Ellie was glad she had told Charles to write to Janie, but didn't know if he would actually do so. It was good to know that Charles hadn't moved on, as Janie hadn't either.

Before Ellie knew it she had to return to the hotel. Luke offered her a hand up, and she accepted it and stood, and was very pleased when he didn't let go as they walked to the Bearcat. She enjoyed having her hand in his. He had been so kind and attentive the entire time she was with him, and she couldn't wait for the picnic lunch at Forest Park tomorrow.

~~~~~~

"She is absolutely wonderful, Luke." Helena gushed the moment he returned from dropping Ellie off. Charles had left to go to his room for the evening.

276

"You think so?" He asked. He really did value her opinions.

"I do. I really think you should formally court her."

"There would be some difficulties, Helena. For one, I live here, and she lives in South Dakota. I know for a fact she doesn't want to leave there."

"Oh, pish posh. There can be a compromise in regards to that. And don't you dare tell me it will be difficult because she's not in your social class."

"In all honesty, that could cause an issue too." He pointed out. "You're smart enough and old enough to realize that."

"Sure it could, but only if you let it." She shrugged. "I know that Aunt Madeline has her own ideas about who you should marry, and pressures you about it, but she had her chance to get married and she chose Uncle Seth. Now it's your turn to choose for yourself."

"Aunt Madeline won't be the only one to object. Besides, I'm not so sure Ellie wants to be married to a man like me. Can you imagine her in society? She would never be happy in that situation."

"Have you asked her?"

"No, but…"

"Didn't you tell me you wanted to spend less time in Chicago anyways?"

Luke ran a hand through his hair. "Helena, I made some mistakes in the past with her, not saying the right things, doing…" He sighed, flustered. "There is just something about her…I really do like her, a lot, yet every time I'm with her I muck things up. Besides, I don't think she likes me in that way. Maybe we could become friends, but I doubt if we would ever be more."

Helena gave him a teasing smile. "Well, I would like to be friends with her as well. She's fun, refreshing, upbeat and a good listener. Not only that, she doesn't just tell you what she thinks you want to hear. Could you at least refrain from chasing her away?"

He smiled back, unable to be disheartened for long when Helena got it in her mind to tease him. It was good to have her in his life. "Well, I will certainly try not to."

Chapter Thirty-Two

Though Ellie was happy that she was representing Longbourn in St. Louis, today the hours were dragging on while meeting with the potential investors. She was anxious to be done so she could get to the picnic with Luke. It surprised her how much she missed him when they were apart. When had that started?

"I do hope you and Aunt Edith don't mind my leaving again this afternoon," she said as she and Uncle Patrick exited the building.

"Of course not. We were talking last night about how you and Luke remind us of when we were courting. You go off and enjoy yourself. Don't worry about us. It is our anniversary trip, after all."

"Thank you," Ellie replied, then smiled when she saw Luke drive up, right on time. Ellie kissed her uncle on the cheek, and had to refrain from skipping to the Bearcat.

"Successful day?" Luke asked. He was wearing off-white trousers and a matching jacket, a navy blue shirt and a boater hat. "You certainly look lovely and dressed for the part."

Ellie looked down at her outfit: professional in her sensible shoes, black skirt and maroon blouse, all capped off with a maroon straw hat with black accents. Even Lindie would have approved.

"Thank you for saying so, though I am much more comfortable in Levis and a flannel button-up."

"You certainly surprised me the first time I saw you in trousers." He blushed, then changed the subject. "I wanted to give you something." One hand on the wheel, he took the other hand and pulled an envelope from his jacket pocket and handed it to her.

"Another letter?" She smiled.

"Not exactly." He had put the top of the car down, and the wind ruffled his hair as they drove down the road. She had never seen a motion picture, but Lindie and Kathy had magazines with images of movie stars, and Ellie thought Luke looked even better than the heartthrob Rudolph Valentino.

She opened the envelope to see an image of herself, taken by Charles's Brownie camera the day they had gone to Custer State Park.

"Charles gave it to me when he got his pictures developed. I hope you don't mind that I kept it."

"Not at all," she replied, but it did make her wonder. He had clearly kept it because he had been in love with her. What did it mean that he was now giving it to her? She wished she had the fortitude to ask him.

"I hope you don't mind that Helena invited the others along today," Luke commented. "Isabella and Louisa arrived today. Isabella wanted to come to the picnic, but Louisa wasn't feeling up to it."

"No, I don't mind at all. It will be nice seeing the Brantleys again, and I really enjoy being with your sister."

"I'm glad. She likes you too." He smiled. "Though we are early, so we will have some time to walk around before they arrive and set up the picnic."

"I read a bit about the park. How incredible it would have been to be here during the World's Fair."

"I've heard many stories of the Fair from my parents," Luke reminisced. "Both the fair and the 1904 Summer Olympics. They made it sound like it was the most fascinating time to be in St. Louis."

"I agree completely. Aunt Edith actually grew up here in St. Louis and was able to attend both. She has told me many stories." Ellie couldn't help but smile as they entered the park. A memorial to Thomas Jefferson stood near the entrance, and it appeared as though some other structures from the fair had remained also, although she had read that most had been demolished.

"Do you know why some of the buildings were taken down?" Ellie asked.

"I believe it was just to make room for the open area or park structures." Luke replied. "I don't know that I've ever really noticed to be honest."

Luke pulled to a stop and got out, trying to get to Ellie's side before she stepped down. Not used to a gentleman wanting to assist her, she smiled apologetically when she realized what he had attempted to do.

"I must try to remember how different our upbringings have been." He tucked her hand into the crook of his arm. "Not that mine was any better, just different."

"And different can be good," Ellie added. "I am just used to being independent, I do whatever I can for myself."

"Indeed." Luke pulled her over to a small pavilion with a long open window and a counter. "Would you like a root beer float? It's my favorite dessert."

"I would." She smiled. "You apparently enjoy everything root beer."

"That is certainly true." He reached into his pocket and pulled out some of the foil wrapped candy to show her. "My father was a big fan of the flavor, and I believe I told you about how root beer barrels helped me to stop smoking."

"You did. It seems you have inherited a lot from your father," she said after he ordered the two floats.

"He was a man to be admired and I do strive to be more like him. I only wish I could have spent more time with him while he was alive. My mother too."

"I can't imagine the sorrow you must have experienced, losing both of your parents." She shook her head.

"It certainly altered my life, but I believe God has made me a better person through it all." He looked off in the distance. "Before they died, I was so concerned with myself and my own goals and what I wanted. I thought I would have all the time in the world to spend with them."

Ellie thought back to her own mother. Perhaps she should show less annoyance with her when she returned home.

"I remember Mr. Bailey mentioning that you almost competed on the Olympic rugby team. May I ask why you didn't do so?" She thought she knew the reason, but wanted to confirm it. Luke took the two floats from the concessionaire and handed her one of them.

"That's simple. I had to take over my father's business and raise a child. I found I had to grow up quickly and give up childish games."

"I can understand how that is. You may recall I spent a year at the college in Spearfish. I was on the women's basketball team, if you can

282

believe that." They began walking down a gravel-covered path. Ellie took a sip of her root beer float. "Mmmm, this is delicious."

"Yes, it is, and I have no problem believing you were an athlete." Luke smiled. "In fact, I imagine you were quite good, but I have wondered why you only took one year of classes. You're certainly smart enough."

"I suppose it's similar to your circumstances, in a way. Papa had a health scare and I was needed at the ranch." Ellie couldn't help but notice the similarities their backgrounds had. "Grandpa Benjamin tried to take on more of the responsibilities so I could continue with classes, but he just couldn't manage by himself."

"I'm sorry you had to give up your education." He nodded. "If you're still interested in athletics, I should take you to a baseball game. Do you prefer the Cardinals or the Browns?" He named the two professional baseball teams located in St. Louis.

"That sounds like it would be fun. I don't know why, but I tend to cheer for the Browns just a bit more." Ellie smiled. They continued walking. It was a beautiful, sunny day, and the park was relatively busy. People rested on blankets, reading or sharing a picnic lunch. Children ran around, tossing balls and flying kites. Many flowers were in full bloom, creating a riot of color throughout the park and adding a sweet and wonderful scent to the air. They strolled by an ornate limestone fountain, with water cascading gently down, and there was a magnificent entrance to a brick pavilion directly behind it. On the other side of the path was a small lake and boathouse. Beyond that were more bodies of water, glistening in the sunlight, creating a beautiful overall view.

"We're to meet the rest of our party on Picnic Island," Luke said as they turned off the main path.

"Clever name," Ellie quipped.

"Indeed."

"This is truly a beautiful park." Ellie raised her face to soak in the sun. "Though I must say, I prefer Hope Gardens. I like the more natural feel that has been created there. Where did you get it's name?"

"I'm glad you like it. It was named after my mother, Olivia Hope. I will always remember that no matter how bad things got, she always had hope, even at the end." Luke was silent for a moment, then brightened. "You are more than welcome to visit Hope Gardens at any time. I really would like for you to see the Japanese garden. Perhaps you and your aunt and uncle would like to join us for dinner tomorrow."

"I must check on their plans, but that sounds wonderful." Ellie agreed. They continued walking, discussing the ranch and some of Luke's businesses.

"I would also like to introduce you to a man I know who deals in livestock." Luke chuckled. "He has some very interesting animals. My favorite are his goats from Tennessee that will faint when they are startled."

"Fainting goats!" Ellie exclaimed. "I read about them in a husbandry magazine and have always wanted to see one. I thought they might be a very interesting addition to the ranch."

They crossed a bridge and Ellie saw a young blonde woman wading into the water.

"Ellie! Luke!" The girl waved, stepped up onto the bank and skipped over to them.

"Good day, Helena." Ellie smiled as Luke's sister grabbed her arm and pulled her towards the water.

"You must come wading with me," Helena begged. "I asked Miss Isabella, but she doesn't believe it is a very dignified pastime."

It figures she wouldn't, Ellie thought, then smiled at the girl. "Of course I'll go wading. I was just thinking that I needed to cool down."

She went to the blanket that had been laid out and greeted Charles and Isabella. Charles smiled enthusiastically, but Isabella's greeting was as frigid as a South Dakota winter's wind. Ellie ignored the flapper and bent to pull her shoes and stockings off.

"I should have known a woman like you would balk at propriety and go wading in public." Isabella sneered.

Yes, because a flapper like you is all about traditional propriety. Ellie wanted to say the words, but didn't want to ruin the day. The grass tickled her feet as she walked to the edge of the water. Once she stepped in, she smiled at how cool and refreshing it felt. It wasn't long before Luke himself had shed his shoes and stockings, rolled up his trousers and joined them. Ellie was surprised at his lightheartedness. So different from the stuffy man she had met a year ago. Charles soon joined them, once again teasing Helena like she was his younger sister.

Time slipped by quickly and soon, it was time for the picnic lunch. Charles lounged on his side on the blanket, Helena near him, Luke and Ellie shared a large rock for a seat, and Isabella sat in a chair, with a sun umbrella shading her face.

"Helena, my dear, you really should take care to keep your face out of the sun. A tanned complexion is terribly unrefined and will cause skin problems in your future years." Isabella didn't look at Ellie when she said these words, but there was no doubt they were directed at her.

"Really? Miss Ellie has a sun kissed face and she looks beautiful." Helena clearly understood that Isabella was suggesting that Ellie was unrefined but the girl would not let her get away with it. Ellie smiled at her in gratitude.

"I keep meaning to ask, Miss Ellie. I heard one of your favorite ranch hands left South Dakota. Davis Martin," Isabella said with her nose in the air.

Luke clenched his jaw and Ellie immediately looked to Helena. The girl had turned white as a sheet, and sloshed some lemonade onto her dress.

"Oh, Helena, I am so sorry, all the napkins are over here, let me help you." Ellie moved to assist the young woman. Isabella continued talking, oblivious to Luke and Helena's reactions while Charles looked between Luke, Helena and Ellie, a bit curious, but too polite to ask.

"I wonder what your family will do for entertainment now." Isabella continued.

"I expect we'll all just continue on with our lives, just as we always do when a ranch hand leaves." Ellie tried to sound pleasant.

"Yes, but if I recall, your sisters…"

"My sisters all have their own duties to attend to and work hard to keep our ranch running smoothly. We don't have time to be frivolous." She wished that were completely true. She had no idea what anyone in her family was actually doing at this point in time. Janie was undoubtedly doing her part, but Kathy and Maria and…Lindie. She didn't even want to think about her. Was she behaving herself with the Foresters?

Luke took Ellie's hand in his once she sat back down, then spoke. "I'm not sure if I mentioned this, but Ellie is here in St. Louis on behalf of her father, conducting business."

286

"Well, isn't that progressive." Isabella's jealousy was obvious. "I suppose when you realize your luck has run out in regards to catching a husband, you must throw yourself into your work, even if it is considered to be a man's occupation."

"Don't be ridiculous, it's almost 1930, Isabella," Charles spoke up. "Many women are stepping out of their traditional roles and excelling at it."

"And just because they do so, doesn't make them any less of a woman." Luke squeezed Ellie 's hand. "In fact, I believe it makes them so much more."

Isabella sputtered and clamped her mouth shut. Charles, Helena and Luke ignored her, so Ellie did as well, enjoying the company of the three.

Before long, it was time to pack up and leave. Helena left with the Brantleys after making Ellie promise she would come to Hope Gardens for dinner tomorrow. Luke and Ellie took the long way back to his car. He remained reflective and continued to tell her more history of the park, as well as improvements he knew were being planned. Once they reached his vehicle, they continued to speak on a variety of subjects as he drove her back to the hotel.

"Would you mind taking a quick stroll through the gardens here?" Luke asked. It was still light out and Ellie couldn't find her uncle's car in the parking area, so they were probably still out and about.

"I would enjoy that," Ellie replied. He helped her out of the car and once again clasped her hand in his. They walked in comfortable silence.

"I apologize for the way Isabella treated you today. Her behavior was rude and inexcusable, but you handled it well."

287

"I happen to remember a time when your behavior was rude and inexcusable." Boldly, yet playfully, she leaned over and nudged him with her shoulder. He stopped and pulled her to face him.

"Then I must apologize for my behavior when we first met. You intimidated me, Ellie." He reached up and brushed a strand of hair from her cheek, then stepped closer.

"I can't imagine why an important businessman like yourself would be nervous around little ole' me." Her heart pounded at his nearness.

Luke slid his hand down to her cheek and his other hand held hers as he gazed into her eyes.

"From the very moment I first saw you, you captured my interest, Ellie. Your eyes captivated me and I was under your spell." He leaned down and kissed her. She pulled back slightly and looked into his eyes, then moved a hand up to his cheek when she heard her name called.

"Ellie, are you back here?" Aunt Edith's voice cut through the garden. Ellie reluctantly dropped her hand, her heart pounding.

"Yes, Aunt Edith." She turned and walked toward the voice, with Luke right behind her. He reached for her hand and they continued together. Aunt Edith smiled when she saw the two.

"Ah, there you are. Beautiful garden, is it not?" The older woman commented.

"Yes, ma'am." Luke focused on Patrick, who had followed his wife. "Mr. and Mrs. Gardiner, I would like to invite you both to dinner tomorrow evening."

"We would be delighted to join you. Thank you for the invitation." Uncle Patrick nodded.

"I would also like to escort Ellie to the Browns baseball game. They play in the afternoon and Ellie mentioned you only have morning appointments." Luke squeezed her hand.

"I think that would be fine, as long as Ellie wants to go." Patrick replied.

"Oh, yes. I've already told Luke I would enjoy it immensely." Ellie smiled.

"That all sounds well and good, then." Patrick stated.

"Until tomorrow." Luke smiled and kissed the hand he still held. Ellie blushed.

"Until tomorrow."

Chapter Thirty-Three

"This is a very large stadium. I have never seen a professional field before. It's amazing." Ellie looked around wide-eyed as they walked into the park. It was a sunny, humid day, and Ellie had chosen to wear a lightweight orange blouse with a brown skirt and a simple straw hat with an orange and brown ribbon around it.

"It is." Luke nodded and couldn't help but appreciate the fact that she had worn the team colors. "The team owner, Philip Ball was so confident the Browns would be playing in the World Series soon, he wanted to be prepared, so he expanded the park a couple of years ago,"

Ellie thought back. "Was it built the year the Cardinals upset the Yankees for the championship?"

"It was indeed, so the World Series was played at Sportsman Park, just as Mr. Ball predicted." The stadium was home to both the Browns of the American League and the Cardinals of the National League.

Ellie looked around, taking in the scene, her eyes shining with excitement. Spectators walked around, buying food, souvenirs and finding their seats. The air smelled of roasted peanuts and popcorn. Ellie had never experienced anything like it.

"Is this your first time at a professional baseball game?" Luke asked.

"Yes, it is. I love athletics, but unfortunately, I haven't been in a position to be a Katie Casey."

Luke laughed and reached over to take her hand in his. Katie Casey was the subject of the popular baseball song, *Take Me Out to the Ball Game*. "Come, I will buy you some peanuts and crackerjacks." As they walked to the vendor, he couldn't help but sing.

> *Katie Casey was baseball mad,*
> *Had the fever and had it bad.*
> *Just to root for the home town crew,*
> *Ev'ry soul Katie blew.*
> *On a Saturday her young beau*
> *Called to see if she'd like to go*
> *To see a show, but Miss Kate said "No,*
> *I'll tell you what you can do:"*
> *Take me out to the ball game,*
> *Take me out with the crowd;*
> *Buy me some peanuts and Cracker Jack,*
> *I don't care if I never get back.*
> *Let me root, root, root for the home team,*
> *If they don't win, it's a shame.*
> *For it's one, two, three strikes, you're out,*
> *At the old ball game.*

As he sang, Ellie smiled and looked at Luke as if she had never seen him before. "I never would have imagined I would hear you sing any song, much less that one."

"I don't do it often. Helena received all the musical talents in the family."

"I'm sorry to say, you are right." Ellie teased, then covered her mouth in mock horror. "I'm so sorry, I forgot the formidable Mr. Callahan cannot be teased." He stopped and pulled her to face him.

"Ellie Bennett, you can tease me whenever you'd like. I will not take offense."

She gave him an admiring look, and if they hadn't been in public, Luke would have kissed her. She must have known what he was thinking, because she blushed, then stepped away. Luke held her hand, then stepped in line to buy snacks and a souvenir program.

Ellie shielded her eyes as she surveyed the field below. "You said we were playing the team from Detroit?"

"Yes, the Tigers. We have a good chance of winning." He handed her the program and led her to their seats, which were in the first row, right behind home plate. Being friendly acquaintances of the team owner had its perks.

"Luke, this can't be where we're sitting." She grabbed his arm, brown eyes in shock.

"Why can't it be?"

"The tickets must have been far too expensive."

"You are worth any expense." Luke smiled, and he meant it. He would give just about anything to make Ellie happy. If only he didn't have concerns about some economic warning signs and breaks in the stock market. Steel production was declining, automobile sales were down and many people were building up high personal debts because it was so easy to buy on credit. Luke felt lucky that his father had instilled in him the value of not owing money to anyone.

Ellie looked at him as they sat down, feeling unsure of his statement. Luke wished he could tell her his true feelings. She seemed much more open to a courtship with him, but he was still hesitant. The last time he bared his heart to her, it was crushed. Perhaps with a little more time...

"When will you be going back to Spearfish?" He knew he had his official meeting with Ellie and Patrick the next day, but beyond that, he wasn't sure of their plans. The day after tomorrow was Independence Day, and would be another good opportunity to spend time with the Callahan family.

"The middle of next week," Ellie replied. Was it his imagination, or did she sound sorry about that? "And I suppose it will be time. I'm not used to sitting around so much. I'll get back to the ranch and not know how to work." She spoke in a teasing voice again.

"True, the walking you've been doing here isn't nearly as strenuous as the paths of the Pisgah Forest."

"Let's PLAY BALL!" The umpire who would be calling balls and strikes yelled out, and the first batter stepped into the box.

"I can definitely tell." Ellie glanced at Luke, then snuck a Cracker Jack from the box he held. He smiled. "Though the parks here are beautiful."

"Did you bring an athletic outfit? If you'd like, I can get access to the local high school gymnasium and we can play some basketball. I would like to see your skills in action. If you didn't, you could borrow some of Helena's and I'd be happy to find you a pair of Converse shoes in one of the stores around here." He smiled at her again. "Unless you're afraid it would be too scandalous to play against a man."

"Only if you won't be scandalized when I win. If you're going to be so generous as to buy me shoes, I'd like a pair of the new Chuck Taylor All-Stars."

Luke laughed. He did enjoy it when Ellie baited him. So few people stood up to him. "Ha! Aren't you the confident one."

"I'm not overconfident, I just know my abilities." She grinned.

"Well then, I look forward to the challenge." He was athletic, but basketball wasn't one of the sports he played a lot. He did have a group of friends who occasionally got together to play for fun and exercise, but she just might beat him.

"Oh, I will give you quite the challenge."

He offered her some more Cracker Jacks and she accepted.

"I believe the advertisements are correct. 'The more you eat, the more you want.'" She popped the molasses-flavored, caramel-coated popcorn into her mouth.

He nodded, and they watched the game for a while, talking about the plays and the players. When the third inning had ended, Ellie turned to Luke.

"I would like to thank you so much for today, as well as the past few days." She sounded a bit nervous. Why was that?

"You are more than welcome, Ellie. I've enjoyed the time we've spent together." They seemed to have an unspoken agreement to not discuss the past, especially the last time they saw each other in North Carolina. Part of him wanted to ask, but he didn't want to spoil what they were enjoying at the moment. They had a new start and he wanted to do everything right this time.

"Luke, I…"

The sharp crack of the bat hitting the ball interrupted her and shouts of 'heads up!' caused Luke to stand and look around to find the foul ball. He saw it dropping down, right over Ellie, who had gotten to her feet also. She jumped out of the way just as he grabbed her to pull her to safety. The leather, yarn and rubber ball bounced on the concrete right where Ellie had been. The quick motions almost knocked them both over. Luke grabbed her waist to steady them.

"Are you all right?" He looked right into her chocolate brown eyes.

"Yes, yes I am. My, that was exciting!"

Luke loosened his grip on her and she stepped away. He looked around for the ball, but it had already been tossed back. The pitcher and batter took their stances on the field as play resumed and Luke and Ellie sat back down again.

"If I had one of those cowhide gloves, I could have caught that ball." She commented.

"I have no doubt." He smiled. "Did you play baseball growing up too? I would guess that you enjoyed the sport."

"I did, actually." She nodded. "My grandfather Benjamin loves the game. He could have probably played professionally, but it wasn't much of an option at the time."

Luke nodded as Ellie continued speaking.

"I grew up playing catch with Grandpa and my father. I also played in the schoolyard with a bunch of the boys."

"I'm sure you kept up with them with no problems," Luke replied.

"I could out-play, out-rope and out-ride most of them." She answered, then frowned. "In fact, my sister Lindie would say that is one of the many reasons I'll never find a husband." She popped some more Cracker Jacks in her mouth.

"Well, all I can say is that those men missed out on something special and your sister doesn't know what she's talking about."

Ellie stared at the field, but Luke couldn't tell if she was engrossed in the game or lost in thought. He suspected that Lindie had treated Ellie like a social misfit, but it was surprising just how much Ellie seemed to believe it.

Just as she was about to speak again, the St. Louis batter, Wally Schang connected with the ball and a powerful crack was heard. As soon as it was hit, the crowd rose to their feet in excitement. The ball flew over the fence.

"Home run!" Ellie exclaimed loudly, jumping up and down, clapping her hands, a huge smile on her face. Luke cheered along with the crowd as the batter ran around the bases.

"Nothing more exciting in a baseball game than a home run!" He exclaimed.

"I don't know; I like it when the fielder dives to the ground to catch the fly ball." She replied. Luke wasn't sure if she was teasing him or not, but he smiled.

"That's exciting as well."

They sat back down as the next batter stepped up to the plate.

"Does Helena enjoy baseball?" Ellie asked.

"She'll come to a game or two every summer with me, but doesn't really follow any sport. Though Wally is her favorite player to watch when we're here." They were back to talking about family, a bit more impersonal than what they had been discussing earlier. *How could she feel unworthy of attention from a man?* Luke thought to himself. She was wonderful.

Chapter Thirty-Four

For the rest of the game, Ellie and Luke talked about small inconsequential subjects, simply enjoying being in each other's company. Unfortunately for the home team, Detroit played a better game and beat the Browns ten runs to four.

"I thought you said the Browns had a good chance of winning." She teased as they walked out of the park.

"We have three more games in the series," he replied. "They'll come ready to play tomorrow."

"If you say so." Ellie grinned. They were almost to Luke's car when she noticed a well-dressed man about twenty feet away. She squinted to see him better, as he looked familiar.

"Do you know that man?" Luke asked. Did he sound just a bit jealous?

"I do believe he looks like Clark Mercer." She looked back at Luke. "He...well, he...you might not remember the conversation back during the Austin barbeque, but my mother was going on and on about how everyone loves Janie and she mentioned Mr. Mercer."

"Ahh, yes. The man who wrote Janie a special song." A flash of understanding hit Luke's face as Mr. Mercer looked at Ellie. Recognition lit in his eyes and he approached the couple.

"Well, well, if it isn't Miss Eleanor Bennett." He smiled. "I'm not sure if you remember me or not, but I met you a few years back."

"Yes, of course. Mr. Mercer. How are you?" He looked well. Tall, handsome, a smooth-shaven face with dark blonde hair and a strong jawline.

"I'm quite well, thank you." He replied.

"Are you still with the government, overseeing the parks?" Ellie asked.

"Yes, I have been moving up quite nicely in the Department of the Interior."

"Good for you." Ellie finally remembered her manners. "I'm so sorry, Mr. Clark Mercer, this is Mr. Lucas Callahan." The two men shook hands.

"Mr. Callahan, your reputation precedes you." Mr. Mercer stood as tall as he could.

"A pleasure to meet you, Mr. Mercer." Luke nodded.

"And how is your lovely family, Miss Bennett? Is Miss Janie doing well?"

"Yes, yes, she is." Ellie glanced over at Luke, who frowned slightly. "She's home at the ranch, as is the rest of my family. Not much has changed over the past two years." Mr. Mercer had spent two months in the Black Hills, surveying the land for the government.

"I am glad to hear that."

299

"Is there anything new in your life? I don't recall you being from St. Louis. Do you have family here?" Ellie wanted to leave, as Clark Mercer had always made her feel edgy for some reason, but she had to be polite.

"My main focus is always on business, Miss Bennett."

"I suppose that's what brings you to town, then?" Luke rested his hand on the small of Ellie's back-dare she hope-possessively?

"Yes, there is plenty of land in Missouri that would be good for the national government to acquire." Mr. Mercer nodded.

"That is certainly true." Ellie nodded.

"Well, I must be going. It was good seeing you again, Miss Ellie." Mr. Mercer ended the conversation quickly. "Will you be in St. Louis long? It would be nice to catch up in more detail."

Ellie's stomach churned. "It would be nice, yes, but unfortunately, my schedule is booked solid until I leave."

"A pity." He nodded. "Perhaps next time I am in the Badlands or around the area, I can call on the family."

"Of course. Until then, Mr. Mercer." Ellie nodded, then steered Luke to his automobile.

"You seem a bit anxious, if I may make that observation." Luke helped Ellie into the Bearcat, started it, then drove off. There was quite a bit of congestion on the road to her hotel, so the ride home took longer than expected. Ellie didn't mind the extra time she could spend with Luke.

"I just never liked Mr. Mercer much, to be honest. There is something about him that I could never put my finger on. In fact, I'm the one who kind of...steered Janie away from him." Her cheeks warmed. She had gotten drastically upset with Luke for doing the exact same thing for Charles. She glanced at him, worried about what he would say. He had every right to call her on it. He glanced at her, but only had understanding in his eyes.

"Sometimes, it's important that we step in to help the people we care about."

She smiled, thankful for his benevolence. He pulled onto a main road and picked up speed.

"I don't mean to sound judgmental, but there is just something about him. Like I said, I never trusted Mr. Mercer." Ellie continued. She looked over at Luke again, and he looked concerned.

"Luke, what's wrong?"

He pressed the brake pedal, but nothing happened.

"Luke?"

"We're not slowing down." He was trying to remain calm.

Ellie's heart pounded as she gripped the door handle. Thank goodness the road they were on was relatively empty. Luke honked the horn, warning others away.

"Ellie, hold on!" Luke shouted, and she moved to grab his arm with her other hand. People died in car accidents, she knew that.

"Lord, be with us." She prayed.

Luke tried to get the car under control and her heart almost stopped when she saw a brick building right in front of them.

"Luke!" She squeezed her eyes shut. He jerked the wheel to avoid the building, and the car began to tip.

"Ellie!" The car somehow righted itself, but slammed into a bushy tree. Ellie was thrown forward and her head cracked on the dashboard. She fell to the floor. The car had finally stopped, but what damage had been done?

"Luke?" She tried to push herself back onto the seat, but her wrist had bent backwards against the dashboard and couldn't support her.

"Ellie, are you all right?" Luke had also been thrust forward but the steering wheel prevented him from hitting the dashboard as hard as Ellie had. Blood trailed from a small scrape on his forehead and she knew right away that his ribs would be bruised, perhaps even cracked.

"I am." She mustered all her strength and pulled herself back onto the seat.

"Do you two need a doctor?" A man in a tan suit ran up to them.

"Yes, we do." Ellie cringed at the pain in her wrist. Luke reached over and wiped his thumb against her temple and it came away red.

"You're bleeding, Ellie." Luke groaned. Some other people gathered around the car and helped both Ellie and Luke out. They assisted them over to the grassy lawn next to the road.

"Oh, Luke, your father's car." She didn't know much about automobiles, but with the smashed front end and shattered glass windshield, she doubted if it could be repaired.

"It's just a car, as long as you're safe. That's all that matters."

She nodded. A crowd had gathered and a police officer pushed his way through to them.

"Mr. Callahan?" He looked surprised. "Are you quite all right? I never thought you to be a careless driver."

"It wasn't Luke's fault." Ellie said to the policeman as a doctor pushed through the crowd and knelt in front of her.

"What do you mean?" The officer asked. The doctor began examining Ellie. He wiped her forehead with gauze he must have kept in his bag and bandaged the cut, then moved to examine her wrist. She jerked

302

slightly when he took her hand in his. Her wrist was at least sprained; she just knew it.

"The brakes stopped working." Luke explained. "We were leaving the Browns game and everything was fine until we turned onto this street. I pushed the brakes to slow down and they just stopped working."

The policeman frowned. "I suppose we'll have to check that out."

"Do you have pain anywhere else?" The doctor asked Ellie as he wrapped her wrist.

She shook her head. "Not that I can feel at the moment." The doctor nodded and moved on to help Luke.

Ellie rubbed her forehead, which was very tender, and she felt the beginnings of a goose egg. Her heart rate finally slowed down and she felt tears threaten. The accident easily could have been much worse, even deadly. "Thank You, Lord, for keeping everyone safe."

The crowd began to disperse, and soon, Luke and Ellie were left with the police officer, whom Ellie learned was Officer Joe Kopfensteiner, and the doctor, Vilray Blair.

"You should both be just fine, though neither of you should be alone for the next day or so in case you become lightheaded or dizzy. You could even pass out. I'm worried you may have head injuries that I can't see." Dr. Blair began repacking his bag.

"That won't be a problem, I have family with me and Ellie has her aunt and uncle." Luke reached into his suitcoat to pull out his leather wallet. "Can I pay you for your services?"

"No, no thank you." The doctor waved his hand. "But please be sure to follow up at the hospital if any of your symptoms change or worsen."

The officer had been examining the automobile. "You won't be able to drive this, but we'll have it moved to a garage to get looked at and be repaired. I'll drive you both to your homes."

"Thank you," Luke nodded and slowly got to his feet, then bent and helped Ellie up. "I'm so sorry about all this, Ellie," he said as they went to the police vehicle.

"It's hardly your fault, Luke," she tried to assure him. "Accidents happen. You were driving quite cautiously."

"I'm not sure your aunt and uncle will feel that way." He helped her into the police vehicle.

"No need for you to worry about it. I know the truth and they'll believe me."

"I hope so, Ellie. I do hope so."

Chapter Thirty-Five

Luke picked up Ellie after her business meeting the next day and took her back to Hope Gardens. She had enjoyed meeting with him earlier in the day for business, and it was kind of fun acting professionally when Luke was smiling at her personally the whole time. He had told her the mechanic had assured him that, while it might take a while, his car would be fixable. In the meantime, he had another vehicle that he was driving, a maroon car with a top and backseat.

"I don't know much about cars, but this seems like another nice one. Newer than the Bearcat, I would think."

"It is. This is a 1927 Willys Overland Whippet." Luke smiled.

"These cars all have such fun names." Ellie commented.

"They do indeed." He nodded. "The Brantley's will be having dinner with some relatives who live in the area, so will not be around tonight. Just your aunt and uncle, Helena and the two of us."

"That will be fun," Ellie said. Aunt Edith and Uncle Patrick would be arriving at Hope Gardens later for dinner.

"Did you learn anything more about the accident?" Ellie asked.

"I was able to speak with Officer Kopfensteiner today and he reported that they believe someone purposely cut the wires that make the brakes work."

Ellie's stomach fluttered. She hadn't even realized that was possible, though she probably should have. Luke's car had been sabotaged?

"Luke?" She said quietly, tracing the bandage around her wrist. "Do you think...is it possible that all these things are connected?"

He tapped the steering wheel. "That has crossed my mind." He took a deep breath. "The cows killed and lit on fire, the shooting at Biltmore, the accident yesterday."

"Naomi being poisoned." She added, then frowned. Had she even told him about that?

"What happened to Naomi?" Apparently, she hadn't.

"Someone mixed green potatoes in her food. That can kill a horse. Luckily, my grandfather's Uncle Aaron was a doctor, so Grandfather Benjamin knew how to help her."

"Ellie, I am so sorry." He reached over and took her hand in his. "I know how important your horse is to you."

"It was bad at the time, but she's healthy now. I just don't understand how or why these things would all be connected and who would be responsible."

Luke's forehead scrunched just a bit in thought.

"What are you thinking, Luke?"

"I don't want to speak out of turn, and I have no real proof, but do you think it could be Davis? Perhaps he learned you and I were getting friendly and didn't like that."

"Possibly, but while that would explain the things that happened at Longbourn Ranch, it doesn't make sense in North Carolina or even here. Davis doesn't have the funds to be able to travel that much."

"True. Besides, I don't want to believe he's capable of something this despicable." He sighed. "I just can't think of anyone else who would want to hurt me."

"I suppose it's possible they could all be isolated events." She nodded. "I just don't know, Luke."

"Well, Sergeant Kopfensteiner is a good man. He'll look into the accident here, unfortunately, I don't believe he'll really be able to find any evidence to bring a charge."

"Let him know he can ask me any questions he has, even though I may not be of much help."

"I'll tell him."

She hesitated, then asked, "How do you usually celebrate Independence Day?"

He grinned. Was it obvious that she wanted to spend time with him tomorrow? "We usually celebrate at our home. A nice barbeque outside by the river, perhaps swimming in the pond, horseback riding. We have a good view of the city's fireworks as well."

"It sounds like a lot of fun." She hoped she didn't sound as if she was begging for an invitation, but she wanted any excuse to spend more time with the man beside her.

Luke glanced at her out of the corner of his eye and chuckled. "Ellie, it would be my honor to have you and your aunt and uncle over to celebrate the day with Helena and the Brantleys and I. As long as you don't have any other plans, and want to, of course. You don't have meetings, correct?"

307

"No, there are no meetings because of the holiday. She nodded and smiled. "And I'll have to ask Uncle Patrick and Aunt Edith, but I believe they would enjoy another day at your beautiful gardens."

Luke pulled up near the entrance of his home and turned to her. He reached up and ran his finger across the bandage on her head. "I'm so sorry if I'm the one that brought all this trouble on you."

"I'm not convinced it's your fault." She smiled, hoping he wouldn't blame himself. He smiled back.

"You're too kind." He leaned forward as if to kiss her, but jumped away when a door banged close.

"Luke! There you are!" Helena's voice cried out. "Oh, Miss Ellie, I'm so glad you're here. Luke told me all about your horrible accident, I am so glad your injuries weren't serious."

Luke sighed and stepped out of the car, then helped Ellie out. She smiled to herself. It would be a most enjoyable evening; she was just sure of it.

~~~~~~

"And over here are some hydrangeas." Helena ran ahead to point out beautiful bushes clipped into neat mounds with large pink flowers. Ellie leisurely walked next to Luke, who kept his hands clasped behind him as Helena gave her the tour of their Japanese gardens. Duchess followed obediently behind them. It was Independence Day, so Ellie and her aunt and uncle were able to spend the entire day with the Callahans. Charles and Uncle Patrick were fishing at the stocked pond, and Aunt Edith was relaxing and reading in one of the gardens near a fountain. Isabella and Louisa had decided to enjoy the celebration in the city.

Just as they were about to cross a pretty wooden arched bridge, one of the men who worked for Luke hastened down the path.

"Mr. Callahan!" He came nearer. "There's a telephone call for you up at the house."

Luke turned to Ellie with a slight frown. "I am so sorry."

"I understand," Ellie said as Helena came and stood next to her.

"I'll watch out for her, Luke." She smiled and took Ellie's arm.

"I'll be back as soon as I can." Luke nodded and followed the young man back up towards the carriage that had brought them down to the garden.

"Now I finally have you to myself, we can have a girl talk." Helena smiled. They began walking down the path again.

"Indeed." Ellie smiled back. She greatly enjoyed spending time with this young woman. It was refreshing to talk with someone so much more mature than her younger sisters. "What would you like to talk about?" She thought the questions would be about Luke, but Ellie was surprised when the girl asked about someone else.

"Did you fall in love with Davis Martin as I did? Or were you smarter than me? Luke didn't really go into detail when he talked about you and Davis, but I could tell he worried that something would happen between the two of you."

Ellie wasn't quite sure how to answer, knowing what she did about Helena's history with the man. She decided to just be honest.

"He is extremely charming and I must admit that I did have thoughts on whether he was the man I might one day marry. He paid attention to me in a way that men really haven't in my past. I'm not terribly popular with the men back home, at least romantically."

"I simply don't understand why that's the case." Helena shook her head. "You're simply beautiful, inside and out."

"Thank you for saying so." Ellie smiled. "Anyways, I did become enamored with Davis and at first, I believed the lies he told, especially the ones about your brother. The fact that Luke didn't exactly make a good impression when we met certainly helped validate what Davis was saying about him."

"Luke rarely makes a good first impression." Helena shook her head.

"I was already a bit negative regarding Luke from our first meeting. I should not have been, and I should never have listened to Davis. But he knew just what to say to sway me towards his way of thinking. I can see how any girl would be taken in by his charm."

"That's comforting to hear." Helena frowned.

"Oh, Helena, you're young. Don't fret, you'll find a man who truly deserves you." Ellie assured her.

"Like you did."

"Helena…"

"Oh, you don't have to tell me anything. I can tell by the way you look at Luke that you love him."

"I do care for him." Ellie looked down, blushing.

"Well, he cares for you as well." Helena smiled. Before they could discuss anything else, Charles came around a bend.

"By golly, I finally found you! Come now, it's almost time for dinner!"

"We'll be right along, thank you, Charles." Ellie smiled as she and Helena headed back to the pond on the grounds where Luke's staff had set up the picnic.

"Goodness, what a spread!" Ellie exclaimed when she saw all of the food laid out on a lightweight table. Deviled egg sandwiches, potato balls, green peas, cucumber salad and raspberry flavored ice cream for dessert. They all ate their fill, and when he was finished, Uncle Patrick leaned back and placed his hands on his stomach. "What a delicious meal!"

"Delicious meal, beautiful landscape, splendid company." Aunt Edith agreed, then sipped some of her strawberry lemonade. "Thank you so much, Mr. Callahan. You have been such a wonderful host today."

Ellie smiled and slid her hand across the picnic blanket to touch Luke's fingers. "It's been wonderful spending time with you all week." She agreed.

"And successful from a business standpoint, I hope." Luke squeezed her hand.

"Yes, indeed." Uncle Patrick nodded. "Benjamin was very forward-thinking, sending Ellie this year. A good businesswoman and a good rancher."

"It's criminal that you can't inherit your own ranch." Helena frowned.

Ellie looked over at Luke who shrugged. "I did tell her about your unfair situation, and I agree with her assessment."

"No one quite understands it." Uncle Patrick agreed. "But I'm sure Mr. Sutton will keep Ellie around when the time comes. He'd be an imbecile not to."

"Thanks to all of you for your support." Ellie smiled.

"Perhaps someday Luke will get involved in ranching and buy a spread and he can hire you to run it." Charles offered.

"That's an idea." Luke smiled at Ellie in a way that made her believe that one day they could indeed have a future together.

𝒟arkness fell and Luke, Ellie, Charles and Helena settled on a bluff that overlooked the Mississippi River as the fireworks began. Uncle Patrick and Aunt Edith had left earlier, as they were both feeling tired. Ellie suspected that Helena was attempting to play matchmaker, as she had pulled Charles to a blanket that was a good fifteen feet from Ellie and Luke's. Luke leaned against a tree and hesitated, then pulled Ellie close.

"I hope you enjoyed yourself today." Luke stated after a bang and blast of color filled the air.

"I did." Ellie smiled. "Thank you so much for inviting me and my family. I have enjoyed every minute of this trip." *Especially the time spent with you.* Why couldn't she say what was in her heart? Another firework exploded.

"I'm so happy to hear that," he answered, "and I know Helena has enjoyed getting to know you."

"She is the sweetest of girls. She could teach our Lindie a thing or two."

Luke chuckled. "So tomorrow is your last day here. What are your plans?"

"One more round of meetings." Ellie replied. "But we should be done by mid-afternoon. I still need to pack, however." Her heart sank just a bit at the thought of leaving St. Louis, but she did miss the ranch, her family, and being home.

Luke shifted just a bit, then spoke again. "Would you like to celebrate your successful trip in the evening?"

"That would be very nice." Ellie nodded. "Although I'm still not sure just how successful we've been. Will Callahan Enterprises be striking up a partnership with the Longbourne Ranch?"

"Oh, I think the owner of that company was extremely impressed by you." Teasing was in his voice. "I believe he can be persuaded to help a ranch that is run by such a competent young woman."

Ellie smiled. "Thank you." A thought occurred to her. "Though I wouldn't want you to invest just because...well, because you and I are friends."

Luke adjusted himself so he could look her in the eye. "Ellie, I like you, a lot, and as your...friend...I would help you in any way. But I am not going to invest in your ranch just because of that. I want to do so because it will be a good, solid investment. Any smart businessman would want to do the same."

She smiled, humbled by his kind words. "Thank you, Luke." His nearness made her heart pound. Or perhaps it was the fireworks bursting all around them.

"You're most welcome." He leaned over as if he was going to kiss her, but then hesitated and pulled back. "Now, about tomorrow. I would like to take you down to hike at the Cliff Cave trails. It's a natural cave located nearby, surrounded by woodlands, wetlands, and rocky hillsides and is near the Mississippi River. It will be challenging, but I know you'll be up to the task."

"Sounds like a perfect way to end the trip." Ellie turned just in time to see dozens of fireworks blasting through the air. The grand finale. Her heart sank. She no longer had a reason to stay in Luke's arms. Helena and

Charles stood and began to fold up their blanket, but Luke seemed just as reluctant to bring her home as she was to be leaving.

Helena skipped over as Ellie and Luke finally stood.

"Miss Ellie, I know you leave tomorrow, but you must come and say goodbye."

"Of course I will, Helena." Ellie pulled the girl into a hug. "Your brother is taking me hiking tomorrow, so I will insist that we have dinner with you and Charles."

Helena nodded. "That will be just splendid."

"Yes, it will be." Ellie said her goodbyes to Charles as well, then she and Luke went to his car. Once they were on the road, Ellie thought back on everything that had happened during this trip. Luke interrupted her thoughts.

"Ellie, when you get home, you need to talk to your father, grandfather, Matthew Shaw, and Sheriff Ingraham. They all need to be aware of what happened here with my car and in North Carolina when we were shot at."

"I had been trying to forget those things." Ellie admitted.

"I'd like to as well, but the fact of the matter is, someone is out to get either me or you. I have a feeling it's me, no one would ever want to hurt you, but I would feel much better if they knew. I believe once you tell your father and grandfather, they will insist you tell the sheriff. It would be wise if they all knew."

"You're right, of course." Ellie shuddered to think of what was happening. The night had been so pleasant that she really hadn't thought of the danger. "I'm still not convinced they're all connected."

"They may not be." Luke agreed. "But we both need to keep a look out."

"I will if you will." She looked at him out of the corner of her eye. He smiled at her, then took her hand in his.

"Sounds like a plan."

It was way too soon when Luke finally pulled up to Ellie's hotel room. He made his way around the car to open her door, and then helped her up, though both knew she didn't need it. She was quickly learning to appreciate the gentlemanly gestures.

"Ellie, I..."

"Oh, Ellie, there you are!" Aunt Edith scurried over to the car from the front door of the hotel, Uncle Patrick right on her heels. "Oh, and Mr. Callahan, perhaps you can help as well. We have the most dreadful news from Longbourn Ranch!" She handed Ellie a note.

"We arrived here to find that Janie had called for us and left a message. Oh, Ellie, Lindie has really stepped in it this time."

Gripping Luke's hand, Ellie read the message.

We have just learned that Lindie has run away with Davis Martin. We fear the worst. There is no trace of them. Mama needs you, Uncle Patrick and Aunt Edith to come home right away. Janie

Ellie's heart pounded and tears threatened. She ran away? With Davis? Had he compromised her? She moved her hand to Luke's arm to steady herself, hating her own reaction, yet not able to do anything about it. He supported her and led her to a nearby bench. Aunt Edith paced back and forth while Luke kneeled in front of Ellie, holding her hands in his yet again.

315

"Ellie, what's wrong, what can I do?" His eyes were filled with concern. She silently handed him the message. As he read it, his concern turned to anger.

"Davis." He growled.

"Oh, Luke, what has Lindie done? You know Davis, you know what he is capable of." A tear fell and he brushed it away. "She has no money, no one to turn to, nothing that will tempt him to actually marry her." She looked up at Luke. "What if we never see her again?"

"Your father will go after her, won't he?" Luke asked.

Aunt Edith answered for Ellie. "Yes, most definitely and Patrick has already gone to the train station to purchase tickets back to Spearfish. He will assist the family however he can, as will I."

"They won't be able to do anything. Not with Davis. I'm sure the damage has already been done." Ellie took a deep breath. Her baby sister would be ruined.

Luke nodded in agreement, then took Ellie's hand and squeezed it. She looked at him solemnly. Just his presence was keeping her calm. There was no one else she wanted at her side. She drew in a breath as she realized that she did love him. But she couldn't tell him now. She had Lindie to think of, and her family. Besides, would Luke even want her any more, with her family disgraced? "I should have said something about him; told her what kind of man he was."

"Ellie, you mustn't blame yourself." His thumb ran over her hand. "She wouldn't have believed you anyway."

Ellie sat up straight, took a deep breath and tried to collect herself.

Luke cupped her cheek. "I do wish I could help somehow."

"Pray." It was always her first response. "And please keep all of this to yourself, except maybe Helena. Please, make my excuses and tell everyone I said goodbye."

"Of course. You know I will."

"We have tickets to leave first thing tomorrow morning." Uncle Patrick stated quietly to the trio. Ellie had forgotten for a moment that he and Aunt Edith were still there.

"I will leave so you can pack." Luke stood and nodded to Patrick and Edith, then looked at Ellie one more time. "Keep me updated. Call me on the telephone if there is anything I can do." He glanced at the Gardiners, then kissed her on the temple. "Travel safely." Then he was gone.

"Lord, please protect Lindie." She prayed. "And please, let me have the joy of seeing Luke again."

Chapter Thirty-Six

"Luke, what's wrong now?" Helena looked up, alarmed, as Luke burst through the door.

"It's Ellie's youngest sister Lindie. She has run off with a man who has a bad reputation. She's just seventeen." He explained. "I feel it is my duty to help locate them as soon as possible."

"Why would it be your duty?"

Luke hesitated. He didn't want to bring up Davis Martin in front of his sister.

"Who is the man with the bad reputation, Luke? Luuuuuke, answer me. Who is the man?" When he still didn't answer, she sighed. "You don't have to tell me. I know. It's Davis, isn't it?"

Luke ran a hand through his hair. "Yes, yes it is."

"Luke, really? One of these days, you're going to have to stop bailing him out of trouble." Helena argued.

"It's not Davis I'm concerned about this time, Helena, it's Ellie and her family. He's probably going to ruin their good name and that concerns me. Besides, it's partially my fault. I should have warned them all about hiring Davis in the first place. Ellie's grandfather Benjamin and I actually got along pretty well before I left. I should have at least told him. He

318

would have believed me about Davis, even if no one else did. He is a very good judge of character,"

"So why didn't you, then?"

"I thought I might seem...petty...to the family, and that's the last thing I wanted at the time. I was thinking of myself."

Helena nodded. "That sounds fair, but there is definitely something more troubling you. Out with it, you can't fool me."

"I have to help for Ellie's sake," he replied. Helena knew this already. "She knew about Davis as well, granted, not until later, but I don't want her to feel responsible."

"You really do love her, don't you, Luke?"

"Very much so."

"I knew it! So let me help too. What can I do?"

"I was going to telephone some contacts I have out west, to see if I can find out where that wastrel may have taken Lindie. Once I locate him, I can try and talk some sense into that worthless...sorry Squirt. I will have to convince Davis to either marry Lindie or bring her home."

"All right, I still have some letters from him..." Luke gave her a wary look and she waved her hand dismissively. "Only to remind myself of past foolishness. I'll go check them to see if there are any clues as to his whereabouts, maybe the postmarks can tell us something."

"Thank you, Helena." He nodded, then went to his study to compose a list of the phone numbers he would need to make calls to tomorrow.

~~~~~~

That night, sleep did not come at all to Ellie, as she continually worried about what the next few days would bring. Her thoughts were so scrambled. She was angry and upset with Davis, but more so with Lindie. What was she thinking? How could she do this to herself, much less her family? Ellie also couldn't deny her own guilt in this fiasco. She should have warned Lindie about Davis, even though Lindie likely wouldn't have listened. Which led her to wonder if her treatment of Lindie in the past had made her act out this way. Perhaps she should have tried harder to understand Lindie instead of always criticizing her. *No*, her mind contradicted, *Lindie is who she is. She would never have listened then and she wouldn't listen now.* And then there was Luke. Thoughts of him interrupted her sleep as well between the worrying for Lindie and the concern for her family. Ellie had finally come to the realization that she loved Luke, and she could tell that he still cared for her, but could he still love her? Would she ever see him again? Would he ever accept her strange and awkward family or would this event remind him of just how inappropriate they could be? Would he now be lost to her forever?

Finally, the first light of day began to peek over the horizon and Ellie could justify getting out of bed. She was already packed so she quietly changed into her traveling outfit, then looked in the mirror and took a deep breath. She looked tired and run-down, but she had no time to worry about herself. She would be with her family soon and they were her main concern.

~~~~~~~

They boarded the early train that morning. For the most part, Ellie, Patrick and Edith traveled in silence, and the same thoughts she held from the previous night continued to roll through Ellie's mind. The unknown was turning her stomach in knots.

320

It was a long, stressful day, but finally the train arrived in Spearfish late that night. Matthew picked them up at the train station with the Model T.

"Is there any news?" Ellie asked the foreman. He shook his head stoically.

"No. Yer father is lookin' for them, and yer ma has locked herself in her room."

"We'll do whatever we can to help." Uncle Patrick said as he, Matthew and Aunt Edith crowded into the cab of the truck and Ellie climbed into the back with the luggage. She sat toward the front so she could hear anything that was said through the window.

The ride to the ranch was quiet until Uncle Patrick spoke through the window to Ellie just as the car neared Longbourn. "I've been thinking,"

She leaned forward and focused on her uncle. "Yes, Uncle Patrick?"

"I'm wondering if perhaps we're overreacting. Davis Martin isn't the steadiest of men, but why would he convince a girl like Lindie to run away with him? He knows the family and knows they will not inherit the ranch. Perhaps they really do love each other."

"Then why all of the secrecy? Why did they run off? Why would they want to hide their courtship?" Ellie shook her head. "It doesn't make sense, none of this does. You're right, though, Davis wouldn't marry a woman unless it was profitable for him. He wants to live the good life, but doesn't want to have to work for it and right now, he can't even afford to care for a wife, much less pay for his own expenses."

"Do you honestly believe that Lindie has so much love for this man that she would give up everything, most notably, her reputation, to stay with Mr. Martin, without being married?" Aunt Edith asked.

"I don't know what to think anymore." Ellie rubbed her temple. "Maybe she's smarter than I give her credit for, but she's so childish and has never really taken on any responsibilities." She sighed in relief to see the familiar land of the Longbourn Ranch, and it wasn't long before they finally reached the house. Janie had come onto the porch the moment she heard the car approach. Ellie jumped from the truck as soon as it stopped and ran straight to her sister.

"Is there any news?"

"Lindie and Davis apparently left the Brighton Ranch on Monday night, no one has heard a word from them since. Father has been trying to track them down, but hasn't had any luck."

"Uncle Patrick says he'll help in the search." Ellie nodded.

"Oh, Ellie, I'm afraid that nothing can be done. Mother is so distraught; she hasn't left her bedroom. You must go up and see her at once."

"Yes, of course." The girls quickly went upstairs and Martha embraced her daughter tightly. She then went on a tangent, blaming everyone for Lindie's predicament, except Lindie herself. "If your father had told her 'no' when she was asked to stay at the Brighton Ranch, he could have prevented all of this. Ohhhh, why did the Foresters ever let her out of their sight?"

Uncle Patrick entered the room and tried to console his sister. "My dear Martha, you must calm yourself. I will head to Cheyenne myself to help James locate them."

"Oh, Patrick, when you find them, if you find them and if they are not already married, you must make them marry. James already knows this. You must also keep James from losing his temper. One punch from

322

that Mr. Martin could kill my beloved. Remind him that I am frightened out of my wits." Martha lamented.

Ellie couldn't stay with her mother any longer. Just the idea of her mild mannered father fighting was ridiculous. If she wanted a fight, they should have sent Grandpa Benjamin. He would have been able to whip Davis into shape.

Ellie and Janie left the room and went down to the porch. Janie sat in one of the rocking chairs while Ellie sat on the top step, leaning back against the post. She stared out across the vast fields. She wanted to go riding, but it was too dark. Ellie wanted to tell Janie all about her trip, about Luke, about meeting Helena, and seeing Charles, but it wasn't the right time. All their efforts needed to be directed towards Lindie and getting her home, safe and secure. Yet if Ellie were to tell Janie that Charles had asked about her, it would get Janie's hopes up, but, then again, at the same time, if Charles heard of Lindie's indiscretions, he might feel that his initial assessment of the family was correct. That thought made Ellie think of Luke again. If he had thought so little about her family before, she didn't even want to imagine how he would feel about them now. A tear slipped down her cheek. She had to stop thinking of Luke. Lindie's dilemma was the most important problem at this time. She must not think of her own problems.

~~~~~~

Some of Luke's contacts had ideas of where Davis could have gone, but he still didn't have any solid leads. Perhaps he should just get on a train and head west. Denver or Cheyenne would probably be good places to

323

start, or even Spearfish, though Mr. Bennett had likely already searched there.

"I found some information that might be helpful, but I don't know for sure." Helena entered the office and set some letters down. Luke scanned through them.

"You know, there's nothing definite, but with what you have here and what I've already learned, I just might have a destination point to start." He looked at a map and pointed. "Casper, Wyoming, here I come."

Chapter Thirty-Seven

$\mathcal{T}$he days passed slowly despite Ellie staying especially busy, taking over her father's duties as well as her own chores on the ranch. The entire household waited with bated breath for any word from their father. Uncle Patrick had left early the next morning, while Aunt Edith and Cousins Sammy and Rachel would continue to stay with the Bennetts. Ellie had offered to go as well, but her mother had insisted that she stay, as she was needed to run the ranch. Martha also wanted her remaining daughters near, as her current greatest fear was that her husband would somehow be killed, and that Mr. Sutton would kick the Bennett women off the ranch before James was even buried.

"Folks in town ain't happy 'bout this Mr. Martin." Matthew told Ellie as they repaired an old fence. Ellie gripped the handles of the post hole digger and thrust it into the ground, then squeezed the dirt and brought it out of the two-foot hole. At least she was able to do some physical labor to take out her frustrations. "I heard he owes many cowboys and businesses around here lotsa money."

"He is much too fond of gambling, I believe." Ellie leaned forward on the post hole digger and pushed her hat back a bit. "And aren't we fickle here because we are all hoping Lindie will end up tied to this chump."

"Sad state of affairs to be sure," Matthew agreed. "Not only did he leave a lot of debts unpaid, he left without fulfilling quite a few promises. He's being called one of the biggest louts west of the Mississippi."

Ellie sighed. "I don't even dare go into Spearfish. It might be cowardly of me, but I just dread what the townsfolk are saying." She felt tears threaten again. "Oh, Matthew, I should have warned Lindie of what I knew about Davis. I don't know why I didn't."

"Ya wanted to keep Mr. Callahan's confidence as ya promised, no one could fault ya fer that," Matthew replied. "Besides, ya know durn well that even if ya told Miss Lindie what ya knew, she wouldn'a listened to ya. She'da probably wandered off with him anyway."

"I could have told her about his character without being specific, but you're probably right. She wouldn't have listened." A tear slipped down her cheek. "I know I've said this before, but perhaps I should have been a better sister to her long ago. I'd always push her away or treat her with annoyance. If I had been kinder to her, perhaps have gone out of my way to listen to her more, she would have been more willing to listen to me. Maybe she wouldn't have felt the need to show off and go out looking for the wrong attention."

"Ya be right. We discussed this before, Miss Ellie, and that's just like ya," Matthew replied. "Feelin' a responsibility fer everyone else. Miss Janie was sayin' the same thing. Maybe what yer sayin' is true, but there's no way for ya to really know. Yer Pa and Ma coulda done a whole lotta things different with her too, but Miss Lindie is who she is. What's done is done, and alls ya can do is pray fer yer sister. If ya think it's needed, ya can always

326

change yer ways with her when she returns, an she will. I got me an inkling."

"Oh, Matthew, you're right again, as usual." Ellie settled her hat back on her head, and continued her work on the fence. Once the repairs were completed, they both rode back to the house in silence. As they neared the driveway, Ellie immediately noticed a familiar form on the porch.

"It's Papa!" She urged Naomi to a gallop and jumped off before she even came to a stop. "Papa! Papa, do you have any news? Did you find them?"

"No, not yet. Your uncle is traveling to Laramie to chase down a lead we have. I have only stopped back here for the day, then will be traveling to Bismarck by way of Sturgis on another possible lead."

"Bismarck? Why would they go there?" Ellie asked. "Or Laramie for that matter?"

"A foreman who worked with Martin in the past mentioned he had friends there."

Ellie tried not to show too much disappointment. She thought for sure when she saw her father, he would have found Lindie. "Well, I'm glad you're home, at least for today. We've missed you."

He nodded stoically. A part of Ellie wondered if he was thinking of the conversation they'd had before Lindie left, when Ellie had shared her concerns about Lindie's behavior. Ellie wished he had listened to her.

~~~~~~~

Luke disembarked from the train in Casper and looked around. It was a smaller town than he had pictured, but that would hopefully play out in his favor. If Davis and Lindie had passed through here, someone would

327

know. He popped a root beer barrel in his mouth and pulled a Bennett family photo out of his bag. Patrick Gardiner had given it to him back in St. Louis. Hopefully, someone would recognize Lindie. He walked to the ticket window.

"How can I help you, sir?" The gray-haired man asked. He was about the same age as Luke's father would have been if he had lived.

"My name is Lucas Callahan, out of St. Louis."

"Of Callahan Enterprises?" The man interrupted.

"Yes, sir." Luke nodded.

"An honor to meet you, Mr. Callahan. I worked for your father many years ago on one of his trains. Started as a porter when I was just a wee lad, then worked my way up to a conductor. Once I started having grandkids I decided to stop traveling so much. I just love these Iron Horses so much though, I decided to transfer here for a ticket job so I could be closer to my family here in Casper. Yes, sir, I did enjoy working for your father. He was a good man, yes sir, he was."

A pang of sorrow hit Luke as it often did when someone mentioned his father. "Yes, he was. I appreciate your kind comments, Mr...I didn't get your name."

"Stoody. Edwin Stoody, sir." The ticket man answered.

"Pleased to meet you, Mr. Stoody." Luke nodded.

"So tell me, how can I help you today, Mr. Callahan?"

"I am looking for a young man, in his mid-twenties. Blonde hair, blue eyes, medium build, a few inches shorter than me. Answers to Davis Martin." Luke showed the man the photograph and pointed. "He would be with this young lady here."

328

The older man frowned. "Can't say as I've seen them, but I would only probably do so if they were to be leaving, buying a ticket and all. But there's only a few hotels in town and they could be staying at one of them if they're here. You should have better luck searching there. I can let you know if I do happen to see them."

"Thank you, that's very kind of you. I'll be staying at the Gladstone tonight." Luke tipped his derby.

The man nodded and Luke continued on his way. He checked into his hotel and spoke with the bellhop and desk clerk, but he quickly learned that Davis and Lindie were not guests. He dropped his baggage off in his room and headed back out.

The other hotels proved fruitless as well. Discouraged and hungry, Luke headed to a diner for some food. A pretty waitress in her late thirties took his order.

"Pardon me, ma'am." He pulled out the photograph. "I'm looking for this young woman here. She's run off with my cousin, who's a bit of a rake. I'm hoping to locate them, have you seen her."

She examined the picture and nodded. "Yes, I believe so. Is your cousin a handsome blonde with a smile too charming for his own good?"

"That sounds like Davis, yes." Luke's entire mood lifted.

"They were both here. The man, your cousin, I saw him later over at the saloon arguing with another handsome gent, this other man, he looked pretty slick."

"They were arguing?" That didn't make sense, but perhaps Davis owed this other man money. That was surely a possibility.

"Don't know what about," the waitress said. "I did hear your cousin say he was staying at the Henning, but he wasn't calling himself Davis. I heard his name was Martin Jones, not Davis. He called the pretty young woman Lindie, I believe."

"That would be the young woman in the photograph." Luke glanced down and couldn't help but notice Ellie's image in the picture.

"I hope it all makes sense, to ya."

"Thank you so much for the information, ma'am." Luke would have to give her an extra tip when he paid his bill.

"Not a problem, sir. I've met a few rakes in my day. I hope your search goes well." She smiled and walked toward the kitchen. Luke sat back. Now that he had found the couple, he had to figure out how to best approach them.

"Pardon me." He asked the waitress as she passed by again. "Is there a telephone nearby I can use?"

"Yes, we have one here." The woman led him to the telephone and Luke quickly placed a call to Patrick Gardiner's hotel in Laramie. He wanted to call Ellie as well, but he and Patrick had spoken about that earlier. After much deliberation, Luke had agreed with Patrick that, if they found the couple, neither would call the ranch until they approached them and learned of their plans. They had also agreed to contact each other. Though Luke hated to admit it, the best thing to do was to get Davis to marry Lindie, and Luke wanted to get that settled before he gave the family hope.

"I found them." Luke said once the call had been connected and Patrick was on the line.

"Thank the Lord. Where are they? Are they married?" Patrick answered.

"I'm in Casper. They are staying at a hotel here, the Henning, and I haven't spoken with them yet. I don't know if they're married or not."

330

"At least you have found them. Do what you can to not let them leave. I'll leave first thing tomorrow morning. I believe it is a three or four-hour drive over there."

"That sounds about right. I'll speak with them as soon as I can. I know Davis, if I promise him money, he won't take off."

"Very good. Thank you, Luke. We'll see you tomorrow."

"See you tomorrow, sir." Luke hung up and headed back to his seat to find his food had arrived. He quickly ate the pot roast and vegetables, left a generous tip, then headed to the Henning Hotel.

"Martin Jones's room, please,' Luke requested. "He's expecting me."

"Of course, sir." The man checked his record book and nodded. "Room 214."

"Thank you." As Luke walked to the second floor, he sent up a quick prayer for wisdom, then knocked on the door. He heard a female giggle, then the door opened.

"Luke!" Davis looked shocked and a little scared. "What are you doing here?"

"I came to talk some sense into you." Luke stepped into the small room. Lindie sat up on the single bed. At least she was fully clothed.

"Mr. Callahan! What on earth are you doing here?" She pouted.

"Apparently, I care more about your reputations than either of you do."

Lindie crossed her arms defensively. "We're getting married, Mr. Callahan. We love each other and my family just wouldn't understand, much less approve."

"That's what he told you?" Luke scoffed. "That he loves you and your family wouldn't understand? My sister believed this scalawag when he told her the exact same story."

"Your sister? Davis, what's he talking about?" She looked over at Davis, who clenched his jaw.

"It's different this time, Luke, I swear." He glanced over at Lindie. "What he says is true, I did court his sister, but it is different this time, darling. I told you I love you."

"Of course, my dearest." She looked at Davis with such obvious and blind adoration, it almost made Luke nauseous. He decided to take another route.

"Lindie, are you all right?" Luke asked.

"Of course I am, Mr. Callahan. Why wouldn't I be? And why would you care anyways?"

"Oh, I know why he cares." Davis smirked. Luke had to hold back from punching his old friend.

"I care because I know your family and I know this isn't what they would want for you." Luke replied.

"You mean being married to a man that loves me? Yes, I know some members of my family don't want me to be happy, but at least I'll be out of their lives now."

"Lindie, that's not true, I promise you. They all dropped everything just to find you. To make sure you're safe."

"Well I am." She shrugged as if she hadn't a care in the world. No wonder she drove Ellie crazy. She was nothing like Helena. Luke turned to Davis.

"And what are you thinking, Davis? Do you have a job? Can you support a wife and family? Because a family is what you will get."

Davis at least had the intelligence to look a bit guilty. "Luke, can we talk over a drink? I know you have a fondness for root beer."

Luke nodded and Davis turned to Lindie. "You stay here, darling. I'll be back straightaway." He kissed her soundly, almost as if he wanted to irritate Luke more, then followed Luke out the door. The men made their way to the Elkhorn Saloon.

"So you claim Lindie is different? Of course, you know she doesn't have a fortune to inherit. That's usually what you look for in a future wife, isn't it? I suspect that when you learned none of the Bennett women would get the ranch is when you stopped paying attention to Ellie."

Davis reddened. "Actually yes, but I'm sure that made you happy."

"What is that supposed to mean?"

"Come now, Luke. We grew up together. I know when you're smitten, though it's only been a time or two, and never quite as intense as what I saw with Ellie."

"My feelings don't matter at this point. Really, Davis, I'll ask you again, what were you thinking, running off with Lindie? She's still a child."

Davis circled his mug with his hands. "You may find this surprising, Luke, but I really do like her."

Luke usually knew when Davis was lying, but he wasn't quite sure now.

"If that's the case, then why haven't you married her yet? You have compromised her, Davis!"

"We had some...unexpected financial setbacks. I can barely afford our hotel room. I didn't realize a marriage license would cost money, but I have found some work, so I'll be able to take care of everything in a few weeks."

333

"Sooner." Luke growled, knowing what he had to do. "And this work you found. Is it permanent?"

"No, just a few weeks, maybe less."

"I'll pay for the wedding. Lindie's uncle will be here tomorrow. He can witness the ceremony for her." Luke thought a minute, then added: "I have an acquaintance at the Old Faithful Inn in Montana, he said he's always looking for friendly help and I bet he would be willing to give you a job on a trial basis. It would only be an entry level position, so you will have to work your way up the ladder, but you have the skills to do so, Davis. You just have never had the ambition or work ethic."

"Never had a real reason to before," Davis said, then took a drink of his root beer.

"I'll telephone him tomorrow morning and make arrangements for you." Luke nodded. "Someone should call the Bennetts as well. They're worried sick about Lindie. Really Davis? How could you be so thoughtless and self-serving?"

"I guess I wasn't thinking it all through, Luke. I'll be sure Lindie calls them tomorrow." Davis replied. "Luke, I...I really appreciate your help, especially with our history and all." Davis actually sounded subdued, but Luke suspected it was an act.

"Use this opportunity to better yourself for a change. You are now responsible for the care of Lindie. Try and become the type of man your father and mine would be proud of." Luke truly didn't think Davis would ever act responsibly, but Luke had to give him one last chance. For the sake of the Bennett family at least.

Davis clenched his jaw again, but kept quiet. They both finished their drinks, Luke paid their tab, and they both returned to their respective hotels.

Chapter Thirty-Eight

$\mathscr{T}$he next morning, the telephone rang and Ellie was just in time to answer it.

"Ellie? Is that you, my dear sister?" It was Lindie.

"Yes, yes it's me." Relief swept through her. "Oh, Lindie, are you all right, where are you?" She leaned eagerly toward the mouthpiece attached to the wooden box.

"Of course I'm all right. Why wouldn't I be? I'm with Davis, in Casper. Uncle Patrick arrived just a bit ago. Is father there?"

"He just left for Bismarck, but I can catch him. Lindie, are you married?"

"Not yet."

Ellie's stomach plummeted.

"But we will be. It's all being taken care of. That's why I'm calling."

Ellie nodded instinctively, though she knew Lindie couldn't see her reactions. "I am so glad to hear that."

336

"Davis found a job, so we will be able to get married very soon."

Ellie leaned against the wall, relief coursing through her. "When and where will it be?"

"As soon as you arrive here in Casper. We want you to be at the wedding, Ellie."

"What? Why? Just me? Not Mama or Kathy?"

"Well, of course we want everyone here." Lindie confirmed. "But we know the whole family won't be able to come. I want one of my sisters to be my witness. I can't have Janie, I don't want her to be too upset that I'm married before her, and Marie won't want to come, she's too much of a homebody, and Kathy won't be able to travel alone. Mama hates traveling by train, and Papa needs to run the ranch. You won't ever marry, so I thought you would be the best choice, please say you'll come."

Her last choice, apparently. She had to get a snub in. Ellie couldn't help but think. "Of course I'll be there for you, Lindie."

"Splendid. Tell Mama we'll come home and we can have a proper reception with everyone."

It still didn't make any sense why Lindie would want Ellie to be the one at the wedding, but if that's what Ellie needed to do, she would do it. She couldn't let Lindie down. "All right, I'll be on the first train headed in that direction. I'll call you when I know the arrival time. It's early enough where I should be able to get there by this evening. Where can I meet you? Where are you staying?"

Lindie gave her the hotel phone number and closed with a quick, "We'll pick you up at the station, see you soon," then hung up the phone.

Ellie hung up too and shook her head. Quickly composing herself, she ran to tell her mother the news, then Janie, Marie and Kathy. Martha was ecstatic to hear about Lindie's call and went down to the telephone right away, no doubt to brag to anyone on the party line about her youngest daughter getting married. Ellie quickly escaped and made her way to the barn to saddle up Naomi. Her father needed to know the information right away and since he had taken the truck, she would need to ride swiftly to catch him, then ride back home to pack and catch the train for Casper.

Ellie's mind drifted to Luke as she rode. A part of her wished she hadn't told him about Lindie running away. The marriage would hide the scandalous part of their escapade, of course, yet he was now aware of another shameful family secret. Ellie knew he wouldn't spread rumors. She trusted him explicitly, which was strange, seeing as how she disliked him not that long ago. She had discovered that he was dependable, kind, and handsome. She gently thumped her fist against her thigh. She wished she could go back in time and accept his proposal.

It didn't escape Ellie that Lindie's marriage would mean that Davis was now a part of the Bennett family. She couldn't imagine Luke wanting to marry her now. The man he despised was going to be her brother-in-law. Luke wasn't the prideful man that she once believed he was, but this development would be difficult to overlook. She leaned down and rubbed Naomi's neck. "Oh, I do miss him so." She spoke quietly to her horse. Naomi nickered as if in agreement. Luke would have been the perfect man for her. He would likely vex her from time to time and she would challenge him as well, but she had no doubt they would have been very happy together. She just couldn't see how it would ever be possible now.

"Father!" She was jerked from her thoughts when she saw the Ford just up ahead. She urged Naomi into a faster run and caught up to him quickly. "Father, we heard from Lindie!"

As he stepped out of the truck, Ellie explained to him what happened. When she was finished, she grabbed his arm. "Apparently, Uncle Patrick is taking care of everything in Casper and Mama and you can plan a celebration here in a week or so."

"I must obviously thank Patrick for his generosity and his success in finding Lindie." His voice was a bit flustered.

"Generosity?"

"Yes, of course. There is no sane man in America that would marry Lindie in this situation, especially a man as dishonorable and greedy as Davis Martin. Patrick must have paid him off quite handsomely to marry your sister."

Ellie bit her lip. Her father was right, and Ellie's spirits sank. What kind of marriage could Lindie hope to have when her husband was paid off to marry her?

~~~~~~~

Ellie had never traveled anywhere on her own and didn't feel comfortable doing so now. Why on earth were Lindie and Davis so insistent that she come to the wedding? It still didn't make any sense. She looked out the train window. Hills rolled by and the Rocky Mountains loomed in the distance. At least Uncle Patrick would be around as well. Still, there was a pit of uneasiness in her stomach. Damage to Lindie's reputation had likely already been done, and would Davis truly treat her right now? Ellie didn't think so.

"Lord, help him be a good husband and help Lindie be a good wife." She prayed, closing her eyes. She had been praying much more of late, ever since she had heard about her sister running away. It helped, but she still worried.

Before Ellie was ready, the train rolled to a stop in Casper. She grabbed her small valise and walked down the train aisle.

"Ellie! Oh, Ellie, here we are!" Lindie waved enthusiastically as Davis stood quietly on the platform next to her. Ellie drew in a deep breath to fortify herself. Lindie actually ran to Ellie and threw her arms around her, almost knocking her over. Ellie hugged her back. She and Lindie had a tumultuous relationship, but they were sisters and Ellie would always love her dearly.

"Are you all right, Lindie?" Ellie glanced at Davis. "You can tell me the truth, I promise."

"Oh, Ellie, don't be a ninnie. Davis has been just splendid. I do hope you're not too mad at me for taking him away from you."

"I...no, why would you say that you took him away?" Ellie tried to interrupt, but then Davis stepped forward.

"Lindie, we must go. Hello, Ellie."

"Davis." She said coolly. "Where is Uncle Patrick?"

"He's at the Henning hotel." Davis took her bag from her. "Come, we'll drive you over." He led her to an automobile, probably rented, and she climbed into the back seat. "It's not far." Davis leaned over and handed Ellie a bottle of Dr. Pepper. "Here, drink some of this. You must be thirsty after your long journey."

Ellie smiled in thanks, took a long sip of one of her favorite beverages, then leaned her head back and rested her eyes. Just for a moment.

The car shifted and was put in park, jolting Ellie from her sleep. "Can't believe I dozed off." She mumbled to herself. She hadn't thought she was that tired.

"Come, Ellie, I'll escort you in. Lindie my darling, you can stay here." He leaned over and kissed Lindie's cheek, then helped Ellie out of the backseat.

Ellie got out and looked around, feeling dizzy and a bit disoriented. "Davis, this isn't a hotel." They must have driven further than she thought, as they were on a dirt road surrounded by trees. A log cabin stood in front of them, not a hotel.

"Come on." Davis roughly gripped her arm. "He's inside, I can promise you that."

"Davis, what about my luggage?"

He ignored her and all but dragged her to the cabin. Ellie's instincts told her something wasn't right, and she started to resist Davis. It was no use, she felt as weak as a newborn calf. He opened the door and shoved her inside. Ellie frowned as the fog lifted from her brain and she saw the last person she ever expected to see.

"I'm real sorry, Ellie." Davis shoved her again and this time, everything went black.

~~~~~~

Luke sucked on his root beer barrel and watched Patrick Gardiner. He had arrived earlier that day while Lindie had been making arrangements for the wedding. Together, they completed the plans and had been able to get the pastor at St. Mark's Episcopal Church to perform the ceremony. Lindie was annoyingly excited for the event that would take place the next day.

Luke still wasn't sure if Davis would make a good husband, but he had to admit, his former friend seemed fairly devoted to Lindie. This actually was somewhat surprising, yet at the same time, brought a bit of comfort to Luke. Davis and Lindie had told Luke and Patrick that they wanted to go out for dinner, just the two of them, so Luke and Patrick had eaten at the hotel dining room.

Now, Patrick was pacing back and forth in the hotel suite, nervous as he had been all day. "Mr. Callahan, I must thank you again for all of your assistance with this business." He had said these same words at least a dozen times already that day. "You have no reason to be involved in this farce, yet you have been most helpful."

"As I said, I should have warned your family about Davis long ago." Luke clasped his hands in front of him, and looked at Patrick, who gave a look that made him suspect that he knew the truth of what Luke felt for Ellie. Luke looked down. He still wasn't sure how or when he was going to approach Ellie with his feelings a second time, but he knew he had to.

"What time do we all need to be at the church?" Luke asked.

"Wedding will take place at 10:00, so just shortly before that should be early enough." Patrick replied. "We'll have the ceremony, then a nice luncheon here at the hotel and after that, I'll head back to Longbourn. Lindie and Davis will have a short honeymoon here and then stop at the ranch en route to Yellowstone."

"I must say that this wedding is definitely not what I would want for my future bride." Luke commented. He would want his family and friends there to celebrate the special day, no matter what. It seemed as though

342

Lindie didn't care about such things, which was surprising since she liked parties so much.

Luke stood. "If you'd like, we can meet in the lobby after breakfast and we can ride together in the car I'm renting."

"That's very kind of you to offer, Mr. Callahan." Patrick answered. "Thank you. I will see you in the morning."

Luke wished the man a good night, then headed back to his own room. He was halfway there when he decided he needed some fresh air. He had more than enough time for a walk before the sun set. As Luke exited the hotel, he saw Davis assist Lindie from his rented car. Luke frowned. What gave Davis the right to drive his car?

"Hello, Mr. Callahan!" Lindie waved, oblivious to everything that was happening around her. Davis's face went pale as he realized he had been caught.

"Uhhh…Luke, I can explain…"

"Explain why you stole my car?"

"I didn't steal it, I was borrowing it."

Lindie brushed her hand down her skirt. "Yes, we had to drop Ellie off at Uncle Patrick's new hotel. Such a pity their room had bed bugs." She glanced at Davis.

Luke's stomach dropped as he glared at Davis. "What are you talking about? I just left Patrick, in the room he's been staying in since he arrived this morning."

"Now, Luke, I said I can explain." The cad took a step back. "I had no choice." Davis held up his hands.

"What are you talking about? What do you mean, you dropped Ellie off?" Luke almost growled. "Why is Ellie even in Casper?"

343

"Oh Luke, don't be a wet blanket. We decided Ellie would be the most logical relative to witness the wedding. Heaven knows she would be no help with planning our reception back home." Lindie suddenly looked a bit frightened.

Luke took a threatening step toward Davis and spoke in a voice that could chill his Aunt Madeline. "Where is she?"

"I had to, Luke, you don't understand, he said he'd kill me and Lindie if I didn't get her here."

"Who? Who would kill you? You're not making any sense." Luke demanded, grabbing Davis by the shirt.

"A man who goes by the name of Clark." Davis grunted. Lindie squealed and grabbed Luke's arm.

"Let him go, you big brute!"

"What in the world would he want with Ellie?" Luke thought back to the only Clark he had ever heard of in regards to the Bennetts, the gentleman he had met at the Browns game. He hadn't seemed especially interested in Ellie at the time. "What is going on?" Luke had never seen Davis so scared, concerned, even a bit repentant.

"I don't exactly know. Really, I don't Luke, I just think…he must have some sort of vendetta against Ellie because he demanded that I assist him. He said she ruined his life and he'd kill Lindie and I if I didn't do as he said."

"You told me he just wanted to talk to her." Lindie whimpered. "He wanted to appeal to Ellie to talk to Janie on his behalf."

Luke ignored the simpering young woman and focused on Davis. "How on earth did Ellie ruin his life?"

"He didn't give me any specifics…look." He pushed away and Luke let him go. "This has just all spiraled out of control, Luke. I tell you, I was living in Omaha and I got into debt, way over my head. I owed this man a lot of money, so he had me do some favors for him to pay it off and before long, he sent me to Spearfish and that's when I met the Bennetts. I had no idea you were there too. I tried getting out, really, I did, but by this time I was in way over my head and he wouldn't let me off the hook."

Luke stepped back and ran his hand through his hair, frustrated and angry. "Where is she?"

"I dropped her off at a cabin Mercer rented. It's out on the North Platte."

"It's quite a nice place, actually," Lindie still seemed oblivious as to how big of a threat Mercer was to her sister. "Like I said he just wants to talk with her, use her to help get back into Janie's good graces. She kind of deserves it, being she's the one that caused all the problems in the first place."

"I can't believe you, either of you! Davis, you abducted her! That's kidnapping! You'll go to jail for a long time! I can't believe this, even from you! If she dies, you're an accessory to murder, both of you."

"Don't be ridiculous, Mr. Callahan, why would he kill her," Lindie insisted. "He just wants Janie back and knows Ellie can make Janie understand that. Mr. Mercer still loves Janie."

If one could explode in anger and frustration, Luke would have. He struggled not to punch Davis. And how could Lindie be so naive? "A man like that doesn't love anyone!" Could the two in front of him really be that ignorant? Or were they just trying to be manipulative. "You both listen to me right now or I will see you prosecuted to the fullest extent of the law." He glared at Lindie. "Lindie, go tell the police what has happened and I mean everything. Make sure you tell them exactly where this cabin is located, then go stay with your Uncle. If you're not there when I return, I will hunt you down and you will spend the rest of your miserable life in jail. Do I make myself perfectly clear?"

Lindie finally looked terrified and nodded. Luke turned to Davis and grabbed his arm.

"You, you're coming with me. One wrong move and you'll wish that you had never met me. Give me my keys, and there better be enough gas."

"There should be." Davis yelped.

He stormed to his car, threw Davis into the passenger seat, jumped into the driver side and started the car then sped away, praying that he wouldn't be too late.

Chapter Thirty-Nine

Ellie's head pounded as she slowly forced her eyes open.

"Ahh, good, you're finally awake." A slightly familiar male voice spoke. Her eyes focused on his face. Clark Mercer.

"What's going on? Where's Lindie?" She tried to rub her head, but her arms were tied together behind her. She tried to survey her surroundings. A large but simple one-room cabin, with a fireplace, dining table and four chairs, some cupboards with a sink and pump were on one side. She was on a bed on the opposite side, and a wardrobe was in the corner. She was lying on her side with numb hands and a pounding in her head that wouldn't subside. The man who spoke sat at the table.

"Your sister is with her future husband, I would imagine. It's kind of funny to know he actually is quite happy to be with her. They seem to complement each other well. They'll be safe, as will your uncle, who doesn't even know that you're in Casper."

"Where am I? What is this place? And why am I here?"

"The where and what is immaterial, Miss Bennett. As for the why? You know precisely the answer to that question. But if I must, I will explain it to you in detail. You're here because you have made my life miserable these past two years. I loved your sister, wanted to marry her and live forever with her. You prevented that. You stole all my happiness, so I will steal yours. I am just repaying the favor." Obsession gleaned in his eyes.

"So you kidnapped me? What..." She wasn't quite sure she wanted to hear what his plan for her was. "How do you plan to take away my happiness?"

"I already have. I took away your precious cattle with a little help from a man you trusted and admired for a time. Davis Martin was so easy to use. He owed me a lot of money because of his gambling and I made sure he paid it back to me. It was an added bonus that you started to fall in love with him so he was able to drop you like you made Janie drop me."

Ellie tried to ignore the fact that Davis was just pretending to like her and focused on the fact that he was the one to set the fire. "Davis set the fire and killed our cattle?" Some of the puzzle started to come together. How could she have missed Davis's involvement? "Did he try to kill Naomi as well?"

"Yes, he tried to poison her, but that didn't work, more's the pity. This Davis really can't do much right."

He was absolutely mad. "You wretch!" Anger boiled through Ellie, pushing away her fear. Clark Mercer laughed like a crazed man.

"Then I tried to take away your new beau, but that plan was foiled as well."

"It was you! You sabotaged Luke's car in St. Louis?"

"I don't do menial work like that myself, dear Ellie. I paid someone to do it for me. I was quite upset he failed also. So many incompetent people in the world."

"Are you talking about Davis again?"

348

"I have quite a few men, and women for that matter, who owe me or are willing to do me favors in exchange for my help. Of course, I never would have had to wreck that beauty of a car if the buffoon I hired in North Carolina had succeeded in shooting your beau. That was wasted money. So now, I have decided to take matters into my own hands."

"How could you?"

"As I said, you stole my happiness! All I ever wanted was to marry my Janie. I love her and you persuaded her to leave me, under false accusations."

Ellie froze. That is how this all started? Was Clark Mercer completely unhinged? "You would kill a man I was friends with because I told my sister I didn't quite trust you? That's all I said to her! She just happened to agree with me! She's the one who started to distance herself from you. She didn't want to hurt you, but that's just how Janie is. She never wants to hurt anyone."

"No! It was all because of you." He crossed the room and loomed over her, threatening.

"Even if I did talk Janie out of seeing you, how is that ruining your life?" She struggled to sit up but was unable to make any progress. "People move on after failed courtships all the time, you are no one special."

"I beg to differ. I love her, there is no one who will ever love her like I do. I also would like to one day own that profitable cattle spread. Janie, being the oldest, will inherit of course."

"Well, then, the laugh is on you. I suppose you should know that it won't be our ranch after our grandpa and father die. Besides, don't you have money and connections through your position in Washington. And, if you really loved Janie, you wouldn't have kidnapped me, that's hardly

349

going to endure Janie to you. Just admit it. This has nothing to do with love or happiness. It's all about your greed and obsession." She paused. "And does Davis Martin really hate Luke that much?" Ellie said more to herself than Mercer. She just couldn't believe any of this.

"No, he was actually working for me before Callahan was even in the picture. That was simply an added bonus for Martin, making his former adversary so jealous."

Ellie finally had to ask. "I still don't understand about..." Without warning, Mercer slapped her and Ellie's head snapped back. She gritted her teeth. This man had to be crazy.

"That is enough out of you!" He bellowed.

"What are you going to do with me?"

"You don't listen well, do you? It's simple. I want to take your happiness from you just as you took mine, but the more I think about it, I believe you need to feel pain."

Fear coursed through Ellie not only at his words, but also the look of evil on his face. She tried to keep him talking so he would be more easily distracted. "So you used Davis once again. You had him run away with Lindie so you could lure me away from home?" It seemed like an awful lot of planning, more than Mercer was capable of. He could have easily had her snatched away from the ranch.

"No, no, no. He ran away with that brat of a sister of yours on his own. I just decided that I could use the situation to my advantage. I gave Davis no other option than to follow my dictates."

Ellie felt nauseous and tears threatened. "Why didn't you just have me killed? Why go through all the trouble to bring me here?"

"I don't want you dead, Miss Bennett. Like I said, I want you to suffer." He reached down and jerked her up by her arm. "I want you to suffer as I have suffered!" She tried to drive her knee into his groin, but he blocked it. He cocked his fist back to hit her and as she was about to duck there was a pounding on the door.

"Ellie!" The pounding stopped. Was that Luke? The door smashed open and Mercer shoved Ellie. She crashed into the side table, then fell to the ground, her shoulder wrenching underneath her. She looked up to see Luke push Mercer, then punch him in the abdomen. Mercer stumbled, then threw a punch at Luke. Luke jumped back then ran at Mercer, tackling him, showing off his rugby skills, then punched him again, this time in the face. Mercer groaned and fell over as Luke pushed to his feet and quickly went to Ellie. He helped her to a sitting position, pulled the folding knife he had received from Helena out of his pocket and cut the ropes from around her wrists. Once her arms were free, she threw them around Luke and felt his arms encircle her waist.

"Luke, what are you doing here?" She never dreamed he or anyone else for that matter, would have found her. Tears of relief filled her eyes as she kissed his cheeks, then hugged him again. How did he even get here so fast? There were still so many questions rushing through her head.

Luke pulled slightly back. "I'm in Wyoming because I was helping your uncle and father track down Davis and Lindie, and Davis just admitted..." A shadow crossed in front of them.

"Luke!" A voice from the doorway yelled just as Ellie shoved Luke away.

"Look out!" She cried.

351

Mercer fell into Ellie, reached over her and grabbed a satchel that had fallen from the table when she had crashed into it. He then pulled a pistol from the side pocket. Luke grabbed Ellie and pulled her behind him to shield her as Mercer cocked the pistol and pointed it right at Luke's head.

"This just makes things so much better." Mercer wiped a bead of sweat from his forehead. "Now I can kill your lover right in front of you." He almost squealed in delight, his focus entirely on Luke.

From behind Mercer, Ellie saw Davis slip into the room and grab a lamp that had fallen off the table. Luke held up his hands.

"Easy, Mercer. I just want Ellie to be safe. That's all."

"Too bad for you, because I just want Miss Bennett to suffer." Before Mercer could pull the trigger, Davis smashed the lamp over his head. Ellie prayed it would knock him out. The gun discharged with the impact, but Luke had been able to pull her to the side with him as he dove away. Mercer fell once again, and Ellie pushed to her feet, quickly went to the bed, stripped the pillowcase off the pillow, tore it into strips, and used it to tie Mercer's hands together.

"Probably should have done that the first time." She looked sheepishly at Luke.

"Yes, probably." Luke finally pushed to his feet, grabbed Ellie's hand, and kissed her forehead, then turned to Davis.

"Davis, thank you." Luke almost looked relieved that the man had actually stepped up to help them.

Though he had just saved their lives, Ellie still wanted to stomp right up to him and slap him across the face, but she thought better of it.

"Why is Davis even here?" She asked Luke as they walked outside.

"Ellie…" Luke was interrupted by automobiles approaching.

"Are you Mr. Callahan?" A tall man with a gray handlebar mustache stepped out of the first car.

Luke shook the man's hand. "Yes sir, I am."

"I'm Sheriff Elliot. We heard you may be needing some assistance."

"We do, indeed." Luke nodded. "There is a kidnapper inside, tied up. He tried to kill me and this young woman here."

"What about him?" The officer nodded to Davis.

"You should take him in as well, but he did help me to find this place. He was helping the kidnapper, but claims he was under duress. He is the one who incapacitated the kidnapper. He came through when it counted."

One of the officers escorted Davis to their automobile, and the sheriff wrote down Ellie and Luke's statements about what happened. Two other officers went to the cabin to retrieve Clark Mercer. Luke and Ellie assured the sheriff that they would both be in Casper through the following day to complete their statements in more detail.

"Let's get you home. Well, to the hotel, that is." Luke took Ellie's hand and they walked to his rented car. Once sitting, she slouched back, exhausted. He started the car and began to drive.

"You okay? What's on your mind?" He asked.

"So much. Clark Mercer's hatred and revenge. You won't believe everything he's done, Luke. I can't believe how much Davis was involved with Mercer. Lindie...I don't understand how she dislikes me so much that she would betray me in such a way."

"In her defense, I don't believe she fully realized the danger she was putting you in."

"I don't know about that." Ellie rubbed her temple, then reached down to take Luke's hand. "Your hand looks like it could be broken. Does it hurt?"

"A bit. It's what happens when you punch someone."

She raised the hand and kissed it, then sighed. "I just cannot believe this has all happened. What will the police do with Davis?"

"Well, he ended up cooperating and saving our lives, and it sounds as though Mercer threatened both he and Lindie to help him here in Casper." Luke explained. "Honestly, though, I'm not sure what will happen."

"Mama will not be able to handle the scandal of a son-in-law in jail. If they even go through with the wedding." She murmured, almost to herself. She felt as though she could fall asleep and not wake up for days. Had they given her a drug to knock her unconscious? Something in the Dr. Pepper, perhaps.

"I'll see what I can do to make sure it all works out." She now knew Luke would do anything for her and her family.

"Thank you, Luke. For being here, for risking your life to help me." She couldn't believe all he had done.

"Don't mention it. Ellie, you must know you mean the world to me…" Her hand holding his loosened as she drifted off to sleep. It had been a long day, and as her eyes fluttered shut, she sent up a prayer thanking God for keeping them all from harm.

~~~~~~

It was almost midnight when they finally arrived back at their hotel. Ellie slowly woke up, then apologized to Luke for falling asleep. He assured her that he understood, then escorted her to her uncle's suite. Patrick rushed to Ellie with hugs the moment the door opened. Lindie approached nervously.

"Oh, Ellie, I am so sorry. I didn't realize just what that horrid Mr. Mercer was up to...I didn't realize...I thought he only wanted to scare you or get you to help him reunite with Janie. Oh, Ellie, you look horrible, but I am so glad you're alright. Will you ever forgive me?"

Ellie wasn't quite sure just how sincere Lindie was being. Her sister often acted like she was a complete ninny, but Ellie had sometimes wondered how much of that was an act. Was it the same scenario here? At any rate, Ellie knew she had to forgive her sister, and figure out what she could do to protect the family's reputation.

Ellie hugged her sister. "I'm all right, Lindie. No need to concern yourself."

Tears welled up in Lindie's eyes, but again, Ellie wasn't sure if they were real. She really had to have more faith in Lindie. "Where is my Davis?"

"He was taken into custody by the police." Luke said. "I'm sorry, Lindie, but you both did take Ellie against her will. That's kidnapping. Davis has a few other charges he must own up to as well. I'm not sure what they will charge him with at this point, but he did help us get Mercer in the end, so I am sure that will be taken into consideration."

"You said you wouldn't turn him in!" Lindie sobbed.

"I never said that. I did confirm with them that Davis ended up helping us, but I had to tell them the whole truth. It's up to the local and federal authorities what happens now."

"Will they...arrest me?" The last word came out as a squeak.

"I honestly don't know." Luke answered.

"Will we still be able to get married? Mr. Callahan, you promised you would make it happen."

"What are you talking about? Luke has no responsibility to you or Davis, Lindie. He has done his best to help in a situation you both created." Ellie tried to keep her temper in check, but the events of the day were piling on her. Luke placed a hand on her arm.

"I did promise, and, if it is possible, I will certainly follow through." He assured the young woman. "I'll pay bail or whatever is necessary, but again, I don't know if or when they will release Davis."

"Luke, you don't have to do that. Why would you offer to help them at all?" Ellie was insistent.

"I have my reasons," he replied, then turned toward Lindie. "You cannot run though, Lindie. As I said before, I will hunt you down, as will the law."

"I'm sure she will stay put," Ellie said quietly.

Lindie clasped her hands in front of her and nodded.

"Right, now." Patrick put an arm around Lindie. "Thank you so much for all you've done, Mr. Callahan, but I believe we should all get some sleep."

Patrick shook Luke's hand one more time, then went off to his room, and Lindie did as well. Ellie looked at Luke as though she wanted to tell him something important. She was exhausted, however. She needed to get to bed and rest.

"Luke..." Ellie began. He smiled and gave a short, stiff bow.

"We'll talk more tomorrow, Ellie. You must get your rest."

She nodded, then headed into her room. Luke turned to go to his own suite of rooms. He needed sleep as well. Tomorrow would most likely be a long day.

Chapter Forty

The following day, Davis showed up at the hotel. Luke had posted his bail, and Davis and Lindie would be married that afternoon. Ellie wasn't the most proficient person to style hair, but she did her best with Lindie's. She still didn't feel she could fully trust her sister, but she was family and Ellie would do anything for her family. She also knew that God could bring good from chaos and this had been a long year full of chaos, that was for sure.

"Are you sure you want to go through with marrying Davis?" Ellie asked. "You know the family would welcome you back home regardless and he still may end up in jail."

"Oh, but Ellie, I do love him, I know you may not believe me, and you think me silly, as you usually do, but I really do love him. Davis loves me as well."

"I don't know if he's even capable of true love." Ellie murmured. She wanted to argue further, but Lindie had clearly made up her mind and Ellie's head still throbbed from her injuries last night as well as the probable drugging.

"Just know that your family will always love you, and if he ever mistreats you, you know where you can turn," Ellie reminded her. Lindie smiled and they continued getting ready.

About an hour before the ceremony, Ellie and Lindie were still doing last-minute preparations at the church. Ellie felt a touch at her elbow and turned to see Luke. She wanted to throw her arms around him, but paused at the look on his face.

"Luke!" She smiled. She had so much she wanted to talk with him about.

"Ellie, I am so glad you're okay. How are you holding up?"

"Still in a bit of shock, I must confess. A bit woozy still, I am sure Davis drugged the Dr. Pepper he gave me."

"Probably. He knew you would figure something out and fight back as soon as you did."

She nodded, glad that he knew her that well.

"And how did you sleep?" Luke asked, concern clear in his voice.

"To be honest, fitfully." She admitted. "I woke many times from nightmares."

"It may take a while for you to adjust. You've been through a traumatic experience."

"And it could have been so much worse if you hadn't come." She stepped closer. "Thank you again, Luke."

"Don't mention it. I should have warned you about Davis when I first saw he was here."

"I probably wouldn't have listened to you." She acknowledged. "And that still wouldn't have stopped Clark Mercer from trying to hurt me."

359

"I suppose." He paused, then continued. "At any rate, you've been through a painful experience. Make sure you don't keep all your feelings inside. Talk to Janie or your grandfather or Matthew if you need to."

She noticed he didn't suggest she talk to him. It hurt, just a little.

"I appreciate everything you have done, very much so. And I'm glad you can stay for the wedding."

"Not quite." He smiled back sadly. "I have some bad news. I must leave shortly, right after the ceremony, as a matter of fact. Family business, unfortunately."

"Oh, dear, is everyone all right? Helena?"

"No, she's fine. My aunt telephoned to tell me that my cousin Anne, you know she's always been sickly, well, Aunt Madeline fears Anne has taken a turn for the worst."

"Well, then of course you must go," Ellie said. "You've done so much for us here already. Much more than was ever necessary. I can't begin to thank you enough."

"I can persuade Davis to marry Lindie, and I can secure him a job so he can provide for her, but I can't make him stay faithful." He frowned. "Though I must say, he seems sincere in his feelings for Lindie."

"She seems quite devoted to him as well." Ellie commented. "I suppose it's proof that God has a plan for everyone." There, she had given him a perfect opening to speak of a future between the two of them.

"I suppose you're right." He stepped forward and took her hand. "Ellie, I'm not sure when I'll be able to see you again. I have so many things to take care of."

"I understand." Her heart fell. Was this goodbye for good?

"I need you to know that I do want to see you again. Believe me. I wish I didn't have to leave. We have a lot we need to talk about."

She held in her emotions. "Of course." But things were as they were. He was a wealthy businessman and she was a cowgirl with calloused hands. They had been in a bubble in St. Louis and even in North Carolina. Perhaps there was no way they could ever be more than friends. "I hope to see you again as well, Luke. Please stop by when you're next in Spearfish. I do hope your cousin has a speedy recovery." She then turned away, hoping he wouldn't see her tears.

~~~~~~~

Luke spent the entire four-day train trip to Charleston deep in thought and prayer. Anne was at the forefront of his mind, but Ellie was not far behind. The look on her face when he was saying goodbye tore at him. He knew she wanted him to tell her he loved her, but he had hesitated. Coward. How he wished he could go back and say the right words, tell her what was in his heart. But family came first, and he had to see Anne, make sure she and Aunt Madeline were okay. Roger would be bringing Helena to Charleston, and Roger's parents would likely be coming as well. He hoped it wasn't that serious.

Luke made it to Charleston and took a taxi to his Aunt Madeline's house on East Battery Street. He handed his bags off to Drummons, the butler, who told him that everyone was in the back garden. Luke quickly made his way there.

"Aunt Madeline, how..." he paused to take in what he was seeing. Helena, Roger and Aunt Madeline all sitting, sipping tea and talking, but also... "Anne?"

361

His cousin sat, looking even more healthy than she had the last time he had seen her in Asheville. "Anne, you look marvelous!"

"Of course I do." She looked at him strangely. "Why wouldn't I?"

Helena skipped up to Luke and hugged him. "I'm glad you could come, Luke. Did everything work out for the best in Wyoming?"

"It's complicated." He dropped a kiss on Helena's head and glared at his aunt, who looked at him with casual indifference. "Aunt Madeline, may I speak with you in private?"

"I don't think it's necessary to do that right now, Lucas. Please sit and enjoy a glass of fresh squeezed lemonade."

"No, Aunt Madeline, I must insist." His muscles tensed in anger.

"Luke, what's wrong?" Helena asked. Aunt Madeline stood slowly.

"Unless you'd like to explain to everyone here why you made it sound as though Anne was on death's door forcing me to to drop all my business plans to come to Charleston."

"Mother, you didn't! Really!" Anne shook her head.

Aunt Madeline lifted her head haughtily. "And would you like to explain to everyone, including your business partners, why you find it appropriate to rush out West to help a man who has done so much damage to you personally and financially and in addition to this, he almost ruined your sister?"

"I told him to go, Aunt Madeline." Helena spoke up. "Ellie's family needed his help."

"Eleanor Bennett is a tart who doesn't deserve help from you, Lucas. Do you know that she actually told Cornelia, Edith and Charlotte Sutton, her best friend, that she could never love you and didn't even like you. She

362

is just using you. Mr. Sutton has informed me that her mother is constantly trying to match all her daughters with wealthy men."

"That might be true of her mother, but certainly not of Ellie. If that were the case, then why didn't she accept my proposal when we were in North Carolina?"

"I knew it!" Helena gasped.

Aunt Madeline's face turned stone cold. "You asked that woman to marry you?"

"Yes, yes I did, and it is of no concern to you."

"Well, she clearly does not have any feelings for you, else she would have accepted. And yet you still act as though you need to buy her love. Why, Lucas, when there are so many fine, upstanding ladies from decent families who would gladly marry you? I've spoken to Caroline Astor and she has a niece…"

"That doesn't matter to me, Aunt Madeline, it never has. I've always wanted a marriage like my parents, one that is based on love and affection, not money or social ties."

"That doesn't mean you can't have both. You need to at least meet women from high society. They desire love as well."

"I am sure they do, but…"

"And besides that, it is clear that Eleanor Bennett doesn't care for you. Go ahead, ask her to marry you again, after everything you've done for her and her family. But if she says yes now, you'll never know if it was for love or because she feels indebted to you."

Luke's stomach fell. As much as he hated to admit it, Aunt Madeline was right. She didn't even know about the fiasco with Clark Mercer yet.

363

"You know I speak the truth, Lucas." His aunt's voice was almost gentle.

He shook his head. "Excuse me everyone. I have some business to attend to." He then retreated back into the house.

~~~~~~

*L*ater that evening, Luke sat on the banks of the Charleston Harbor at White Point Gardens. Fort Sumter loomed in the distance. The bombardment of that fort had started the War Between the States and he was fighting his own inner war. The irony wasn't lost on him.

"Guide me, Lord. Please let me know what I should do?" He clasped his hands together in prayer.

"Well, for one thing, you shouldn't listen to Aunt Madeline. I don't think she'd know true love if it womped her in the head." Helena plopped down next to him.

"Be charitable, Helena, she's just doing what she feels is best." Like he had done with Charles and Janie.

"But she's wrong. Ellie likes you a great deal, I just know it. I would be willing to bet that she even loves you. She's just afraid of her own feelings."

"What makes you think that?" Luke asked.

"We had a conversation or two without you lurking about," Helena replied. "She all but admitted to me that she was wrong about her initial assessment of you. Did you see her in South Dakota? How did she react to you?"

Luke explained what had happened in Casper. "Strange thing is; I believe Davis will be a better man because of all this. Maybe, at least I hope so."

"One can only hope." Helena drew her knees up to her chest and hugged them. "Heavens, Luke you could have died!"

"But Davis saved me."

"Well that's actually a turnaround from his normal actions."

"Indeed. All the same, I can't help but wonder if that's something else she would feel indebted to me for."

"Tell me true, Luke, why did you really do any of it? For what purpose?"

"It's simple. I love her. I want to do everything in my power to make her happy and keep her safe."

"Even if she never marries you?"

"Even then."

"Oh, Luke, you are quite the romantic, at least where Miss Ellie is concerned. Perhaps you just need one more grand gesture, to show her your feelings. To show her that you really do care for her."

Luke thought for a moment, and a few ideas popped into his head. "You know, Helena, you may be right." He paused. "And you're certain Ellie was speaking fondly of me. I don't want to push her too much, I mean, if she has no feelings for me."

"No, of course you don't and yes, I'm quite sure."

"And you really wouldn't mind a country girl for a sister?"

"If she's a country girl named Ellie Bennett, I'd quite prefer her." Helena smiled and threw her arms around her brother. "So what will your big plan be?"

"To start with, I need to correct a big mistake, I'm afraid," he sighed. "I need to admit to Charles Brantley that I was wrong."

~~~~~~

The day after Lindie's wedding, Ellie returned home to Longbourn. She filled her family in about the wedding, but left out the part about Clark Mercer. Uncle Patrick would stay with Lindie until Davis's trial, which was most likely going to end in a plea bargain. It sounded as though he would have his sentence reduced to probation as he was going to be the key witness against Mercer. Ellie was sure this was all possible thanks to Luke's influence and connections. She still didn't know why he had gone out of his way to find Lindie and Davis, and then make sure their married life started out on the right foot by securing him a job where he could advance as far as he was willing.

As Ellie spoke, she couldn't help but notice the looks on Janie's, Aunt Edith's and Grandpa Benjamin's faces. She might be able to hide many of the facts from her preoccupied father and self-absorbed mother and sisters, but not Janie, her grandpa or her aunt. As the family dispersed after the discussion, Grandpa Benjamin stayed back with Janie, who took Ellie's arm.

"Mama and Father might be so happy and relieved to not question why you were the only one invited to the wedding and why Uncle Patrick is staying and what on earth happened to your face, but I, for one, am very curious. What happened in Casper, Ellie? Out with it."

Ellie looked from her sister to her grandpa. They had a right to know, and Luke's advice about being able to talk about her bad experience was sound. She might as well start now and tell them the whole story.

366

When Ellie finished the tale, Janie simply pulled her into her arms and hugged her tightly.

"Oh, Ellie, how terrifying. How could Lindie and Davis have done such a thing? And Clark Mercer? Oh, goodness, I am so sorry. This is all my fault."

"It is hardly your fault, Janie. He is much worse than when he was courting you. He's truly mad. I can't imagine what your life would be like if you married that lunatic."

"Never liked that Mercer fellow." Grandpa Benjamin said gruffly, then moved across the room and hugged both Ellie and Janie. "Don't like that Davis Martin either, but it appears we're stuck with him, unless he gets what he deserves and is thrown in prison."

"Unfortunately, Grandpa, that would destroy Lindie and Mama as well." Janie pointed out.

"Would do that girl some good, to know that her actions have consequences." He replied.

"Well, there's nothing we can do about it now." Ellie stated. We can just be there for Lindie if she needs us."

"And that is what we shall do." Janie nodded. "You should tell Aunt Edith all of this as well, Ellie. She should know. Father should as well."

"I'll talk with each of them tomorrow." Ellie agreed. "I'm too tired to retell it all right now, and most likely Uncle Patrick will be calling Aunt Edith to discuss in more detail."

"Well, by George, young'un, you definitely need a good night's sleep after your adventure." Grandpa said. Ellie couldn't agree more.

~~~~~

367

$\mathcal{T}$wo weeks after the wedding, Ellie received a phone call from Uncle Patrick, informing her that Davis would not serve any further jail time. The newlyweds would be arriving in Spearfish by the end of the week, and Martha immediately finalized the reception for the couple.

The day of their arrival, Ellie tried to stay busy so she wouldn't have to see either Davis or Lindie much. It was unavoidable that evening, however, as she had to eat dinner with them.

"Good gracious, how exciting this has all been!" Lindie was insufferable. Ellie didn't know how Davis could tolerate her.

"Yes, me being kidnapped and almost killed was great fun." Ellie muttered under her breath so that only Janie heard her.

"Who could have ever guessed I would return home from Brighton Ranch a married woman? And the first in the family at that." Lindie laughed as Kathy and Martha continued to prattle on, telling her of the plans for their big celebration tomorrow.

As they enjoyed the steaks Hattie had prepared for the meal, Ellie watched Davis. He acted as though nothing untoward had happened, that he hadn't run off with a young woman, hadn't kidnapped her and hadn't used a good, kind man to get him out of trouble time and time again. He hadn't even attempted to apologize to anyone. The whole situation nauseated her.

That evening, the family congregated to the sitting room. Lindie and Davis had gone to their hotel in Spearfish. Martha had wanted them to stay at the ranch, like the Gardeners were, but Lindie wouldn't have it. She wanted to prove to her family and neighbors that Davis could indeed support her. Ellie knew for sure the room was probably being paid for with Luke's money.

"I must tell you again. Your Mr. Callahan is a very special man. You do know that, right?" Aunt Edith pulled Ellie aside to speak more privately.

"Of course I do. He bailed Davis out, paid his legal fees and is the one that got his jail time suspended. He paid for the wedding. He used his influence to get Davis a job at the Yellowstone National Park and secured them housing. Oh, yes, and he saved my life, and still I don't understand why he would do any of it. He certainly didn't have to." Tears formed in Ellie's eyes. "Oh, Aunt Edith, I am afraid I will never see him again. What must he think of me? Of this family?"

Aunt Edith hugged her. "Your uncle and I both agree that he is a man of integrity, a man to be admired and there is obviously a reason he feels the need to help this family. You know very well what that is. Believe me, I don't think we've seen the last of Mr. Callahan."

"We owe him so much." Ellie replied, more to herself than her aunt. "I feel so ashamed of every unkind thing I ever said to him or about him." Unlike her aunt, Ellie couldn't help but feel strongly that she would never have the chance to tell him how she truly felt.

Part 7: Fall of 1929

Chapter Forty-One

Lindie and Davis left a week later, and the Gardiners left two days after that. Ellie had spent much of her time working. Whenever she looked at either Davis or Lindie, she remembered Clark Mercer and the small cabin and the fear she had felt, believing she would die. She continued to wake from her sleep occasionally with nightmares.

The reception for the married couple had been outlandish and exasperating. Lindie had relished being the center of attention, and would tell everyone in dramatic fashion about their elopement. She even included parts about Clark Mercer. According to Lindie, Mercer was a dastardly man who had tricked both Davis and Lindie into bringing Ellie to Casper, but then Davis saved Ellie and became the hero of the day. Ellie had longed to correct Lindie's version of the story or at least add in the parts about Luke, but was too frustrated to do so. Not only that, but any time that Ellie tried to get a word in edgewise with her mother, she was ignored. Ellie found great comfort in the fact that many in her family knew the whole truth. Still, she spent much time praying for the wisdom to deal with her sister and Davis and the humility to forgive them as well as to give thanks to those who really deserved it.

371

"I admit, I still find it hard to believe that anyone would hire Davis with the reputation he has acquired," Janie said one afternoon a few weeks after Davis and Lindie had departed. She and Ellie were running errands in Spearfish. Their youngest sister had written about how they were settled in their new home. Yellowstone was beautiful, but Lindie had complained about how secluded it was and that Davis wasn't getting the respect he deserved at work. Ellie wasn't surprised. He was the kind of man that would never take responsibility for anything that ever happened, which made him a perfect husband for Lindie, as she was the same way.

"I thought I explained it all to you." Ellie shook her head. "Maybe I didn't, with everything else that happened." Ellie had apparently left some things out when she told her story. "Luke vouched for him. I hope he won't end up regretting it."

Janie shuddered. "I still find it hard to believe that all of this even happened. I know you have nightmares about it; I can hear you across the room." She paused and looked at her hands. "Ellie, I am so sorry. I still feel responsible for everything Mr. Mercer did, I know it's all because of me. I never would have imagined it possible."

"It's hard for me to believe as well. Thank the good Lord it all worked out the way it did."

"Ellie! Janie!" Angelina Ingraham ran over to them. "You will never guess what I just heard." She smiled broadly.

"What is it?" Janie asked.

"Mr. Charles Brantley has returned to Verbena Meadows," Angelina replied.

Janie immediately blushed. "That's wonderful for him, but it doesn't affect us one way or another." She tried to brush the news off, but Ellie could tell Janie was again trying to conceal her feelings.

By the time Ellie and Janie met up with Martha and Kathy at the truck, their mother had heard the same news about Mr. Brantley. She nagged Janie about seeing Charles the whole way home.

"My dear, it is imperative that you visit Mr. Brantley as soon as possible and we must invite him to dinner."

"I don't know if that's such a good idea, Mother." Janie tried to hide her apprehension, but Ellie saw through it.

The excitement continued when they arrived home as Martha immediately told James the news. "You must plan to visit Mr. Brantley as much as possible, my love."

"Yes, yes, of course, dear," James replied, then made his way back into his office. Ellie grabbed her hat from the peg and turned to go back to work as best she could with her mind extremely distracted. Why was Charles returning? Hadn't his sisters said that he planned on selling Verbena Meadows?

As soon as she stepped back out onto the porch, she saw a cloud of dust on the road being kicked up by a familiar Phantom. She smiled and poked her head back inside to tell the family.

"Good heavens!" Martha exclaimed, knocking her chair over as she stood quickly. Ellie turned back outside to welcome Charles. Her heart sped up when she saw someone in the passenger seat. Luke. What was he doing here? She took a deep breath and waved. Luke looked even better than he had in Casper, wearing Levis, his Harvard letterman sweater, cowboy boots and a dark Stetson. How could he look so at home in so many different settings? Ellie longed to run into his arms, but knew she must refrain. He had put his life on the line for her, then walked away. She needed to let him make the first move. She needed to be patient, even though she wanted to talk with him about what had transpired in Casper.

"Gentlemen! Welcome!" She smiled warmly.

"Miss Ellie, it is so good to see you again." Charles smiled back. Luke was reserved and merely tipped his hat.

"My mother and sisters are in the sitting room, please come in and join us." The two men followed her and the newcomers and the Bennett women greeted one another. Ellie couldn't help but notice that Martha ignored Luke as she told Charles the news of the county. Ellie stepped next to Luke, needing to be near him. He smelled of leather, sandalwood and the ever-present root beer.

"And my Lindie is married as well, though we weren't able to celebrate as we should have been able to do."

Ellie tuned out her mother's babbling and discreetly glanced at Luke. He was looking at her with an expression she couldn't quite decipher. She noticed that Charles was staring at Janie with tender admiration in his blue eyes. The one-sided conversation continued when suddenly, Martha stated:

"Now, gentlemen, you must join us for dinner."

"We would enjoy that very much, however..." Charles was interrupted by Martha.

"You remember, you promised when you were here last summer. I haven't forgotten."

"Yes, of course, but as I was about to say..." Charles started to assure her and then glanced at Luke, then to Janie. "Forgive me, but we must be on our way. We already have dinner plans for tonight, but perhaps another time, possibly tomorrow."

"Tomorrow it is, gentlemen!" Martha exclaimed before Charles had a chance to change his mind.

Ellie smiled to herself when he said 'we'. Surely, that meant Luke would be coming as well. She and Janie walked the men out to the car; Charles still couldn't keep his eyes off Janie, reminding Ellie of a little puppy. Ellie knew Luke was responsible for bringing Charles back to South Dakota. One more thing to thank him for.

"I...I'm so glad you were able to visit, Luke. I haven't had the opportunity to ask. How have you been?" She wondered why he had bothered to come with Charles to the ranch, when he hadn't even said a single word. Before he left Casper, hadn't he said that he wanted to talk? Had he changed his mind about her? Was he upset about what had happened in Casper?

"I am quite well, thank you," he replied quickly, but smiled, and it warmed her heart.

"We will see you ladies tomorrow!" Charles tipped his hat to them and the two men got into the car and drove off.

Janie tried to hide her excitement, but Ellie could tell how happy she was.

"Oh, Ellie, I cannot wait for dinner tomorrow!" Janie grabbed Ellie's arm and spoke in hushed tones. "Though I am sorry he brought Luke with him I know he annoys you."

"I wouldn't say that..." Again, Ellie had the opportunity to tell Janie everything she had learned about Luke over the past few months. She was conflicted, however. Had their time together in St. Louis meant more to her than it had to Luke? He had come to the rescue in Casper, but was it only because he felt a responsibility for Davis Martin? Luke hadn't spoken to her today, and barely answered her one question. True, her mother really had not allowed anyone else to speak of course, but he could have said something.

"Ellie! Janie!" Martha's screech broke into Ellie's thoughts. "Girls, stop dallying, we have much to do before tomorrow. Dinner must be perfect if we are to get Mr. Brantley to propose to Janie."

"I'd say that won't be a problem. Did you see the way he was looking at you?" Ellie smiled and nudged Janie as they went their separate ways.

~~~~~~~

"*L*uke, what's wrong with you?" Charles asked as they drove back to Verbena Meadows. "You were so quiet at the Bennett's. You're acting like you did when we were here the first time."

"Hard to get a word in edgewise with Mrs. Bennett so excited that you're back in town."

"Janie...she looked beautiful today, didn't she?" Charles couldn't hide his grin.

"She did, and I must say, she looked very happy to see you. I told you I was wrong about her."

"It didn't take much to persuade me back then. I should have listened to my heart in the first place and discussed the situation with Janie instead of just leaving without a word."

"Well, are you now convinced of her feelings?"

"I am." Charles ran a hand through his windblown hair. In another few weeks it would be too cold to have the roof down. "What about you?"

"What about me?"

"You barely said a word to Ellie. I know how difficult it was to speak, as you said, but you could have tried when she walked us to the car."

Luke thought for a moment. "I thought I was ready to come back and talk with her, but when I'm around her, especially here...I don't know." It had been so easy to talk with Ellie in St. Louis, he felt comfortable with her there. In Casper, he had been so focused on his mission that he hadn't had time to think about his actions, and then Aunt Madeline had interfered and he had lost his courage just when he needed it most. His talk with Helena had given him some confidence, but his aunt's words continued to cause him doubt. What if Aunt Madeline was right and all Ellie ever felt for him was simply gratitude?

~~~~~~

The next day, Ellie took more time than usual with her toilette while dressing for dinner, without making it obvious. She wore a dark blue skirt with a white silk blouse that had intricate floral embroidery across the collar. She even had Janie do her hair in a functional yet elegant updo instead of her trademark braid. Luckily, Janie was so excited that Charles was coming that she didn't question Ellie 's extra preparedness.

When the men arrived, Charles greeted everyone warmly, especially Janie. From there, they went directly into the dining room. Charles made sure he sat next to Janie, and was attentive to her during the entire meal. Ellie had the feeling that a proposal would be imminent.

Unfortunately for her, Luke was seated as far away from Ellie as possible, though not by choice. Somehow, he had the pleasure of sitting between her mother and Grandpa Benjamin. Ellie could tell the seating

377

arrangement irritated Luke, having to sit there and listen to Martha, who rambled on about Charles and Janie and totally ignored Luke. How could her mother be so rude? If only she knew just how much Luke had done for the Bennett family, especially while in Casper. Luckily, Luke had Grandpa Benjamin to talk with. The two men seemed to get along quite well.

After dinner, the group congregated in the family sitting room. Ellie watched Luke as he walked from one corner of the room to the other after speaking to Charles and Janie. He now was holding a conversation with her father. Ellie wished he would speak to her and couldn't understand why he was avoiding her, and more than that, she wished she had the courage to speak to him. Ellie finally found an excuse to approach him when her mother asked her to serve coffee.

"Is your sister still in St. Louis?" Ellie asked when she brought Luke his cup.

"Yes, until Christmas, at least." His fingers brushed hers as he took the cup and saucer. Her mind went blank of anything else to say, and he remained quiet as well.

Thank you. I'm so glad you're here. Why won't you talk to me? I love you, Luke.

Why couldn't she voice any of her thoughts? She never had issues expressing her opinions to others before, and Luke seemed to actually like that about her. What was holding her back?

Time passed quickly and suddenly, it was time for Luke and Charles to leave, but they promised to visit again soon.

Chapter Forty-Two

"*I* don't understand why he's being so distant, Matthew," Ellie said as they worked the next day. October had finally arrived, and the weather was getting cooler. "I also can't understand why I'm being such a ninny? Why have I been so hesitant to talk with Luke? What's wrong with me?"

"Must be love, Miss Ellie, can' t be anything but love. Don't ya worry none. It'll all work out. Once the ice is broken, ya two'll be actin' like ya were back in St. Louis."

"If he ever decides to talk to me again," Ellie replied.

When they returned to the house, an unfamiliar truck was parked in front. What was even stranger was that Charles stepped out of the newest Ford truck model.

"Mr. Brantley, what happened to your Phantom?" Ellie asked as she dismounted Naomi.

"I have a special delivery for you, Miss Ellie, one that I could not bring in the Rolls Royce." They both walked to the back of the truck and Ellie smiled when she saw three small goats.

"What on earth?"

"Boo!" Charles jumped at the goats suddenly, then laughed. At the outburst, the goats stiffened, then fell. They laid there for about half a minute, then rolled back onto their feet. Ellie laughed in pure joy.

"Fainting goats? Where in the world did you get them?"

"They're a gift for you." Charles smiled. "They're from Luke."

"Luke...for me?" Ellie couldn't believe it. He had not only remembered the small comment she had made, but he'd bought her livestock? To most girls, that wouldn't mean much of anything, but it meant the world to Ellie.

"Thank you for delivering them, Charles, but where is Luke? Why couldn't he be here to deliver them himself?"

"He planned on being here when you received them, but he was called away on business, quite unexpectedly, and very urgent." Charles didn't look too concerned, but Ellie still had to ask.

"Is everyone alright? His sister? Is it Anne again?" Luke hadn't told Ellie anything about his trip back to Charleston.

"Oh, no, everyone is all right, he had to go farther east. New York as a matter of a fact. Helena is just fine. It's a four-day trip, so he'll be gone for over a week, unfortunately."

"Well, I thank you for bringing these kids out." Ellie reached out and scratched the closest one on the head. He was a chocolate brown color and very friendly. She loved them already.

"It was no problem." He smiled sheepishly. "I wanted to come out here anyways."

"Janie will be so happy to see you." *As will my mother.*

"Charles! Good afternoon." As if right on cue, Janie came onto the porch and waved as Charles's face lit up.

"Janie." He reddened just a bit. "I was hoping to take you for a stroll."

Janie smiled. "That sounds wonderful. Let me just grab my jacket."

"Shall I help you get these goats out?" Charles offered. She shook her head.

"No, you go on. I've got these guys. You go for a walk with Janie."

"Thank you." He nodded, then jogged over to Janie, who was exiting the house. He offered her his arm. Ellie smiled. She had a feeling she knew what Charles was going to do.

Ellie brought the goats into the barn, thankful they had some extra space where they could keep them. Her mother, Marie and Kathy wandered out of the house.

"Where on earth did Janie go?" Martha asked. "And whose truck is that?"

"Mr. Brantley rented it. He brought me some fainting goats. He and Janie just left for a walk."

"Why on earth would he bring you goats?" Martha asked.

"They're actually from Mr. Callahan." Ellie smiled. "I mentioned my fascination with them once. In regards to Janie, I think we all know why Charles is taking Janie for a walk."

Martha clapped her hands, and Ellie was glad that her mother didn't ask about the goats in more detail. How could she explain to her mother why Luke had gotten her goats when she didn't even understand it herself?

The women enjoyed watching the fainting goats, and Kathy quickly came up with a slew of possible names for them. It wasn't long before Janie and Charles returned, all smiles, and Janie was blushing. As the women approached the couple, Charles excused himself to go into the house, no doubt to speak to James.

"My beautiful Janie, where on earth has Mr. Brantley gone?" Martha took both of Janie's hands into hers. Janie laughed, tears of happiness in her eyes.

"Charles went to speak with Father. He asked me to marry him."

Martha and Kathy squealed and hugged Janie. Ellie smiled, so happy for her sister, glad that everything was settled. The past year's suspense and heartache was over, at least for Janie. The group moved inside, Martha, gushing over how happy Janie would be, was already planning an engagement dinner. Charles and James soon joined them in the sitting room. Ellie hugged Charles, and there were congratulations all around. It was one of the happiest days in the Bennet household that Ellie could remember.

That night, after Charles left, Ellie wandered out to the barn to see her new goats. She sat down in their pen and let them crawl into her lap. She couldn't help but think of Luke, and tears of longing formed in her eyes. The gift of the three animals was very telling of the fact that he should still heve feelings for her, but then why had he left without a word?

"Ellie, are you in here?" Janie called into the barn. Ellie wiped her cheeks with her palms.

"Yes, I'm over here." Ellie stood and moved to climb over the gate as Janie walked towards her.

"What are you doing out here? What's wrong? Were you crying?" Concern filled Janie's voice.

"I'm just so happy for you, Janie. You and Charles were made for each other." She tried to paste a smile on her face, as she moved to Naomi's stall to pay her some attention.

"I wonder if one can die from happiness." Janie giggled. "I can't believe he loves me. The kindest, most handsome man I have ever met wants to spend the rest of his life with me." She shook her head. "You know, he told me that when he left last November he already loved me then. He only left because he didn't believe I really cared for him." She laughed again. "Can you believe that? I am so glad that he finally knows just how much I love him. Oh, Ellie, God is good!"

"He is indeed." Naomi nudged Ellie with her muzzle.

"I only wish you could be as happy as I am. We must find someone special for you."

Oh, Janie, I do have someone. If only he were here with me... She shook her head. "Well, I did meet Mr. Sutton's cousin in Asheville. Perhaps he is the one for me." Naomi gave a nicker and shook her head as if in disagreement and Janie and Ellie laughed.

Chapter Forty-Three

The next week passed by slowly for Ellie. Charles was a frequent visitor to the ranch, often staying all day. He drove Janie, Martha, Kathy and even Marie over to Devil's Tower in Wyoming one day, but Ellie stayed behind to work on chores. She was happy for Janie, but it hurt seeing Charles and Janie together and so much in love. It made Ellie realize just how much she missed Luke and all they could have had, if she weren't so stubborn and opinionated.

She had just finished feeding her new goats when Grandpa Benjamin poked his head into the barn.

"Ellie, you have a visitor," he said.

"Who is it?" She wiped her hands on her trousers and followed her grandfather.

"A Madeline Day Burger or some such person. She's pretty high-falutin'."

Ellie froze. Madeline VanRensselaer? In South Dakota? Ellie walked as quickly as she could to the house.

"She's in the sitting room!" Her grandpa called after her.

Ellie caught a quick look at herself in the entryway mirror and shuddered. She looked as if she had been working on a ranch all day, which was true. Oh well. It would have to do.

"Mrs. VanRensselaer. I must say I am surprised to see you have traveled all the way out to South Dakota. Are Luke and Helena all right?"

"They are." Mrs. VanRensselaer looked with clear disdain at Ellie's appearance. "I hope you are as well as can be expected with your station in life."

"Yes, ma'am." She let the insult go. "Can I get you anything in the way of a refreshment?"

"No, thank you." She gestured for Ellie to sit. "You must know why I have come all this way, Miss Bennett."

Ellie sat down. "Actually, I have no idea, ma'am."

"Do not trifle with me! I have heard that one of your sisters recently married under suspicious circumstances, one is on the verge of a very advantageous marriage, and lastly that you, Miss Eleanor Bennett, you will be marrying my nephew, Lucas."

Ellie's stomach fluttered. Mrs. VanRensselaer continued.

"I know this to be a scandalous falsehood. You must deny it at once. Tell me it's not true."

"I have no idea what you're talking about. I don't know where you could have heard such a thing." Had Luke made a comment to someone?

"Can you deny that there is no foundation in this claim?" Mrs. VanRensselaer demanded.

"Not to be rude, but I don't have to tell you anything or answer any of your questions."

"That is an outrageous answer!" Mrs. VanRensselaer barked. "Has my nephew proposed to you? I have the right to know about his future."

Ellie couldn't believe she was having this conversation. Anger and frustration bubbled inside her. "Maybe that's true in your world, but here

385

in my home, you have no right to ask me anything!" She spoke firmly, trying not to shout.

"Let me be clear with you. A marriage between you and Lucas can never be. It simply cannot happen. He is engaged to one of the Astor girls."

Ellie felt like someone punched her in the stomach. Was that why he had distanced himself from her? Had she just been a challenge for him? He once said he loved challenges. Was she just a diversion, especially while in St. Louis? Self-doubt crept through Ellie.

"Now what do you have to say about that?"

Ellie tried not to let the woman's words visually affect her. "I only have to say that...well, if he really is engaged to an Astor, then he never would have proposed to me, so again why are you even here?"

"Their engagement is...quite particular. It was pre-arranged long ago. Now that they are both of age to be married, it appears that you are trying to prevent this union!"

"With all due respect, they are both adults and can make their own decisions."

"I will not have this union prevented by a... backwoods hoyden with no connections or money."

Ellie threw a hand in the air in exasperation. "Why does any of this concern me? Besides, you and the Astors may have planned a marriage, but Luke isn't obligated to marry anyone. After all, this is the twentieth century! In America! For crying out loud! If Luke isn't interested in marrying someone his aunt chose long ago, and if he never made a specific promise to this Miss Astor, then he is free to choose whomever he wants. And if, for some extremely odd reason he were to choose me, why should I not accept him?"

"Because honor and decorum forbid it." She stepped closer. "If you care one wit for Lucas at all, you will stop seeing him at once. A relationship with you will only bring misery and hardship on him. He would be shunned by everyone he knows because of you. His business would suffer dramatically without the proper contacts. Your sister's engagement to Mr. Brantley is quite bad enough, but at least she has grace and poise and womanly attributes. You on the other hand would be a complete and utter embarrassment. Your marriage would be a disgrace and you would ruin his chances of becoming the most notable of businessmen."

Ellie knew that most of the words out of this pretentious woman's mouth were untrue. Luke's true friends would remain loyal to him no matter what the circumstances. "That would be unfortunate, indeed, if it were only true, but I am sure that Luke will be extraordinarily happy when he finds the woman he truly wants to marry, no matter what her social status is. He is a kind and wonderful man and his worth is much more than his bank account and properties. If I were to be lucky enough to win his heart, I can assure you he would never regret it."

"Headstrong, foolish girl! You should be ashamed of yourself. Is this how you thank someone for trying to do what's best for all involved? I am most definitely not used to being treated in this manner."

"That is unfortunate for you, ma'am, but neither am I."

Mrs. VanRensselaer stepped closer and spoke in a low, threatening tone. "Again, let me make myself perfectly clear. Miss Astor and my nephew are meant for each other. She has been raised to be the wife of a great man and that man is my nephew. They both have pure, untainted

387

pedigrees as well as great fortunes. You on the other hand, are the exact opposite. The Callahan line cannot be thus polluted."

Ellie tried to hold her emotions in check. She couldn't believe this woman talked as if people were animals. Her horses had pedigrees, she didn't. Ellie didn't know why she was even arguing when Luke had given her no indication that he ever wanted to see her again. Still, her stubbornness wouldn't let her give in. "Whatever my pedigree may be, if Luke doesn't care about it, then why should you?"

Mrs. VanRensselaer smiled smugly. "I do not have time to argue about trivial things. Will you promise to stay away from Lucas and never agree to an engagement with him?"

"No, I will not." She replied firmly. "I won't be intimidated by you. I have a right to choose my own friends, as does Luke. All of your arguments are ridiculous."

"If you are quite finished, I have one more thing to say, Miss Bennett." Mrs. VanRensselaer's voice sounded as if it could freeze water in July. "Just remember I know every sordid detail about what happened in Casper. Do you honestly believe Lucas would want a girl like you whose family is completely deranged?"

Ellie took a shaky breath, her anger and frustration simmered over in her. How had she even heard about the Casper incident? "You have insulted me and my family in every way possible. You can't possibly have anything further to say, so if you will please now leave." Ellie made her way to the door and opened it and made a sweeping gesture inviting the old women to exit.

"So this is your final response? You must have no consideration whatsoever for my nephew. You obviously have no care that you will disgrace him. You are selfish and undeserving of even his friendship."

"I only want Luke to be happy," she replied honestly. "You, on the other hand, want to control him, so I don't really care what you think."

"You are determined to ruin him then?"

I love him! She wanted to shout the words, but if she were to ever speak them aloud, she wanted Luke to be the first to hear them. "No... the last thing I want to do is ruin him, unfortunately it's been made quite clear to me that he doesn't want me. So you should be ecstatic about that!"

"Do not imagine, Miss Bennett, that you will ever marry Lucas. I came here hoping you would be reasonable. Rest assured, I will not stop until I put an end to such an outlandish union." The woman stormed out of the house to a waiting car where the chauffeur drove her away. Ellie flopped down onto a chair. Had Mrs. VanRensselaer really come all the way to South Dakota from Charleston just to break off a possible engagement? Did she really consider Ellie that much of a threat? How would Luke feel about his aunt's interference? Did he send her, did he agree with her? Was that why he hadn't really spoken to her when he was here earlier? Did he still love her and if so, was he willing to stand up to his aunt? Oh, so many questions.

Grandpa Benjamin stepped into the sitting room cautiously. "Everything all right, Ellie?"

"I have absolutely no idea." Ellie quickly told her grandpa everything that had transpired. "I just don't know what to think anymore. If Luke doesn't come back, then I will know he doesn't care."

"I don't believe that. From what I can tell he's a good, solid man who was very interested in you the first time he was here. I much enjoy conversing with him. Perhaps you should ask Charles, he would know more about Luke's feelings. They have been friends for a long time."

"Yes, that's a good idea, and Charles would give me much more reliable information," Ellie replied, then looked out the window to see her father pull up to the house in the Model T.

"How is everything in Spearfish?" Ellie asked as he walked up the porch steps, grandpa still standing at her side.

"Well, I received an interesting letter from Mr. Sutton today." He rubbed his mustache and chuckled. "The first piece of news is that he has sold his rights to Longbourn Ranch."

Ellie's stomach dropped. "What? How can you laugh at such news? This is awful." Ellie was astonished. How was this possible? Mr. Sutton had said multiple times that he would never give up the ranch. "Who did he sell to, Papa?"

"He didn't say, only that we would learn 'all in good time'."

"Really Papa, and you're...okay with this? I can't believe you are so calm; this is devastating news!"

"It may be, but he wrote nothing more. I'll certainly write and inquire about it further."

Ellie needed to know more, and she needed to know it now. She shook her head. "What else does Mr. Sutton have to say?"

"You will find this most interesting, my dear. He writes that all of Asheville and Biltmore Village are talking about how you are going to be wealthy and powerful beyond measure."

"What?"

"He says that there is a rumor that you will be marrying Mr. Callahan, and that Mrs. VanRensselaer is none too happy about it."

"That much I know to be true." Ellie mumbled under her breath.

James then laughed out loud. "Imagine, you marrying Mr. Callahan! I don't think he ever paid you a lick of attention, much less ever really looked at you as a woman. He's certainly not the romantic one, that's for sure. I find this whole letter just far too amusing."

Ellie tried to force herself to laugh with her father. Grandpa Benjamin just looked at her curiously.

"Sutton continues to say that it is his duty to warn us all, that you, my dear Ellie, should not rush into such a union." He laughed again. "What a foolish man. Then he goes on to say how glad he is that Lindie's unfortunate business was hushed up. He thinks we shouldn't have allowed them back at the Longbourn Ranch so soon after the scandal. Says it's almost as if we were encouraging their bad behavior, but then he reminds us that, as Christians, we must forgive them, but we also must be careful about allowing them to visit." James folded the letter. "Those are his ideas about Christian forgiveness! Ellie, as much as I despise that Davis Martin, Mr. Sutton is in a class all his own. I cannot wait to reply to this."

James looked at the letter one more time. "How silly he is, Ellie. Mr. Callahan is most certainly not interested in you, and you don't like him any more than he likes you. This is all so absurd." He handed her the letter. "There is a message from Charlotte in here for you as well, my dear." He beamed as Ellie scanned the letter, then shrieked with happiness for her friend. Charlotte was with child, and he or she would arrive in early May. Charlotte wrote that she couldn't be happier about bringing new life into the world.

Ellie read the rest of the letter herself, wondering how all of Asheville knew about her relationship with Mr. Callahan. First Mrs. VanRensselaer's visit, and now this news. She wished she knew what was going on in Luke's mind. His actions, especially over the past month, must be proof that he still cared for her, but more importantly, she now had the wisdom to know that she had loved Luke all along. Would she ever get a second chance with Luke? Would she have the courage to tell him of her love for him?

Chapter Forty-Four

" Ellie, your presence is requested up at the house."

Ellie finished feeding the horses, kissed Naomi on the nose and turned to look at Marie. "Why? What's going on?"

"Mr. Brantley is here and he brought that Mr. Callahan. They are traveling down to Custer and they want you to drive them. Janie will be going as well."

"Luke is here?" Ellie smiled and her heart sped up. It was all she could do not to run up to the house and throw herself into the man's arms, but she had to keep her composure. She didn't have any time to make herself presentable, but Luke didn't even seem to mind her appearance. Luke greeted her warmly with a smile.

"Ellie! I hope you don't mind being our chauffer today." Charles had his arm around Janie's waist, and they both looked incredibly happy.

"I don't mind at all. It will be fun, and the weather is perfect." It was unseasonably warm today.

Luke's hand brushed hers as they walked side by side to the car. He looked relaxed, wearing his usual attire while in South Dakota, but he also had on a brown leather jacket.

"I want to thank you for the fainting goats, Luke. They are a wonderful addition to the ranch." They all climbed into the Ford, Janie and Charles in the back, Luke took the passenger side and Ellie slid behind the wheel. On the outside, this appeared much like their previous trip to Custer, yet so much had changed.

"I'm glad you like them. I found a breeder down in Tennessee and just knew you would appreciate them." He smiled.

The conversation for most of the hour drive focused on Janie and Charles's wedding, which would be held in Chicago the following spring. As they neared the state park, the conversation turned to the economic tragedy that had occurred just yesterday, which Ellie hadn't heard about. The way Luke and Charles were talking, Tuesday, October 29, 1929 would go down in history. Billions of dollars had been lost on the New York Stock Exchange, wiping out thousands of investors. Ellie wondered if Luke or Charles had been affected much, but felt it wasn't her place to ask.

Charles decided that they would walk around Center Lake, which was one of Ellie 's favorite places in the Black Hills. They left the picnic dinner in the truck for after the hike. The trees surrounding the lake were mostly evergreens, and their reflection off the clear blue lake was beautiful to behold. Tan rock formations dotted the shore of the lake and Ellie knew from personal experience that they would need to either hike around them, which would be a challenge, or climb over them. She preferred to climb them, and hoped at least one of the others was up to that task. Preferably Luke.

Charles and Janie lagged behind, wanting some privacy, which gave Ellie some time alone with Luke.

"I am constantly amazed at the beauty to be found in South Dakota." Luke commented.

"The most beautiful place in the United States, in my opinion," Ellie agreed. "Which reminds me, are you still planning to build a resort in the area? What with the stock market problem and all?"

"Unfortunately, that project is on hold for now," he replied. "I have acquired the land and the blueprints are ready, but you're correct, with the financial crisis sweeping the country, I'll have to take stock of all my business holdings and simplify things for the time being."

Ellie bit her lip. "And I suppose Lindie and Davis caused more of a financial burden on you." She glanced at him. "I...I have been meaning to thank you again for everything you did for them and me in Casper. I am so grateful, you...like I said before, you saved my life..."

"You would have done the same for me." He sighed. "But Ellie, you only need to thank me for yourself, not your family." He took her hand to help her over a fallen log. "You must know I did it all for you. I would put my life at risk seventy times seven more for you."

Ellie wasn't sure what to say and moved to step away, but he held her hand and pulled her closer. "When I was here a few weeks ago, it was because I wanted to support Charles, but I also had to see you. I wasn't myself because I was worried about the impending economic crisis I knew was coming. I had taken precautions, but I was still preoccupied. There were also some...family concerns. Then there is also the fact that...I didn't want you to feel obligated to me in any way because of what happened in Casper."

"I...I don't understand. Why would I feel obligated?"

"Because I helped with the Lindie and Davis fiasco. Often times, people do whatever they can to pay me back. I don't want that from you." He paused. "I know you don't care about wealth, and you have your own interests, but I want to be able to give you everything your heart desires, everything you deserve." He took a deep breath. "You must know Ellie, that my feelings haven't changed since we were in North Carolina. I love you more now than I did then. The real question is…" He took another breath. "Do you care for me? Have your feelings changed since we were in North Carolina? I am so hesitant to ask because my aunt has put some negative thoughts in my head. She says I may never know if you are being kind to me because you truly care or if you just feel indebted to me and that marrying me is the only way that you can return the favor."

"That most certainly is not true." Ellie shook her head, and Luke continued.

"I still love you with all my heart. I want to spend the rest of my life with you. Say you have changed your mind about me?" Luke's eyes were pleading.

"I'm sorry, Luke, I'm afraid I haven't changed my mind at all." Ellie replied. Luke's face fell. "You see, I actually came to the realization that I have been avoiding my own feelings for you since I met you. I do believe that I started to fall in love with you from that first party."

Luke heaved a sigh of relief.

"Ask me again, Luke, please."

"Will you marry me, Eleanor Bennett? Will you make me the happiest man in the world?"

Yes, Luke." Ellie threw her arms around him and then stood on her toes to kiss him. "Oh, yes, I love you. So much. I was so wrong about you at the beginning. You are the kindest man I have ever met and I would be proud to be your wife."

He smiled and kissed her, then hugged her so tightly that he lifted her off her feet, knocking both their hats off.

"So much to think about! Where will we live? Chicago? New York? St. Louis?" Ellie questioned Luke, so happy to be in his arms.

"I've always stayed with friends while in New York, and I've already sold my home in Chicago. While I'll need to travel at times, I was thinking we can split our time between Longbourn and Hope Gardens."

"You would do that for me? Honestly? I can stay here and keep working on the ranch?" Ellie was elated.

"How does building our own home on the property here sound to you?"

"Well, I don't think that's advisable because once my father dies, oh, goodness! I forgot to tell you that not even Mr. Sutton will take over the ranch. You won't believe this, but he actually sold his rights to the land after saying he never would and now he won't even tell my father to whom he sold it. Just like him, to simply take all the money. He didn't even give Papa a percentage of the sale. The family can still live here until Papa dies, of course, but then we will have our home taken away. We will be forced to leave. I think it prudent that we build over on your investment property."

Luke reddened just a bit, released her and picked up their hats. "You and your family won't ever have to worry about losing your home, Ellie. It was me. I convinced Mr. Sutton to sell me his interest. The Longbourn Ranch will always be yours. Charles drew up all the necessary paperwork and I have already signed it over to you. All they need are your signatures, yours and your father's, of course. The papers are at your house now; your father was reviewing them when we left. I must say he was quite confused."

"Wait…" Her excitement and gratitude at not losing the ranch was quite overshadowed by a thought. "What if I had said 'no' to your proposal again?" *Heaven forbid I make that mistake twice.*

"I would still have given it to you. The will was balderdash. I don't understand why your great-grandfather would do such a thing, but the ranch is now yours. You deserve it." He said this as if it were common sense. She couldn't process the thoughts swirling around in her mind. *He bought me a ranch. My own ranch. He bought me my ranch.*

"Oh, Luke." She hugged him tightly again, tears of joy and gratitude in her eyes. "You are simply the best. Can you afford it? With the economic crisis I mean? Are you sure you'll be all right with your wife running a ranch?"

"It's already done. And in regards to you being in charge here? I wouldn't have it any other way. It's what you were born to do." He chuckled. "I have to tell you, last week, I still wasn't convinced that you had changed your mind about me. That was another reason I didn't say much to you. I didn't want you to say yes simply out of gratitude. I have since learned I was wrong about that."

"What on earth, other than just asking me, could have changed your mind?" She asked. They began hiking again, hand in hand.

"My aunt Madeline came to see me in St. Louis." He shook his head.

"Oh, goodness, I didn't tell you about that yet either." Ellie admitted.

"She stopped to see me after she came out here to confront you. I must apologize to you for her behavior, but most of what she told you was a lie, a last-ditch effort to keep you away from me. She told me of your

398

conversation and your refusal to deny your feelings for me. Just as she initially put doubt in my mind, she unwittingly gave me hope that I might have a second chance with you."

"That second chance has been ready and waiting since your last letter." Ellie looked at him guiltily. "I was so foolish. Please forgive me."

"Well, I must admit, I really didn't make the best first impression." He admitted.

"Now, that is a fact." She stated playfully. "I took your insults quite personally. When I think back, though, I believe I wanted to impress you even then."

"You certainly did impress me. I just didn't know how to respond. I felt so awkward and I liked you in spite of myself. I did not have the courage to approach you."

"I'm just glad we found the wisdom to communicate now." She squeezed his hand. "If only we were honest with ourselves and each other from the beginning, we could have saved much heartache and headache."

"A good dose of humility is never a bad idea either." He chuckled. "We must always remember that lesson. I was miserable when you refused me in the spring. At first, I was angry. It never even crossed my mind that you would turn me down. I couldn't believe anyone would do so. After I thought it through, I realized you were absolutely right about me. That's why I wrote the letter."

"Communication." She nodded. "I wanted to talk to you about your letter in St. Louis, but I didn't want to ruin how well we were getting along. Like you said, we can learn from our past mistakes and look forward to a future of hope."

He smiled at her. "And always remember the good times, like those very pleasant memories in St. Louis." He pulled Ellie to a stop, kissed her, then continued walking.

"Mmm, those were very good memories." She brushed a strand of hair from her cheek. "Like I said, I knew I loved you even at Biltmore, but I was so shocked when I learned you were the reason for Charles leaving Janie. When you asked me to marry you, I completely overreacted. I regretted it almost right away." The couple continued walking, taking in the sights around them. The lake was so clear and still today that the landscape was reflected like a mirror in the water. The weather was turning cool, but the sky was a clear blue with a dazzling sun. The entire day could not have been any more perfect.

"I knew I would never be able to get you out of my mind when we rode out and saw those buffalo so long ago." He grinned. "And good heavens, when I first saw you in those trousers. What a sight you were." He blushed. "And then that bathing costume. You, ahh, definitely have a figure to admire."

"I remember you being speechless in regards to my trousers. I just thought you were appalled! But with the bathing costume, well...let's just say I was very uncomfortable myself." This time, she blushed, thinking of seeing his broad shoulders in his bathing costume, she quickly changed the subject. "Did you speak with Charles? Are you the reason he returned?"

"Yes. Once you pointed out my mistake about Janie and her friend and I realized how much Janie cared for him, I felt I had no other option. I tell you though, it took me some time to build up the courage to talk to Charles and admit that I made a mistake. Helena was there for moral support, but honestly, I believe Charles would have made the decision to come back for Janie on his own eventually. He really does love her."

"Thank you, Luke, so much, for everything."

They continued walking, talking and laughing until they made it back to the car. Ellie was glad to find that Luke also liked the challenge of climbing up and over the rock formations instead of going around them. They set out the picnic quilt and food and waited for Janie and Charles to return. Luke couldn't contain his excitement and told them both about their own engagement the moment they reached the picnic area.

"How can this possibly be, Ellie! I remember only that you despised him." Janie exclaimed to Ellie without thinking. She quickly covered her mouth and looked at Luke, who simply waved his hand dismissively.

"We were both quick to judge each other." Ellie admitted. "But the more I got to know Luke, especially in St. Louis, I was able to see all of his finer qualities. I love him with all of my heart."

"Well, then, I will be proud to call you my brother." Janie smiled at Luke.

"And you and I will finally be family." Charles slapped Luke on the back good-naturedly.

"I just wonder how Mama and Papa will react to the news that you are engaged to Mr. Callahan," Janie stated.

"I believe your father already suspects, since I mentioned my intentions offhandedly when I gave him the legal documents," Luke replied.

"Goodness, you had papers drawn up for your marriage? Why on earth would you need those kinds of documets?" Janie asked.

Ellie quickly explained, and Janie was clearly excited and relieved at the prospect of the family not losing the ranch.

401

"I'll speak to your father officially when we return." Luke smiled at Ellie. "Charles feels obligated to have a long engagement because of his family and their expectations, but do you want to wait that long?"

"I haven't had time to think about it." She paused. "I suppose as long as Charlotte can make it, and my family, which includes Matthew and his family. I would be content with just a small ceremony, but I would prefer it to be in a church. Would that be okay?"

"That's all I require as well." He smiled.

"I should be able to make all of the arrangements in a month or so." Ellie smiled back.

"How about a Christmas wedding in St. Louis?" He asked. "Hope Gardens would be a splendid place for a small reception and the pastor at the Basilica of St. Louis is a good friend of the family."

"I think that's a splendid idea," Ellie replied. "The winter is a slower time on the ranch, so father and Matthew could both leave for a little bit, but not too long. Travel is more difficult in December, but St. Louis is a good central place for our friends and family. Charlotte and many of the guests invited could even stay at Hope Gardens."

"And I already have decided where I'm going to take you on our wedding trip." He could barely contain his excitement. "If you approve, that is."

"Won't most places be cold?" Janie asked.

"Mississippi should be quite mild at that time, and Natchez has some wonderful hiking from what I hear. Then we can work our way down to New Orleans."

"I have always wanted to go there." Ellie smiled. "Won't most people expect us to go to Italy, France or Spain?"

402

"I suppose, and if you want, we could." He looked a bit surprised and concerned. "Yes, definitely. I just didn't know if you would want to travel out of the country for an extended trip. I thought a Mississippi River tour would be better."

"Luke, don't worry. If I ever get a longing to hike through the Alps, I will let you know. But truly, I think your idea is perfect." She took his hand in hers. "I have read so much about the Mississippi River and its history, and I have always wanted to travel its length especially beyond St. Louis." Ellie couldn't believe how happy she was, knowing that she would spend the rest of her life with Luke. It was a good thing that God knew more than the both of them and had brought them together when they couldn't have imagined it themselves.

Chapter Forty-Five

After eating their picnic lunch, the two couples packed up their supplies and leisurely drove back home, taking a more scenic, yet bumpy route through the Black Hills National Forest. When they returned to Longbourn, Luke went directly to James's office to ask for Ellie's hand. His heart pounded. He hadn't thought far enough ahead to worry about the possibility of Mr. Bennett denying him his blessing. He assumed that Ellie wouldn't need her father's permission, but he also knew she loved her family and if James said no, she may reconsider her answer if...he shook his head. No. They had been through enough. He knew he would never be good enough for Ellie, but he had to at least show her father that he would love her and treat her as well as he could for the rest of her life.

"Mr. Bennett, may I have a word please?" He asked. James looked up, confusion in his face, and waved him in.

"Yes, yes of course." He reached over and picked up a packet of papers and gestured for Luke to sit down. "I just finished reading through these. It answers a lot of questions I had, especially about who convinced Sutton to sell his stake in the ranch, but it now brings up a slew of other issues. Tell me, what is this all about?" He pulled out a pipe and lit it.

Luke sat. "Well, sir, to start, I believe your grandfather's will was extremely unjust and have felt that way since the first time I heard of it. Over the past year, I have gotten to know your daughter quite well. She deserves to run this ranch. I was simply righting something I saw was wrong."

James sat back. "There are many wrongs in this world that you could be fixing, Mr. Callahan. Why this? Why Ellie?"

Here was the moment. "Well, Mr. Bennett, I love your daughter, and somehow, I have won her heart as well. I know she and I had a rocky start to our relationship, and I had some preconceived prejudices that kept me from showing Ellie my true feelings. I had much to learn, I'm afraid."

"My father made comments about how well the two of you would suit. He's a good judge of character, but I always laughed it off. I didn't even realize you'd had any conversations with Ellie that didn't end in disaster or annoyance and one of you storming off."

"That did happen quite a bit in our early days of knowing one another, sir." Luke admitted. "But I do love her and I have already asked her to marry me and she has agreed, but Ellie and I would both like your blessing. She values your opinion very much, sir, and I promise I will do everything in my power to make her happy." He felt like a teenage boy again.

"Yes, that is quite apparent." James held up the packet of papers in acknowledgement of that fact. "And you say she loves you and has accepted you? It does make it clear in these papers that you're giving her the ranch with no strings attached, as you apparently passed the documents over before she answered." Was he just thinking out loud, or did he want answers? Luke sat and nodded and listened, not wanting to

405

interrupt. "Well, my boy, I must say, I did not see this coming. If it were any of my other daughters, I would have to think about it and talk it over with my father and my wife as well, but as I said, my father already approves and I know my wife will. Beyond that, I value Ellie's opinion and know she has a good head on her shoulders, however, I will speak with her. This is a matter of great importance and, as I said, comes at a great surprise to me."

"Of course, sir. I would expect no less."

James stood and held out his hand. Luke followed suit and shook it.

"No matter how this turns out, young man, I do appreciate you undoing what my grandfather did. I can't imagine any son of mine doing a better job of running this ranch than Ellie and the thought of it falling into Sutton's hands always distressed me. I thank you for that from the bottom of my heart."

"You're very welcome, sir. I'll tell Ellie you'd like to see her." He then turned, heart full of happiness and relief.

~~~~~~~

Janie and Charles had gone directly to the sitting room, but Ellie wanted to stay near Luke. She paced the hallway in front of her father's office. After what felt like hours, but was likely only a few moments, Luke emerged with a smile on his face. He dropped a kiss on Ellie's forehead.

"He wants to see you." He whispered. She kissed him on the cheek, then hurried into the office. Her father had a concerned look on his face.

"Ellie, are you out of your mind? You've accepted Lucas Callahan? I thought you disliked the man immensely."

"I have, Father. Accepted him, I mean."

406

"Is it because he's wealthy? Are you doing this for your mother? That's not like you. Will he make you truly happy? I've only known him to be a snobbish, arrogant man, but if you really like him, that would certainly change things. He seems to care for you. For crying out loud, he gave you the ranch!"

"Yes, Father, he did. I like him quite a bit, actually. In fact, I love him. I was so wrong about him, Papa, and I spoke untruths. You don't know what he's really like. The way he makes me feel, the many things he has done for our family."

"Our family? Like what? Buying the ranch for you?" James asked, confusion apparent on his face.

"That and so much more." Ellie explained everything that had transpired during the past year and how she finally listened to her heart and not her mind as she got to know him. She didn't leave out what he had done for Janie and finally, most of all, what he had done for both Ellie and Lindie in Casper. When she was finished, James sat back in his chair, astounded.

"Luke Callahan did all that? I know he assisted in locating Lindie and Davis, but not that he helped to that extent. I'm a bit surprised that Patrick didn't give me more of the details. Good Heavens, knowing this will save me a world of trouble, but now I find I must pay Luke back. He said nothing to me when asking for my blessing."

"He won't let you pay him back, Papa" Ellie said. "And I am sure he wanted your blessing based on his merits and personality, not for what he has paid for."

"I know, I know, but I would have repaid your uncle, so I at least must make the offer. It speaks well of him that he didn't brag about the other

407

details." Her father grinned and shook his head in wonder. "I really had no idea, though your grandpa tried telling me there was more to Luke than what appeared. It is good to know that he is a man of honor and that you love him. Oh, my girl, I could not have given you up to anyone less worthy. I wholeheartedly give my blessing," he chuckled, "and I'm sure your mother will love the news."

"I hope she will," she replied.

"No time like the present for you to go speak with her. She was in the sitting room last I saw her." James nodded, then stood and kissed Ellie on the forehead. "I love you, Ellie. I am truly happy for you."

"Thank you. I love you too, Papa." She took a deep breath, knowing he wouldn't come with her to talk with her mother. She left the office to find Luke leaning against the same wall she had been pacing in front of earlier.

"I told him everything, and he is very grateful to you. He gave us his blessing, but now we must break the news to Mother."

"We?" He looked a little squeamish.

"You chose me, Luke, and my family comes with me." She grabbed his hand and all but dragged him over to the sitting room. Martha was knitting and Kathy was reading. Janie and Charles sat in the corner, talking and Ellie could see Marie right outside, working in the garden. Her mother glanced up, then scrambled to her feet when she saw Luke.

"Mama, Luke has asked me to marry him and I have accepted." Ellie simply blurted out. Martha plopped back into her seat, silent for once in her life. Ellie clung to Luke's arm and pulled him closer.

"Mrs. Bennett, I..." Luke started to speak, but was interrupted by Martha.

"Lord, you have answered my prayers! Ellie, you have always been the smartest of all my girls, though severely lacking in feminine grace. I will never know how you snared a man like Mr. Callahan, but you chose well."

Ellie was relieved to hear her mother say those things, though not completely surprised. She knew her mother liked the match because of Luke's wealth, but she also knew that Luke would prove to Martha that he was more than just his bank account. Ellie smiled up at her fiancé. He looked down at her with love in his eyes. Martha stood, her hands clasped together in delight.

"We are planning on having the wedding at Christmastime in St. Louis." Ellie informed her mother, then proceeded to tell her the rest of the wedding plans. Martha uncharacteristically listened politely, though did interrupt with her own ideas from time to time. She was respectful, almost as if she were afraid Luke would run away and take his proposal with him if she did anything improper. Perhaps there was hope for her mother to change after all.

~~~~~~

That evening, Luke and Ellie sat in front of the sitting room fireplace on the settee, his arm around her shoulders and a wool blanket wrapped around the both of them. She snuggled close, and looked into the flames dancing in the fire.

"I never believed I could be so happy." She paused. "Why do you love me? You have yet to tell me the particulars. Is it my country spirit?"

"I admire your wit, and the fact that you challenge me." He squeezed her shoulder.

409

"So you don't prefer women who will always agree with you, and tell you what you want to hear?"

"I don't like that from anyone, man or woman. I prefer someone who is willing to speak their mind," Luke agreed, "but you, you were different from the start, and that caught my interest. There has always been something about you that drew me to you. I can't explain it. Who knows why people fall in love? I've just come to the conclusion that God brought you to me." He kissed her temple. "Your passion, your love for this land, your competence. The love you show your sisters, parents and grandfather. I'm glad all these ranch men overlooked you. Had they seen what I see, you would have been married long ago. You have always been special to me."

They fell into a comfortable silence, just enjoying the presence of one another. She had just closed her eyes when he sighed and rubbed at his temple.

"What's wrong, Luke?" She asked, straightening. He leaned forward and put his elbows on his knees.

"I shouldn't bother you with my business concerns, especially today."

"Lucas Callahan." She leaned forward and gently pulled his face over so she could look him in the eyes. "We are going to be man and wife and I am not a delicate, shrinking flower. You can tell me anything. If it affects you, it affects me."

He smiled. "Another reason I love you. You're practical and don't run away from a challenge." He sat back, clearly tense. Ellie stood and moved to stand behind him, then put her hands on his shoulders and began massaging them.

"So what is worrying you? The economy?"

"Yes. I fear this will be very bad. It's the reason I left, the day your goats were delivered."

"I figured that." She leaned down and kissed his head. "Which, by the way, my goats, I must tell you again how much I love them."

"I am glad." He chuckled. "Like I said, I couldn't resist them either." He continued. "I wanted to bring them to you personally, to see your face when you saw them, but I had an urgent business matter to attend to. I'm afraid that our country will be in for some very bad times over the next few years. Perhaps even decades. I have been reading and keeping up with what's happening in the United States, but there are problems in Europe as well."

"What exactly is happening? I must admit, I don't know much about the whole situation."

"In all honesty, there are many things that have contributed. Over the last few years, people have been buying too much on credit, with the encouragement of the banks, unfortunately, but now, production of goods has declined and many men may lose their jobs. The problem is, they still have debts and now they have no money to pay them off. Some farmers are already starting to struggle a bit. It's all interconnected. Everyone has become too dependent on the banks and borrowing and the stock market."

"I had no idea." Ellie bit her lip. "Will Charles be alright with his businesses?"

"We'll all lose some, but he and I will be just fine. We both are more cautious than most with our business decisions. I will have to make further adjustments, but we won't be affected much. I have enough saved, and not just in the banks, which will probably crash soon. It will be a downhill slide for all, I'm afraid."

411

"You mean people could lose all their money in the bank?" Her stomach fell.

"Unfortunately, yes, and many other problems will come trickling down from the top as well, but with the grace of God, we will get through this. Together."

Epilogue: Winter of 1929

St. Louis

December 14, the scheduled date of Luke and Ellie's wedding quickly arrived, and they couldn't have been more ready. It was a simple affair, and although Madeline VanRensselaer and Anne didn't attend, all of the people who really mattered were there. The ceremony was at the Basilica of St. Louis, and the reception was in the conservatory at Hope Gardens, all as planned. Helena had overseen the Hope Garden decorations and really had a knack for design. The conservatory looked beautiful. Evergreen trees with electric lights on strings wound around them were strategically placed throughout the greenhouse, and pine garland had been draped on almost every flat surface. The girl had even hung a few sprigs of mistletoe, which gave Luke many excuses to pull Ellie under for a kiss. A fire roared in the fireplace, offering comfortable heat. The tables were covered in starched white cloths and garland. White dishes with a thin red trim and beautiful silverware graced the table. Luke had purchased prime rib for the meal, and the cooks had prepared it to perfection. The whole day had been like a dream so far.

"I tell you, my dear, I knew you and Luke were in love back in St. Louis." Uncle Patrick laughed. "And I know you remember me telling you so."

Ellie blushed and Luke squeezed her hand.

"I knew before I even met you, Ellie." Helena piped up. "The way Luke talked about you, I just knew you were special to him."

"Smart girl." Luke smiled.

Helena gave her new sister an admiring look. "And I have never met anyone who has been such a challenge to Luke. You keep him on his toes. It's good for him."

She couldn't help but laugh. Ellie knew that she and Luke would still have their arguments, but they were far beyond where they had been a year ago.

Luke smiled at Ellie. "I find her challenges invigorating."

Ellie had enjoyed getting to know her new sister-in-law even more over the last few weeks. Helena was a sweet girl who had lived a sheltered life. She couldn't wait to visit Longbourn, and Luke would allow her to choose whether to live at the ranch or at Hope Gardens or both. Ellie had a feeling Helena would choose the Black Hills. She could only hope that her new sister would be a good influence on Kathy.

Marie and Angelina Ingraham would be traveling back with Charlotte and Richard Sutton to stay at Biltmore Village for a while to help Charlotte prepare for the baby, though it was still months away. Knowing Marie and remembering Mr. Sutton's cousin Edward, Ellie couldn't help but wonder if she would soon be married as well. They would be a perfect match.

Ellie continued to look around the room full of people. The future was uncertain, with more and more people losing their jobs every day. Nothing would ever be perfect, and there would be many challenges ahead, but Ellie knew that she and Luke could get through anything as long as they were together. She couldn't help but think of the passage from Proverbs they had chosen for one of their readings earlier that day… "When pride comes, then comes disgrace, but with humility comes wisdom." Luke and Ellie had overcome much of their pride, yet realized they would have a constant battle keeping it at bay. Humility was neither of their strongest attributes, but she was content to know that with the love of God and their friends and family, they would be able to live by these words.

Author's Note

Jane Austin's Pride and Prejudice is by far one of my favorite stories, and there are hundreds of different retellings of it. In fact, I believe most romance novels have a similar storyline. I couldn't help but feel as though this story could be told once again by me, this time taking place during such an interesting time period in our country's history. So much was changing in such a short period, both good and bad.

I was able to travel to Spearfish, South Dakota, and the Black Hills on a vacation several years ago and I fell in love with the landscape. The stark contrast in the scenery from one area to another is beautiful. The views and sunsets are magnificent. Mount Rushmore, Devil's Tower and the Custer State Park are truly sights to be seen.

Another family trip took me to North Carolina where the Biltmore Mansion was my favorite stop. I could have spent weeks there, hiking and visiting. The Asheville area is a tourist attraction and while the Biltmore House is pricy, the grounds are worth it. It was fun to be able to use both of these locations as my settings for this novel. If you get the chance, you should add them to your bucket list of places to visit.

St. Louis is also a great destination to visit. Beyond the modern Gateway Arch National Park, botanical gardens and zoo, there are many beautiful parks to explore, like Forest Park, Tower Grove Park and City Garden Sculpture Park as well as several beautiful state parks. I was fascinated by the fact that they hosted the World's Exposition and the Summer Olympics in the same year of 1904, although the Olympics were poorly under-represented at that time. It must have been an exciting place to live and witness all the marvels that had been constructed. I only wish they could have left more of the facilities standing so that future generations could have enjoyed the same experiences.

I hope you all enjoy my version of a timeless tale of love and it's many complexities. As always, let me know what you think!

Luke's Photo Album
arranged by
Helena Callahan

Wally Schang

Sportsman's Park

Biltmore Manor

Cornelia Vanderbilt

Biltmore Lagoon

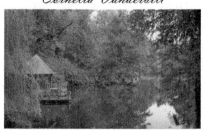

The Biltmore Boathouse

Buttes of South Dakota

Devil's Tower, Wyoming

Black Hills View

Ellie at Custer State Park

Center Lake, Custer State Park

Bison at Custer State Park

The Badlands

Needle's Eye Rock Formation

419

Other Books by

Marie LaPres

	The Turner Daughter Series
Though War Shall Rise Against Me	The war between the states has finally come and the civilians of Gettysburg hope the battles will stay as far away from them as possible. But the war will touch them all more than they can imagine. Four friends, old and new, will find themselves looking to God and each other to get them through.
Be Strong and Steadfast	Kate, America Joan, and sisters Belle and Elizabeth enjoy their lives in the safe, "finished" town of Fredericksburg, Virginia. Then, the Civil War breaks out and their lives will never be the same. Will the Civil War affect the women and their town? Will they lose faith, or always remain 'Strong and Steadfast'?
Plans for a Future of Hope	The citizens of Vicksburg never wanted secession, much less a war, but when Mississippi secedes from the United States, they throw their support behind the Confederacy. They hope the battles will stay far away from their bustling trade center, but they realize the importance of their town, perfectly situated atop a hill at a bend on the mighty Mississippi River. Then the siege comes...
Wherever You Go A Prequel Novella	As the United States are being pulled apart, one Southern belle must decide between love and comfort. Will Augusta Byron let her family down and risk social rejection from friends? Or will the problems facing the nation keep her from the man she is falling in love with?
	Middle Grade Novel
Whom Shall I Fear? Sammy's Struggle	Twelve-year-old Samuel Wade's life has never been easy, but the coming of the American Civil War makes it even more difficult. Then the war comes to his hometown of Gettysburg and he must make quick decisions that could mean life or death.

The Key to Mackinac Series: Young Adult Novels	
Beyond the Fort	16-year-old Christine Belanger has always loved learning about the past, but she may get more history than she bargained for when she finds herself at Colonial Michilimackinac in the year 1775. While there, Christine helps uncover a plot to eradicate all the French settlers. It falls to Christine and her new friend Henri to save the French settlers, and possibly change the course of history.
Beyond the Island	Raphael Lafontaine thought he could live in the modern world but not even a year after leaving the 18th Century, he finds himself missing his family and friends, as well as the freedom of his past voyageur life. When Rafe decides to go back in time, he doesn't count on Sadie Morrison following him and they quickly realize that nothing is as it should be.

About the Author

Erica Marie LaPres Emelander is a middle school social studies/religion teacher and lives in Grand Rapids, MI. Erica has always enjoyed reading and writing, and with her love of history and God, she has incorporated all four loves into her writing. When not working on and researching her books, Erica can be found coaching middle and high school sports, being a youth minister, and spending time with her friends and family.

Find Erica on:

https://sites.google.com/view/marielapres/home?authuser=1

Facebook: "Marie LaPres"

e-mail~ericamarie84@gmail.com

GoodReads: Marie LaPres

Instagram: marielapres

Made in the USA
Middletown, DE
05 December 2022

15932615R00239